CASIDDIE WILLIAMS

Never Fear Again

Contents

Preface

Content Warning:

This book contains sensitive matters including but not limited to sexual, mental, and physical abuse. Stalking. Mention of rape. Violent dreams. Kidnapping. Characters engage in sexual acts such as pegging, anal play, lactation kinks, and masturbation.

This book contains characters that are in polyamorous relationships including FFM and MMMMF.

Characters in this book are fictional, and although there is neurodivergent representation, it is not meant to downplay or be insensitive to anyone with this diagnosis. Autism and ADHD are a spectrum, and everyone's experiences are different, including the characters in this story.

Your mental health matters. You are Enough!

Acknowledgement

And we're here. We've come full circle as the series comes to an end, and what a wild ride it's been.

Many hands, eyes, and brains have been with me along the journey that started with Annie and her sub, Blake, and ended with baby Emory Tucker.

Many boatloads of thanks need to go to my ride or die, the niggle in my ear, my "but wait" woman, KK Moore. Between the random sex toys that show up at my door for inspiration and your "don't overthink it" attitude, my books wouldn't be nearly as interesting.

My Beta and ARC team has expanded and contracted with each book in this series, and I want to thank everyone who took a chance on me and then stuck around to see how each of the characters got their happily ever after.

I love every single one of you!

Always remember, no matter what…YOU. ARE. ENOUGH!

~Casiddie

1

Spencer

Today has been long and draining. The rain barely let up, but we were finally able to go home. Miller is making dinner, and we're relaxing together after our showers.

As we're enjoying some much-needed peace, the noise of our phones chiming with various sounds pierce the room.

"What the fuck?" Tucker is the first to open the message, and his posture stiffens while anger mars his face.

As more texts come through, the sounds of pissed-off grumbles flood the air.

"What's going on?" Everyone stares at their screens while my phone is still across the room. I can't get to it fast enough. Something is wrong, and no one is speaking.

"Where are you?"

I turn my head toward Tucker's demanding voice to see he has his phone to his ear. There's a pause as he listens to whoever is on the other line.

"We got pictures...from an unknown number," he growls.

More pictures? Shane's never sent them to our phones before. They're always left on our cars.

I unlock my phone and scroll through a new group chat. The photos would seem innocent enough if they didn't imply so much. He was there with them.

"He sent them to all of us in a group text, but you're driving right now, right?"

So, these pictures happened earlier today? Why send them now?

"The first picture was Katy with a blue baby outfit over her belly. There's one of you both getting pizza. Dempsey, one of them, has Katy alone in the food court. Please tell me you were just out of the frame." Tucker's anger elevates as he listens to Dempsey's response and I step up next to him. His body relaxes slightly when I curl into his chest, but he's still tense. "That's all it takes, Dempsey."

Something makes him tense up again. "Katy, what's wrong?"

More listening. I wish he had put it on speaker. Everyone in the room is focused on Tucker and his phone call. "Dammit, Dempsey. Get her home safely but as soon as possible. She's precious cargo."

He hangs up the phone and pulls me into him. "They'll be here in ten minutes. We need to figure out what this asshole wants and why his focus seems to be geared toward Katy now. He was *there* with them."

I'm comfortably wrapped in Tucker's embrace when my phone rings minutes later. Tucker and I look at the screen and exchange equally curious looks.

"Dempsey?"

"No, Spencer. It's Katy. We had to pull over. A car bumped

us in the rain, and Viktor is out talking with them."

"Are you alright? Is there a lot of damage?" She sounds a little shaken up but otherwise calm.

"I'm fine. It wasn't a big bump, so I don't think there's a lot of damage. It's just raining like crazy. I want to get home and change into something warm and dry."

"Where are you? I'll have some fresh hot chocolate waiting, or if you'd rather take a bath, I can get that started." I step away from Tucker with a nod and walk into the kitchen.

"Um…I don't think we're far. It's hard to see through all the rain. Oh. This is the parking lot with the skating rink. We're only a few blocks." That's a relief. They should be back soon.

"Miller just pulled dinner out of the oven. It smells Italian and cheesy."

"My favorite! Is there garlic bread?"

"Of course. He always makes carbohydrates with carbohydrates." She laughs, and I smile as Miller puts the bread in the oven.

"Let me crack the window and see how much longer. It's raining so hard, and it looks like they're just standing out there." I hear rustling, and then the mechanical sounds of the window rolling down. "Can we go yet, Viktor?"

"Close the fucking window, Katy."

Whoa. Why is Dempsey talking to her like that? There's a lot of noise through the speaker because of the rain then—
Bang!

My body stiffens. That was a gunshot. I'd know that sound in my sleep.

"Katy? Dempsey? What's going on? What the fuck just happened?"

3

I'm a trained professional. I've been through hours of classes and courses to be able to hold in my emotions and work the scene. The sound of a gunshot, followed by Katy's audible screaming, just ripped me in two. Every piece of medical knowledge has left my mind; all I can think of is getting to them.

My body numbly takes me to the front door and I fumble several times to get my keys off the key ring. A weight cages me in, and I truly feel like an animal when I whip around and almost punch Lincoln.

"Dream Girl, what's going on?" I lift my trembling hand and hit the speaker button.

Katy's scream guts me again, and I lose it.

"Someone fucking talk to me!"

"Spencer?" I almost drop the phone, but Lincoln catches it and pulls me into him. My entire body shakes with fear and adrenaline. That voice. *His* voice. I feel the blood metaphorically drain from my face and ice run through my veins.

He can't be there. That can't be Shane. She's safe. Dempsey has her, and she's safe.

Lincoln's arms hold me up as my body shuts down from fear and anxiety.

"Spencer, I've come to collect our girl. I'm going to be taking her with me. I'm sad to say I don't think Dempsey is going to make it. He's losing blood fast."

I'm suddenly surrounded by my men. Axel, Tucker, and Miller each put a hand on me for support. Tucker pulls up the GPS map on his phone to find Katy's location, and I shake my head and whisper, "Skating rink."

"Spencer, my love. Do you really not know? I thought I

4

was making it so obvious."

My love? I was never his love. And what should I know? That he has continuously sent us pictures from all over town? We've kept that fact from Katy because we didn't want her to worry. She's never alone, and we have all our faith in Dempsey that he would keep her safe and protect her. But right now Shane said he's bleeding out, and we need to get to him.

"The baby is mine. I took her in that alley. I'm finally getting my little boy, Spencer."

A terrible cracking noise echoes through the speaker. It sounds like bone breaking and I hear Katy scream.

"You fucking bastard," I rage into the phone, but it disconnects. My only thought is to get to them. Get to her.

We all run to Miller's truck. I don't know how it's decided, but his lights are the ones that flash and we leave the house in a rush.

"The skating rink parking lot. That's where she said she was. Break all the laws, Miller. Shane is with Katy and he said Dempsey was bleeding out. If he…I can't…"

The words aren't coming. My brain is fogging over. I need to stay focused, but my body is telling me to retreat. My mask is refusing to come down and let me compartmentalize what's going on. It's too close to me. I heard Dempsey get shot. I…I…

"Breath, Little Miss, or you'll pass out. What are the facts? What do we know?"

"I-I don't…"

"Okay, listen to me. We know Shane has Katy, and we know Dempsey is wounded, most likely from a gunshot. What do we do first when someone is bleeding, Axel?" Tucker is trying

5

to help me deal in facts and put my emotions aside. It's exactly what I need.

"Locate and assess the wound," Axel responds. "Cut away any clothing necessary."

"Then?"

"If needed, pack the wound with a sterile cloth. If not, apply pressure to the wound with a sterile cloth. Elevate above the heart if possible." I focus on Axel's answers, and he goes through them step by step.

"Is he right?" Tucker gently massages my shoulders to ground me.

"Yes."

"Anything you would add?" While there are many more steps I could add, Axel covered the basics, and Tucker did what he set out to do. My mind has cleared, and my mask has slipped into place. I may know who we're going to be helping, but they are still patients and need me at my best.

"Rescue and police are on their way, but we'll get there first." Lincoln hits a button on his phone, ending a call. I didn't hear him talking to anyone; I was so far gone. "Everyone be safe out there."

"I've got your backs since the rest of you have medical training." Tucker checks his gun on his hip and nods his approval at what he sees. As much as I want to protest, he's not wrong. A club owner can't do nearly as much as a paramedic, firefighter, nurse, and a police officer. Whatever we're about to drive up to, they're in the best hands.

Pulling into the parking lot, Dempsey's black sedan sits alone with the front doors wide open. The rain has let up, but it's still a steady, cool drizzle.

I check in with myself and make sure my mask is fully in

place because once I step out of this truck, I can't be a pseudo-mother to whatever state my seventeen year old is in. I need to go out there and RATE. Recognize. Assess. Treat. Evaluate. Hopefully, the ambulance will be here soon.

As prepared as I am, seeing Katy covered in blood with a gun in her hand and her entire body draped over Dempsey almost makes my mask falter.

Almost.

"Spencer," Miller calls. "Take care of Katy. We'll work on Dempsey."

We have to pry a screaming Katy away from a lifeless Dempsey, but once I've secured the gun, the guys lift him out of the front seat and into the bed of Miller's truck, which is covered by a cab. It may not be very tall, but it's dry, and they can lay him flat and assess him better.

"Katy, are you hurt?" She watches them load Dempsey before she collapses into me—my insides war with myself. Be professional and keep your mask on, or be the person she needs right now.

"Katy, where did Shane go?" If she can't tell me if she's hurt, I at least need to know if we're safe.

"I-I shot him. I have no idea where, but he left in his car." She peers out the back window where he must have been parked, but there's no longer another vehicle there. And now I know why she had a gun in her hand.

"Are you hurt anywhere?" Her hand comes up, and she rubs the back of her head. "Did he hit you?"

A chuckle escapes her, and I momentarily worry about her current mental state.

"No. I head-butted him. I'm pretty sure I broke his nose. It was really hard."

I palpate the area and find she has a bump on the back of her head, and I'm inwardly proud of her for being offensive in a defensive situation.

"Is he...is V-Viktor going to be okay?" We both stare at Miller's truck, and I can tell by the steady rhythm of the rocking that someone is doing CPR. Hopefully, Katy doesn't notice it.

"I hear the sirens." Moments later, a police car followed by an ambulance pull up. Tucker directs them where to go, and I continue to get ignored while trying to ascertain if any of the blood on her clothes belongs to her.

"Katy, he's in good hands. Please let me look at you."

"Spencer, I'm fine. I..." She turns to me with wide eyes. "The baby. Spencer, I haven't felt him move this entire time. Oh god, do you think he's okay?"

Patient care. Patient care. Patient Care.

Katy recognizes my silence and covers her mouth.

"Holy shit. I'm so sorry Spencer. I didn't mean to. I wasn't thinking. It was so stupid of me to say."

"It's fine. You are allowed to own your feelings. You're already taking a trip to the Emergency Department to get checked out. We will have him looked at by ultrasound as well. Don't worry about me."

The ambulance backs up to Miller's truck, and Dempsey is quickly pulled out onto the stretcher, with Miller jumping right back on top of him doing compressions.

Katy has already been through so much, and I've seen the bond she's forming with Dempsey. I hope for her sake he makes it through.

2

Katy

I can't breathe.

The arms around me are too tight.

The rain is too loud.

There's so much blood.

I'm so wet and cold.

He's not breathing. Why isn't he breathing?

Bang!

My hands. My hands are covered in blood. Who's blood? There's so much of it; I don't know where it's coming from. My ears are ringing, and the rain is pouring down and…and…

Viktor!

"No, Viktor. Viktor, wake up. Wake up!"

Arms wrap around my stomach. "Get away from me!"

"Katy."

They won't let go, no matter how hard I shake.

"The baby is mine. You can't have him. He's mine."

"Pepper, wake up."

No. Viktor needs to wake up. He's so pale. Why won't he

wake up?

"Katy, sweetheart, you're dreaming." Gentle hands caress my cheeks, and they feel nothing like the harsh grip of the man trying to steal me and my baby. "Shhhh. Wake up for me. Open your eyes."

I can't open them. My baby is safe right now. Viktor is still here. He's hurt, but he's here.

The air around me thins, and I feel like I'm flying. I'm surrounded by warmth. Have I died, too? Is this heaven? I'm too young. I didn't get to live.

A finger sweeps across my cheek, and I feel wetness.

"Come on, Pepper. Wake up for me. You're safe. I'm fine, and Owen is sleeping." The voice is gentle and soothing.

Owen. *Owen!*

I sit up with a gasp, sucking in air.

"Owen." A baby monitor is handed to me, and I see an angelic, dark-haired toddler sleeping in a crib. I put my hand to my stomach—my flat stomach.

My groggy brain tries to connect all the information in front of me. I'm not pregnant. There's a sleeping baby in a crib, and I'm... I look under me and realize I'm in someone's lap. I follow the line of his shirtless body to a scar on his abdomen. Further up is a muscular chest with almost translucent hair. A light blond beard surrounds his jaw, and his thin lips are slightly turned down.

I can pretend everything I'm seeing is still part of my nightmare, but when my brown eyes lock with his silver-blues, I take a breath that feels like I was drowning before I saw him.

"Viktor." I throw myself into his chest. He's here. He's not bleeding out on the front seat. His body isn't cold and lifeless in my arms. "Viktor." His name is a sign of relief. His large hands smooth over the back of my tank top, and I finally feel grounded back into reality.

"Are you back, Pepper? That was a bad one." I nod into his chest and inhale his rich, spicy scent.

The realization of what I'm doing comes flooding into my consciousness, and I jump off his lap, putting distance between us.

"Viktor." I look around the room and realize I'm in the pool house, which means Owen is safely down the hall, asleep in my old bedroom. "You're shirtless."

He sits up, giving me a sheepish look, and rubs his hand on his chest.

"Yeah. Sorry, I got hot. If you're okay now, I'll leave you to get back to sleep." He moves to stand, and without thinking, I grab his thigh.

"No. Please stay." Realizing what I'm doing, I swiftly pull my hand back. "Sorry, just…please stay for a little while longer. You're right. That was a bad one."

Torture flashes through his eyes as I'm sure he knows what my nightmare was about.

"Sure. Come here." He moves back to lean on the headboard and lifts his arm in offering. I scoot across the bed and curl up into his side.

At night, when we're most vulnerable, is the only time he allows himself to accept any comfort. Despite doing everything he could that day, he holds onto all the guilt. He officially died that night, but my family brought him back.

For months after his discharge, he came and slept on the couch in the living room of the big house. Some nights, I'd wake up, and he'd be asleep on my bedroom floor.

To him, his scar is a constant reminder of his failure two years ago, but to me, it's a reminder that I'm alive because he saved me. And by saving me, he saved Owen. Viktor allowed me to be a mother.

3

Dempsey

I bolt up from my bed on the fold-out couch, feeling disoriented. It's dark outside. I listen, trying to figure out what woke me up. I don't hear Owen, but...

"No, Viktor." *Katy.*

I grab my gun and hastily, but with all the silence I can manage, creep into her room.

She's alone and dreaming. Or, more specifically, she's having a nightmare. I retreat from the doorway to put my gun away and return to the room. She's thrashing around. I try to let her work out her nightmares on her own, but this seems like she's struggling.

I crouch next to her and put a hand on her lower back.

"Get away from me." I know the panic isn't for me. She's reliving the night of the attack. These nightmares are always the worst, and I can't help feeling guilty knowing I caused this one.

"Katy." She's shaking under my hand. "Pepper, wake up." Her eyes squeeze shut harder, and her breathing increases.

13

"Katy, sweetheart, you're dreaming." She's crying. I hate when the nightmares pull her in this deep. It's almost impossible to pull her out, and I never know if it's worse to wake her or let it play out to completion. I don't see a difference either way.

"Shhhh. Wake up for me. Open your eyes." Standing, I scoop her into my arms and sit back on the bed, cradling her.

It wrecks me to be this close to her. She's suffering in her sleep because I didn't protect her. My guard was down and Shane got the jump on me.

I don't deserve to comfort her, but it's torture to let her suffer like this alone when I can do something as simple as hold her while she relives this experience.

Most nights, she stays asleep, and once she calms down, I slip back out. As I swipe the tears from under her eyes, I don't think it will be one of those nights.

"Come on, Pepper. Wake up for me. You're safe. I'm fine, and Owen is sleeping," I whisper, not wanting to startle her. I need to find a way into her subconscious.

"Owen." She sits up and gasps, and I grab the baby monitor off her nightstand and hand it to her. She stares at the screen, looking over the tiny boy asleep in his crib. Her hand moves and rubs her stomach.

Slowly, her eyes glide up my body, stopping at my scar. The bullet was a through and through and didn't hit any major organs, but I almost bled out. The blood made my heart stop, and if Spencer and her men hadn't shown up when they did, there would have been no chance of me surviving.

Katy's eyes continue to roam up my body. The living room was still hot from the casserole I made earlier, so I removed my shirt. I didn't think to put it on before I came in. I was focused on her.

Only at night. It's the only time I allow myself to be soft and vulnerable with her. I hate myself, but in the shadows of the night, I can be thankful that I was the one to get shot and not her. Grateful Katy understood me and grabbed the gun from the glove compartment after head-butting him and probably breaking his nose. And fucking ecstatic that the few times we gave her gun lessons, she paid attention and knew how to turn the safety off and got a good enough shot that Shane ran off.

I allow her to peruse my body. I can tell she isn't fully awake, and there's a chance she won't remember this come morning.

When her eyes meet mine, she inhales a sharp breath.

"Viktor." Katy throws herself into me, and I don't hesitate to wrap my arms around her. I fucking love when she says my name. Everyone calls me Dempsey or Vik. But not Katy. She calls me Viktor because she wants to. "Viktor." She says my name with such reverence that, for a moment, I allow myself to believe we could have this together. Me holding her, giving her comfort.

I run my hand over her back, hoping it's offering her the comfort she needs.

"Are you back, Pepper? That was a bad one."

She nods into my chest, and I hear her inhale my scent.

Suddenly, something sets her off, and she jumps out of my lap to the farthest corner of the bed.

"Viktor." She glances around the room, trying to get her bearings. "You're shirtless."

I readjust so I'm sitting against the headboard and rub my chest. Katy's fully awake now, which means I've overstayed my welcome. It's time to retreat to my sofa bed.

"Yeah. Sorry, I got hot. If you're okay now, I'll leave you to

15

get back to sleep." I reluctantly lean forward to stand and get startled by the warmth on my thigh—Katy's petite hand.

"No. Please stay." She pulls her hand back, probably regretting that she even touched me. "Sorry, just…" Katy is struggling to put into words what she wants to say. I hate when she lacks confidence. It could still be the nightmare floating around in her head or the situation of finding me in her bed, holding her. "…please stay a little while longer. You're right. That was a bad one."

Fuck. I knew it was. I wish there was something I could do to take all the terrible memories of that night away from her. No matter how badly I know I should get up and leave, I can't deny her.

"Sure. Come here." I open my arm, and she crawls into my side. I instantly feel better with her in my arms. The guilt I carry around on a daily basis always disappears during these fleeting moments.

Katy burrows into my chest, and her hand rests on my stomach. Slowly, her fingers inch over until they covers my scar. She inhales a ragged breath, and I pull her closer.

"I'm okay, Pepper. I'm here."

"I know. But the dream was so real, and parts of it actually were."

We sit in silence for a while, her hand warming my scar while I caress her back. I'm going to soak up every second of this interaction because I know, come morning, she'll go back to being just my job.

Katy's breathing slows, and a soft snore whispers through the room.

Sixty more seconds. That's all I'm giving myself before I go back to my pull-out couch. My self-imposed dungeon.

I was happy sleeping on the regular couch. I just needed to be close enough to Katy to prevent any other potential situations. The guys understood, as everyone was on edge for a while, so they upgraded me to a sofa bed.

When Spencer's guys were discussing giving up their apartments since they all live together now, her father, Eddie, offered Katy the pool house and said he would take over one of their leases. My sofa bed was the first piece of furniture brought into the house for us. There's an unspoken agreement that I'm watching over Katy now. Someone continues depositing money into my account, but I'd still be here even if they didn't pay me.

I hate that it's been almost two years without contact from Shane. He sent a picture of Katy coming home from the hospital with Owen, but nothing specifically from him since. Occasionally, a package will arrive without a name and with baby items in the box. Tucker's P.I. has looked into them, but all roads have been dead ends.

My sixty seconds are long gone, but I'm having trouble extricating myself from this beauty's grip. With a final sigh and a kiss to the top of her head, I roll her onto her other side and slip out of the bed.

4

Katy

My alarm rings, and without opening my eyes, I can feel his presence gone. The void that he leaves behind when he exits a room is palpable. I know he comes in here when I have bad nights; I feel him more than he probably knows.

Rolling over, I silence the alarm and glance at the monitor to see if Owen is still asleep, but I don't immediately see a lump or a head of dark hair. I sit up, rubbing the sleep from my eyes, and search the monitor again. The crib is empty, and I stare at the screen in disbelief because there's no way he crawled out of it.

Panicking, I jump out of bed and rush out of my room, only to come to a halting stop. Standing at the kitchen counter, still shirtless, Viktor sways with Owen on his hip, making pancakes on the griddle.

I take a moment to catch my breath, but also to calm my mind because it immediately went to the worst-case scenario. I know the security in the pool house and the main house is as good as it can get, but until I know that Shane no longer walks this earth, there will always be that nagging suspicion in the back of my mind.

Shane told me the night of the attack that Owen belonged to him. It wasn't until after the fact, when I really thought about the words he said, that I realized he was my rapist.

Shane, Spencer's ex-fiancé, raped me in the alley across from my high school when I was sixteen.

I can say that now. The words are still hard, but I can do it. It took me a long time to admit that to myself but it's another thing I can thank Viktor for. I knew I needed help the night he found me hysterical in the corner of my room with Owen crying just as loudly in his crib. We were still in the big house, and Owen was only a few months old the night it happened.

It's three a.m., and Owen's crying wakes me up. I groggily walk over to his crib, but when I reach down to pick him up, I freeze.

The shadow cast from the moon outside drapes the lower half of his tiny body in darkness, and my mind registers it as a stain. A stain like the one I watched spread over Viktor's stomach as he bled out in the front seat of my car from a bullet wound.

"Katy?" Viktor barges into my room after hearing me scream. A sound I wasn't aware I was making until he arrived.

Viktor's eyes frantically bobbing between Owen and me, not sure who he should go to first. With a shaky hand, I point at the crib, and Viktor scoops up Owen, looking over every inch of him for the source of my current state.

When he's confident there's nothing visibly wrong with the baby, he comes to me and crouches down, giving me a once-over.

"What's wrong, Pepper?" His voice is soothing but laced with concern.

"I...blood...you." *I struggle to get words out through my hyperventilation, and the ones I am managing are just making him look more worried.*

"There's no blood. Owen is fine. I checked him over. Do you want to look?" Viktor pulls Owen away from his chest to hand him to me, and I shake my head. The image of both of them covered in blood is too much for me to handle at the moment.

"Okay, Katy, I'll hold him. What can I do?"

I have no idea. I just need to get this image out of my head before it snowballs like it's done in the past.

"Sh-shower."

"You want to take a shower? Okay. Let me get Spencer. Will you be okay until I get back?"

His words send me deeper into a flashback of the day I was raped, and Spencer helped me shower.

"No Spencer. I-no. I don't want her." *He looks torn with what to do, and I don't exactly know what I'm asking of him either, but I know I don't want Spencer.*

"Okay. Can I bring Owen to them so I can help you?"

I close my eyes and dig the heels of my hands into the sockets until I see stars. I just want to forget that night. Why can't I just forget?

"Katy?" Viktor's hand pulls at one of my wrists. "You're going to hurt yourself, Pepper. Please let me help you. I'll be right back, okay?"

I allow him to pull my hands away, and seeing his silver-blue eyes, very much alive and staring at me, calms my nerves. I nod, and he stands with Owen and leaves the room.

It feels like he just walked out when he returns. Without a word, he scoops me in his arms and carries me to the bathroom. Viktor doesn't let go as he turns the water on and adjusts the temperature.

He cradles me in his arms while I cling to him like a koala. Once again, I'm reminded of being in a similar position and feeling with Lincoln. The thought of Viktor putting me down so I can undress and get into the shower is terrifying.

He must sense how I'm feeling because he opens the shower door and steps inside, clothing and all. If I had any protest in me, I would have used it, but I don't.

Viktor angles us so the hot stream of water beats on my back, and his body keeps my front warm. Neither of us speaks. He holds me without effort, and our clothes cling to our bodies.

"Katy."

"Not yet."

"Pepper, I'm not letting you go, but I'd like you to listen. Can you do that for me?" Burying my head deeper into his chest, I nod. "I think you need to talk to someone. You're an amazing mother, and Owen deserves you to be as healthy as possible, both physically and mentally."

Therapy has been mentioned more times than I can count. I don't want to talk about it. I don't want to remember it at all.

"I'm fine."

"You're not fine." His previously soft tone has turned firm. "Katy, you've been through more in your seventeen years than most people go through in a lifetime. Talk. That's all I'm asking. Your strength in the past few years is stronger than any man I've ever known, but admitting to yourself you need help isn't a weakness. It's the most strength you can possibly have. Strength for yourself and strength for Owen."

After that conversation, I reached out to Justin. While our traumas are completely different, I knew he was the best one to point me in the direction I needed. Viktor gave me the initial push, and Justin held my hand.

I lean against my door frame in awe at the ease my Viking Viktor cares for my son.

Not mine.

My bodyguard, my babysitter, my pain in the ass protector, even my nightmare chaser, but not mine.

Owen's arm reaches up, and I think he's going to grab at Viktor's ear, but he goes a little higher and pulls at his hair. He yanks hard enough that a big chunk comes out of Viktor's bun. Rather than complaining about what my son just did, he tugs at the hair tie and lets all his hair cascade down to his shoulders.

I must have made a noise because Viktor's head turns over his shoulder, and a sweet smile forms on his lips, but then suddenly freezes. He must have remembered that the sun is up, and he isn't allowed to be nice to me unless we're under the cloak of darkness.

My attitude sours at the whiplash he gives me.

"Pepper—"

"Don't Pepper me. I still think it's the stupidest nickname, but whatever. I get it. You're on the job. Can't be nice to me. I don't understand why you do nice things, like obviously waking up with my toddler, but you treat me like I'm nothing to you. After close to three years, Viktor, you'd think we could at least be friends?"

"Katy." My name is a little firmer.

"What?"

"You're shirt—"

"Yeah, yeah. It's morning. I know I look like shit. I'm sorry I didn't have time to put on a full face of makeup when I looked at the baby monitor and saw my kid was missing from his crib."

He looks at Owen and then back...past me? He can't even look at me now? Great. Awesome.

I charge toward him, and he turns his body as I approach so Owen's frame is in my line of sight. I take him off Viktor's hip, and he still looks in the opposite direction.

"What the hell is your problem?" I wipe at my cheeks. "Do I have drool crusted on my face or something? I'm sorry I'm not as cute and vulnerable by the light of day."

"Katy." My name is clipped from his mouth.

"What?" I bark out. "I can match your energy if you want me to."

"You're shirt—"

"Jesus Christ, Viktor. What is your obsession with my pajamas this morning? It's just a tank to—"

"Look. Down," he growls.

I growl back in frustration as I look and immediately turn my back to him.

Rule number one of having big boobs. Tank tops at night are just small torture chambers your boobs will escape from at all costs. I've never been a part of the Big Titty Committee before having Owen. Breastfeeding has almost tripled my bra size, and there are some new things I've never had to deal with before.

Exhibit A- My left tit is flapping in the wind. How did I not notice? I just flashed Viktor, and by the look on his face and the way he reacted, he's not happy about it.

5

Dempsey

My body naturally wakes up with the sun. As I walk to the bathroom, I see Owen sitting up in his crib, playing with his stuffed navy blue bunny. Bun-Bun is his comfort toy and goes with us everywhere. Nicole bought him, as well as five backups when Katy was pregnant.

Katy. He goes with *Katy* everywhere. I'm not part of an *us*.

I relieve myself in the bathroom, hoping to get to him before he makes too much noise and wakes Katy up. Quietly, I sneak in his door, and when Owen sees me, he stands, smiles and outstretches his arms.

"Vik." His face lights up with a smile.

"Shhh. We don't want to wake Mommy. Let's go."

He's the cutest kid. He has dark brown hair and eyes, just like Katy. He has a handful of teeth and must be getting more because the front of his shirt is soaking wet. I need to change his clothes and diaper, but I don't want any more noise from the monitor to wake Katy.

As we leave the room, with Bun-Bun in hand, I close the

door behind us and go to the diaper bag hanging by the front door. I know everything I'll need to get by will be in there.

"Morning, Little Man. Did you sleep well?" Owen reaches up and rubs his hand on my beard. He almost never pulls. He likes to rub his hands on it, and I'm not going to lie; the comfort he seems to get from it could bring a grown man to his knees. I've seen the mock resentment in Katy's eyes on a few occasions when she couldn't seem to console him, and I'd take Owen to give her a break. He would instantly calm with his head on my shoulder and a hand on my beard.

Did I think at twenty-four I'd be a glorified, overpaid nanny? Hell, no. Is Owen the cutest kid I've ever met, and would I lay my life on the line for him as much as Katy? Fuck, yes.

Once he's clean and fresh, I know I have a small window to feed him before he fusses. Katy usually breastfeeds him in the morning and before bed, but he's eating big people food, too, so I think I'll let her sleep just for this morning.

As we walk into the kitchen to find some breakfast, he squeezes his little fist in my face, looking toward Katy's bedroom door. Milk. He's using the ASL sign for milk. Maybe Katy won't get to sleep in this morning after all.

Katy has taught him basic signs since birth, and he uses them often to communicate. Milk, more, and all done are his frequent ones.

"Mommy is sleeping. How about…pancakes?"

"Kay-kays." He smiles and jumps in my arms. I know the way to his heart.

I gather all the supplies we need one-handed. When I try to put him in his highchair, his face scrunches with protest and I resign myself to continuing my morning with only one available limb.

I talk Owen through everything I'm doing. I read in the baby books that's how they learn at this age. When I knew I wouldn't be leaving Katy's side anytime soon, I did all the research I could on babies. Guns, tactical gear, maps, and strategies, I knew well. Babies, diapers, and sleep training, not so much. It's been a learning experience for us all.

I feel Katy walk into the room before I see her. Her presence makes the air shift, but she doesn't say anything, so I continue making our pancakes and wait for her to announce her presence.

She watches us for several long minutes before I hear her gasp when Owen pulls at my hair, and I take it down. I turn to greet her with a smile and freeze. The tank top she's wearing shifted in her sleep, and her left breast is gloriously hanging out on full display. I steal my face because, holy fuck is this small glance of her body gorgeous.

"Pepper—" She cuts me off.

"Don't Pepper me. I still think it's the stupidest nickname, but whatever." I try not to smile at her rant because this isn't the time or place. She may think the nickname is stupid, but it perfectly describes her. Sometimes sweet, sometimes spicy, and other times, the heat sneaks up on you when you aren't expecting it.

"Katy," I try again, but a little firmer. "You're shirt—"

"Yeah, yeah. It's morning…" She's not going to listen to me. She's woken up spicy. Maybe like a jalapeno. If I stay away from the seeds, she won't be as hot. I stare past her in an attempt to give her some modesty, but it seems to only make her madder.

Katy charges toward me, and I look away, using Owen as a

buffer between us. Her fucking beautiful breast, full of milk and motherhood, stares at me the closer she gets. She takes Owen from me, and I continue to look away.

"... I'm sorry I'm not as cute and vulnerable by the light of day." Fuck. Does she think that's why I won't look at her?

"Katy." The last of my control comes out with her name.

"What?" She barks back. "I can match your energy if you want me to."

"You're shirt—"

"Jesus Christ, Viktor. What is your obsession with my pajamas this morning? It's just a tank to—"

"Look. Down," I growl, the last bit of my restraint shredding into pieces.

She groans her frustration but judging by the subsequent rush of air I feel when she spins, she's finally realized her wardrobe malfunction.

"Is it safe to turn around now?"

"Why didn't you tell me, Viktor?"

Okay. I guess this is my fault. "I tried to. Several times."

"Mama, mik?"

I glance over my shoulder to see if she's decent and find a smiling Owen using the sign for milk. Katy's cheeks are bright red, and her innocence behind the scowl she's giving me is fascinating. How someone could go through the experiences she has and still keep the innocent pieces of herself is beyond me. I know Owen has brought a bright light into her life, and I'm grateful for him every day.

"I can finish the pancakes if you want to go feed him?"

She tries hard to keep the edge to her face, but I see it softening when she looks at him.

"Sure. Thank you. We'll be right back."

27

I watch them retreat into Katy's bedroom and shake my head at the last few minutes. I shift on my feet, adjusting myself in my loose lounge pants. I'm glad I was standing behind the counter because I might need a cold shower after what I just saw.

Katy's body has retained a lot of her motherly figure after birthing Owen. I watched as her hips widened and her breasts swelled while she was pregnant. She struggled to breastfeed him at first, but it was something she was passionate about doing, and Nicole, Annie, and Blake were a huge part of her success. When she got discouraged and wanted to give up, they didn't let her, and when Owen started latching on properly and gaining weight, we all celebrated with her.

Latching. Another thing I knew nothing about before Katy. How she's taught me more about life than any of my military training is awe-inspiring. Living life truly is the realest form of experience.

Owen comes running out of Katy's room just as I finish the last of the pancakes. He jumps into my awaiting arms. I put him in his highchair and give him the plate I already have ready for him. I made a big batch, so we have leftovers for snacks.

Not we. She.

I made extras so Katy has snacks for Owen or breakfast for them another day. I don't need to do any of the things I do for her, but I want to. Her safety is my job, my priority, but I also relish in being able to help her in any way possible. All I ever want in return is her happiness.

The comment she made earlier struck me hard. *"I'm sorry I'm not as cute and vulnerable by the light of day."* She's feeling the effects of my own nighttime vulnerability.

During the light of day, my role in her life is obvious. I'm on alert for their protection. My duty is to make sure they are safe from all harm, and I take it extremely seriously. I won't ever let her down like I did that day in the rain. I'm here 24/7. Justin and Spencer have talked to me several times about hiring someone else to help me, but I refuse every time. They are my responsibility.

At night is a different story. She's wrong. I'm the vulnerable one. I can't keep my defenses up when I know she's having nightmares I caused. She's seeing the man that raped her because I was unprepared. She's remembering all the blood from my wound. The worst ones, like last night, are when she remembers clinging to my near-lifeless body in the car.

I can't stay away when she screams my name out in desperation from her dream state. Those are the nights she falls asleep in my arms and wakes up alone.

Nights like those produce mornings like this. The silent awkwardness between us. It's not about her wardrobe mishap when she comes out of the bedroom and makes herself a plate without talking to me. It's the cold shoulder and scowl I have firmly etched on my face because it takes my mind longer to forget each time I hold her.

It's not fair to her, and I'm aware of it, but I have no choice. Before the incident, there was already tension between us. I saw her attraction to me, even if she was too young to think about entertaining her crush. Maybe that's why I was sloppy that day. Our banter in the food court was fresh in my mind. Was I too much of a love-struck puppy to notice a car following us? Was my mind too much in the clouds watching her look at baby stuff that Shane was able to take several pictures of us without my knowledge?

I obviously was, and because of that, she could have been kidnapped or worse.

That will never happen again.

6

Katy

O kay, so that happened. I've managed to go all this time without a nip slip. Why now? I went through months of feeling like a dairy cow, nursing on demand, raw nipples, and Viktor never saw anything, at least to my knowledge. One random panicked morning, and I lose my ever-loving mind and apparently my tit.

When Owen is done nursing, I let him out of the room to eat. I watch from the crack of the door to make sure Viktor sees him. When he scoops him into the highchair, I decide to take a quick shower.

I know I rely too much on Viktor. I'm supposed to be raising Owen as a single mother, but in reality, I've never been one. I'm single in the aspect that I have no significant other, but I had six extra sets of hands when I lived in the big house, and here I have Viktor.

Having him here affords me the luxury of sleeping in or showering whenever I want to. I'm more than grateful for everyone in my life, and I'm fully aware of my privilege in that aspect.

When I'm done in the shower, I quickly get dressed in an oversize green t-shirt and black capri leggings. Today is Tuesday, and two days a week, I work at a preschool. I take Owen with me and Viktor, the Viking broods in the hallway outside our classrooms.

No one wants me to work, but I'm nineteen and a mother, and I can't have my pseudo-parents paying for everything despite all of their protests. It's not a lot, just enough money to make me feel like I'm contributing to my life, and it gets me out of the house for a few hours a week.

Stealing my resolve, I enter the living room and smile at the two boys in front of me. Viktor is sharing sausage slices with Owen, who is happily grabbing each piece from a fork.

"Morning."

"Morning," Viktor replies without looking at me.

"Mama!" Owen's excitement is contagious. He saw me fifteen minutes ago and is still excited to see me. "Kay-kays." His little fist offers me a smooshed pancake, and I pretend to eat it from his hand, making him giggle.

"I need fifteen minutes to get ready, and then we can leave," Viktor says with no emotion.

He still isn't looking at me. I can see how my morning will go.

"Take your time. We don't have to leave for a while." I peek out the front window and see several cars still at the big house. "I think Owen and I will walk up to see everyone, and you can join us when you're ready.

"I'll walk you."

I exhale an exaggerated sigh. "I can walk up the driveway

without an escort. I'm not a child."

"Pep—"

"I can walk. Up the driveway. Alone." I pick Owen up from the highchair and disappear into his room, locking the door behind me. I squeeze my eyes shut, trying to will the prickly feeling of tears to subside. Owen wiggles, and I slide down the door, releasing him when my butt hits the floor.

It feels like everything is one step forward and two steps back with Viktor. My mind can't bridge the gap between the day and night man. Every morning, I wake up thinking today is the day he won't let his guilt consume him, and we can go back to the easy-going relationship we had before the accident. Hell, even during his recovery.

We spent hours on the couch watching movies and playing board games while he recovered. He became my best friend.

He got cleared to return to regular activity around the same time Owen was born. I don't know if it was the all-clear or Owen's birth, but he flipped a switch and became this grumpy, overprotective asshole.

I've lost so much in my lifetime, and having Viktor go from being my best friend back to my bodyguard and nothing else, hurts.

The tears silently fall as I get Owen ready for the day. Maybe I can visit Nicole after work and spend time alone without him. Being Spencer's best friend, Justin's house is one of the only places I'm allowed to be unsupervised by Viking Vik. Justin takes the security of his wife, Nicole, and their two children, Hannah and Miles, very seriously. I'll text her a little later. If I do it now, someone will contact Viktor, and then I'll have to deal with him all morning being even grumpier. He hates when I'm out of his sight—big oaf.

When I open Owen's door, the shower is running. I pause, wondering if I should tell Viktor I'm leaving, but decide I'm too mad to care. Grabbing the diaper bag off the hook near the front door, I take Owen's hand and leave. I know when he gets out of the shower, he'll have a notification on his phone from the security cameras of movement outside. That's me. I'm the movement. He can watch and see we got to the house safely because we do.

Coffee. That's the smell that invades my senses the moment I open the back door onto the three-season porch of the big house.

"Everyone descent? Little eyes coming in."

"Come on in, Katy girl. Where's my favorite little guy?" Axel pulls down a mug for me from the cabinet before crouching and lifting Owen into the air.

"Morning, Owen. Are you having a good morning? Are you taking care of your mama?"

"Ac-el." Axel's face beams at his name. He leans and kisses the top of my head, saying morning to me as well. I know I come second seat to Owen around here, and I'm perfectly all right with that. I'll never complain that someone puts my son first. Everyone here has helped me raise him as much as I have.

"Who's home?" I don't know whose cars are in the garage, if any.

"Everyone. Have you eaten? I'm about to make biscuits and gravy." He looks behind me, most likely looking for my shadow.

"We ate, and we left him in the shower. I needed a break." He nods in understanding. I've expressed the whiplash the man gives me, but after this long, even I agree that no one

34

could protect Owen and me better than Viktor can. I'm not going to give up self-preservation over some peace and quiet.

"Everything okay?"

I open my mouth to respond, but we're interrupted by laughter in the other room.

"Katy and Owen are here," Axel calls as a warning to whoever is coming our way. Miller and Lincoln come in, both wearing nothing but pajama bottoms. A look at Axel shows the same attire, only he has a tank top on.

"Did I miss the memo that it's PJ day? Shouldn't at least some of you be getting ready for work?"

"Hey, Cupcake." Miller throws an arm around me and kisses my temple.

"Off, off, range recertification." Miller points at himself, then Axel, and then Lincoln on the last word.

"So, a lazy morning. Got it."

Lincoln kisses my cheek and stops in front of the coffee pot. "Coffee?"

"Yes, please. I haven't had any yet."

"Uh oh." Miller looks out the back window to the pool house. "Trouble in paradise?"

Lincoln hands me my coffee, and I flop onto the stool at the counter.

"There was a little mishap this morning, and it turned Mr. Grumpy into Mr. Steel Wall."

Axel sits next to me with his own mug and smiles. "This sounds juicy. I want all the gossip."

Once again, I open my mouth to tell him about my morning when we're interrupted. Owen runs out of the room, and we hear an "oomph."

"Katy. What are you doing here?" Tucker comes into the

room, holding Owen in his arms. Unlike the other three men, Tucker has on jeans and a t-shirt.

"Oh, look. Someone knows how to put on clothes." Tucker's brows furrow as he looks around the room at everyone's state of dress.

"Katy was about to give us some juicy gossip. Sit and listen." Axel is all too invested in my morning woes.

Tucker kisses my cheek and passes Owen off to me, who immediately throws himself at Axel. Owen loves all of them, but Axel is the biggest goofball of all Spencer's guys, and he has a special relationship with Owen.

"Well, now that the gangs all here…" I'm not embarrassed to tell them what happened. Nothing can embarrass me with any of them. It's the fact it's Viktor that has me hesitating. "Viktor saw my boob this morning."

The room is quiet. No one is saying anything. Why aren't they saying anything? Shit. Maybe I shouldn't have told them.

"Oh, good morning, Katy." Spencer enters the kitchen, and no one moves. She looks around the room, confused. "Is something wrong? Why do they look broken?"

With my elbows on the counter, I rest my head on my fists. "It's my fault. I told them I had a nip slip with Viktor this morning."

"Just this morning? I'm surprised that hasn't happened before. You breastfeed and live together. It was bound to happen." Spencer is logical as always but, ugh.

"We don't live together," I protest, but there's no conviction behind it. He lives *with me*. At least, that's what I keep telling myself.

"There's a difference between seeing your breast and a nipple slip. Which one was it?" Tucker finally speaks up, breaking the stale air of their stares.

"Well, I had a tank top on, and ol' lefty was just flapping in the breeze."

Axel bursts into laughter next to me, breaking the tension in the room. He clasps my shoulder and takes a few breaths before speaking.

"Well, that explains why you're here so early in the morning. You're running."

"I can't just want to come see my favorite, overbearing people in the morning?"

"Nope." Miller pops the P, grabs Lincoln's hand, and heads toward the stairs. "Love you, Cupcake, but I have to get my man ready for work." Miller stops in front of Spencer and presses his lips to hers. "Morning, Smithy." He leaves the room with a smiling Lincoln and a breathless Spencer.

"I need more details of this incident this morning."

"Uh oh, Daddy Tucker is taking charge," Axel teases. With one look from Tucker, Axel slides off the stool, kisses him on the cheek, and retreats from the room. I can't help but chuckle at their relationship. It's obvious of the four men that Tucker is the most dominant of them but there isn't a hierarchy in their relationship when it comes to outside the bedroom. Inside is a different story. I've had many conversations with Spencer about their bedroom dynamics. I never ask for specific details, but it's fun to hear who's in charge sometimes.

"I wore a tank top to bed last night, and apparently, one flopped out while I was sleeping. I panicked when I woke up and saw Owen wasn't in his crib. I ran from my room without thinking and found him with Viktor, who informed me I was giving him a show."

"So it was an accident." A wave of relief washes over Tucker's face, and for some reason, it annoys me.

"You know, I think I'll head back to my house. Thanks for the coffee."

Spencer shoots Tucker a look, and it's obvious he doesn't understand the reason for my reaction. Do I?

"Katy, did I—"

"Yes. You did. You know I'm a woman, right? I'm nineteen, and I have a child. I've never dated anyone. I've never had a real first kiss. The look of relief on your face when you realized I didn't intentionally show Viktor my breast was… was…ugh! Frustrating. What if I wanted to show him my boobs? What if I wanted to strip naked and show him all of me? I have that right as an adult. I can kiss whoever I want. I can show my body to whoever I choose. You aren't allowed to look relieved that I get to stay sweet and innocent in your mind."

A throat clears behind me, and why wouldn't it? I'm sure Viktor heard my entire rant.

Fuck it. I'm seizing the day.

I jump off my stool, charge over to Viktor, and with a last glance at Tucker, I ball my hands into Viktor's shirt, pull him down, and plant a kiss on his lips.

There's nothing special about the kiss. Our lips don't move. There's no swapping of spit between our tongues, but the electric feeling exchanged between us is charged.

"Katy," Tucker's warning voice booms behind us. I pull away and pat a dazed Viktor twice on the chest.

"Have a great day, Tucker. Viktor, please grab Owen, and I'll meet you in the car." I pick up the diaper bag that I left on the porch and power walk my way back to my house.

All of the bravado I had a few minutes ago drains as I watch Viktor and Owen make their way toward me across the lawn.

What did I just do? What did I *do*?!

Viktor opens the back door and secures Owen in his car seat before getting into the driver's seat.

"Viktor. I'm—"

"We aren't going to talk about it, Pepper." Every nerve in my body wants to protest, but I know that tone. He's seconds away from chastising me like a petulant child if I try to force the conversation. I don't blame him. I deserve it. I acted like a toddler throwing a tantrum, took an already sticky situation, and made it worse.

"I'm sorry." I let the words rush out in a hushed whisper. I don't care if he hears it or not, it needs to be said.

I'm sorry that our first kiss was done out of petty frustration and not lust and passion.

7

Dempsey

I've never been so grateful that Katy and Owen are in different rooms in the preschool building. If I had to spend the next three hours consistently staring at her, I would lose my mother fucking mind. Being able to pace the hallway between the two gives me something to do with my body as well as my mind. I'm always on high alert having them separate, but the extra space is welcomed today.

What the fuck was she thinking? I only walked in at the tail end of the conversation, but it was more than enough to know she was upset.

"What if I wanted to strip naked and show him all of me?"

Him being me.

This morning was already too much. My restraint has its breaking point. The vision of her naked breast and now the kiss that still lingers hot on my lips is getting to me.

I heard her apology this morning and wanted to ask what it was for. Was it the kiss, the accidental flashing, or maybe hearing her words? Whatever it was for, I never in my wildest dreams thought Katy would kiss me.

"Mr. Dempsey?" Shelly, one of the teachers in Owen's room, calls from behind me. She's an older woman with white hair and kind eyes who loves the children here as if they were her own.

"Shelly, is Owen okay?"

"He's fine, but he had a diaper blowout, and there isn't an outfit in his bag to change him into. Could you ask Katy if she has any spare clothes for him?"

Shit. I completely forgot I used his spare and forgot to tell Katy.

"Is there another option? It's my fault there aren't clothes in there."

"No, unfortunately not. All we have spare at the moment are little dresses."

Of course. "Can he just walk around in his diaper?" She gives me a sheepish look because she knows I know the rules. "I'll go talk to Katy."

"Thank you, Mr. Dempsey."

I grunt a response and reluctantly head to Katy's classroom. She works with the two year olds and is sitting on the floor building blocks with a few children when I lightly knock.

Katy smiles toward the door until she sees me, and her face falls.

"Can I talk to you for a moment?" Katy glances at her co-teacher, who nods and tells the children she's playing with that she'll be right back.

"What Viktor. I'm working."

I see she's still being salty with me. "I made a mistake this morning—"

"This isn't the time or place for a conversation like this. I'm

41

working."

"...with Owen's diaper bag. His clothes." I can see I need to get right to the point before she comes to the wrong conclusion again. "I used his spare outfit when I dressed him this morning, not wanting to wake you, and forgot to replace it. He had a blowout and now has no clothes. Ms. Shelly wanted me to come ask you if you have anything else."

Katy sighs in frustration. "You know that I don't. That's what the diaper bag is for. They should have a few spares in the classroom."

"I already asked. All they have are dresses."

"Well, then tell Ms. Shelly to put him in a dress. I'm sure he'll love it." She spins, and I feel her dismissal. She may be acting nonchalant right now, but I know her wrath will come later.

When the morning is over and we're walking to the car, I can't help but admire Katy while she proudly holds Owen's hand as he walks in his little yellow dress. She was right; he loved it. I watched him twirl in circles with some of the other girls wearing dresses in his class. Ms. Shelly had to scavenge the dress-up bin for some skirts so other boys could twirl, too. It was an adorable sight to watch.

"Please take me to Justin and Nicole's house."

"Excuse me?"

"I said, ple—"

"I heard what you said, but why?"

"You don't get to ask why, Viktor. I asked you to take me. Or you're welcome to hand me the keys, and I'll drive myself, and you can find your own ride home."

Damn. I really fucked up. This wasn't a planned visit. She's running from me. She knows I'm not needed there and have no reason to go inside. Why is she being so infuriating? I'm not the one who flashed me or kissed me. I'm the fucking victim here, yet I'm being treated as the villain.

"As you wish, Miss Katy."

Three...two...

"Are you freaking kidding me with that? *Miss* Katy? That's how it's going to be? Fine. Fine! Take me to see Nicole, *Dempsey*." She crosses her arms and huffs back into her seat.

Fuck. I asked for that. Maybe a few hours alone will do both of us some good. It's been a volatile morning. Hopefully Justin will be there, and we can have a burger together. I don't ever have girl problems, not that this is exactly that, but I'm at a loss.

When we pull up to Nicole's house, it feels like she's out before I even put the car into park. I can almost see the steam rising off her as she takes Owen out of the back seat.

"Katy?"

"What, Dempsey?"

I close my eyes and sigh. I don't want to fight. "I'll let you have your time. Just please let me know when you're ready to come home. Please." I see her soften the tiniest fraction, and she gives me a curt nod before walking the path to the front door.

I wait until the door opens, and Justin lets Katy in. He steps out and waves.

"Hey, Vik. Want to come in?"

"Thanks for the invite, but I think Katy wants some time without me around." Justin looks inside the house then closes the door behind him, heading to me in the driveway.

"Wanna talk about what's going on with you and her?"

"There's no me and her." My comment comes out more

forceful than I mean it to. Justin raises his hands in surrender but cocks his head and arches a brow at me.

"Okay, how about this. Blake is in there with Rose and the twins, so there are three women and six kids. Why don't we go find a burger or taco place and grab some lunch, and you can tell me all about what's *not* going on between you and Katy."

"Yeah, sure." He runs into the house and is back out a few minutes later.

I have a lot of respect for this man and the things he's done for Katy. He convinced Katy's deadbeat mother to sign away her parental rights, and Spencer immediately adopted her. Owen was a few months old by the time the courts made it official, but in everyone's hearts, she was already Spencer's.

"So tacos or burgers? Either works for me." Justin stares at me waiting for a response.

"I can't drink." No idea why I felt I needed to say that out loud.

"Wouldn't try to convince you otherwise, Vik. I'm only asking about your food preference."

Dammit. I'm so on edge I can't seem to have a simple conversation.

"Burgers sound good. I know a place." I smirk, but he doesn't see it. I know the perfect place to help lift my mood.

"This is where you want to eat? I'm thoroughly amused." Justin shakes his head as we walk through the front doors of the Fifties-themed diner, Debevics. I can't help but plaster on a huge smile at Ziggy, the hippy-dressed man at the host stand. His brown suede vest with fringe on top of a tye-dyed t-shirt wouldn't be complete without the pink heart-shaped glasses.

"You come in at lunchtime? I hope you don't expect great service. Sit wherever you can find a spot." Ziggy flails his arm to the crowded restaurant. Justin takes the lead, and we find a booth that needs cleaning, but I know it will make the experience even better.

"Ever been here before?"

Justin's head is on a swivel, taking in the atmosphere. "Only picking up patients. This is the place where everyone is rude to you, right?"

"Okay, listen up." Rebel, a greaser-looking guy with slicked-back hair and a leather jacket, slides up to the table. "I have a girl in the back waiting for me. If you could give me your entire order now, I can get back to what I was doing before you interrupted me."

"Justin, any allergies or dislikes?"

"Nope."

"I don't have all day." Rebel taps his foot and looks over his shoulder toward the kitchen.

"I got this. We'll get a Route 66 and a Kiss My Heinz burger. Fries with both. I'll take a root beer, and he'll have…" I spin my hand in a circle, encouraging Justin to pick a drink quickly.

"Oh. Me? Um, I'll have a Coke." *Oh no.*

"Ugh. Nope, you'll get water. We don't serve that gross stuff here." Rebel turns to walk away, and I spew out the rest of what we'll need.

"Rebel, he'll have a Pepsi, and we'll take napkins and ketchup with our food."

He rolls his eyes at me and scowls. "Newbies are so much more fun."

"Why are we here, Vik? What's going on?"

Justin might as well be Katy's dad. He's the closest she's

ever had to one. I don't know why I thought I could talk to him about my Katy situation.

"Come on, Vik. I know something's going on with Katy. Should I call the guys and get the info from them? You know how much Axel likes to gossip."

I meet his eye and instantly know. "He already told you, didn't he?"

"The moment your car left the driveway this morning."

I throw my back into the seat and huff. I should have known. His invitation for lunch was just a ploy to get my side of the story. He doesn't seem mad, so I'll take that as a good sign.

"If you know why we're here, then give me your thoughts, Justin. I can take whatever you have to throw at me."

"What are your intentions with my Katy?"

Huh? That's not at all what I expected him to say or ask. My intentions. Do I have intentions? Katy and Owen's safety is my number one priority. It always has and will be.

I want Katy to be happy. Period. I want her to have everything in life she could ever want. Her past was terrible. Honestly, terrible isn't even a strong enough word to describe it.

Katy was neglected by the people in her life who should have been taking care of her. I may not have neglected her that night, but I let her down, and that's just as bad in my books.

"Damn, Vik. You shouldn't need to think about it that hard. I won't bite. I know you're a great guy, and I'm sure whatever your feelings are for Katy, you're fighting them hard. You've been fighting them for a while." He cups one hand over his mouth and whispers. "We've all seen it."

"What do you mean? Seen what?" How would they see anything? I never let my emotions get the best of me. Not since...

"No man can sit and watch hours of chick flicks without there being ulterior motives. Even Axel, and he loves those kinds of movies."

My recovery. Katy and I grew close. Despite not being able to protect her physically, I knew I was helping her heal mentally as much as I could with what I had. Friendship.

"I have no negative intentions or ill will for Katy or Owen."

"I know. Trust me, *we* know. If any of us had doubts about you, we wouldn't allow you to still be in the position you are. The fact that you care about her to whatever degree that might be right now means you'll protect her even more than if she was just a job."

"But she needs to be just a job."

He looks shocked by my curt response. "Why?"

"Here's your food, your *napkins,* and your *ketchup.* You take all the joy out of my life, you Viking look alike. If you want anything else, speak now or forever hold your pen—ees. Hold your piece, 'cause I got a lady in the back who's about to hold mine."

"Thanks. Everything looks great. Enjoy your...peace."

"Why, Vik?"

"Why? Oh, I ordered two of the best burgers and figured we could split them in half and share. Unless you had a preference for one over the other?" I'm fully aware of what he's asking, but I hope I can avoid or distract the question with food.

"Splitting is fine, but you know what I'm asking."

Fuck. I knew I couldn't get away with it. Grabbing a knife, I cut my burger in half, buying myself a few more moments of peace before I have to pour my heart out in the middle of a diner that prides itself on minor degradation. Seems fitting actually.

"I failed her." Those three words sum up everything I feel about that night. All the weeks that I recovered because I failed her. It's bad enough she lives with the memory of my injury, if I had died...

"You saved her."

"I fucking didn't!" Heads turn at the level of rage behind my words. Lowering my voice, I try again. "I didn't save her that night. I wrecked her. We were arguing about stupid bullshit. My guard was down. I was being a friend and not her bodyguard and...fuck. She watched me fucking die because I was upset that she walked off on me at the mall and flirted with some little boy. Then the pictures were sent, and I was out of my mind with worry. I let my fucking guard down. Even if I wanted to pursue anything with Katy, I don't deserve her. She deserves the best of the fucking best, and that's not me."

8

Katy

"How do you both do it? I have one, and I'm exhausted." As I sit on the couch in Nicole's living room and admire the stone floor-to-ceiling fireplace, I can't help but be in complete awe at how well put together these two women are.

Blake is managing to hold a conversation, a glass of wine, and watch her twin five year olds, Ruby and Rory, while also keeping an eye on her almost two year old, Rose.

Nicole looks as cool as a cucumber, letting Hannah, her five year old, wrangle all the little kids while her almost three year old brother Miles plays happily on the floor with Owen.

"Blake is the pro. Ask me again in five months when we have our third wandering around." Nicole rubs her baby belly and looks at her bump adoringly.

"I'm not a pro, trust me. The terrible twos almost broke me with the twins. I don't know if it's easier with Rose because there's only one of her or because she's honestly just a good toddler."

Nicole laughs. "Or maybe it's because she made you wait an extra eight days for her birth." Nicole takes a sip from her wine glass. She's drinking a fruity cocktail of cranberry and pineapple juice to feel included. Blake and I both have wine. I may be underage, but they know I'm responsible and always have a ride so they allow me to indulge on occasions.

"Are either of you planning more kids?" Blake almost spits her wine back into her glass and pats her chest. I pat her back to help her regain her air. "Should I take that as a no?"

"Cole wants a football team. Since Annie had her tubes tied after having the twins, that leaves me to carry all the babies. I have one more in me, but Rose was a lot on my body. We agreed to start trying again when she's three. Until then, we just practice a lot. We've also talked about adopting after having one more."

"I didn't know Annie had her tubes tied. And that's great about adopting."

"Yeah, with her hip injury, we didn't want to take any chances. The twins were enough of a miracle. None of us wanted to tempt fate another time." Blake looks off into the distance, lost in a memory.

"I want all the babies," Nicole says nonchalantly.

"All?"

"As many as my body allows. My hubby happens to like me being pregnant. He's got a total breeding kink."

"That's probably more information than I needed to know." I put my hands over my ears and sing "lalalalala" making us laugh.

"How about you, Katy? Thoughts on any more? You have plenty of time." Blake asked such an innocent question, but it sparks immediate anxiety.

I was sixteen, boyfriendless, and a virgin in high school when I was raped. I was more worried about graduating and getting away from my mother than a future beyond that. I never allowed myself to think about kids because my childhood was so broken.

I wanted a relationship first. I wanted what Nicole and Justin have; a stable home and a support system. I always told myself I would worry about kids once I had that. The universe had other plans for me, and while I wouldn't change being Owen's mother for anything in the world, I still haven't allowed myself to think ahead for a future.

A gentle hand covers mine, stopping me from rubbing the tops of my thighs. I hadn't realized I was doing it. My anxiety doesn't usually present itself on the outside.

"Hey, I'm sorry. I didn't mean to ask a difficult question. You don't have to answer." Blake's eyes are sincere. Her question shouldn't have elicited such an extreme response from me.

"It's okay. I just haven't really thought about it. A baby usually requires a partner, and I'm nowhere close to dating or having a boyfriend. But…I think I'd like Owen to have a sibling. I'm an only child and sometimes wonder if things would have been better had I not been alone."

"Trust me. Have another. When they have a playmate other than you, it's a life changer." Nicole rubs her stomach again and I'm wondering just how many playmates she plans to provide for her kids.

"So what's the potential for some Viking babies in your future?"

My jaw drops at Blake's question, and I whip my head to Nicole, who's sipping her wine glass, pretending the curtains have all her attention.

"How...who..." I sigh.

"Axel," we say simultaneously.

"I swear that man should have his own gossip column." Nicole's smirk tells me she knows more than she's letting on.

"Nicole?"

"The call was almost immediate. I don't think he even waited until your lips were dry from the kiss."

"Eww. Seriously?"

Nicole shrugs, and I can't blame her. I made an irrational, childish decision this morning, and I'm going to have to live with it.

"Are you okay, Katy?" Blake looks at me again with sympathetic eyes. "What are you thinking?"

"I stole my first kiss, and it wasn't even good." I'm suddenly surrounded by two women who are instantly doting on me.

"You didn't steal anything Vik wasn't willing to give," Blake protests.

"That man is head over heels for you, and you probably knocked him flat on his ass," Nicole encourages.

"It's not...it's not like that. I'm basically his employer. His job is keeping me from trouble, not giving me my firsts." I empty my glass of wine because the thought of Viktor giving me any of my firsts spikes my anxiety. Blake quickly grabs the bottle of red wine from the coffee table and refills it.

"At this point, we can all see that it's more than just a job for him. I bet that's what my husband is lecturing him on right now."

"What?" My head pops up to meet Nicole's eyes. "They're doing what? They're out talking about me? No. No. They can't do that. No." I stand from the couch and pace the length of the living room.

"Katy, you're both adults. What's so bad about it?" I can only gawk at Blake.

"It's not real. What he feels is guilt and a survivor bond. He only thinks he has feelings for me. He feels an emotional attachment to me because we both survived a trauma together. I don't know if that's the right term for it, but it makes sense in my head."

I've thought about this a lot. We didn't have much of a relationship before the night of the incident. Sure, we were friendly, and I gave him a hard time, but I was a smartass teenager, and he was an authority figure that was being paid to take my shit.

After he got out of the hospital, things changed. He was attentive and friendly to me. We hung out and became friends. I thought it was his way of protecting me the best way he could, being out of commission with his gunshot wound. But once he got the all-clear, he became cold and aloof.

Except at night. At night, we're both vulnerable. He holds me, and I let him comfort me. And maybe it's comfort for him as well. Two survivors of a shared traumatic experience leaning into each other for support. A survivor's bond.

"Katy, that's not it at all." Nicole stands and takes my hands, encouraging me to sit with her on the couch. I finally relent and join.

"Katy, I know your story with Justin. Do you think you have a survivor bond with him? Or *my* story with Justin? Trauma is all around us. Especially in the field that our significant others work in. But they *all* have coping mechanisms. Justin goes to therapy, Annie goes to therapy, and Axel and Miller use their humor. I don't know about Lincoln, but I imagine, at the very least, the department made him go to therapy after his injury."

"I...no, I don't feel that way about Justin, and I don't think you have that with him either. It just can't be real. Even if it was, I have nothing to offer him. I'm a young, inexperienced single mother with a GED and half a job, living in a pool house."

"Katy, oh god." Blake throws her arms around me. "You're so much more than all of that. Yes, you're a single mother, but that makes you strong and resilient. You may only have a GED, but you earned it a year early while pregnant. Your age doesn't mean anything. You've lived so much of your life already."

"I get it but—"

"MOMMY!!!" The three of us whip around to see a disheveled Rose covered in pink sparkles from head to toe.

"Rosie. What happened to you?" Blake stands and carefully approaches her glittery toddler.

"Mommy, she was in the bathroom with this." Rory opens his hand to present us with a pink glitter bath bomb.

Nicole's hand flies to her face. "Blake, I'm so sorry. Miles never plays in Hannah's bathroom, so I didn't even think to move those." Blake is trying her best not to laugh at the hysterical sight of Rose.

"Nicole, it's perfectly fine. Can we use your shower?"

"Of course. Use whatever you need. We'll watch the twins. Do what you need."

Nicole and I hold it together long enough for them to leave the room before we burst out laughing.

"Who wants a snack? Apples, cheese, and peanut butter?" Nicole heads toward the kitchen with several children cheering on her heels.

"Mommy, can we have donuts too?" Hannah asks.

"Apples, cheese, peanut butter, and one donut." Little squeals erupt through the room, and I help Nicole get everyone set up while she makes their snack.

They've given me a lot to think about. I don't know how much of it I believe, but I'll think it all over, and maybe I need to have a conversation with Viktor about it.

9

Dempsey

What a fucking nightmare. How could Justin think I'd be any good for Katy? I want what's best for her and Owen. It's not me.

I can't wait to get home and create some distance between us. Katy will do Owen's nighttime routine, breastfeed him, and then put him to bed. Depending on the night, sometimes she'll join me on the couch, and we'll talk or watch a movie. Tonight, I'm going to have a quick drink, then pull out the couch while she's in her room so she knows I want to be alone.

I'm lying on my back after finishing my second glass of whiskey when Katy comes out with a sleeping Owen in her arms.

"Do you need help with him?"

"No, I've got him," she whispers back. I breathe a sigh of relief, knowing I can get some sleep, hoping Katy sleeps through the night. Except Katy has other plans. I should have known. I saw her take a sippy cup filled with breast milk into the bedroom. She didn't want him to nurse after she had been drinking. When I picked her up from Nicole's house, she was tipsy. Maybe a bit more than tipsy, but I wouldn't say she was drunk. She still had her wits about her to know that she shouldn't feed him.

I'm just rolling over when she returns to the room.

"Can we talk, Viktor?"

Fuck. I can't say no to her, but after downing those two glasses, I might be a little worse than her.

"Of course." I sit up and rest my back against the pseudo headboard. She crawls onto the sofa and sits cross-legged in the middle of the bed.

"How was your day?" Her voice is low and sing-songy.

My day was fucking terrible. You kissed me, you were angry with me, Justin thinks I should go for it, and all I want to do is forget about today and fade off into my alcohol-induced haze that's slowly getting worse.

"It was fine. Lunch with Justin was nice. How was your day?"

Fucking generic conversation. I don't need this right now.

"There wasn't too much tragedy, so it was good."

"Good. Pepper, I'm tired. Was there something specific I can help you with?" I'm trying my best not to be curt with her, but I'm exhausted from the day.

"I'm sorry."

"You have nothing to be sorry for. You're a little tipsy and should probably get some sleep."

"Viktor." She closes her eyes, and her chest heaves with her sigh. "I shouldn't have kissed you, or whatever you want to call it. I'm sure it meant nothing to you, and you probably kiss your aunts the same way, but it was disrespectful of me to do that to you."

I don't notice I'm growling until Katy's chocolate brown eyes flash to me. "You think it meant nothing to me?"

She shrugs, and her entire body deflates. "It was so simple, and I've never kissed anyone before. There wasn't anything to it, so I just stormed off. I was mad, and it wasn't at you in that moment. I feel like I disrespected you, and I wanted to apologize."

Without thinking, I'm on top of her, arms pinned above her head and her body glued under mine from chest to toes. Her eyes remain closed, but I don't need to see them. I can feel her warmth under me. She's soft and curvy everywhere I like.

Using one finger, I caress her cheek, coaxing her to open her eyes. I want to see the heat I'm feeling from our close proximity. Instead, I see her bottom lip tremble and realize it's not just her lip but her entire body.

What the fuck am I doing?

I jump back from her to the farthest corner of the couch that I can squeeze into.

"Fuck, Pepper. Fuck. Fuck. I'm so sorry. Are you okay? God. Fuck. Of course not."

She's still lying on her back, eyes closed. I need her to say something. Anything. This. *This* is the exact reason I'm no good for her. I have no self-control over this woman. She's my own fucking siren.

"Please, Pepper, say something. I'm so fucking sorry. I have no idea what came over me."

With her eyes still closed, she lowers her hands from above her head and rests them on her stomach.

"I'm okay, Viktor."

"Oh, thank fuck."

"Just let me have a moment."

"As many as you need."

She intertwines her fingers together, and I can tell she's concentrating on her breathing. I absentmindedly breathe the same pattern. Our breaths become more shallow and calm, and I know she's relaxing.

"Will you sit up for me? I just…god, I feel so fucking terrible. This isn't about me. I'm sorry." I need to stop. I triggered her. I just laid her flat without consent or permission. She asked how my day was, and I basically attacked her.

Fuck.

My hands fly to my head, and I pull at the roots. I can't watch. I can't see her lying there suffering because of me. The bed shifts, and I can't force myself to look up. I feel her warmth when she's close enough to touch me.

Katy's fingers glide over my fists and she softly whispers, "Relax before you hurt yourself."

My fingers instantly loosen from her gentle tone. Why is she comforting me? This is all wrong.

"Fuck, Katy. I—"

"Shhh. I'm fine. I-You just took me by surprise. It wasn't you, I promise."

Is she serious? How was this not me? There wasn't some other grizzly of a man pressing her body into the mattress.

Katy tugs at my hands to remove them from my hair. She pulls them to her lips and kisses each one. Each press of her lips feels like a tornado of lightning jolting through my body.

"Katy."

"Please believe me. It wasn't you. I was trying to push down the feeling that I know doesn't belong here." She drops our hands into her lap.

"Katy—"

"Can I get this out first?" I bob my head. "You know my story. I haven't done anything with anyone, so that one... incident, it took everything from me. It's the only baseline I have, and that's really shitty."

"You've never kissed anyone? Not even...before?" Her head slowly shakes.

I drop my head and stare at the ceiling. I took that from her. I gave her nothing back this morning. Not that I had the forethought to plan it.

"Will you..."

Is she about to ask me to kiss her for real? Fuck. Can I give that to her? Can I handle it? I'm a man trained to kill by the government, and despite being dishonorably discharged, this petite thing is about to bring me to my knees.

"Katy. Be very careful with what you're about to ask me, and make sure you're confident in your question. Some lines can't be redrawn."

Please don't ask. I'm a weak man, Katy. I won't tell you no. I'll give you everything you want and things you didn't even know to ask for.

"I want you to kiss me, Viktor."

"Pepper."

"Please." She squeezes my hands in hers, and it sends a jolt straight to my cock, which isn't restrained very well behind loose sweatpants.

"Katy."

"If you don't want to, I understand, but please don't hesitate because you think I might not want to. I do."

"You do?" She nods at me and holds my gaze.

"Please erase the only image I have in my head before this morning."

She wants me to erase the image of Shane's lips on hers. I'm conscious of the growl this time and hold it back. I pick up a hand and rub a thumb over her bottom lip. They part, and a small breath escapes.

"We've both been drinking, Pepper. This is a terrible idea. Probably the worst one you've had." I can't help but stare at her soft, inviting lips. They're a rosy pink with a deep cupid's bow. When I run my thumb over it, my touch tickles her, and she draws her lips together, sucking the tip of my finger into her mouth.

I feel a swipe of wetness when she touches her tongue to my thumb. "We can regret it in the morning. You don't like me when it's light outside anyway. Right now, it's dark. Kiss me in the dark, Viktor."

Slowly, I slide my hand from her jaw to the back of her head. I lean in torturously slowly until our lips almost touch.

"Are you sure, Pepper?"

"I'm sure. But...what if I suck?"

"What if you're heaven?" I close the tiny space between us and press our lips together. Nothing more than this morning. The same sparks are there, but I'm prepared. They don't almost knock me on my ass this time.

With a shuttered breath, she opens her mouth, and a hesitant tongue explores. Katy licks my bottom lip, and I sweep my tongue across hers. She gasps before leaning into me farther. Her movements are still hesitant, but god damn if it isn't heaven.

I shift to move close and run my hand up her thigh to her waist. Katy pulls back.

"Viktor?"

"We can stop. I'm sorry. We should probably stop." I pull my hand away from her thigh, and she stops me.

"I'm okay. I am."

Is she trying to convince me or herself because I'm not sure?

Katy picks her hand up from her lap and touches my shoulder. Her fingers trail down my arm, leaving goosebumps. When she gets to my wrist, she grabs it and pulls my arm behind her back, where my hand was already heading when she stopped kissing me.

"Can I kiss you again?" Her chocolate eyes are full of so much hope that even if I wanted to, I couldn't say no. With my hand on her lower back, I pull her to me so she's straddling my legs on the bed.

"You're in control, Pepper."

She gives me a shy smile and runs a hand across my beard. When she reaches my chin, she tugs, pulling me forward. Why the fuck do I like that so much? Our lips meet, and she parts hers almost immediately this time. She already has more confidence in the strokes of her tongue, and I'm eager to see how far she explores.

I don't have to wait long. She pulls away again, and I sigh, thinking the kiss is over, but she surprises the fuck out of me by pulling off her tank top. I stare at her eyes, unwilling to look down at her body, no matter how badly I want to.

"It's your turn." Katy's eyes roam my t-shirted chest. She arches a brow and tips her head silently, saying, "Let's go."

"My turn, huh?" Her hands drift to the hem of my shirt, and she tentatively lifts. I sit forward, allowing her to remove it.

"You're beautiful, Viktor." I preen under her roaming hands on my chest and abs. I want to close my eyes and relish in her soft, gentle touch, but the growing heat and admiration in her eyes are captivating. "Why won't you look at me?" Her hands freeze on my pecs, and her brows knit together.

"I am looking at you, Pepper."

"All of me. You're looking through me."

"I'm looking *into* you. It's fascinating to watch you experience things for the first time. And not just watch, but feel." Her fingers twitch at my words, and her pinky brushes my nipple. I suck in a breath at the sensation, and she pulls her hands away.

"Come back. That felt...god I liked it."

Katy lifts a hand and intentionally swipes a thumb over my now erect nipple, and I moan. A smile bursts across her cheeks, causing me to do the same. There's so much joy in that one simple gesture.

"What does it feel like?" She does it again, and my abs constrict, causing her to giggle. "You're so reactive."

When I sat Katy on my lap, I made sure she was far enough back that she wasn't sitting on my cock. If she were, she'd be able to tell exactly how reactive my body is to her.

"It feels like you're shooting fireworks straight to my cock." Her cheeks flush, and her mouth forms an O.

"Show me. I mean, I don't have a dick, but I wonder if I'd get the same sensation to my clit."

Fuck. Me.

Katy should not be saying dick and clit in the same sentence to me. I want nothing more than to touch her and give her every pleasure in the world, but I'm not the conductor of this show.

The longer I take to respond, the more worried she looks. I need to make a decision right now whether I'm going to give her what she's asking or disappoint her and send her to bed. I know the right choice, but my cock and my mind are at war.

"Unless you don't want to."

Katy's retreating hand snaps me out of my mental debate. Decision made.

"Tell me what you want me to do."

The spark is back in her eyes, and so are her roaming hands.

"Before you do anything, you need to actually look at me, Viktor."

She's right. She's so fucking right, but if I look, there's no turning back. I'm already so far gone for this woman with just a kiss. Even if it's only in the dark of night.

"Look at me. Please."

Slowly, I allow my eyes to drift from her chocolate eyes down the slender slope of her nose. Her slightly swollen lips from our kiss to her neck that I want to explore every inch of. Her chest begins to heave, and before I can fully take everything in, my eyes are on her breasts.

I saw a glimpse of one this morning, but that doesn't compare to what I see right now. They're full—so beautifully full and round. Her areolas are a light shade of brown, contrasting with the dark pink of her nipples.

My mouth waters at the sight. I know she's so full because she didn't breastfeed Owen tonight.

Katy pulls my bottom lip from my teeth that I hadn't even realized I was biting.

"Show me." Her eyes flash to mine in confusion. "This is all about you. Show me what you want me to do to your body."

"Like Shadow?"

Shadow is a game she plays with Owen. It's like Simon says without having to say Simon says. Katy does something, and Owen copies it.

"Exactly like Shadow."

She smiles, half innocent, half devilish. She begins to move her hands, and I stop her by placing mine over them.

"Safeword. We need a safeword. You say it, and we stop. I want you to be one hundred percent comfortable and confident that you're in control."

"Okay." She draws out the word in thought. "How about bunny?"

"That works but why?" Such a strange option for a safeword.

"Because it will make me think of Owen's stuffed animal, and what's more of a mood killer than a kid in the room."

Well damn, she's got me there. "Bunny it is. Now, let's start our game of Shadow, Pepper."

10

Katy

This is unreal. I'm topless in front of Viktor. My courage is coming via liquid form—or, more specifically, wine.

Despite being slightly tipsy, I know what I want, and now that we have an established safeword I'm confident to play his game.

I reach up and brush my finger along the tops of his shoulders from neck to tip, then move them to the middle of his chest to give him room to copy my movements.

Viktor's hands are rough, and his fingers feel large over my small shoulders. I shudder at the line of heat he leaves behind. My next movements bring my pointer fingers from the base of his neck, between his pecs, and I stop when I hit the waistline of his pants.

I'm unprepared for the sensation I feel low in my belly when his fingers shadow mine and run between my cleavage. It's an aching need for more.

My fingers dance across the top of his pecs, wanting to

touch his nipples again, but I'm nervous about him touching mine.

"Viktor, he's the only one who's touched me here." I placed my hands flat across each of his pecs. "I want you to erase the pain he gave me and turn it into pleasure."

Rage flashes through his eyes. I revealed a lot with my request. The question is, will he accept it?

"It would be my honor."

I glide my hands down his body and wait. And wait. Viktor is hesitating. He wants to move. I can tell by his fingers flexing on my stomach. Ever so slowly, his hands ascend my body. He follows my previous path and brushes my chest as he works his way up my cleavage then around the swells of my breasts. Large hands rest on top, and my nipples harden, wanting to feel him.

"Touch me." Viktor's hands curve around the outside of my breasts, and he lifts them from the bottom, feeling their weight. His thumbs move and graze my nipples, and holy fucking fuck. My entire body jolts, causing his hands to squeeze my breasts and...

"Oh my god. I'm sorry. I'm so embarrassed." I shift to move off his lap, convinced he'll be horrified, but he stops me with a look, and I obey.

Viktor's thumb wipes up the breast milk that leaked from his gentle squeeze. My jaw drops as he lifts his thumb to his mouth and sucks off the drops.

"It's...sweet."

He repeats his action with the leakage from my other nipple, closing his eyes as he enjoys more of the taste.

"Fuck, Pepper. I think I could devour you."

The thought of his mouth all over my body sends a shiver

down my spine.

"You can try more if you like."

"That's for Owen. I can't do that."

"Not tonight, it isn't. I was planning to pump and dump to make sure the wine is out of my system. You could...help me with it."

If there was a picture to go with the definition of feral, the look on Viktor's face would be it. His tongue darts out, and he licks his lips.

"Are you sure?"

Even those three words show the restraint he's barely holding as they have a slight growl to them.

"I'm sure." I'm sure I want him to touch me in every way possible. There's a small part of me that's apprehensive about whether it will feel good. Can my mind switch from the sensation of breastfeeding Owen to Viktor sucking on my nipples for sexual pleasure?

As his mouth descends on my breasts, the sight alone leaves me with little doubt I can make the distinction between the two. But when his lips wrap around my nipple, and his mouth makes the first pull, I feel every spark and firework explode in my clit.

"Holy hell." I grab the back of his head and pull him in closer. It's unlike anything I've ever felt before. He switches sides, feeling me leak on his hand from my other nipple, and the hum of appreciation he makes causes me to giggle.

Viktor pulls away, holding each breast in his hands, and his eyes dart between them in admiration.

"Why does that taste like the last meal I ever want to have? What happens if I—*Oh shit.*"

Now I'm laughing out loud as he just squeezed my left

breast, my overachiever, and she squirted all over his face. His silver-blue eyes meet mine, and they're wild with lust.

"Pepper. Is that normal? Can I fucking shower myself in your breastmilk?"

His question makes me laugh harder. The mental image I have of this Viking on his knees in the shower as I squirt breastmilk all over his naked body is powerful.

"Next time. I promise." Viktor shoots me a look because I just eluded to us doing this again. He shakes it off and hungrily brings his mouth back to my breasts. The feel of his tongue on my overly sensitive nipples has other parts of my body reacting in ways that are new to me. My clit tingles, and my inner walls are pulsing.

Can I come just from his oral stimulation of my nipples alone? It sure feels like it.

"You're killing me, Pepper. You gotta stop grinding on my lap." I freeze. I hadn't even realized I was doing that. My body has a mind of its own right now.

"I can't help it. Everything you're doing feels amazing. I don't want you to stop." Viktor licks at my nipple then blows cold air onto it, causing my entire body to convulse with pleasure.

A smile forms on his lips, and he quietly chuckles and does it again to the other nipple.

"More. I want more." I can feel my buzz starting to fade, and if this is the only chance I get to be with him, I want all of him.

"You can have whatever you want. Just tell me. Or show me."

Show him? Okay. We can continue our game of Shadow. I move my hand up his thigh and over the very prominent bulge in his pants. I stroke up and down a few times with the heel of my hand, and he hisses.

"It's your turn."

His Adam's apple bobs as his eyes wander down my body.

"Don't ask me if I'm sure. You know what the answer will be. I need you, Viktor. There isn't anyone in the world I trust more than you." It's mildly humorous that this big man is acting like he's afraid of me. His hands skim my thighs and toy with the edge of my shorts.

Grabbing each side of his face, I flex my fingers through his groomed beard to get his full attention. I've seen a myriad of emotions in his silver-blue eyes tonight, but this one is different. Is it awe? Wonderment?

"Penny for your thoughts?"

"Pepper, you're…"

"Trusting you, wanting you, asking you to take my pseudo virginity, Viktor? I know we haven't gotten that far yet, but that's the direction I'm heading, and there's no use sugar-coating it. I. Trust. You."

His eyes dart between mine. His face hardens as he considers my words. Part of me knows he'll say yes, but another part fears he'll say no.

"You started calling me Pepper for a reason. Sometimes spicy, sometimes sweet. I want to be spicy. Shane took this from me as a child. Give it back to me as a woman, Viktor. Make love to me."

I press my lips to his, but he's slow to return the kiss. I've just asked him for a lot, for everything. But I still need him to know the choice is his.

"Or, we can go to bed and chalk this up to some drunken foolery."

70

"No."

His objection is quick and confident. With more purpose than his hands have had, he encircles my hips and pulls me up his lap until I'm sitting on top of his length, pressed between my legs.

"Oh god."

Viktor's hands coax my hip to move over him. Bracing my hands on his shoulders for leverage, he hums when I take over the movement.

"I'll give you whatever you want, Katy, but you're in charge. I need to know everything we do is what you want."

"Okay." I shift off him and stand, almost laughing at the sad puppy face he gives me. I see more of this man than anyone else does. The softer side. He just gave up total control for me. Something he would never do in his everyday life. My nighttime Viking.

"Come. My bed is more comfortable than this." I offer him my hand, and he stands, pulling me in for a kiss. It tells of what's to come as his tongue twists and explores with mine. I pull away and drag him behind me toward my bedroom. Once we cross the threshold, he closes the door, and I drop his hand.

I don't want to play games. I want this. Tucking my thumbs into my last piece of clothing, I push my shorts over my hips. Gravity takes them, and they pool around my feet.

"Fuck."

"Your turn," I tell him.

His lip twitches and he takes a slow perusal of my body before pushing his pants off.

"Well, that's not fair." I pout at his underwear and cross my arms over my chest. I don't miss how his eyes flare when my tits push together.

"It's not my fault you weren't wearing any underwear. I have nothing left to shadow, so I guess these are for you to take off."

It's my turn for my eyes to peruse his body. I was a confident, badass woman out on the couch, but my bravery slips a bit. The bulge he's sporting is significant. The only thing standing between me and a naked, extremely muscular man, tattooed..."

"Holy shit, Viktor." Peeking out of the bottom of his black boxer briefs and running the entire length of his right leg is a tattoo with intricate knots or tribal work. I squat in front of him to get a better look in the low light of my bedroom, and he curses under his breath. My position probably has him thinking dirty thoughts, but I only want to look at his tattoo right now.

"It's gorgeous."

Viktor's fingers stroke through my hair, "Yes, it is."

My cheeks heat at his compliment. He reaches down and pulls me to standing.

"You don't belong on your knees for me. That's where I belong."

Before I can fully register his words, he kneels before me, and his hot lips find their way to my stomach. He pulls me in closer by the back of my thighs and kisses from one hip bone to the other.

"Has anyone ever kissed you here? Tasted you?" His nose nuzzles skin that feels forbidden. He knows the answer to his questions, but I understand it's a silent request.

"You'll be the first." His forehead flattens on my stomach, and he inhales. When he exhales, I giggle as the air tickles the trimmed triangle of hair I have between my legs.

"I love that you aren't shaved bare." His fingers lightly brush over the hair, and I shudder at how close they are to my aching core.

"Viktor."

"Can I take care of you? Would you like that?" He nips at my hip bone, and I have to will my legs to keep me upright.

I bob my head more frantically than I mean to, and his lips twitch, attempting not to smile at my eagerness. He stands and grips the back of my thighs on the way up, lifting me off the floor. A squeal escapes me, unprepared for the distance between me and the floor.

"I've got you."

"I know." He means more than me currently being in his arms. *He's got me.* In every way.

Viktor crawls us to the top of the bed and gently lays me on my back. His lips feather kisses down my body, stopping to pay more attention to my nipples and his new favorite snack.

"I know what I said earlier, but I might not be willing to share with Owen."

"If he can learn to share, so can you." Once again, he stares at me at the implication that this might be more than a tonight-only event.

Moving further down my body, I feel like every nerve ending is on fire. His beard scratches my sensitive skin, but his lips and tongue soothe it. When he reaches my belly button, he swirls his tongue inside as his hands open my thighs to accommodate his broad shoulders. I pull my knees up, giving him better access, and when he finally takes his first look, I brace myself for his reaction.

"Are you fucking kidding me, Pepper. When did you do

this?" His words are a growl, and I know it's curiosity, frustration, and lust.

"Um. Blake took me about a year ago. Not long after I turned eighteen." He's staring intently at my triangle piercing. When I decided to get a genital piercing, I did my research. The Isabella and the Triangle were both said to give the most pleasure. Both piercings run behind the clitoris, but one is horizontal, and one is vertical. I chose the triangle because I liked the look of wearing an open hoop rather than a curved barbell.

"Does it...can I..."

A flustered Viktor is sexy.

"It's completely healed. It doesn't hurt, and it's basically a bullseye for your tongue."

"Fuck." He says the word as if it hurts. "You're going to be the death of me, Pepper."

"Let's hope not."

He slowly moves his hand up my inner thigh, and I hold back the giggle as he tickles me. I don't want to ruin the mood. He looks so serious. When he moves around the horseshoe jewelry, I shudder in a hard breath. Viktor's eyes flash to me with worry.

"That felt incredible. No one's ever touched it but me, and I'm a little sensitive right now. Please don't stop."

His fingers explore the piercing, continuously brushing my clit until I'm starving for his touch.

"Fuck. Please, Viktor."

"Shhh. I've got you, Pepper."

Finally, I watch his head disappear and feel his hot breath before he licks me for the first time. My hands fly to his hair, grabbing fistfuls. I feel his smile as he licks me again. I don't even recognize the noises coming from me as he sets a rhythm, occasionally sucking my jewelry into his mouth, making sparks fly behind my eyes.

The build-up of my orgasm is quick, and Viktor can tell because he pulls away.

"No," a needy whine escapes me, and I try to pull his head back.

"Pepper, calm down. I'm not done with you. But if you still want me to make love to you, I need to prepare your pussy to take me. I'm a big man. I don't want to hurt you."

11

Dempsey

How the fuck did I get here? How am I a lucky enough bastard to have my face between this Queen's legs, preparing her to take my cock that wants to explode just thinking about being inside her?

I press a finger to her soaked entrance, and she inhales.

"Pepper, remember your safeword is bunny. Don't be afraid to use it."

"I know. Thank you."

Reaching up, I lace my fingers through hers as my other hand pushes a finger into her pussy in a slow rhythm, going deeper with each pump. She's tight. I expected her to be, but there was no way for me to prepare for the ecstasy that comes with it.

This is such a fucking gift that she's giving me. I haven't touched a woman since I came into Katy's life. Not solely because of her. She was a child when I became her bodyguard. Because this world is fucking cruel, and women have it worse than any man. Putting my protection into Katy and then

Owen has been my sole purpose, and I've put everything I have into it. Except for that day...

"Hey?" Katy caresses my hair, and I look up her body into her eyes. "Where'd you go?"

Leaning down, I suck her clit into my mouth. I don't want to talk or think about that day. I want to be in the here and now and savor every second of this once-in-a-lifetime opportunity she's trusting me with.

When I enter a second finger, she clamps down on me, and the thought of my cock feeling this makes me safeword in my head.

Bunny. Bunny. Bunny.

Think of that blue fucking bunny because I can't blow my load before I'm even inside her.

By the time I manage a third finger, she's a writhing mess.

"You're almost ready for me. How about an orgasm to get you the rest of the way there?"

"Oh, fuck. Yes, please."

Her neediness is evident in her breathy plea. I don't make her wait and go back to devouring her pussy. The piercing shocked the fuck out of me, but I honestly shouldn't be surprised. Katy is bold and ballsy, and piercing her genitals is right up her alley. And it's hot as fuck. She wasn't kidding when she said it was a bullseye. The jewelry is pierced right under her clit, and the opening of the horseshoe ring directs me exactly where to go.

Her moans are the most erotic thing I've ever heard, and my eyes occasionally drift to the baby monitor, hoping she doesn't get too loud and wake up Owen.

I move my fingers in a "come hither" motion, and Katy almost lifts off the bed.

"Oh my god. What…what are you doing?"

Her breaths come in short quick puffs as I stroke her G-spot and suck on her clit. She's right on the edge. I can feel her walls fluttering around my fingers, ready to tip over the edge of release any second.

"Fuck. Oh, Viktor. Oh fuck. Ahh."

The dam breaks. Her pussy convulses around my fingers and sucks me in. I can't wait for my cock to feel this.

Katy's orgasm begins to subside, but I'm not ready to give up my treat. I continue to lazily lick her after reluctantly pulling my fingers from her dripping pussy.

"Strip."

"What?" Her forceful tone takes me by surprise.

"I said, strip. I won't ask again."

Holy fuck. I won't make her ask me again. I sit up on my knees and awkwardly take off my boxer briefs. She watches me with hungry eyes.

"Any surprise piercings for me to find?"

Brat.

"Why don't you find out for yourself." To my surprise, she shifts her position and grips my cock without any hesitation.

Not a brat, clearly a vixen.

I stare at the ceiling as her fingers explore. There's nothing to find, but I didn't expect her to so willingly look when I told her to. She once again surprises me.

"Pep—FUCK." I clamp a hand over my mouth to contain my outburst as Katy's hot mouth surrounds the tip of my cock. "You just…oh fuck…you could've fucking…warned me. Fucking Christ."

My soul has left my body via her mouth. Just the tip. That's all she has in her mouth. One hand squeezes the base of my cock while her tongue laps at the pre-cum that I know has to be leaking out.

She pops off, and my body convulses.

"It's salty."

Oh fuck. Now she's talking about my pre-cum. I'm having trouble holding my shit together. I'm a grown man struggling with prepubescent boy problems. She licks my tip like an ice cream cone, and I praise every deity I can think of. This woman is going to kill me.

"Katy," I plead through gritted teeth.

"Pepper. Call me whatever you want during the day, but at night, when you're mine, you call me Pepper." She sits up on her knees and pulls me in for a kiss. I can taste remnants of me on her tongue. "The level of spice you'll get will depend on how good of a boy you are."

Gone.

Fucking fried.

Mush.

What's a goddamn brain?

I don't even have thoughts to explain what those two words just did to rewire my brain chemistry. I'll bow at her feet and be her good boy any fucking day.

"I'm yours, Pepper."

"Good." She caresses my beard and taps the tip of my nose with her finger. "Go sit against the headboard." I open my mouth to question or object, but she puts a finger over it. "Now."

I shuffle around her and lean my back against the headboard. Her smile is beautifully devious as she crawls up my legs. My heart stops at the sight of her swaying breasts, and I need my mouth on them again. The moment she sits up, I do just that. The sweet taste of her breastmilk flavors my tongue, and I moan around her nipple. I suck like I'm a starving man.

Katy's hips move forward, and her wet pussy glides over my cock. My jaw involuntarily clamps, and she gasps in pain. Horrified I hurt her, I pull away, or try to. Katy grabs my head and pulls me back to her nipple.

"Do it again."

I suck her nipple deep into my mouth and bite down. Milk squirts in my mouth, but it's overshadowed by the guttural moan of pleasure Katy makes.

Fuck she's perfect.

Her hips grind over my cock in rhythm to my sucking and biting, and I'm losing my mind. It's all too much. I can't concentrate on one sensation over the other.

Katy reaches up and pulls out my hair tie, running her fingers through and pulling at my roots. I'm a madman lost in lust and pleasure when I feel her hand curl around my cock again. Her hips rise, and my tip coasts over her entrance.

I want inside her. I want inside her so fucking bad.

She lowers. She lowers so. Goddamn. Slow. It takes everything in me not to buck up and drive myself into her. Katy's hips sway back and forth, edging me inside her. I know my biting has become more aggressive, but she makes no move to stop me—her panting and moaning increases with each passing second.

I know she's taken all of me when she's seated and breathes a long, contented sigh.

"Tell me what to do up here. What do you like, Viktor?"

"I. Like. You." I punctuate each work with a small thrust, and her hands fly to my shoulders for leverage.

"Looks like I don't have to do all the work up here myself."

She sways her hips in a circle, and I see stars.

"Pepper." I grit my teeth, and I growl her name in warning.

"Does it not feel good?" She rocks side to side, and I grip her hips to stop her.

I drop my head to the headboard and take a few cleansing breaths.

"Hey, Viking? I don't care if you come in five seconds or fifty minutes. You've already given me an orgasm. It's your turn. Chase your pleasure. You have my permission to be rough if you need to be. That's why I'm up here. Ultimately, I'm in control."

She's giving this to me. Katy's letting me take my pleasure from her. She's trusting me.

"I'm so feral for you right now. I don't think I can handle anything more than quick and dirty."

She rests her forehead on mine and smiles. "Then it's a good thing I have a shower." She scratches her nails through my beard, and I buck my hips up, causing the sexiest moan. "Again."

"Hold on, Pepper." I dive my lips to her neck and tighten my grip on her hips before taking us both for a ride.

She feels so fucking good surrounding my cock. I want to feel her come all over me again, her pussy sucking my cock.

"Can you come again?" She bobs her head furiously, and I sink lower onto the bed. Adjusting our angle, her piercings rub against my body stimulating her clit. I'm teetering closer to the edge than I'd like. I want to make this as good for her as it is for me, but I'm struggling.

"Tell me. Tell me when you're going to come. I'm waiting for you, Pepper. Get there for me baby."

"Close. I'm so close."

I know what will help, and I want one more taste. I lean down and capture her nipple between my teeth. I suck it in and feel her walls clamp down on me.

"Oh fuck," I mumble around her peak in my mouth.

"I'm coming. Fuck Viking."

Thank fuck. I pump twice more before my cock fills her. Her pussy milks the come from me and it's fucking, hot and sexy and…messy. It's *messy*.

"Fucking shit, Katy." I pull her off me and push her down my thighs. I stare in disbelief at my very naked, glistening cock.

Naked.

No condom.

Fuck. Fuck. Fuuuuuck!

"What the fuck, Viktor?"

"We…there's no…we didn't use protection." My brain is mush for a completely different reason than before. "I'm so fucking sorry. Shit." I crawl out from under her. "Fuck I'm an idiot."

"For which part? The sex? Sex with me? I'm clean and on birth control."

There's venom in her questions. She's pissed, and I can't blame her. I took advantage of this situation.

"I-we shouldn't have. Fuck. I'm an asshole. I'm sorry." I can hear her protesting, but I can't comprehend the words. Leaving her room, I go straight to the guest bathroom and lock the door.

Fuck.

12

Katy

He didn't...he just...left. I deflate on the bed, trying to figure out what happened. Should I go after him? No, I'm pissed off. Everything we did, I asked for. How could he just leave?

Against my will, all my emotions stream down my cheeks. The biggest one is anger, followed closely by regret. Regret that I gave him something he obviously didn't take as seriously as I do, but I understand that's a me problem.

I don't know when I drifted off to sleep, but as my alarm rings, I feel the weight of my swollen eyes. I contemplate staying in bed since I have no reason to get up, but I like to keep a schedule with Owen. Peeking at the monitor, I can already see Owen stirring. He's used to the schedule we keep.

I quickly jump out of bed to grab him before he wakes too much and freeze when I remember I'm naked. Flashes from last night smack me in the face, and I gasp.

Get it together, Katy. You're bigger than this. You've survived worse. Walking into the bathroom, I quickly relieve myself and grab the bathrobe off the back of the door. I tiptoe into the living room and see Viktor is still asleep. He's usually up when I am, but I'm thankful he's not.

Owen is rolling in his crib, playing with his bunny, when another wave of emotion hits me. Why did I choose that as a stupid safeword?

Owen smiles at me as I change and dress him, remembering to grab an extra outfit to put in the diaper bag. When we're ready to leave the room, I cross my fingers and say a little prayer to the universe that I can creep back into my room and leave the house before Viktor wakes.

Make it to my room-Check.

I put on a burgundy, flowy dress and sandals in record time. Owen follows me into the bathroom, where I throw my hair up into a messy bun and try to conceal the bags under my eyes as best I can.

"Come on, buddy. Let's go see who's home at the big house." I scoop up Owen and tiptoe to my bedroom door. "Can you be quiet for Mama?" He smiles, which isn't exactly an answer, but he probably doesn't fully understand me either.

I open the door with trepidation and keep Owen's back to Viktor. He's somehow still asleep. Walking backward, I make it to the front door. I grab the diaper bag from the hook and shove Owen's extra clothes in it before slinging it over my shoulder.

Leave the house without waking Viktor-Check.

I glance over my shoulder before closing the door, and stormy blue eyes stare me down.

Not check.

I hold his eyes for a moment before closing the door. My shoulders deflate as I hold Owen's hand, and we walk across the lawn.

Was he awake the entire time and avoiding me like I was him?

My phone vibrates, and I pull it out, hoping it isn't Viktor.

Babs: I'd love to meet my beautiful grandson soon.

Seriously? Not that I even want to talk to my mother, but any morning other than today would have been preferable. She doesn't have a right to call him her grandson. She gave up her rights to me, therefore forfeiting her rights to claim Owen as her family.

She reaches out about once a week. I know she's trying to wear me down, and it kills me to admit that it's working—slowly, but it's working. I never knew my grandparents. Hell, I barely know my mother. But, although I'm angry, I'm not cruel. She *sounds* like she's trying. I haven't answered any of her texts, but sometimes, she gives me updates on her life.

The house is quiet when I walk in. I put Owen in his high chair, and he gives me the sign for milk.

"Mik, Mama. Mik."

Shit. In my hasty retreat, I didn't sit down and breastfeed him.

"Buddy, do you want milk or waffles?" Axel loves frozen waffles, and so does Owen, so I know they're in the freezer without looking.

"Faffle."

I lean down and smack several kisses on his cheeks, making him giggle. "Okay. Mama will make some waffles."

While his breakfast is in the toaster, I make a pot of coffee and cut up some strawberries, trying my hardest not to think back to last night's devastating disaster. I wish I knew what went wrong.

When the toaster pops, a large hand reaches around me and snags a waffle, and I stiffen.

"Linca," Owen yells, and my body sags in relief.

"Morning, Katy. I was wondering why I smelled coffee." Lincoln kisses me on the cheek and grabs two mugs from the cabinet and a sippy cup for Owen. "What's little man drinking?"

"Whole milk if you have it."

"Of course. Always for Owen." He looks around the room, and I'm surprised he's just now noticing. "Where's your shadow?"

I shrug, and he looks out the window to the pool house. I know he's seeing the car still there, so he knows Viktor is somewhere nearby.

"Trouble in paradise?"

If Viktor and I didn't regularly butt heads, I might have read more into his question. Unfortunately, me showing up here with Owen solo isn't an unusual occurrence.

"Something like that." I can tell he wants to ask more questions, but he knows me well enough to know I'll talk when I'm ready.

I give Owen his breakfast and pop in more waffles. Picking up my mug, I gingerly sip my coffee and lean back against the counter, a myriad of questions swirling in my head.

"Linc, can I ask you a question?"

"Anything." He leans on the island across from me. I know he had a hand in the hiring process of Viktor. Justin consulted with him to find the right person to guard me.

"Why Viktor?"

He stares at me for a moment, studying my face.

"That's a loaded question. Can you be more specific?"

"Why did he get picked out of all the other candidates? What made him more qualified? He's so young."

His lip twitches. "He was one of the least qualified actually."

"That's…interesting. Then why him?"

He thinks for another moment as the toaster pops. We each grab our waffles and sit at the table.

"I take it, if you're asking, then he hasn't told you? Has he shared anything about himself in the last three years?"

I think back to everything he's shared with me and realize it hasn't been much. He's an only child. He was in the military, though I don't know what branch or why he no longer is. I just learned his entire leg is covered in a tattoo.

"Not much, apparently."

"Maybe you should be asking him these questions." He eyes me patiently, waiting for me to spill the reason I'm here.

"We aren't exactly speaking right now."

"I'm all ears when you're ready to talk."

"Up. Uppie." Owen wiggles his hands, showing the "all done" sign. I clean him while pondering if I can share with Lincoln without judgment. I wouldn't talk to Tucker or Spencer. Axel would high-five me, then tell me he's an asshole, and he'll come around. Miller doesn't often get mad, but I think this is something that would enrage him.

"Linc? Can I talk to you as a friend and not a father figure?" While none of them have taken over the official role of Mom or Dad, their dynamic has. "I need a judgment-free, levelheaded conversation."

"Do you need friend or cop? Do I need to prepare to kick some ass?"

His hand closes into a fist, and I rest mine on top of it.

I chuckle at his reaction and shake my head. "Judgment-free. I'm an adult, and as much as you want to protect me, I just need a friend."

Lincoln closes his eyes and takes a cleansing breath. His fist unclenches, and he turns his hand over and laces our fingers together.

"What's going on, Katy girl?"

I go over some of the events from last night, and he listens, like I expected he would, with little emotion and few questions. His only tell that he's affected by some of my words is the slight clenching of my hand in his. I'm talking to him about sex. I know it's probably hard for him to hear, especially since this exact tragic act is how Lincoln and I connected.

"I don't understand why he ran out, and I have all kinds of feelings that I can't put a finger on because they're swirling everywhere. I need…I'm not even sure. Answers? Advice?"

"A frying pan?"

We stare at each other before bursting into laughter. The tension that built during my story dissipates. Lincoln releases my hand and stands.

"I'll wash you dry? I need to be doing something to get through this."

"Of course."

I turn on some cartoons for Owen and meet Lincoln back at the sink, dry towel in hand.

"You asked me a question earlier. Why was Vik hired? While I didn't and still don't feel it's my story to tell, I think you need some answers because right now, all you have is questions."

Lincoln's phone chimes in his pocket. He pulls it out, types a message, and returns it to his pants. He tests the water temperature and picks up his first dish to wash.

"Vik worked in private security, which is how Justin got his information. As I said, he wasn't the most qualified, but his circumstances made him uniquely qualified to protect and watch over you."

"I don't understand."

"Just listen and dry." He hands me a plate and smiles.

"Did you know he was dishonorably discharged from the Marines?"

I shake my head, and my forehead scrunches. *Dishonorably?* What had he done?

"Vik was planning to be a career military man. He was moving up the ranks quickly, and one day, he wasn't." I open my mouth to ask what happened, and he hands me another dish. "Dry and listen."

"Okay. Okay."

He chuckles and continues. "Vik assaulted his Commanding Officer."

I gasp and almost drop the coffee cup he handed me.

"His CO had been accused of raping a fellow female Marine, but there was no proof. It was her word against his. Vik overheard him at a bar bragging to his friends about the lock of hair and her panties he had kept. The woman was a friend of Vik's, and he reacted without thinking."

His friend was raped? That's what Lincoln meant by Viktor was uniquely qualified.

"Vik served no jail time because the female Marine's items were found where the guy was bragging he hid them, but his career was over. Despite what his CO did, he was still superior to Vik."

"Wow. So that's why Justin hired him?"

"Yes. He still has an exemplary record, but after speaking to him, we knew he could and would protect you to the best of his ability."

"He doesn't think he did. He blames himself a lot for the night in the rain."

Lincoln sighs as he grabs another towel to dry his hand off. "I've seen that. Are you leaving anything out about last night? He doesn't seem like the kind of guy that would regret a decision like that. He's been a patient man when it comes to you."

"Seriously? Has everyone seen it but me? You all just let me live in my own little bubble of ignorance?"

"What did you want us to say? 'Hey Katy, your bodyguard has a crush on you. Want to live out your romance book fantasies?'"

"Eww." I shove his shoulder, and he barely moves. Tossing the towel on the drying rack, he crosses his arms and leans against the counter.

Did I leave anything out? I did. One minor detail, but I didn't think it was a big deal.

"We…" Lincoln looks at me expectantly. "We didn't use protection. He was caught up in the moment and didn't realize, and I didn't care to stop him."

"Katy." He says my name with accusation and drops his hands to his sides. "Did you talk about any of that first?"

My head slowly shakes side to side.

"Okay. I get it now."

"Care to share with the class, Professor?"

He pulls his phone out of his pocket and swipes on the

screen several times.

"Come on. I'll walk you back to your house."

"No. Wait. What? Why?" I don't understand. I haven't gotten any answers yet, and now I'm being sent home.

"Because our time is up unless you want everyone down here. I can't hold them off any longer, and Vik is chomping at the bit to make sure you're okay."

"What?" I look around the bottom floor. No one is down here but us.

"Vik texted the group chat earlier to make sure you were here, and I requested everyone stay upstairs. You looked like you didn't want a crowd."

My chin drops to my chest. There are definite downfalls to this wonderfully big family that adopted me.

"I'm not ready to face him, and you haven't given me any answers."

"You need answers from him, Katy, not me."

I sigh heavily, and he places a hand on my shoulder and squeezes. We both look up when we hear footsteps upstairs. "You're keeping them from their caffeine. The natives are getting restless. Come on, get the diaper bag."

Lincoln picks up Owen from the couch, blowing raspberries on his belly. He's giggling when they return to the kitchen.

"Let's go." He takes my hand with Owen's in the other and leads us to the back door.

"Fine."

Each step we get closer to my house fills me with dread. Lincoln stops mid-walk and turns to me.

"Okay, so here are my thoughts, and they are just my own, so you still need to talk to him. Vik is an honorable man. You said you were both drinking last night—"

"But we weren't drunk. I'm aware of every decision made. I could have stopped him and said something, but I was okay with it for that one time."

"And that right there is the reason he's upset." Huh? What reason? "*You* were aware of every decision, but he wasn't. Can I make an assumption that last night was your 'first time' since..." He uses air quotes when he says "first time" because we all know Shane took that from me.

Owen tugs at Lincoln's hand, wanting to be let go to run free. The pool is completely fenced in, so Lincoln let's go. The worst that can happen is a scraped knee on the driveway.

"Mama, buf-fy." Owen runs off giggling and chasing after a blue butterfly.

"It was."

"Talk to him and give him time. I'm sure, somewhere in his mind, he's comparing himself to Shane." I try to protest, and he holds up a hand, stopping me. "He's not him. We know that. Trust me, we've all talked about you two. If we had any concern, he'd be gone."

"Why does everyone think they can meddle in my love life?"

He arches a brow at me. "Love life?"

I shove at his chest to move him along. "It's a figure of speech, and you know it." He chuckles and puts his arm around my shoulders as we walk closer to the house. "I'm not ready to face him. I still have too many emotions about it that I haven't figured out yet."

He stops and turns us so each house is to our left and right.

"One man," he points to my house. "Three overbearing men and Spencer." There's no contempt behind his plain description of Spencer. She'll tell me exactly what she thinks, and I usually love it, but I don't think I can handle that right now. Everything is too raw.

I point to my car because it is mine, I just don't ever get to drive it. "Or there's four wheels?"

"My dear, are you trying to flee without your bodyguard?"

"Could you blame me right now?"

Lincoln chuckles. "No. Escaping seems like the lesser of those evils." He looks to his house, where we can see movement on the back porch. They really wanted their caffeine. "You're trying to get me in trouble, aren't you?" Lincoln squeezes me into his side.

"I wouldn't say no to a little trouble." I wink at him, and he groans.

"Where would you go if I let you leave alone with the car right now?"

"Hmm. The Bahamas sounds nice."

"Of course. The most natural choice. It's a good thing we got those inflatable tires put on last winter. They'll work nicely, floating you across the ocean."

"Please." I fold my hands together and give him my best puppy dog eyes. He's close to caving. I can feel it.

"Can we compromise?"

I'm so close to freedom. "Whatcha got?"

"We'll watch Owen, and you can go out without a body-guard if you take Miller and Axel."

Hmm. No kid *and* the goofballs. That does sound like fun. But...

"Counter offer. You keep my kid, and I'll take *one* of yours."

He tries hard not to laugh but loses, and we both end up doubled over.

"Is that your final offer, Katy?"

With confidence, I say, "Final offer."

"I think I can live with that. I know Axel will love it. Do you need to grab anything from your house before we go back?"

"Nope."

13

Axel

I'm so excited to have a faux girl's day with Katy. I miss her being around the house. She handles my "high definition" like no one else.

"Do you promise me I wasn't a consolation prize? You didn't want to do this with someone else like Spencer or Lincoln since that's who you were talking with this morning?" My leg bounces, and she places a hand on my arm to calm me.

"First off, you're never a consolation prize. Secondly, could you see Lincoln sitting in this chair with his feet soaking in lavender water? And third, you're going to splash the poor woman if you don't stop fidgeting."

I look at my feet and give the pretty, dark-haired woman doing my pedicure a sympathetic look. "Sorry."

"Your girlfriend is pretty." My nail lady points at Katy, who almost chokes on air, and starts waving her hands.

"No. No. Not my boyfriend. He's my…" She tilts her head at me, trying to find the right words. I'm not her father or uncle. I'm more than a friend. We've never labeled what everyone's role is to Katy. We are all just family.

"We're family," she settles on. The lady smiles and goes back to my foot massage.

My heart swells with pride that we thought of the same word. Katy and Owen are both our family. I couldn't imagine considering them anything else.

I jumped at the chance to have one-on-one time with Katy. We used to hang out a lot when she lived with us, but since she moved out, even though she's only in our backyard, we see much less of each other.

"How much of my conversation with Lincoln do you know?" There's a shyness to her tone that I'm not used to. I don't know anything about their conversation, unfortunately.

"He wouldn't tell us anything other than he told you Vik's history. Believe me, we tried."

After the texts, we were all chomping at the bit to get downstairs this morning.

Group Chat D:

Dempsey: Katy left the house and didn't tell me where she was going. I assume she's there. Can you please confirm?

Lincoln: She's here. No need for you to come, Vik.

Group Chat 5:

Lincoln: Please stay upstairs until I give the all-clear. Katy seems like she needs to talk, and I think it would be better if she didn't have a big audience.

Spencer: 10-4

Lincoln's second message came to our house group chat, leaving us to believe he didn't want Dempsey to read that particular message. Our minds were spiraling, wondering why she was here again without him.

There's been tension between them for a while, but we know he would never be anything less than honorable with his intentions toward Katy. None of us would allow him to stick around if we thought otherwise.

"Lunch at the place that makes the frozen Piña Coladas? It's not a conversation for an open audience."

"You had me at all you can eat chips and salsa."

"But I didn't even say—"

"You didn't have to." She chuckles at me, and we relax and enjoy the rest of our pedicures.

"Two Piña Coladas. One virgin, please. And an order of queso for the chips to start us off."

The pretty blonde waitress flashes me a flirty smile. "Sure. Can I see your I.D. handsome?" I reach into my back pocket and grab my wallet. I hold my I.D. between my index and middle finger on my left hand when I give it to her to make sure she sees that my left ring finger is taken.

We can't legally all marry Spencer, but we decided last year to have a ceremony of commitment to each other. Blake hosted it, and Annie's party planner did a fantastic job decorating their backyard. It was an amazing day. Miller, Spencer, and I all wear silicone bands most days because of our jobs, but I have my silver band on today. Five diamonds along the top represent each of us in the relationship. We each have one in the metal of our preference.

I see the recognition on the waitress's face when she notices my ring. She quickly glances at my I.D. and walks away, telling us she'll be right back with our drinks.

"What's so funny?" Katy tries to contain a laugh behind her

hand, but her shoulders shake, giving her away.

"You just had to flash the ring and crush her, didn't you?"

"I'm a happily committed man. Now tell me why I shouldn't kick Dempsey's ass for whatever reason you ran away today." As Katy is about to speak, her phone vibrates on the table. She looks at it apprehensively before turning it over and sighing.

"It's my mom again."

"Again? Your mom has been texting you?" I had no idea she even had Katy's phone number. Why is Babs texting her? "What does it say?" She turns the screen to me.

Babs: 120 days sober today. I'd love to have coffee together. Or tea or hot chocolate if you don't drink coffee.

"She's sober? Do you believe her?"

Katy places the phone back on the table and gnaws on her bottom lip.

"I have no idea. I was never enough for her to get clean. I can't imagine she would do it on her own. Justin told me at one point, he offered to send her to rehab if she ever wanted to go, but to my knowledge, she never went. At least not that anyone told me."

"Want me to ask Tucker to have his P.I. check her out?"

"Tucker has a P.I.? Actually, that doesn't really surprise me. Um, yeah. I don't want to be that person who doesn't allow someone to see their grandkids, but I also have to make sure Owen is safe. I think I'd like to give her a chance if she really has turned a corner."

"I'll ask him for you."

The waitress drops off our dip and Piña Coladas, and Katy sips at her drink with a far-off look after the waitress takes our orders. She's so brave to want to allow her mother to meet Owen despite her childhood. Although I want to get back to the Dempsey drama she's already lost in thought, and I don't exactly know *what* the drama is. I don't want to bring her down any more.

"So what's next?" We didn't make any actual plans. We've just been going with the flow.

"We should probably get home. I don't want to leave Owen with them for too long."

I reach across the table and grab Katy's hand. She looks guilty for leaving Owen with them at all. "Absolutely not. Lincoln went to work, and Spencer has recertification training, but Miller and Tucker are home. Owen is getting absolutely spoiled right now and probably doesn't even know you're gone."

"Well, that doesn't make me feel any better."

I roll my eyes at her sarcasm. "Should we ask for a proof of life picture?" She perks up and nods.

Group Chat 6:
  Axel: Katy needs proof of life pictures of Owen.

Katy chuckles when she reads the text on her phone. We have several group chats going between us, and they are all labeled by who or how many people are in the chat. For everyone in my household, it's Group Chat 5 because there are five of us in it-Spencer, Miller, Lincoln, Tucker, and me. Group 6 adds Katy, and Group 7 adds Dempsey. There are also Group Chats D and K. D includes my household, and Dempsey and K is my household, as well as Katy. It sounds complicated, but really, it's the easiest system we could come up with after

Katy and Vik were privy to a few too many mistaken texts. I laugh at one in particular, and Katy gives me a strange look.

"What's so funny?"

"I was remembering the time Tucker asked Spencer to send us a video of her pleasuring herself." Katy groans as she remembers the same text.

"Please don't remind me. The secondhand embarrassment is still strong."

Before any of us realized that he sent it to the text thread Katy was also in, Spencer sent back a video. Katy was asleep because Tucker sent it late at night, but when she woke up, we all got an earful of her screaming at us through the house. She couldn't understand why we were all laughing until we finally convinced her to open the video. Spencer had been cleaning her guns at the time and recorded it because it was her idea of pleasuring herself, and that's the video she sent us. It became the last straw, and we decided that labeling the group chats would avoid any more confusion or mishaps.

"You can't look back at it and laugh yet?"

"No. I'm still traumatized."

Our food arrives, and so do several texts with pictures of Owen happily playing. The relief is evident in her posture. I know she thinks she has to do all of this on her own, but we do the best we can to reduce that burden from her. She never got to be a kid herself.

"I had sex with Viktor."

I almost spit my cheesy burrito out of my nose. Grabbing a napkin, I quickly chew and swallow while gasping for air.

"Could you warn a man before you throw around life-changing sentences like that?"

She looks apologetic but also smug about the reaction I

gave her.

"Okay, now that my mouth isn't full, do you want to try that again? You slept with Dempsey? Wait, let me say that again. You. Slept. With. Dempsey. Okay, yeah. That doesn't sound any different the second time. Do you want to talk about it?"

Of all the things I expected her to say, that isn't one of them. Do I want her to talk about it with me? If anyone is capable of taming Katy, it would be him. He has confided in me about her nightmares, and I know he helps her at night. They could be good together if they allow themselves, but I know about the guilt he carries.

"I talked about it with Lincoln. I don't really have any more answers or questions. I do have lots of emotions, though."

"Do you want to talk about those?"

"Feelings suck. That's what got me here in the first place. Well, that and wine."

"Katy." My tone is harsher than I mean it to be.

"I wasn't drunk. Calm down, *Dad*."

There's a pause between us before my face sours, and we both break out into laughter.

"*Anyway*. I was fully aware of everything I was doing and thought he was too."

"Thought? Was he drinking too?" I'm liking this story less and less. I thought Dempsey was more respectable than that. I drop my hand to my lap, and my fingers curl into fists. She said she was aware, but was it consensual? She's obviously upset about something.

"Axel. I see you panicking. Please stop." She reaches across the table and takes my hand. "I wanted everything that happened, and so did he. It was *after* that was the issue."

I inhale a deep breath and close my eyes. My fist opens on my thigh, and I rub out the tension.

"Okay, tell me what happened."

I'm a little shocked to hear his reaction. More shocked that Katy would have sex without a condom despite being on birth control.

"I don't know if I should be a dad figure or friend. Which response do you want?"

She eyes me, weighing her options.

"Lincoln went, friend. Give me your best dad advice."

"Okay." I sit up in my seat and straighten my back, folding my hands on the table. "Young lady." Katy's lip twitches, and I almost crack, too. Clearing my throat, I try again. "Young lady, you know better than to have unprotected sex. That poor boy probably freaked out because he thinks you're trying to trap him with a baby." Katy's smile falls, and she drops her eyes to her lap.

"Do you think he thinks that? Is that what happened? Because it's the furthest thing from the truth."

"From what I know of Dempsey, no, I don't think that was it. He knows you're on birth control. He's seen your entire medical records file." She cringes at that thought. "The only person that can honestly tell you why he freaked out is him. And that would require you talking to him and not hiding out with me."

Katy sighs and flops back against the booth. "Is there another option? He's so broody."

"Katy?" A pretty, petite strawberry blonde stops at our table. She looks to be about Katy's age with hazel-green eyes.

"Hey, Meghan." Katy jumps up from the booth and throws her arms around the girl's shoulders. "Oh my god, how are

102

you?"

"I'm great. I missed you senior year. It wasn't the same without you." Meghan gives Katy a shy smile and looks around the table, pausing at me.

"Oh, Axel is family. Axel, this is Meghan. We went to school together. Owen, my son, is at home with more family. We're just out having lunch."

"Sorry, I missed meeting the little guy. I bet you're the best mom and deserve a little grown-up lunchtime." She hugs Katy again. "I really missed you. What are you doing tonight? I know it sounds totally crazy for me to invite you out somewhere after not seeing you for almost two years, but some friends and I are going to The Beat Brew Cafe. They're having an open mic night and then a D.J. after. It's just a relaxed night. We are meeting at nine if you're interested."

"That sounds like so much fun, but I'm not sure. I've already been away from Owen for several hours. I'm not sure I want to ask for more."

"Go," I tell her. "We've got Owen. He can even spend the night."

"But I—"

"Katy, she's right. You're an amazing mom, and you never do anything for yourself. You know Spencer would love the chance to hang out with Owen. She was salty that she had her training today and was missing out on all the fun. We can go home now, and you can spend time with him, then go out with Meghan."

Her face slowly lights up. Her entire life revolves around Owen. She barely asks us to watch him, and we tell her all the time we are ready and willing whenever she wants. I think she just needs this little push.

"Are you sure, Axel?"

"Do you want me to ask Spencer now to make you feel better?" Katy nods, and I pick up my phone. The girls exchange numbers while the phone rings.

"Axel."

"Hey, Tails. Katy ran into a friend who invited her to hang out tonight. I told her we would happily watch Owen and have a sleepover, but she wants to hear more confirmation from someone other than me."

Spencer chuckles. "Put me on speaker." I click over and tell her to go ahead. "Katy, go be a teenager. Owen will be fine here tonight. And next time any of us tell you we've got him, don't question us. We will always watch Owen."

Katy's smile beams. "Thank you, Spencer. We'll be home soon. I'm not going out until nine."

There's a round of "I love you's," and I hang up.

"So, I'll see you at nine?" Meghan confirms.

Katy's shoulders fall. "Not just me. I'll have a babysitter with me. But he won't get in the way. He just watches like a stalker from the corner."

"O-kay?"

I hate that Katy and Dempsey are having issues, and that's her current thought of him.

"We love Katy and always want to make sure she's safe. She has a bodyguard because of some issues we've had in the past. He's a good guy and won't bother you ladies unless he sees trouble."

Meghan still seems a little apprehensive, but she's obviously excited to go out with Katy. I'm not sure how this will work with the added tension between them tonight, but I know Dempsey is a professional, and *hopefully*, he won't let his feelings get in the way of keeping her safe.

14

Dempsey

What a fucking nightmare. I listened to Katy sneak around the house this morning and pretended to be asleep like some coward. I thought the coast was clear and opened my eyes, not expecting her to look back but she did. She saw me looking at her.

Fucking coward.

You can't even face the woman you made love to last night. All the beautiful words exchanged, down the fucking toilet because you ran from her bedroom like a little chicken shit when you realized you had taken her bare.

How could I have been so caught up in my feelings that I didn't think about a condom? I wanted her to be in control and completely comfortable that I forgot the most basic rule of sex. Protection. Fucking protection.

I've never had sex without one. I knew it felt different with her, but I assumed it was the emotion behind it, not the literal rawness without a condom.

I couldn't handle it. Knowing I took a decision away from

her. She had already had it taken once from her. We were so lost in the moment we were making stupid decisions. I know she's on birth control, and neither of us has been with anyone else, so I'm not worried about diseases.

Does she feel like I took advantage of her? She didn't follow me when I ran out, so maybe she felt the same guilt I did. The fact that I even allowed myself to touch such a fucking goddess is enough to throw me into the pit of despair. I promised myself I'd never cross that line with her. She's been through enough, and as much as I'm attracted to her inside and out, I needed to be her safe space, and I took that away. She made that very clear by hiding from me all day.

I was losing my mind when she walked out, and I had no idea where she was going. I couldn't make myself get up to watch her walk across the lawn. Although I assumed that's where she went, after a while, I needed the confirmation and messaged the group chat. I was relieved to know she was over there with them.

Lincoln came by after she left with Axel to let me know they were going out, and Tucker was watching Owen at their house. She didn't even ask me to watch him, and that hurt.

I had no intentions of going over to the big house since I wasn't sure what, if anything, she had told them, but judging by the look on Lincoln's face, she definitely told them something. He didn't say anything to me about it, which I respect. I'm also happy she felt comfortable enough to confide in at least one of them.

After twiddling my thumbs all day, not knowing what to do with myself if my purpose wasn't to protect Katy and Owen, I'm watching her get ready to go out. She came home a few hours ago but didn't come back to the pool house until about an hour ago.

Spencer told me she was going to The Beat Brew Cafe with Meghan, a friend from high school, and I was to be scarcely seen and not heard while I was there with them.

They have been in the bathroom for what feels like forever, getting Katy ready to go. At least I get to play with Owen before they take him for the night. I don't like being without him for long. He's not mine, but I treat him as if he was my blood. I've been here since the day he was born and will hopefully be in his life after Katy is no longer my job.

"Vik, Vik. Gag. Doggie." Owen lays his head on Gage, Spencer's German Shepherd, who's lying on the floor next to my feet. Gage puts up with everything Owen does to him, but I've also seen him protect Owen when people come around who he doesn't know. Spencer has him trained well.

"Mama, pitty."

A few minutes earlier, Owen was in Katy's room. I wonder what she's doing in there?

"Your Mama looks pretty? I bet she does. Is she wearing blue?" His face scrunches as he thinks about my words.

"No boo."

"Is she wearing pink?" He knows some basic colors, and I work with him every chance I get, as does Katy. He loves guessing colors when you point them out.

"No peek."

"Hmmm. Is Mama wearing yellow?"

"No lellow."

The more I guess with Owen, the more my anxiety increases. I haven't seen Katy dressed up since her seventeenth birthday, and she looked stunning that night in a pink, flowy, strapless dress. I know she's only going out with friends, but I have a feeling, based on how long she's been in the bathroom with Spencer, that she's dressing up.

"I don't know, buddy. You've got me stumped. I wonder what Mama will be wearing."

"Geen!"

"Green? Mama's wearing green? Good job." I lift my hand to him, and he gives me a high five.

She looks gorgeous in green. It contrasts beautifully with her chocolate hair and eyes.

Fuck. I shouldn't be thinking things like that. Lines were blurred last night. No, fuck that. Lines were obliterated last night, and I need to get my head straight. I need to be on high alert at all times, and I can't let last night cloud my judgment.

It's eight forty-five, and I know they have to be done soon, or we'll be late. Axel came home with her friend's information, and between everyone's connections, Meghan was fully background-checked and vetted. Not that I was worried about a nineteen year old girl having ill will, but I can breathe a little easier knowing that Katy's friend, at least on paper, has pure intentions with her invite tonight.

"Mama!" Owen jumps up from his lounging position on Gage and runs to her.

Fuck.

Katy looks...I have no words.

"Hi, buddy. What do you think?"

I know she's talking to Owen, but I can't help but stare. Katy is wearing white pants and a bright green sleeveless top that ties at the neck. Her hair is curled into big waves, and her eye shadow matches her shirt and makes her eyes pop.

My mouth is dry. Katy looks gorgeous. She's wearing a casual outfit but also looks ready to take on the world. My

109

breath hitches when she tucks a curl behind her ear, and I see she's wearing the earrings I gave her for her eighteenth birthday last year. A pair of diamond studs that I convinced her weren't real because I knew she wouldn't have accepted them if she thought they were.

They sparkle like she does. A growl of possessiveness creeps up my chest, and I cover it with a cough. She's marked by me tonight, and I like the idea of her walking around wearing something I gave her. Did she do it on purpose? Is this an olive branch?

"Alright. You better go before you're too late." Spencer picks up Owen and shoves Katy toward the door. Once Katy walks out, Spencer stops and turns to me.

"You will be on your best behavior, Dempsey. No one has shared with me what caused her to be upset this morning, but I know it involves you. If you or Katy want to talk, I'm here, but we respect each other's privacy, so I won't pry. Can you handle this?"

This is why I fucking respect Spencer. Straight to the point. No B.S. She understands there's a problem, and she's confronting me with it.

"Spencer, you know I take my job seriously, and if there ever comes a point where I don't feel confident in my abilities, I'll excuse myself."

"You're a good man, Dempsey. Go watch over our girl."

Spencer steps aside and allows me to walk out ahead of her. I don't miss the use of the words "our girl." They probably have a different meaning to Spencer, or maybe not. She's highly perceptive, and I know they have discussed the relationship between Katy and me. Spencer was probably the first one to notice.

When I get in, Katy is already in the car waiting and playing on her phone. She ignores me, as she's been doing all evening. I feel the weight of her anger heavy on my chest as her presence takes up all the air in the car. She smells like vanilla and sunshine. It is so uniquely Katy and only a scent she wears on special occasions.

"You look beautiful, Pepper."

Her fingers clench around her phone, and her crossed leg shakes. I can't decipher her mood right now, and the tension is killing me.

"Thank you."

I might as well have told her she looked ugly with the monotone response she gives me. I know I fucked up, but if we are going to get through tonight, there needs to be some semblance of peace between us. I always do my best to stay out of her way when she's out with others besides me, even with any of the five from the main house. When I'm on duty, protection is my number one focus.

"Katy, can we—"

"No. We aren't going to do this right now. I'm going out with friends and having a good time. I want you to be seen and not heard. Please."

I don't miss the identical phrasing Spencer used on me earlier. "Seen and not heard." I can play my role as bodyguard tonight, but after, we're talking. I can't allow the silence to linger between us any longer than necessary.

"Alright. I'll respect your wishes. But we *will* talk about it."

Katy stares out the window for the rest of the drive, ignoring me.

From the outside, the Beat Brew Cafe looks like a regular coffee shop, but the atmosphere is entirely different once we step inside. The walls are decorated with old instruments, sheet music, and coffee paraphernalia. There's a small stage in one corner and a DJ booth in another.

Someone waves at us near the stage, and I place my hand on the small of Katy's back, directing her toward the table. She shimmies her shoulders, trying to shake me off, but I shoot her a look, and she rolls her eyes at me.

"Katy!" A strawberry blonde-haired girl greets her with an exuberant hug, and I assume this is Meghan.

I extend my hand to the young lady and introduce myself. "Hello, I'm Dempsey. I'll make myself scarce, but if you need me, I'll be in the corner." I point to a dark place where I can stand and view the room without looking like a creeper.

She smiles and shakes my hand. "I'm Meghan. Glad to meet you. You can join us if you want to."

Before I can object, Katy does it for me. "He's fine in the corner." I smile and nod at the girls, and Katy gives me her back as Meghan introduces her to the others.

Three other people are at the table, all looking to be around Katy's age. She recognizes the brunette female, and they hug before she's introduced to the two boys sitting at the table. One kid wears a too big for him button-up shirt and gives Katy a polite smile. The other kid wears a backward baseball cap with dark hair curling around the edges and a band t-shirt. He stands and offers Katy a quick hug before they all sit. I can't tell by her interaction if she knows him, but I don't like someone else touching what's mine.

The night goes by uneventfully, and when the open mic ends, the DJ plays music that makes people move tables and chairs around, and a small dance floor is formed in the middle of the room. It makes me uncomfortable not being able to see Katy as easily as I could when everyone was sitting.

I go to the coffee counter and order two bottles of water. After drinking mine, I slowly make my way toward Katy. I've only seen her drink a coffee, and she's been dancing for well over thirty minutes. She needs to hydrate.

"Pepper?" She jumps when I lean over her shoulder to speak in her ear.

"What?"

There's venom behind the word, and it's obvious she doesn't appreciate being interrupted. I hold up the bottle of water, and her brows scrunch. She wants to be mad, but she also wants the water. Which one will win?

"Thank you. Now go back to your corner."

She dismisses me and gives me her back. The brunette with them comes up next to me and trails her eyes up my body.

"You got one of those for me too?"

"No, ma'am, but I'll happily get you one as well." She hooks her arm into my elbow and tilts her head toward the counter.

"I'll come with you."

I don't like the idea of taking my eyes off Katy, but it's a short walk before I can turn and see her again. I nod to the brunette, and we walk together. I feel Katy's eyes staring at my back. When I reach the counter with her friend and turn around, Katy has her arms around the kid with the backward hat, dancing far closer than I'm comfortable with.

"I'm Sara, by the way. Your name began with a D, right?" I can feel her leaning close to me to be heard over the music.

"Dempsey, yes. Who are the friends you are with?" She follows my line of sight to the four people she's here with.

"Meghan and I went to school with Katy. Jace and Logan go to the community college with Meghan. I think they have a class together or something. Jace seems sweet on your girl."

I fucking see that. He's getting way too comfortable with his hands on Katy's lower back. A few more inches, and he won't be on her back anymore.

"Did you want something?"

"Huh?" We've reached the front of the line, and I need to order. "Oh, two waters please. Thank you." I swipe my card, keeping my eye on Katy the entire time. Sara takes the two waters from the barista and tries to hand one to me. "That's for Meghan. You should all hydrate."

"Do you want to come and dance with me?"

"No. I have to keep an eye on things. Go have fun."

She runs her pink polished hand up my chest and stops to fiddle with the collar of my gray v-neck shirt.

"Are you sure?"

Is she flirting with me? I came here with Katy. Okay, fine. Not exactly *with* Katy, but she had to see that I'm here doing a job.

"I'm sure." She pouts an exaggerated pout and saunters back to their group on the dance floor, handing Meghan the water, who gives me a big wave and thumbs up over the crowd. I smile back and find another corner to stand and watch.

I feel like a stalker. I don't usually feel that way, but tonight feels different. Maybe last night changed something, and it's making me struggle to watch from the wings, but that's my job, and I can't let my actions interfere with that.

Katy continues to dance with the douchebag. He could be a great guy for all I know, but he's holding what's mine, and I don't like it.

The night slows down, and closing time approaches. Their group has been sitting for a while, talking and laughing.

Douchebag's hand is over the back of Katy's chair, and he keeps whispering in her ear. She's blushed and giggled more times than I'm comfortable with, and I've been chanting our safeword in my head over and over, convincing myself I have no right to go over there and sling her over my shoulder like some caveman staking my claim.

My phone rings, and I answer it without looking.

"She looks pretty in green, doesn't she?"

I pull the phone away from my ear and see it's an unknown caller. "Who the fuck is this?"

"Awe, Dempsey. Don't insult me. We know each other far too intimately for you to not know who I am. I've seen your insides. Or rather, caused them to spill."

I'm seeing red. Shane is here. Or he can see her, which isn't much better. I scan the room looking for him but don't see anyone even remotely resembling Shane.

"What the fuck do you want?"

"Get her away from that asshole. I don't want any more competition."

"How—" The call disconnects, and I'm already heading toward Katy's group without conscious thought. When I approach her table, she looks up at me towering over her with pure disdain.

"What do you want, Dempsey?" I fucking hate it when she calls me that, and she knows it.

"We have to go."

She scoffs. "I'm not ready to leave. We still have another hour before the cafe closes."

"Katy, we need to go."

I don't want to explain the reasoning behind our hasty exit in front of her friends. "You know what? You have twenty minutes."

"I'm not a child. You can't just give me a countdown…" I walk away, leaving her ranting behind me, and pull out my phone.

"Dempsey. What's wrong?" There's loud music in the background, and I hear a door close before there's silence.

"Tucker, Shane called me. He knows Katy is here. She won't willingly leave, but I realized it's probably not good to leave in our car anyway. I'm sure he knows which one is ours, and I'd rather have safety in numbers because of the last time."

"Say no more. You're at The Beat Brew Cafe, correct?"

"Yeah."

"Don't let her out of your sight. I'll be there in ten."

Tucker hangs up, and I continue to stare at Katy and her friends. She's going to be pissed off that I called Tucker but fuck her feelings right now. This is about her safety. Feelings come second.

True to his word, ten minutes later, the cowboy hat-wearing, muscular man walks through the front door, and Katy's eyes beeline right to him. Like a teenager caught after curfew, she jumps with panic in her eyes. He holds his gaze with hers for a few tense moments before releasing her and finding me. We shake hands when he approaches.

"So what's going on, Dempsey?"

"He called me from an unknown number. Taunted me by saying Katy looks good in green, then told me to get her away from the asshole because he doesn't want any more competition."

"Fucker."

"I tried to get Katy to leave calmly, but she's pissed at me

116

right now and will do anything to disagree. I'm sure the fact I called you is only going to piss her off more."

He places a hand on my shoulder. "You did the right thing. It's not always the easiest." His hand squeezes a little too hard for my liking, and he leans close to my ear. "And the next time you make love to my daughter, she better walk away happy. Not whatever is going on between you two right now."

My head snaps to look at him.

"Who—"

"No one has said a word. I know the face of a woman scorned. I don't know what you did, but fix it, or you'll be out of a job."

"Yes, Sir."

Fuck. Me. I should have known that nothing gets past Tucker.

"How much longer till she can leave?"

"I told her twenty minutes when I called you, but she wasn't happy."

"Well, her happiness isn't my concern right now, and she was warned. Her time is up."

Tucker stares in Katy's direction and waits for her to look over at him. It doesn't take long, and when she does, he simply tips his head toward the door, walks to it, and waits. Without hesitation, she tells her friends she has to leave.

After her goodbyes, Katy glares at me like I ran over her puppy or tattled on her. I imagine she does feel like I've tattled. From her perspective, without all of the information, that's exactly what it looks like.

She hugs Tucker, and he whispers in her ear. Her face softens as she watches me approach, but then her head whips to Tucker, and her eyes widen in panic.

"Here."

"We believe so. Dempsey didn't want to take a chance that he tampered with your car, so he called me." Tucker tucks her under his arm and opens the door for them to walk out.

"I'll drive everyone home in my truck," Tucker calls back to me once we're all outside.

"If it's alright with you, I'll drive Katy's car back. It will probably make her more comfortable to be without me."

Katy stays under Tucker's arm as he looks at me over his shoulder. For a long moment, we stand and stare at each other before he concedes, clearly seeing in my eyes what I'm trying to convey to him.

He nods, and we take off in different directions toward our vehicles.

15

Katy

So much of me wants to be mad at Viktor, but I now realize he wasn't being an ass telling me we needed to leave. He was trying to keep my past out of the situation in front of my friends. I respect him for that. He didn't have to. I've given him nothing but grief all day, and he still tried to be a good person, which only makes me feel more like shit.

"We aren't being followed or anything, are we?" I can't help but feel nervous. The last time I heard from Shane, I shot him.

Pulling my knees into my chest, I wrap my arms around my legs and try to become as small as possible in the passenger's seat.

"Calm down, sweetheart. The only one following us is Dempsey." Tucker rubs my arm as I stare out the side view mirror. I've been watching my car follow us. I know it's him, and although I'm still mad at Viktor right now, I wish he was in the truck with us so I would know for sure he's safe.

"Is he back? Is this starting over?"

There was something in the look on his face when he just glanced at me. Shane did stop, didn't he? No one has said anything to me about him other than he hadn't been found after our incident in the rain. The police called all of the local hospitals and gave them a description of Shane. I didn't know where I had shot him, only that I had, so they didn't have that information to help if he showed up.

I speak in barely a whisper because I don't want to believe that it's true. "Did it never stop?"

Tucker's knuckles turn white on the steering wheel, and he sucks in a ragged breath.

"No, sweetheart, it never stopped. We still occasionally get photos. We've intercepted a few packages before you've seen them as well. All presents for Owen. That's why Dempsey hasn't been relieved of his duties. Shane hasn't stopped being a threat."

I puff a big breath of air from my lungs and curl myself tighter, staring at my car. I thought this was over, but if I were Shane, I'd probably just be more pissed.

"Why tonight?"

"He told Dempsey to get the asshole off of you because he didn't want more competition."

"Tucker, I'm so sorry I acted like a brat. You came from work, didn't you? That's how you got to us so quickly. He called you because I was being a spoiled brat and didn't want to listen to him because I'm holding a grudge like a toddler. I should have known something was wrong, but I thought he was just jealous that I was talking to another guy. I know I was jealous when Sara pulled him away—" Holy word vomit. Appalled, I bury my head into my knees. I didn't mean to confess any of that. Least of all to Tucker. "Please ignore those last few sentences."

"Too late, Katy. I heard it all. And I know more than that."

I groan into my knees. Of course he does. He's the all-knowing Tucker.

"Go ahead. Say whatever you want to say." I wait and wait. And just when I'm ready to burst with anticipation, he speaks.

"It's not my place."

What?

"Um. Okay. What does that even mean, 'it's not your place?'"

"Katy, you're a grown woman. He's a grown man. I can't tell you what you can and can't do together. I can tell you that if he hurts you,"—he turns and his eyes roam my pill bug state—"any more than whatever is going on right now, he'll have hell to pay. If you want to talk, I'm always here with a nonjudgmental ear."

Wow. The person I was the most worried about finding out seems to already know and isn't giving me the third degree.

"Thank you." I don't know how else to respond.

To say this day has been a rollercoaster would be an understatement. I woke up pissed, had a great conversation with Lincoln, pedicures and Piña Coladas with Axel, and then had a fun night out with friends. Now, I just want to curl up in bed and sleep, but I'm so wired with adrenaline that I have no idea how I'll manage.

"Are you still okay keeping Owen for the night? I'll feel safer knowing he's surrounded by all of you."

"Of course. He's always welcome. You can stay too if you'd like. I want you to feel safe. With or without Dempsey."

"No, I'll be okay. I'll come over a little after seven when my alarm goes off. I have work tomorrow, or rather today since it's already tomorrow." The clock on the dashboard glows a green 12:37.

As we pull into the driveway and park, Viktor parks next to us. I reach for the handle, and Tucker puts a hand on my arm.

"Wait. Let Dempsey sweep the house just in case."

I slump back in my seat, feeling defeated and anxious. What if Shane is in there? We already know he has a gun. I can't watch Viktor get hurt again. My anxiety rises as the front door opens, and he disappears inside. This is torture. The seconds pass by, feeling like minutes, as I see him sweep across the house by the lights turning on and off in each room.

"It's okay, sweetheart." Tucker holds down my shaking leg. I hadn't realized my nerves were showing an outward appearance.

"I know, but why isn't he out yet? There haven't been any lights turned on in a while." In reality, the clock only now says 12:41. Four minutes isn't really that long, but it feels like forever. I just want him to give us the sign that it's clear to come inside.

Where is he?

Finally, the front porch light comes on, and Viktor stands under the glow, his blonde hair shining, making him look almost ethereal. He nods and gives us a thumbs-up.

"I'll walk you in."

"I'm good. I just want to get inside and go to bed. It's been a long day."

"Alright. Let any of us know if you need anything. I love you, sweetheart."

"Love you, too, Tuck. G'night." Tucker leans over and kisses my forehead. I open the truck door, still apprehensive of my surroundings, and power walk to my front door. Viktor holds it open with his arm, and I duck under him to swiftly get inside.

I stop midway to my bedroom and listen to the door lock click and the beeping as Viktor turns on the alarm. When the robotic female says, "Armed," I exhale a breath that leaves me boneless. All the adrenaline seeps out with the confirmation that I'm safely inside my house.

My back is still turned to Viktor, but I feel him approach. I don't have the energy in me to fight or argue, or even talk about anything right now. My body is a live wire of stress and nerves.

"Pepper?" Viktor's voice is low and gravelly. He knows I need to be handled with kid gloves right now. But maybe I don't.

I look out the back window, knowing I'll see nothing because it's dark. It's nighttime. It's *my* time.

Spinning around, I grab Viktor's hand and pull him behind me. He follows without hesitation into my bedroom.

"Lay down on your back." He looks at me, confused. "Actually, take off your shoes and shirt and lay on the bed on your back.

"I—"

I turn and look him directly in his eyes. In this moment, our height difference doesn't matter. He sees my determination. "Viking, do as you're told."

He mutters "fuck" as he toes off his shoes and removes his shirt. Once he's done, he lies on the bed and waits.

"Move closer to the headboard." He shifts his body higher and stares at the ceiling. I untie the neck of my shirt and remove it but leave my lacy blue bra on. Next goes my shoes, pants, and matching blue panties. I know how much he loves my breasts, but this isn't about him; it's about me, and he doesn't get rewarded for his bad behavior.

I crawl onto the bed, and Viktor's head turns to watch me. His pupils are blown with lust, and when he tries to speak, I cover his mouth with my hand.

"Don't talk, just listen and nod yes or no. Do you understand?" He nods under my hand. "Good boy." I pat his cheek, and he leans into my hand, sighing.

I kneel up next to his head, and his eyes widen.

"I'm stressed. About last night, about tonight, about *you*. Since you're a big reason for that stress, you're going to help me relieve some of it. I'm going to sit on your face, and you'll make me come so I can get a good night's sleep. Do you remember our safeword?" He slowly nods. "Say it." He hesitates. I lean closer to his ear and whisper, "You have my permission to speak."

With a shuddering breath, he says, "bunny."

"Such a good boy. Since you're behaving so well, as long as you can concentrate on what your tongue is doing, I'll allow your hands to do what they need to for you to get some relief as well. *But*, my breasts are off limits, as you can tell by my bra still being on. Do you understand?"

I swear I hear the man whimper before he nods.

"Do you need to use your safeword right now?"

His head shakes vigorously, and I smile. Mounting his head, I think of all the smutty scenes I've read in my romance books. I have no idea what I'm doing, but I know an orgasm will make me feel better, and if I act confident in what I'm doing, I'll be confident. Fake it till you make it, right?

I lift my knee, chanting to myself not to kick him in the head. Viktor grabs my legs to help guide me into position. I want to yell at him to keep his hands to himself, but I also appreciate the assistance.

I grab the headboard, the reason I told him to lay closer to it and wait for the first feel of his tongue. It doesn't come. I feel him putting pressure on my legs, and I look down at him.

"Lower."

I should chastise him for speaking out of turn, but I don't understand what he wants me to do.

"What?"

"I need you lower, Pepper. If you're going to sit on my face, I need you to sit, not hover."

I thought I was sitting. I don't want to smother the man, which is also a common thought for the heroins in my books.

Be confident, Katy.

Viktor's hands shift to my inner thighs, and he pulls them apart, lowering my core closer to his face.

"You smell like fucking Eden."

"You aren't supposed to be talking."

"Then put your pussy in my mouth and fill it up so I can't."

Fuck his breathing. I let myself fully down over his face. He knows the safeword and can physically remove me if he needs to.

My move seems to please him because he hums into me, and I almost jolt away. If it wasn't for his grip around my thighs, I might have.

Viktor's tongue comes out, and the pressure of gravity makes it feel like he's everywhere. His tongue licks, and his lips suck. I'm mad at him, and so fucking turned on that all the lines in my head are blurring. The emotions mix, all being wrapped together by pleasure.

The warmth of his mouth lowers, and he spears his tongue inside me. I gasp at the invasion. Viktor's hands move, and there's suddenly pressure on my clit. I'm overwhelmed by his tongue and his finger touching me at the same time.

I'm pulled out of my pleasure bubble when I hear Viktor's zipper lower. I told him he could do what he needed to relieve himself, and it seems like he's listening. Except his hand comes back to my thigh.

Why is he touching only me and not himself?

The question drifts off as my pleasure heightens. Folding one arm over the headboard, I rest my forehead on my hand. Viktor's hair is too tempting not to touch, and I reach down, pulling out his hair tie.

I can't see much of him as he's fully committed to being buried beneath me, but I run my fingers through his loose strands, pulling at the roots. The guttural moan that the pulling produces vibrates my entire core and forces a groan out of me.

My orgasm is rapidly growing, and I'm warring with myself. I want it so bad but I also want it to last longer. Fuck. I don't know what I want more of, but it seems my body is making the decision for me. My toes tingle as the warmth pools low in my belly. My hand tightens further in his hair, and my hips grind across his face. Viktor's beard rubs along my inner thighs, and the scratchiness only heightens the build-up.

"Fuck, Viking. Fuck, I'm gonna—Oh god." The wave of euphoria crashes through me. I'm practically humping his face, but I can't stop myself. It feels too fucking good. My moans borderline screams, and I'm happy we're alone in the house, and nothing can stop this moment from playing out

126

completely. Viktor moans loudly beneath me, and it sounds like he's enjoying himself as much as I am.

Viktor is relentless, drawing out my orgasm with his tongue as long as he can, and only stops when I make him.

"Enough. I can't take anymore. Stop, please." The words come out between pants and gasps. There's barely any air in my lungs, and I remember he probably hasn't had a full breath in a long while. I push myself back to slide down his chest when he stops me.

"I'm a mess."

His face glistens with my come, but I don't understand why that would stop me sitting lower on his stomach. He shakes his head at my inspection of his face. "Not up here."

Not up here? *Oh.*

I peer over my shoulder and find come all over Viktor's stomach and chest. I guess his moaning wasn't just from my pleasure but also his.

"Let me get something to clean you up."

He opens his mouth to speak but thinks twice about it; his silvery-blue eyes holding mine.

"You have permission to speak freely."

"Thank you, Pepper. I'll just go take a shower in the guest bath and go to bed. I know you're tired."

Is he dismissing me? Is he dismissing himself? Is he playing our little game better than me? I still have no idea what I'm doing and what happens *after*. I carefully hike my leg over his midsection and sit next to him.

"If that's what you'd prefer, you're free to leave."

There's long moments of silence and staring. I don't want him to leave. I'm still upset and confused about last night. I want him to ask to stay, but even if he did, I'd have to tell him no.

He seems to come to the same conclusion as I do and nods before carefully shifting off the bed. Viktor picks his shirt up off the floor and wipes his stomach and chest clean. Stepping up to me, he pauses before kissing the top of my head and whispering, "Goodnight."

I got what I wanted, and at the moment, it felt so right and so fucking good, but now I feel empty and like I used him. I know if he felt that way, he still wouldn't have stopped me.

Did he do that against his will?

All the stress he just relieved has been replaced with new stress and anxiety.

16

Dempsey

K aty was fucking stunning. She told me exactly what she wanted, and I was all too willing to give it to her. I was so turned on I came when she did, and I'm not even ashamed of it. She came apart so beautifully on top of me that I couldn't stop my body from enjoying her pleasure.

I had no intention of touching myself, even though she gave me permission. The only reason I even pulled my cock out was because it was straining against my pants, and I wanted to be free. My orgasm was the cherry on top of the icing on the cake.

Unfortunately, when it was over, I had no misconception of what it was and wasn't. She told me she needed relief, and I gave her that. I didn't want her to clean me up. It was my mess, not hers. I needed her to understand that I know my place with her.

I shower quickly and set up my bed. I consider sleeping on the couch, but I can't make a habit of that. I have a bed for a reason, even if it's only a fold-out one.

As I drift off to sleep, I almost wish I hadn't taken a shower so I could still smell her on my skin. My memories of devouring her pussy will have to be enough.

"Viktor. No, Viktor. Come back to me."

I jolt straight up at Katy's yelling and grab my gun like I always do. I never assume it's only a nightmare because the one time I let my guard down could be the day he's come to take her.

"Viktor!"

It hurts my fucking heart that it's always my name she's yelling when she dreams. The door pushes open easily since I didn't shut it when I left. It makes me more comfortable to know I can do exactly this without any extra noise. Silently, I creep in and visually sweep the room. There's no one in here but a thrashing Katy twisted in the covers.

Since Owen isn't here, I move to the side of the bed and tuck my gun in the back of the nightstand drawer, confirming the safety is on before I close it.

"Pepper. Katy, wake up, baby." She never responds to her name, but I always try, just in case. I don't want to fully startle her awake; I know it can make a nightmare worse if it doesn't work. Calling her name first makes me feel like I'm gently walking into her subconsciousness.

Reaching over, I rub her back gently, again trying not to startle her. Once I've come this far and she's still in her nightmare, I pull her to me. I love getting to hold her in the middle of the night. Sometimes, relieving her dream is as simple as holding her like this. Other times, like tonight seems like it's going to be, I have to wake her gently.

I struggle with this part because she's having a nightmare about me, and waking up to me holding her usually causes crying. It's relief that I'm not in whatever nightmare her subconscious put her in, but I hate when she cries, nonetheless.

"Wake up for me Katy." I caress my fingers down her cheek. Every touch is gentle, trying to make the transition from sleep to awake as easy as possible. Tonight, though, she's fighting against me.

"Don't touch him. Get away from me."

Her arms thrash, and she kicks at the blankets. Keeping my hold firm around her, I lean us over so I can untangle the blankets from her legs. Hopefully, that will help her not feel trapped.

"Viktor."

Her yelling has turned to pleading, and tears stain her face.

"Sweet Katy, please wake up for me. I'm right here, and I'm safe. I'm safe. Shhh." I kiss her forehead as I rock us, continuing to whisper that I'm safe.

Her body relaxes in my arms, and I know she's coming out of her nightmare, or at least down from it. Sometimes, she wakes up, and other times, she drifts back to dreamless sleep.

"Viktor?" There's a slight rasp to her voice from the yelling.

"I'm right here, Pepper. I've got you." I always use her nickname when she wakes. She told me once how it helps ground her because it's not a name Shane knows. When she hears Pepper, she knows she's safe.

"God, Viktor." Katy's hand balls into a fist, but there's

nothing to grab onto. I didn't bother putting on a shirt. Instead, I grab her hand and lace our fingers together. I'll give her comfort however I can. She stutters a breath into my chest, and I feel the wetness from her tears.

"I've got you, Pepper. I've always got you. You're safe. I'm safe." I kiss her forehead again, and she looks up at me.

"My Viking."

"Your Viking."

"Kiss me."

"What?" She must still be asleep.

"It's nighttime. That's my time. Kiss me."

Shit. She's awake enough to remember her self-imposed rules; I'm going to assume she knows what she's asking for.

I lean down, and she lifts her chin more to meet me halfway. When I close the distance, and our lips meet, Katy sighs a sound of pure relief. She removes her hand from mine and slides it up my chest, neck, and into my hair as she lifts her body to straddle mine.

"Katy?" I mumble into her mouth as she takes over the kiss.

"Shhh."

Her breath on my lips tickles, and I can't help but smile. She's definitely awake and kissing me willingly. As she melts into me, I realize she's completely naked. How I hadn't noticed that until this moment shows the level of protection I have for her when it's needed.

"Touch me, Viking."

That fucking nickname. I know it's what I look like, and she's certainly not the first person to ever call me that, nor will she be the last, but knowing that she uses it as a level of control over me has my cock twitching. "Touch me." There's a whine of neediness to her tone, and I can't deny her.

132

My hands run along her sides straight to her incredible breasts that she denied me of earlier. She fed Owen before she went out with friends, but that was hours ago, and I can feel the weight her breasts now hold. I want to taste her so fucking bad, but she only asked me to touch.

I softly caress her nipples, running the pads of my fingers back and forth, and she arches into my hands.

"More."

"Pepper, tell me what you want, and I'll give it to you. Anything. Just ask." She places her hands over mine and squeezes—not too hard, but just enough that she leaks. I stare at the creamy liquid leaking over our fingers, and I feel like a starved man.

"Clean it up."

Without hesitation, my tongue darts out and laps at her sweet offering. It's as heavenly as I remember, and I know the more I taste it, the harder it will be to stay away.

Katy moans and her fingers trail up the back of my neck into my hair. I love the feel of her fingers flowing through my locks. She grips my hair and pushes my head further into her breasts.

"Pepper, I'll take it all if you're not careful. I'm trying to restrain myself."

"Take it all. I'll make more by morning. Please don't stop. I love the feel of your mouth on me."

Her words are killing me. I want to give her everything she wants, but she knows her body better than I do. If she says she'll make more, then I'm going to enjoy myself. Taking her left breast in both hands, I latch onto her nipple and suck long and hard.

"Fuuuuuuck."

Katy throws her head back and moans the word. I feel her milk squirt in my mouth, and the carnal side of me takes over. I alternate between her nipples, taking and taking everything they offer me. Katy grinds on my lap, rubbing herself over my erection. I'm grateful for my orgasm earlier, or I'd probably be making a mess in my pants right now. Though it's not stopping my cock from stiffening to uncomfortable proportions.

Katy's breathing grows ragged, and I can tell she's close.

"Are you going to come from grinding your needy pussy on my cock, Pepper?"

She shakes her head erratically. "No," she breathes out. "Your...mouth."

I growl as I dive back in and drink my fill. Her fists tighten in my hair, and the pain at my roots makes my scalp tingle.

I would give anything to be inside her right now. To feel her walls flutter around me as she orgasms. But after last night, I don't deserve that part of her. She gave it to me, and I reacted horribly. Orgasms I can give and I can give them freely and often.

Katy's face tenses as her orgasm crests, and her release dampens my pants. I slow my assault on her nipples until her grinding stops, and with one last kiss to each rosy tip, I sit back.

Her chest heaves as she catches her breath, and I mourn the loss of her fingers when she releases my hair.

Katy leans down and rests her forehead on mine, smiling. "Stay with me tonight."

Not a question. A statement.

"That's—"

"Not against the rules if you leave before the sun comes

up."

It's hard to argue with that logic.

Katy leans over and picks up her phone. I groan as she rubs over my still-hard cock.

"The sun rises at 6:17. If you leave by six, we aren't breaking the rules."

A glance at the clock shows me it's just after two, which gives me more hours than I deserve to hold her in my arms.

"Okay." I gently remove Katy from my lap and stand, walking around the bed.

"Where are you going?" Her eyes follow me, and I walk across the room.

"Getting a warm cloth to clean you up. I don't want you to get a yeast infection."

She stares at me with a shocked expression, furthering my guilt that I left her last night and didn't do this. I left her alone with my come leaking from her and didn't clean up the mess I made. A mistake I'll never make again, swearing to myself to worship Katy from head to toe every fucking chance I get. Even if it's only at night.

When I return, Katy is lying in bed staring at the ceiling. I sit on the side and caress her leg.

"Open for me." She tries to sit up, and I place a palm on her chest. "I've got it. Open your legs." She relaxes back in the pillows and spreads for me to clean her.

A hum slips past her lips, making me smile. "Does that feel good, Pepper?"

"Mmhmm," she purrs. Doing this for her is almost as satisfying as giving her the orgasm that made the mess a necessity to clean up. "I set an alarm for you."

"Thank you."

I toss the cloth into the bathroom and crawl over Katy.

"Little spoon or chest to chest?"

She answers with actions instead of words. Katy crawls into my chest, tangling our legs together. There's been many nights that I've fallen asleep in here after one of her nightmares, but tonight is different. Tonight, she asked me to be here with her, and even if I have to leave before the sun comes up, I'm still going to cherish every minute I can with my little Pepper in my arms.

17

Katy

My alarm goes off, and I blindly swing my arm until I find my phone and hit the snooze button. I need a few extra minutes this morning. Rolling over, I take a deep breath and smell something musky—like a man. I nuzzle into the smell as my brain takes a few extra moments to catch up with my nose.

"Viktor." I sit up and frantically look around the room as the memories from last night come flooding back to me. I'm staring at my pillow, the one he slept on that holds his smell, when I see movement from the corner of my eye.

"Katy? Are you okay?" My eyes flash to a fully dressed Viktor standing in my doorway, then down to the empty bed beside me where I left my barely clothed Viking a few hours ago.

"W-what time is it?"

"It's seven. That was your morning alarm that went off." He walks over to my side of the bed and drops off a mug of coffee. I can tell by the color that it's made perfectly to my liking. The liquid is a peanut butter color, and the smell of French vanilla fills my nose.

Viktor steps back, giving me space, and I remember that I'm naked. I pull the blanket up my chest, but feeling like I shouldn't be embarrassed. He's seen me topless several times now, but it's daylight outside.

"I woke up before the alarm you set for me and turned it off. I wanted you to sleep as long as you could. I'm ready whenever you are." With a slight smile, he leaves the room, closing the door behind him.

The coffee warms me from the inside out as I take my first sip. I need to shower and get to Owen. I love the fifteen minutes each morning and night we bond through our breastfeeding. It's not something that I ever considered before getting pregnant. I'm not sure any sixteen year old does, but in my effort to be as small of a burden as I could, I was determined to do it. Any money I could save Spencer and the guys was a win for me, and breastfeeding was the simplest thing I could do. And nothing compares to the bonding I feel with Owen when I do it.

I'm fortunate that my body was able to nourish my son and continues to do so, even if we had a rough start. However, it's not everyone's journey.

I shower and dress in a dark red maxi skirt and a graphic t-shirt knotted at the front. Simple, easy clothes work best for the continuous up and down with the kids in my class. I packed extra clothes in Owen's diaper bag before I left so I wouldn't have to worry about it this morning.

One last peek in the mirror before I leave, and I look at the woman before me. She looks confident and happy. Someone I never thought I'd see staring back at me. I smooth my hands over my hair, missing the waves from last night, and remind myself to have Spencer teach me how she did them. Or, more specifically, I could ask Nicole because I'm sure she's the one who taught Spencer.

"All set?" Viktor's smile warms my belly as I step out of my room.

"Yeah. You could have gone ahead without me. I'm capable of walking across the lawn alone."

His apologetic half-smile leaves me with a feeling of dread.

"Sorry, Katy. New orders state you aren't allowed to do anything alone. I'm with you at all times. Even if you're out with one of them."

There went my good mood. "What? Why?"

"Because of the phone call last night. He's getting close again, and we need to keep you and Owen safe."

"But you're with me and not Owen right now. How can you be in two places at once?" I thought my logic was good, but his face tells me otherwise.

"You'll meet Patrick when we get to the house. He'll be accompanying us to school today, so you and Owen have eyes on you at all times. When I'm with you both, his job is the main house."

"You've got to be fucking kidding me? This is ridiculous."

"I'm sorry, Katy. I'm just following orders."

"Whose? Whose orders are you following?" Viktor stays silent. Did he have something to do with this? At this point, I don't even know who signs his paychecks. I know he was hired by Justin, but that was almost three years ago.

"It's for your protection."

"Fuck my protection. I'm not a prisoner. I have to have a life outside these four walls where I'm not being followed by

139

guard dogs." Viktor flinches at my comparison, but I don't care. That's what it felt like last night to have him stare at me while I was with my friends. His job is to watch my surroundings. Not me.

"Viktor, does this have anything to do with last night? Did you tell them about your jealousy seeing another guy pay attention to me?"

"What? Not at all. Tucker saw the same thing that I did last night. I just follow orders. If you want to yell at someone, it's him you should be directing your anger toward."

I know he's probably right, but he's in front of me, and some of my jealousy seeing him with Sara is bleeding out right now. I have no claim on him any more than he has a claim on me, but he's *my* Viking, even if it's just at night.

"Viktor, were you jealous last night?" Now I need to know. His Adam's apple bobs as he swallows hard. It's the only tell that he's affected by my question. I stalk toward him, and he holds his ground. "No answer for me, *Viking?*" I run my finger down his chest, feeling the rippling muscles under his navy shirt.

"*Katy.*" He grabs my wrist, stopping my hand, and leans close to my ear. "The sun is up, and that means it's *my* time. If you're changing the rules of our arrangement, there are plenty of things I am happy to do to you right now. But I think you like how our dynamic is and that means you don't get to use your charm right now and expect it to work."

Fuck. He's right, and he knows it. I give him a saccharine smile, and he releases my wrist as I step back.

"There's breakfast waiting for us at the big house. Let's go."

Viktor turns, and as he expects, I follow.

Patrick is a brick house of a man. There's no hiding in

the shadows for him. He's tall, dark, and broody and gets interesting looks from the kids in the preschool. One of the three year olds asked him if he was a G. I. Joe because he's dressed in all black, with cargo pants and a "meanie face." My laughter couldn't be contained, and even Viktor cracked a smile.

The G.I. Joe wannabe followed us to work in his own car, and I was told that's how it would be from now on. Always two cars wherever we go. Some people would enjoy the attention of having two gorgeous men follow them around all day, but not me. I've always done everything on my own. I willingly accepted Viktor several years ago because I was still a traumatized little girl and clung to anyone that I knew was safe. Now, I have two overgrown babysitters, and one was already bordering on too many. Although, based on the looks that Viktor keeps tossing at Patrick, I'm not sure he's too happy about the addition, either. Patrick has a scar that runs from his right temple past the front of his ear and disappears at his jawline. I was looking at it during breakfast, and Viktor eyed me suspiciously. It seems he didn't like me looking at another man, and I think I'm going to like this little jealous streak he has.

"Can we go to lunch? I have a feeling this could be my last meal out." Viktor is on high alert as we leave the preschool and walk to the car. He insisted he carry Owen, who's happily enjoying the ride from one of his favorite people.

"I didn't have any intentions of going anywhere but home."

"Please. I need a last hurrah of my freedom. There's two of you and one and a half of us. How bad could it get?"

Viktor looks at me, and I feel instant guilt from my statement. I know how bad it can get. I was there, and it was bad—so very bad.

"Fine." Maybe this is a fight I won't win. I understand the cons outweigh the pros sometimes, but I was really hoping this wasn't one of them.

Viktor opens my door for me and moves around the car to buckle Owen. I dream of the day this nightmare is over, and my little boy can have a completely normal life. He doesn't know the difference, but I do, and I want better for him.

"Vik. Hug me." My heart swells as Owen wraps his little arms around Viktor's neck and pulls his hair.

"Thank you, buddy." Viktor tickles Owen's stomach in an attempt to get his hands to release his hair. It finally works after several wincing faces, and I turn my head to look out the window so Viktor doesn't see me laughing at him.

Viktor turns the car on with a sigh and pulls out his phone. "You planned that, didn't you? Where would you like to go to lunch?"

Did my kid just win me a ticket to lunch? *Hell yes.*

"How do you feel about mild degradation?"

"No. Absolutely not. Pick somewhere else."

"But—"

"Katy, I'm happy to take you straight home, or anywhere else but Debevics. Your choice."

"Fine." I don't want to push my luck. "How about S'morgasm? They have delicious sandwiches." And a back room that maybe I can get my Viking to explore with me.

No. You can't think like that, Katy. Viktor reminded you of that this morning.

"Maybe." Huh?

"Maybe, what?"

"You're so easy to read, Pepper. Yes to S'morgasm. Maybe

142

to the blue door. And that's a big maybe."

Holy shit. He said maybe. I don't care how small of a possibility it is; the thought of exploring the sex shop at the back of S'morgasm is exhilarating.

Viktor sends a text and looks in the rearview. He stares momentarily before nodding at his reflection, and we drive away. He must have been having a conversation with Patrick.

18

Dempsey

Tell me why I agreed to this? S'morgasm is a favorite coffee shop among the group. Everyone enjoys coming here. I know this is a philanthropy for Annie, and they stock the ingredients to make Nicole's pumpkin spice lattes even in the middle of summer at Annie's request.

While the food and coffee here are top-notch, it's the blue door that Katy keeps glancing at that's the true reason all the girls love this place. Behind the unassuming blue door is a private sex toy shop. I don't think Katy has ever been back there before. At least not with me, but she obviously knows what it contains. I wouldn't be surprised if Blake has taken her back there, as it's her favorite place. I've heard rumors that Annie's card is on file, and Blake can purchase anything she wants at anytime.

The coffee shop keeps both businesses very separate, and if you don't know what's back there, you'd be clueless. I only know because Justin warned me the girls might want to visit when I'm here with them. None have so far. Going through that door would be as new to me as it will be for Katy.

Despite my maybe, I know it's what she wants, and I'll go with her as long as G. I. Patrick agrees to watch Owen, which he will because it's his job. It's also the reason we parked in the back and walked to the front. The toy shop only allows you to exit from the back of the store.

"Are you ready? Do you have your I.D. on you?"

"Why do I need—Oh. My I.D. Of course." Katy's face lights up with excitement as she digs through her purse. In order to gain entrance to the back, you have to show your ID to the baristas, who allow you access through the blue door. It's a fantastic system.

"Patrick, are you all good with this little guy?" He grunts as I hand him a sticky toddler who instantly grabs for Patrick's cheeks.

"No hair." Owen's forehead scrunches, and he reaches back out to me. I lean in, knowing what he wants, and he tugs at my beard. "Hair."

I shrug at Patrick. "He knows what he likes. We'll meet you out back. I don't know a time frame, but I'll keep you updated via text."

As a man of little words, he grunts again. I hand him the diaper bag and pull out the wipes, waving him away. I join Katy in line to show our I.D.s, and soon, we're entering the blue door to the sex toy shop.

I've never been back here before. It's much larger than I expected and well organized. Katy's head rotates around the room, and I wonder how much of this is new to her. I know she's an avid romance reader, and I've glanced over her shoulder a time or two to know the things she's reading aren't vanilla.

"Where should we start?"

We. Interesting. It's probably just a slip of the tongue because she knows I'm going wherever she goes, but I can think Katy means "we" as in us.

"Wherever your heart desires. And don't look at the price tags. I'm taking care of this trip."

"What? No." She spins on her heels and plants her hands on her hips. "You can not pay for me. I have no idea what I want to buy, and everything here is...*personal*."

I allow my eyes to roam over her body and don't stop the hunger from shining through.

"Is that supposed to be a deterrent? Would it make you feel better if you pretended it was nighttime outside?"

A beautiful blush creeps up her neck and turns her cheeks rosy. I hum my approval as I glide my thumb across the blush on her face. "I'll let you pick anything your little heart desires and you can use it on me, Pepper."

Katy's eyes scan my face. She's imagining something more devious than I think I'm giving her credit for.

"Anything?"

"I'm going to regret this, aren't I?"

"*Any*thing?"

Fuck, she already knows I'll give her anything *and* everything.

I sigh, giving in to her. "Yes, anything. Always, Pepper."

She hops several times and claps her hands. It's adorable to see her skirt fluff around her. Katy practically skips off into the store, and I dutifully follow.

"Really?" I feel like we've roamed the entire store three times, and she keeps coming back to this section. "This is your choice?"

Katy's smile is mischievous as she stands in front of the display of strap-on harnesses and dildos.

"You said anything." She's acting sweet and innocent, but her dirty mind is anything but.

"I thought you'd pick handcuffs or blindfolds, not straight to pegging."

"Wait, are those options too?" Her eyes widen with excitement and I regret giving her more ideas.

I drop my forehead to my hand and groan. "Of course they are." I've created a monster. I walk over to the counter and pick up a hand basket. I extend it to Katy with a huff. "It sounds like we are going to need this."

Her responding giggle is all I need to feel better about whatever activities this goddess has in mind for me. I trust her, and she trusts me. Even if it's only under the light of the moon.

Two hours. That's how long we stayed in the store and left with three bags of toys and accessories. Patrick wasn't too happy when we finally emerged from our not-so-little shopping trip, but I didn't care how he felt when I could feel the anticipation vibrating from Katy.

"Pepper, you know some of the things we bought need build-up and training, right." I'm honestly afraid that she thinks I can take something up my ass without prep work.

"What? You mean you can't just take it like a man. I do?"

"Um, Pepper. My ass is a virgin, and this isn't a conversation we should be having in front of Owen." I glance in the rearview at Owen, who's happily eating his snack and utterly oblivious to what's happening up front.

I turn up the music and lower my voice. "You know I'm more than happy to explore with you, but you can't just ram things up there all willy-nilly."

Katy bursts into hysterical laughter, and without knowing why, I join her.

"I'm not naive, Viking. Nor do I plan on doing anything *willy-nilly*. I can't believe you used that term. Right now, all I can imagine is me kneeling behind you, swirling my hips with a dildo spinning between my legs like a helicopter."

"Holy fuck, Katy." The image she just painted in my mind has my cock swelling, and it's not an appropriate time for that to be happening. I also shouldn't be so turned on by the thought. I'm already nervous knowing that she has the tools to do things to me that I've never even dreamed of experiencing, and now she wants me to do them just from a simple visual image.

Katy's hand slides across my thigh, and I stop whatever she thinks she's trying to do.

"The sun is out. It's not your time, Pepper."

Her bottom lip pops out, and fuck, do I want to kiss the shit out of it.

"It's not going to work. Stop trying to be a brat during the day."

Katy slides down the seat and grabs handfuls of her skirt. Inch by fucking inch, she pulls it up until her knees are exposed, but she doesn't stop there. She continues to expose her creamy thighs, and I glance in the rearview again. First, at Owen, who has dozed off, and then at Patrick, who's following behind us.

"What are you doing, woman?"

"Being a brat." Her hands disappear under her skirt, and lacy purple panties appear, sliding down her legs.

I shift in my seat, attempting to make room where there is

none for my cock.

"I'm just being what you accused me of—a *brat.* Do you want to watch or participate?"

"What are you talking about?" *What is she talking about?* Is she asking me...

"Viking, don't be coy. You're a big boy and know exactly what I'm asking."

Katy's hand disappears again under her skirt, but I know there's nothing under there this time.

"Suit yourself." She closes her eyes and releases a low sigh. "Stop."

One eye pops open, but she doesn't stop the movement between her legs.

"What if I don't want to?"

"Pepper, I said stop. *I* make the rules during the day and you better be a good girl and follow them."

She smiles, and I don't know if it's because I used the words "good girl" or because she realizes she's getting to me. Either way, I need to take control of this situation before she thinks it's okay to be a complete brat.

I have to admit I like the contrast in our relationship from day to night. I initially meant that during the day, she wouldn't question my choices as her bodyguard, but it appears the lines are blurring, and I'm not fucking complaining one bit.

"So, have you decided to participate?"

"No one touches your pussy without my permission. She's mine."

Reaching over, I trail my hand up her neck and rub her earlobe where my diamond earrings still sparkle my ownership. She smirks, letting me know she wore them

149

on purpose last night.

"Then do something about it, Viking. She's ready to purr for you?" Katy sucks in her bottom lip, and her chest heaves. She huffs a few times before she covers her mouth, trying to dampen her laughter. "That was…eww. Can we pretend I didn't say that? I think I just grossed myself out."

I glance one more time in the rearview to check that Owen is still asleep before my hand slips up her skirt, and her laughter turns into a gasp. Katy is already slick with her arousal. This is more than a few swipes from her fingers.

"How long have you been this wet, Pepper? Were you imagining all the naughty things we would be doing? Did that soak this pussy for me?"

Katy's head rests on the back of her seat, her bottom lip tucked firmly between her teeth.

"Answer me, Pepper."

"Yes."

It's more of a whisper than a word, but I understand it. I want to make this good for her, but we aren't far from home, and I don't want to have to explain an unnecessary detour to Patrick.

Pushing in one finger, she accepts me easily, and after a few pumps, I add another. Katy lifts her left leg onto the center console and angles her hips in my direction, giving me easier access. It's still awkward for my arm, but I'm making do.

"I need you to come for me, beautiful. We don't have much time. Wanna help me out?"

Katy's hand joins me, and she plays with her clit while I massage her inner walls. She's getting close. If her breathing wasn't already giving her away, the small thrusts of her hips are.

"That's it, Pepper. Take what you need." Her finger quickens, and she's riding mine as best she can within her seat belted lap. Katy's hand rises and covers her mouth as her inner walls clamp down on my fingers, and she comes. Her breaths are long and controlled, and I can tell she's holding in as much noise as she can. The adorable little squeaks sneaking through make my cock twitch, and I'm going to have to do something about it as soon as we get home. This isn't the type of erection that goes down on its own.

"Good girl." Katy melts at the praise as her body relaxes from her release.

Removing my fingers, I bring them to my mouth and suck them clean.

"That shouldn't be so fucking hot."

Katy's words sound sleepy, and I wouldn't blame her if she needed to take a nap when we get home.

"Everything about you is hot, Pepper, especially your taste." I grab the hand she had under her skirt and lick them clean as well. "You're my favorite flavor."

19

Tucker

"Any new news?"

I wish I had something to give Justin. I have no idea how Shane is such a ghost after more than two years of stalking Katy and almost a decade of Spencer before that.

"No. The call to Dempsey was from a burner phone. It was turned off immediately after they hung up."

"Shit. What more can we do? How's Patrick?" I can hear the defeat in Justin's voice, and it runs as deep as mine. I hate that this asshole is still out there and taunting our girls.

"He's broody. Doesn't talk much. He's doing his job well." With the new development between Katy and Dempsey, we thought it would be good to have another set of eyes around at all times. Not that any of us believe that Dempsey would be a less efficient bodyguard for her. It's actually the opposite. We know he'll be on higher alert. He has more to lose now. We hired Patrick in hopes that he would share the burden. It also gives us peace of mind when they're out, or she's separate from Owen.

"He's overqualified to be a babysitter for Owen, but he has the skills if they are needed. And I pay him well, so he has nothing to complain about."

"I have no doubt, Justin. How's my niece and nephew?"

"Wonderful as always. You should all come over for dinner soon. We've seen a lot of Katy but not the rest of you."

We hang up with the promise of an evening together, and I text Dempsey. I saw them come home not that long ago, and Patrick is walking the grounds.

Tucker: Need to talk outside.

Dempsey: 10-4

Patrick nods at me as I pass him in the yard. As I approach the pool house, Dempsey steps out, closing the door behind him.

"How are they?" I nod to the door.

"Napping. We went to S'morgasm for lunch. How was Owen last night?"

"An angel as always." We love having Owen over. We treat him as our own, and he's completely spoiled. Would I have loved to have children with Spencer? Absolutely. But it wasn't in the cards for us as a family, and I don't regret it. Spencer is the love of my life, and I'm pretty fond of those three other assholes too.

"My guy checked all the cars, and no tracking devices were found. I also had him check the security systems, and everything is locked down tight. I wish I had more news for you."

"I always appreciate good news."

A silence falls between us, and I wait to see if he'll confide in me about Katy. He didn't flinch when I referred to her as my daughter last night. Dempsey knows I'm fiercely protective of Katy. Blood or not, she's my daughter.

"I'll do right by her, Tucker. I promise. As long as she'll have me, I'll be good to her."

"Did you work out your issue?"

"I think we've come to a comparable agreement." I noticed a difference between them when they came to pick up Owen this morning, so whatever agreement they came up with seems to have made them both happy.

"Good. And Patrick? Is everything working out well with him?"

I can tell by the look in his eyes he appreciates my change of subject. I trust him. If I didn't, he'd be gone, and he knows it.

"He wasn't a fan of our little outing today because he had to watch Owen alone for a while, but he seems good at his job."

"Outing? I thought you went to S'morgasm? Why would he have to watch Owen alone if you all went together?"

Dempsey's face pales.

"Um…"

He's nervous. I've never seen him this way before. What happened at the coffee place that has him jittery?

"Dempsey, what aren't you telling me?"

He looks toward the pool house and rubs the back of his neck.

"Do you not know about the blue door at S'morgasm?"

Blue door? Blue door?

I have no idea what he's talking about. I'm particular with

my coffee and prefer a specific roast. I only drink at home, Katy's house, or at Midnight Moonshine because I make sure it's the specific coffee I like. I've never been to S'morgasm other than dropping others off. I know it's a place where you can make s'mores at your table, and they have a free cup of coffee program. I've never heard anything about a blue door.

"I don't. Would you care to enlighten me?"

Dempsey looks even more nervous, if possible. He's sputtering for words when the door opens behind him, and a sleepy-eyed Katy squints at us through the sun.

"What's going on out here? Are we having secret meetings?"

"Dempsey was just telling me about the blue door at S'morgasm."

Katy's eyebrows shoot up, and she looks at him. "Which part were you telling him about? Was it the silk blindfold? Or maybe the candle that melts into massage oil?"

She stares Dempsey down, and his eyes shift everywhere but at me.

"Oh! Wait, it must have been the vibrating cock ring."

I'm beginning to see a pattern and why Dempsey's previous pale complexion is turning shades of red the more she talks. He's begging her with his eyes to stop talking, but Katy seems to be having too much fun.

"No. I got it." She steps up to his chest and dips her head to meet his gaze. "You told him about the nine-inch strap-on we bought so I can peg you."

Katy smiles a triumphant smile while a barely audible "fuck" hisses from Dempsey.

"Sir, I—"

"Stop. I don't think I want to know what goes on behind your closed doors." I point a finger at Katy, then Dempsey.

"Be safe, and if you have any questions, ask anyone but me."

I adjust my hat and turn away from them with too many thoughts swirling through my head.

Group Chat 5:

Tucker: Tell me about the blue door at S'morgasm.

Miller: Oh shit.

Lincoln: Who told you?

Axel: Is it time to take Daddy Tucker shopping?!

Spencer: It's an adult toy store.

Tucker: If I have to know, so do y'all. Our daughter went there with Dempsey and bought a vibrating cock ring and a strap-on for pegging.

I close my phone and place it in my pocket. The vibrations come quick and so does my smile, knowing tonight should be fun.

20

Katy

Babs: I miss you. I just know you're the best mother. Have coffee with me, please? It could just be me and you, and you could show me pictures of my grandbaby.

Ugh. This is not the text I want to see when I first wake up. Especially after waking up alone and the infuriating night I had.

After the stunt I pulled with Tucker, Viktor ignored me the rest of the night. I couldn't help myself. I knew I was crossing a line, but everyone was fine with Viktor and I…what? What are we?

No. It's too early in the morning for those kinds of deep thoughts. I'd rather think about the sweet torture Viktor put me through, as infuriating as it was.

He waited. Viktor's patience knows no bounds. This man had to time things exactly perfect…

"Pepper." Viktor stalks to me in my room after pretending for the last several hours that the only other person that exists in this house besides him is Owen.

"Viktor." Some of the breath leaves my lungs as he cages me against the wall. "Or should I say Viking?"

His nose nuzzles my neck, and his breath tickles my hair. "Look outside."

I turn my head to see the orange and pink hues of the sky as the sun goes down.

"It's dusk."

"Mmhmm. Not quite day, but not yet night."

The heat of his mouth surrounds the sweet spot where my shoulder and neck meet, and I let out a low moan. I just put Owen down to bed and can't be too loud.

Viktor kisses my neck and jaw, and his warm hand snakes to the front of my skirt. I've never been as grateful for elastic waists as I am. His hand easily dips into my maxi skirt, and my body responds by arching into him. He growls when he realizes I never put my panties back on in the car.

"You have until the sun goes down."

"Huh?" I must have heard him wrong. What am I being timed for?

"You have until the sun fully goes down to come. What do you want me to do to make it happen? My mouth? My fingers? Do you want to help again? Tick tock. Times a ticking."

I'm struggling to form any coherent thoughts with his lips on me.

"Ugh. Um. M-mouth." His lips disappear, and my skirt fluffs in the air as Viktor dives between my legs.

The feeling of his tongue, but not the sight of him, is jarring. It's like being blindfolded but still having sight. My fingers itch to

158

grab his hair and run through it, but he's fully immersed under my shirt.

Viktor's hand smooths up my inner thigh and lifts it over his shoulder. I gasp as he flicks my piercing, teasing my clit.

"Tick-tock, Viking."

He doesn't like getting a taste of his own medicine, and it's evident by the growl he makes and the suction on my clit.

"Oh, fuck. God, you feel so fucking good." I'm dying to touch him. I feel like my hands are tied up, but all he's doing is hiding under my skirt.

Note to self: wear more skirts and dresses.

My breathing increases as Viktor's mouth teeters me closer to the edge. I need more—his fingers inside me, his hands on my breasts. Just as I'm about to ask him for either of those things, I hear an alarm going off and feel the emptiness of his loss, as Viktor stands up.

"W-what are you doing?"

He turns his head to the window, and the beautiful colors are gone, now faded to blues and blacks.

"Time's up, Pepper."

"I-but. Then that means it's my time. I want you to get back down there, Viking. Finish what you've started."

His smile is devious as he boops me on the nose.

"No can do, Katy. Maybe next time think first before you embarrass me in front of one of the people who signs my paychecks.

Grrr. I'm frustrated all over again thinking of how he left me. He wasn't wrong. I deserved it. My intentions absolutely were to knock him down a peg and embarrass him. I guess it worked a little too well.

I finished what he started last night and made sure he heard me, but it wasn't nearly as satisfying as what an orgasm with my Viking would have been.

A light knock at the door has me sitting up. When the blanket falls from my chest, I don't flinch because I have pajamas on. Sleeping alone is much less fun and sexy.

"I thought I heard movement in here. You're up early, Pepper."

"My mom texted me, and the noise woke me up."

Viktor sits on the end of the bed and finds my leg, rubbing it over the blanket. "I heard that too. What did she want this time?"

"Is Owen up yet?" I need a few more minutes to process her request before I get someone else's opinion.

"Still sleeping." Viktor's eyes flash to my very full breasts. The tank top I'm wearing has negative support, and there are miles of cleavage on display.

"My eyes are up here, buddy."

He smiles before tracing the lines of my neck to my eyes. He needs to adjust himself after his perusal, and I chuckle.

"Was last night just as much of a tease for you as it was for me?"

He holds my eyes, daring me to back down, but I won't. He sighs, looks away, and I straighten my back at this mini victory.

"I was perfectly fine until the show you put on after we went to bed. You moaned my fucking name. It wasn't fair."

I did. Several times. I tried everything I could to break his resolve, but nothing worked. "All you had to do was walk through the door."

More lines are blurring every day. Our shopping trip yesterday was the biggest one. I'm still flabbergasted that he let me buy a strap-on to use on him. I'm oddly excited about the thought of it. He's a big guy, and I'm…not. But he has no trouble following my direction in the bedroom, and the idea of Viktor the Viking giving himself over to me completely is exhilarating.

"Viktor, tell me three things you like about me that have nothing to do with physical appearance."

He's taken aback by my abrupt topic change, but it's always something on my mind. I often doubt my self-worth despite knowing all of the obstacles I've already tackled in my life.

"Three things. Hmm." He shifts further onto the bed and begins to crawl up my body. I love seeing him crawl. It's so fucking powerful to watch a man on his knees. "You're fiercely independent in a way that is a strength, not a weakness."

"One."

Viktor kisses the exposed skin between my shorts and tank, licking a trail and blowing on it to make me shiver.

"You have the kindest heart of anyone I've ever met. Watching the patience and love you have with your preschoolers is an inspiration to anyone who sees it."

"Two."

His nose nuzzles my hard nipple, and all I want is to feel his mouth on me, but I know he won't. He's been very specific about never wanting to take anything away from Owen, and it's morning, and he hasn't nursed yet.

"I love your tenacity. You had so many options when you got pregnant, and you chose him. You took your situation and blew everyone away with your strength and courage. You're a fucking fantastic mother."

"Three."

Viktor's mouth finally hovers over mine, and my body vibrates, waiting to feel his lips when my alarm goes off, and he disappears. I blink, and he's standing beside my bed with a shit-eating grin.

"Time to wake up and get the *day* started, Katy. Coffee is ready whenever you are. Unless you'd like me to bring you a cup in here?"

He knows exactly what he's doing—first last night and then this morning. Viktor is playing a losing game because I can hold out longer than he can.

As I'm getting dressed, Owen's sweet voice floats from the monitor.

"Mama. Mama, uppies."

I love his sweet little voice. Nothing is better in life than hearing him say my name.

"Morning, little man. Did you sleep well?"

"Vik. Uppies."

Well fuck. That's definitely a close second.

A minute later, there's a soft knock on my door, and Viktor comes in carrying Owen. When I come out of the bathroom, both have huge smiles on their faces, and it melts my heart and my panties for very different reasons.

"Mama. Mik." Owen's arms outstretch toward me as he squeezes his fist, signing "milk." I grab the wiggling bundle, and we get comfortable on the bed, ready to nurse. There's a moment of embarrassment as Owen tugs on my shirt, but Viktor has seen me naked on multiple occasions now, and this seems like another one of our lines that are about to blur.

I lift my shirt and unclip my bra so Owen has access to nurse. Viktor dips his chin as he heads back out to the living room. Just before he leaves, he turns and glances at us one more time.

"Admiration or jealousy, Viking?" His lip twitches as his eyes bounce between Owen and me.

"Both." He turns to leave, but I stop him.

"Hey, Viktor?"

"Yes."

"I think I'd like to have coffee with my mother today. Can we figure out the best way to make it happen? I don't want to bring Owen just yet."

"Of course. If you're sure?"

Am I sure? Not really. But it feels like the right thing to do.

"Yeah. It's time."

If S'morgasm is my favorite coffee shop, The Hippie Bean is a close second. Lincoln introduced me to this place because the owner, a hippie named Flower, makes the best apple fritters. This also happens to be where Spencer met Lincoln and Tucker, despite their meeting being of an unusual nature. I don't think most people can say their relationship started with a robbery, but it feels like a very fitting story for them.

I asked my mom to meet me here at two, during Owen's nap time, so Patrick didn't have to do any actual babysitting. I think his grunt was a thank you. He really doesn't say much.

On a regular day, the colorful tapestries lining the walls would calm me, but at the moment, I think it's increasing my anxiety. I can't seem to find a single object to focus my nervous energy on.

I haven't seen my mother since the day Owen was born. She somehow found out where I was, and the hospital nurses let her into my room. None of us thought to put her on a no-entry list because she hadn't tried to make contact with me since I left.

"Pepper, it's not too late to leave."

Viktor gently pulls my hands apart, stopping me from picking at my cuticles. I give him a small smile of thanks and shake my head.

"It's overdue. She's been reaching out and offering olive branches. I have to at least hear her out."

"You don't *have* to do anything in regards to her, but I understand your reasoning."

My mother isn't due to arrive for another ten minutes. I wanted to get here early to give myself time to change my mind if I decided to.

"I'll be in the corner if you need me." Viktor brushes his thumb across my forehead. "Imagine that was my lips giving you a kiss for strength."

Damn. Why does he have to do things like that? Now my belly is all warm and tingly. Viktor winks at me and takes a seat a few tables down.

I sit and wait, glad I had already ordered my coffee when she's ten minutes late. At the fifteen-minute mark, my phone rings.

"Hello?"

"Oh, honey. I'm so sorry. I missed the bus, but I'm on my way. I'll be there in about fifteen more minutes. Will you wait for me?" Sighing at her obvious excuse, I rub my forehead.

"Fine, but I don't have a lot of time. I don't want to be out much later than Owen's naptime."

"Of course. Of course. I'll be there soon." She hangs up, and I feel Viktor's presence behind me.

"Is everything okay?"

"She'll be here in about fifteen minutes. Said she missed the bus." He looks at his watch and frowns. "I know. I told her I didn't have a lot of time."

"We can leave whenever you're ready. Would you like an apple fritter while you wait?" I smile up at him and nod. This man knows the way to my heart.

I'm three bites into my fritter when the bell jingles for what feels like the hundredth time, but finally, the woman standing in the doorway looks familiar.

I say familiar because she has the same eyes and smile, but instead of the bottle blonde that I've known all my life, her hair is a muted brown. Similar to mine, but there's no life in the color. Her normal grayish skin tone has color to it that I'm not used to seeing either. She looks…healthy.

"Katy! Oh my god Katy. Look at you."

My mother almost trips on the wheel of a stroller as she tries to get to me. Her arms spread wide, and a gift bag dangles in the crook of her elbow. When she finally reaches me, I'm engulfed in a suffocating hug. Even if I wanted to return her hug, I can't; she's squeezing me too tight.

Her smile is wide when she finally releases me, and my mind is having trouble associating this woman with the one who raised me. Babs didn't smile unless it was to get something she wanted. Her eyes were always bloodshot, and the constant drinking always left a lingering scent of staleness on her skin.

The woman who stands before me looks bright and vibrant. She still looks older than her years, but there are some things you can't reverse with makeup and perfume.

"Babs. You look…well."

My mother smooths down the front of her paisley-patterned dress, fussing over her outfit.

"Please call me Mom."

Her eyes look sincere. I thought the texts she'd been sending me were all bullshit, but Babs is a terrible actress, and even on her best days, she couldn't pull off this put-together woman.

"Um. I can try...Mom."

Babs sighs and places her hands over her heart. Her eyes flash down to the gift bag she's carrying as if she forgot it was there.

"This is for my sweet grandson. It's just something that I saw and thought he might like. You can open it now if you'd like."

She passes me the bag and we sit at the table.

"Did you want to get coffee?"

"No, Dear. I don't want to waste a minute with you." She reaches out and takes my hand. My gut reaction wants me to pull away. This woman, my mother, is the least affectionate person I know. As a child, I yearned for her love, but she was always too busy with her booze or her boyfriends. Justin handing me a bowl of mac n cheese was the first genuine affection I ever felt from someone who wasn't obligated to give it to me like a teacher or a doctor.

Slowly, I pull my hand from hers and place it on my lap. Her face falls for a second as she watches my reaction, but she blinks a few times and shakes it off, putting a smile back on her face.

"Tell me about you. About my grandson. Is he walking? Talking?"

She's so out of touch with my life. Does she not have any

idea what a typical one and a half year old is like?

"Um, we're both doing good. He's been walking for over six months and is a little slow to talk, but his pediatrician said boys sometimes talk slower than girls. He still has a good vocabulary, though, so we aren't worried."

She's smiling so wide I don't know how her cheeks aren't hurting.

"That's wonderful. I'm sure he's just doing things on his own time. What does he look like now? It seems like I haven't seen him in forever. Does he have your dark hair?"

She takes a piece of my hair and curls it around her fingers. I'm frozen. I have no idea what's going on, but at any moment, I feel like someone is going to jump out from behind a coffee display and tell me I'm on some game show and my mother has won an acting award.

"So when do I get to meet him? I've been trying to decide what I want to be called. Grandma makes me feel old, and Babs is too informal. Do you think I could pull off Gigi, G-ma?"

"Stop." My voice is a whisper. Who does she think she is?

"What, Dear? I'm sorry, could you speak up?"

I breathe in a much-needed breath of air and sit straighter in my chair.

"I said, stop." This time, there's more force behind my words, and my mother's brows pinch and her eyes dart nervously around the room.

21

Dempsey

Katy's raised voice catches my attention. I've been trying not to look like a creeper, watching their entire interaction, but I can't ignore her protest.

"I said, stop."

Babs looks shocked by Katy's tone, and I stand there waiting to see what happens next.

"You-you don't get to pick a grandparent name because you aren't his grandparent. You aren't a mother; how could you expect to be a *grand*mother?"

Pride swells in my chest as Katy sticks up for herself.

"Now Katy, I may have made some mistakes, but—"

"You abandoned me," Katy hisses. A few heads turn, and I know she doesn't want to cause a scene, but I also know she needs to do this for herself. "I was your responsibility, and you abandoned me. You gave me away. Sold me for money."

Fuck. I didn't think she knew about the arrangement Justin made with Babs. Did someone tell her? I know Justin and Spencer had her sign an NDA about the details of Katy's adoption. The paperwork is public record, but the terms of her termination of parental rights aren't.

"Katy, I didn't—"

"No. It's fine. I'm great." Katy's voice is calm and collected. It's as if an acceptance has washed over her. "I really am." Katy reaches out and takes her mother's hand. "Thank you for being such a terrible mother so I can be the opposite of you. You don't get to be a grandmother, but I'm not a heartless bitch. I'm also not your daughter. *My son* can call you Babs like the rest of the world does. I'm not ready for you to meet him, but I'll say I'm impressed. I hope whatever improvements you've made in your life stick because I'd like my son to eventually meet the woman who gave birth to me."

Babs' mouth flaps like a fish as Katy lets go of her hand and stands. She glances at me with a barely perceptible nod and turns to leave, knowing I'll follow, but Babs grabs her arm.

"I deserve all of that, and I understand. I'll be here. Please give him my gift. I'd like him to have it from me." She picks up the gift bag and angles it in Katy's direction. Katy wars with the idea but relents and takes it.

"It was nice to see you, Babs. I'll speak to you soon."

Katy walks out, and I follow behind her, trying not to look too obvious. As soon as we turn the corner, out of the view of the coffee shop's windows, Katy spins and collapses into my arms.

"Viktor." Her voice cracks, and I want to take it all away for her.

"I've got you, Pepper." I scoop my hands under her legs and carry her to our car. She's quiet, but I feel the dampness of her tears through my T-shirt. When I squat to place her in the passenger seat, she tightens her arms around my neck

169

before letting me go.

"Thank you for the strength."

I stare into her chocolate eyes and then kiss her forehead for real.

"I'll always give you strength, and when you don't have enough, I'll take the burden for you." I reach over and buckle her seat belt, and she brushes her hand through my beard as I pull away.

Katy stares out the window the entire way home. I won't push her to talk. I heard most of the conversation and can fill in the blanks. Her mother is a piece of work, and I'm so damn proud of her for putting her foot down. She deserves better, and I'll give it to her.

"Do you want to take Owen to the park after his nap? I know his giggles always cheer you up." A small smile creeps on her lips, and I imagine she's thinking about those giggles.

"Yeah. That sounds nice." She looks over her shoulder to the back seat where I put the gift bag from her mother. "What do you think is in there?"

Shrugging, I look in the rearview. "Only one way to find out."

"I guess the question is, do I care? And unfortunately, the answer is I do. She's my mother, and as good and as terrible as that felt, I can tell she's trying, and I'll give her credit for that. But it felt like she was trying to take something she hasn't earned, and I probably overreacted." Out of my peripheral, I see her chin dip to her chest.

"None of that, Pepper." I tilt her chin up with my knuckles. "Own your words. Your feelings are valid. You were too much for her. Not that she couldn't handle you, too much in a way that you shine brighter than she ever will. Don't let her

170

dull your shine." I know I sound like a greeting card, but she needs to know she's so much more than her mother could ever think of her.

I can see she's still a little down on herself, so I try one more tactic.

"Pepper, I want you to say three good things about yourself."

She huffs and crosses her arms. I can feel her gaze boring a hole in the side of my head, and I try not to react.

"You're evil. Using my own words against me? Fine. Three things." She taps her finger on her bottom lip as she thinks, and it's adorable. I wish I could watch her face while she thinks, but I need to stay focused on the road and our surroundings.

"I'm a decent shot."

She is. I've been with her a few times with each of the guys as they taught her about guns, and she learned quickly. After the Shane incident, she wanted to make sure she never hesitated again. We still aren't entirely sure where she hit Shane, but there was plenty of blood, and his subsequent retreat let us know she did enough damage that it saved us both.

Midnight Moonshine sits on a large piece of property, and despite the law requiring her to be twenty-one to handle or own a firearm, none of them were going to stop her from learning. Tucker set up a makeshift range there with Spencer's approval.

"One. And I can practically hear your eyes roll."

"Ugh. Why is this so hard? I...have pretty hair?"

"That doesn't count, and you know it. It's hard because we are the most critical about ourselves, but if we don't think positively about our self-worth, how can we expect others to? Give me another one, Pepper."

I smirk to myself as I hear her mumbling about how Vikings shouldn't be allowed to make so much sense.

"I'm helpful in the kitchen. I may not be the best cook on my own, but I follow directions well."

"You are a good cook on your own, but I'll give you that one. Two. One more. Dig deeper."

She gnaws on her bottom lip as she thinks, and it's the cutest thing.

"I'm an excellent student, at all things in general, but I did well in school and...I miss that I didn't get to finish traditionally. I-I think maybe I'd like to look into college."

Something about that idea sparks a flame inside her. She turns in her seat so her body faces me and becomes animated with her enthusiasm.

"Viktor. I think I want to go back to school. I always wanted to be a teacher growing up. School was my only safe space, and I would make up stories in my head about my teachers being my mom because anything was better than what I had at home. I wanted to be that for a child someday. Do you think Spencer would help me?"

"Yeah. I think she would. I know she would. Any of them will help you, and you know that."

She turns back in her seat and stares out the window, deep in thought.

"That's three, Pepper. And I think it worked."

"What worked?"

"You feel better about yourself, don't you?"

"Huh. I do, actually. Thank you."

Katy's smile is bright, and I can tell she feels lighter. I have no doubt that if she decides this is what she wants, everyone will stand behind her. She'll be a fantastic teacher for the exact reasons she stated and more.

"It's your turn."

"My turn for what?" A glance in her direction shows her beautiful smile, and I temporarily forget that she even spoke.

"Give me three things."

"No ma'am. This was about you. I'm not going to overshadow your moment. Ask me another day. Let's get home and take our boy to the park."

Fuck. *Our boy?* I didn't mean to say it that way, but if I'm being honest with myself, I liked the way it sounded far more than I probably should have.

When we stop at a red light, I pull out my phone and send off a text.

Group 6D:

Dempsey: Katy just mentioned to me she thinks she wants to go back to school to become a teacher. Wanted to give you all a heads up. I don't know how serious she is, but I think we should encourage her.

Spencer: She has my complete support.

Axel: Fuck yes!

Miller: That's my girl.

Lincoln: That would be perfect for her. Keep us updated.

Tucker: Anything she wants. Tell her to pick a college and I'll send a check for tuition.

Katy gives me a suspicious look as my phone buzzes. She glances at her phone, realizing she hasn't gotten any texts, and pouts her plush bottom lip.

"Are you talking about me?"

"Me? I would never do that, Pepper."

"You lay in a bed of lies, Viktor Dempsey. What's going on over there?"

I put my phone in my pocket before she can swipe it.

"Just know that everyone in your life will support your dream if you choose to pursue it."

She freezes, getting an idea of what I messaged everyone about.

"You didn't?"

"I did, and I don't regret it. You'll be an incredible teacher one day. We all support you. Go for it, Pepper."

She stares out the window again, hopefully, lost in the thought of decorating classrooms and reading books during carpet time. I don't have to ask to know she wants to teach elementary school, just like I didn't need to send the heads-up text. I know everyone in Katy's life supports her dreams.

22

Katy

I could be a teacher. It's all I've been thinking about since my conversation a few days ago with Viktor. There would be a lot to juggle with Owen, but it's a real possibility.

As exciting as my mind has been with my future education, right now I have a stubborn little boy who insists he wants to use the big boy potty. He's been following Viktor into the bathroom and trying. Viktor has been an absolute saint about it and encouraging him. I'd be lying if I didn't admit to myself how absolutely fucking sexy it makes him as a man to see the way he treats Owen.

"Mama. Pidey-man."

"You want Spiderman undies?" Owen points to a package of underwear that catches his attention amongst the huge wall of options. I thought we might as well give this potty training thing a try if he's going to be so interested. Why fight it if I can save money and not have to buy diapers anymore?

"Vik. Pidey-man, too."

I bite my lips to contain my smile. The mental image of Viktor in a pair of Spiderman briefs is just too funny.

"Sorry, little man. Spiderman is just for big boys like you." Viktor takes a pack off the rack and hands them to Owen. "Is that even the right size?"

"Not for you." The laugh I was holding bursts out. Viktor groans at me as Owen giggles at the package in his hands.

"Don't be a brat, Pepper," he whispers in my ear. A shiver runs up my spine and I need to decide what role I want to play right now. It's technically daytime, but he melts so easily when I take control.

"Then you better be a good boy, Viking."

That's all it takes. His pupils dilate, and I hear the low rumble in his chest.

"What else do we need for potty training?"

I'm once again holding in a laugh as he speaks through gritted teeth. I love when I say or do something that tests his control.

"We need another stool, something for a rewards chart, and probably several more packs of these." I reach over and grab a few different character undies for Owen.

"Vik, potty?" Owen holds up his pack of undies to Viktor.

"Do you need to go potty now?" Viktor scoops Owen up into his arms as Owen hugs the package close to his chest.

"Pidey-man!"

"We'll be right back. Don't take your eyes off her." Patrick grunts per usual, and Viktor smiles at me before disappearing down an aisle to take Owen to the bathroom.

I forgot Patrick was with us. He does an excellent job at being inconspicuous. I sometimes wish he was friendlier, but then outings like this wouldn't be as fun. Viktor doesn't feel like a babysitter or a bodyguard, though I know he's always on alert when we're out. He's phenomenal at his job.

I wander the arts and crafts aisle, looking for something to use for a reward chart. I already picked up a poster board and markers, but I want something fun. I come across the star stickers and instantly have fond memories of school and receiving a sticker on my assignments from my teachers. I reach for the gold ones but veer left to a packet of holographic rainbow ones right next to them.

"Perfect." I'll make a chart and reward him with these colorful stars. He'll love it.

"Mama? Where Mama?" I hear Owen's sweet voice calling for me, and I roll my cart to the end of the aisle to see Viktor holding Owen's hand. They both smile when they see me, and my heart warms. Viktor releases Owen's hand when he tugs, and a few seconds later, a little body crashes into my leg.

"I pee pee potty, Mama!"

"You did? What a big boy. Look what I found." Owen's eyes light up when he sees the stickers in my hand. I open the package and put one on his shirt. He tugs it off his body so he can peer at it in awe.

"Did he actually pee?" I ask Viktor in a hushed tone. He shrugs.

"He dribbled a little. But he refused to put a diaper on, so he's wearing a new pair of underwear."

"Oh. I guess we better hurry along this little shopping trip before it turns into a disaster." We are in no way ready for diaperless outings yet, but I also don't want to discourage Owen.

Four accidents. We went through an entire pack of new

undies before Owen finally went to bed—with a diaper on. I'm exhausted but also excited for him because he successfully used the bathroom twice. He loved the stickers even more when he got to put them on the chart I created for him. It feels like progress, and I'll take it.

"Movie? What do you have there?"

I glance up from my seat on the couch at Viktor, who's holding a remote in his hand.

I finally opened the gift bag from my mother, and to my shock, inside was an identical bunny to the one that Owen loves. It's a popular stuffed animal at any baby store, which is why Nicole chose it for him. She knows the plight of a lost lovie.

"The present from Babs. Funny huh?" I lift the toy, and he takes it, looking it over before tossing it on the coffee table.

"So, movie?"

"Are we talking about an actual movie or a Netflix and chill kind of movie?"

His smile could melt ice cream in the middle of winter.

"I guess that would depend on you since the sun just went down."

The combination of being simultaneously turned on and exhausted seems like the soundtrack for motherhood.

"Honestly, I think I'd like to shower above anything else. I can still smell pee despite washing my hands more times than I can count. I think the smell is stuck in my nose hairs."

Viktor chuckles, and I can't blame him. I've already showered once today after Owen peed on my leg while I read him a book.

I still praised him for letting me know he had to pee…after we were both wet. But I know just feeling the sensation is progress. Baby steps.

"I understand that. Do you want to watch a movie after, or I can make you some tea for bed?"

It's nighttime. It's my time.

"Would you like to join me?"

Viktor looks at me with a shocked expression. We haven't done anything like this, openly naked in front of each other for a purpose other than sexual gratification.

"In the shower?"

Why does he look so surprised? It's just a shower. Although I know us, and it will most likely lead to *something*.

"Yes, Viking. In the shower. I'm not the only one who had to deal with pee today." He cleaned up Owen while I showered earlier, and I was grateful for the help. I'm always grateful.

It's always fun watching this big man look nervous because of me. His exterior is tough and intimidating. I remember the first few weeks when Justin hired him, and he was just like Patrick, quiet and all work. Our relationship has come so far.

"Who's asking? Katy or Pepper?"

"Both." He likes my answer based on his smile and the hand he offers to help me stand.

As we walk into my bathroom, we stand and stare at each other, unmoving. There's sexual tension between us always, but something about this doesn't feel sexual.

I take the hem of his shirt, and he bends so I can lift it over his head. I roam my finger over the dips of his chest. He's so pretty.

"You're beautiful." The corner of his lip tugs at my compliment, and he sighs a contented sound. I trace the scar on

179

his abdomen—the entrance wound to the bullet that almost took him from me. A wave of guilt floods me as it always does when I see it. He must sense the change in my mood and interrupts my thought process.

"Your turn." Viktor removes my shirt and unclips my bra. He mimics my actions, and fingers roam my body, avoiding where he knows I want him to touch me the most. This isn't meant to be a sexual experience, but my body still yearns for his touch.

He pulls back his hands to undo his belt and jeans, and I do the same. We silently watch each other as we strip, eyes roaming over every piece of exposed skin.

Viktor turns the shower on, but neither of us is in a rush to get in. Even when the mirror fogs and the air in the room thickens with humidity, we stay lost in each other's eyes, hands caressing our now slick skin.

"I don't deserve you, Katy."

How could he think that? I'm the one undeserving of him. He laid his life on the line for a stupid teenager. He's been by my side every step of the way through the last few years of my life. I'd be lost without him.

"I've never heard words so far from the truth. You deserve so much more than I have to offer, Viktor."

His head slowly shakes, disagreeing with me, but he doesn't vocalize his protest. Instead, his fingers caress down my arm until he reaches my hand and laces his fingers with mine. He steps into the shower and pulls me in with him.

Viktor angles me under the spray and gently tips my head back to get my hair wet. His actions are wordless as he guides my body to do what he wants. Without asking, he takes my shampoo and lathers his hands. Weaving his fingers through my hair, he massages my scalp, and the feeling is heavenly. His large hands are so graceful and tender. He washes his hair after he rinses mine and then conditions it.

When he reaches for the body wash and loofah, I stop him.

"Let me." He nods, and I pour the rain-scented soap onto the sponge. I wash Viktor from head to toe. I never knew lathering someone's body could be so sensual. I drop the sponge to the floor and use my hands to wash away the suds. The tension between us feels like it's moments away from snapping, but I don't want it to. We're in a haven of adoration and comfort, and it feels more monumental than anything we've done up until this point.

Viktor bends, picking up the loofah, and it's his turn to wash me. Once the cleaning part of showering is done, he pulls me into his chest and kisses the top of my head. Pure joy and contentment are my only thoughts as we embrace each other under the stream of warm water. I feel like I'm meant to be here. He's meant to be here, with me.

The sound of glass breaking and the high-pitched squeal of the alarm jolts us from our bubble.

"What the fuck." Viktor is out of the shower and throwing on pants before I can register what's going on.

"Katy, don't move."

"Owen." I'm trying to pull on my robe as Viktor grabs a gun from the nightstand.

"I've got him. Stay here."

23

Dempsey

The adrenaline my body just dumped has me vibrating. To go from a serene moment with Katy in my arms to dread is not a good feeling.

"I've got him. Stay here."

"But—"

"Katy. Stay here and lock the door behind me. Now."

Turning off the safety to the glock Katy keeps in her drawer, I quietly stalk to the bedroom door. Katy is safe behind me as I hear the lock click, and my next priority is Owen. The light is on over the stove, and I can see the kitchen window is smashed. It's not enough for someone to have come in through it, but that doesn't mean it wasn't a distraction. My senses are on edge as my eyes scope every dark corner and crevice in the room on the way to Owen's.

He's crying, no doubt, because of the piercing sound of the alarm. My nerves calm a fraction, knowing he's still in the house. I clear the laundry and bathroom before finally entering Owen's. The moment he sees me, he throws his arms in the air, and I scoop him up.

A noise from the other side of the house catches my attention, and I put him back into the crib. His wail of disapproval crushes my heart, but I can't take him with me if there's danger on the other side of the door.

I peek around the doorframe of Owen's room down the small hallway and don't see or hear anything.

I listen for a few heartbeats before the alarm suddenly stops. The immediate silence is as defining as the alarm. My ears ring from the loss of sound, and it's almost disorienting.

"Katy?"

I know that voice. "Spencer?"

"Dempsey? Where are they?"

I should have known they would get the alarm notification. The systems are linked.

"Katy is in her room, door locked. I have Owen. It's all clear back here."

"Clear in here, too," Lincoln comments back. It seems like the cavalry is here. I tuck the gun into my jeans and turn to pick up a now hysterical Owen. I feel terrible. He has no idea what's going on.

"Come on, little man, let's take you to Mama." He buries his face into my neck as soon as I pick him back up, his hand clenched around his bunny. Tucker appears in the doorway and looks around.

"Just the kitchen window?"

I nod my response, and he steps aside to let me out of the room. Everyone is huddled in the kitchen looking at something when I knock on Katy's door.

"Pepper? It's safe. I have Owen."

The door flies open and arms tightly grip around me and

183

Owen. I pull my arm out from her hold and wrap it around her back.

"Shh. It's okay. Everyone is here."

Her worried brown eyes peer up at me before they roam the room.

"What's going on?"

I'd like to know myself.

"Not sure. I came right to you with Owen. Let's find out. Do you want him?"

Owen is curled into me as much as Katy is. She shakes her head, and we walk as a unit to the others.

"What came through the window?" Miller turns at my question with a strange look on his face.

"Underwear?"

"More underwear?" Katy questions, sounding frustrated. I'm sure she's remembering her seventeenth birthday party when Shane left an envelope with pink panties on Lincoln's truck outside of Midnight Moonshine.

"Not quite." Miller holds up a package of little boy's underwear.

"What the actual fuuuuu-dge." I quickly stop myself from cursing and pull Owen closer to me.

"All clear." Everyone's attention whips to the front door, where Patrick silently stepped in.

"Nothing?" Tucker asks. He sounds annoyed, and I can't blame him. "Did you check the cameras?"

"Yes. There's a figure dressed in all black. He runs from the neighbor's house, throws the brick, and runs back. He barely stops. Breaking the window seems to have been his entire intention."

I'm momentarily shocked because I think that's more words

than I've ever heard Patrick say. He looks pissed off. He's been taking it upon himself to patrol at night. Tucker told me he doesn't like to be idol, and Patrick has downtime during the day unless Katy goes out, so staying up at night isn't an issue for him.

"So this asshole throws a brick with kids underwear through a window? It doesn't make any sense." Axel runs a hand through his curly hair, as frustrated as the rest of us. "And more importantly, why are you both wet?" He pauses as his eyes dart between us. He forms an O with his mouth and gives me a quick thumbs up.

A glance at Katy, who has clothes on, unlike me, who's just in jeans, shows her cheeks are tinted with color from his question.

"Please tell me they don't happen to be Spiderman?"

"Pidey-man?" Owen perks up at the mention of his favorite superhero, and Katy gasps when Miller flashes the colorful package.

"No. Viktor?"

I tighten my arm around Katy as Owen excitedly reaches for the Spiderman undies identical to the ones we bought him this afternoon.

"Would someone like to tell me what I'm missing here?" A pissed-off Lincoln is never a good one.

"We bought this exact pack at the store earlier today to start potty training with Owen."

I hear a "fuck" muttered off to my left and see Patrick clenching his fists. He's feeling the same possessiveness I am right now. Shane was close enough to them that he saw the products we bought.

"Enough playing around. Pack your bags." Tucker storms

185

in the direction of Owen's room, and Katy looks at me wide-eyed.

"Um, what?" Katy asks me as if I have any idea what's going on.

"That's a good idea, brother." *What's a good idea?* "Sleepover at our house."

"Lincoln, no. This is my house, and I won't let him run me out."

Miller approaches us and places a gentle hand on Katy's shoulder. "You have a broken window that we can't do anything about right now, Cupcake. It's not safe for you to stay here tonight. I think Dempsey and Patrick would agree. There's plenty of room there for all of you until we can figure everything out. Let's all get some sleep and approach this tomorrow with fresh minds."

"He's right, Pepper."

I can see in Katy's eyes she wants to object, but she looks at Owen and knows it's the best situation for him.

"I'll go pack a bag." Katy tries to pull away, but I hold her for a second longer. She gives me a sweet smile, and I kiss her forehead. I don't care who's in the room with us.

"All my strength, Pepper." She nods, and I can't help but see the glossy haze that overtakes her eyes.

This needs to end. We've all been living on edge for too long. Shane has been toying with us for so long that we're almost desensitized to it, and I bet that's what he's banking on. Minor escalations and then months of silence. He was too close tonight and even closer this afternoon. I'm fucking done.

Axel comes to me, extending his arms. "I'll take him while you pack a bag."

"We're just going to be across the lawn. I don't need anything I can't come back and get."

"Dempsey." My eyes snap to Tucker as he walks back into the kitchen with a large bag from Owen's room. "You aren't leaving Katy's side, even to walk across the lawn. Let Axel take Owen and pack what you need."

Even if Tucker wasn't my boss, he's right. I hand Owen to Axel and grab a duffle bag from the closet. It doesn't take me long to pack, and I notice Katy still hasn't come out of her room yet.

"Pepper?" I don't see her when I first walk in, and a glance into her bathroom is empty. "Katy?"

"In here?" Her response comes from behind me. She's in her closet.

"Katy, what—Katy." I drop to my knees in front of her. She's flushed from the amount of crying she's done. I wrap her in my arms and pull her into my lap.

"I'm sorry."

"No. Shhh." My chest muffles her quiet sobs. "You have nothing to apologize for. We've been doing this for so long, and it's stressful. You're allowed to take a moment and feel your emotions."

We're in the closet for several minutes when I hear footsteps enter the room. Miller appears in the doorway, and his face falls into one of concern. I shake my head and raise my finger, signaling for him to give us a minute. He nods in return and leaves.

"Pepper, we should get over to the big house and get Owen to bed."

"Okay. I'm okay."

"Hey, look at me." She tilts her chin, and the sorrow in her

187

eyes almost crushes me. "No one is asking or expecting you to be okay. We just need to get that little boy back to sleep, or he'll be a bear tomorrow."

She smiles in agreement, and I kiss her still-damp hair before I stand us up.

"Did you get to pack?" Katy points to a bag on the floor, and I pick it up.

"I need to grab my bathroom stuff."

I put her duffle on my shoulder and lace my fingers through hers.

"I've got you, Pepper. I always will."

24

Lincoln

The smell of sweet, buttery goodness in the morning always makes me happy. As much as we don't have a schedule for the cooking in the house, it's almost a guarantee that I'll be making pancakes when it comes to Sunday morning breakfasts.

"You're up early." I shiver as Miller's lips graze my neck.

"I have four more people to feed. I want to make sure everything is done by the time they all wake up."

"It smells delicious, Baby. So do you." I feel the sting of his teeth as he nips my shoulder.

"Down, Fireball. I'm busy." Firm hands squeeze my hips, and I feel him chuckle into my neck.

"So am I."

Just as I begin to give in to his temptation, we're almost knocked over by a squeal of delight crashing into our legs.

"Milyer. Linca. Kay kays!"

"Hey there, buddy." Miller picks up Owen, who leans closer toward me to see the pancakes on the griddle.

"Yummy. I hung-ee."

I open the microwave, pull out the overstacked plate I've already filled, and then grab a stack of plates from the cabinet. Miller buckles Owen into the highchair, tucking his bunny safely into the seat next to him, and makes him a plate.

A half-asleep Dempsey walks into the kitchen and huffs a sigh of relief when he sees Owen happily getting sticky syrup in his chair.

"There you are. You snuck out. Someone please tell me there's coffee."

I've never seen him look so unkempt.

"Rough night?" I pour a cup of coffee and hand it to him. He smiles and takes a big gulp before answering. I can tell he's a bit nervous, and I know it has to do with whatever is going on between Katy and him.

"They were both restless last night. I didn't get much sleep."

"Viktor, I know this isn't an ideal situation, and you are both used to your privacy, but please consider this your home, too. We all know you slept in the room with Katy and Owen. We aren't judging."

"I respect your daughter." He looks Miller and I firmly in the eye, not a quaver of uncertainty in his statement. The fact that he called Katy our daughter shows the level of respect he has for us as well. Blood doesn't make Katy our daughter, but love does, and we love the fuck out of her and Owen.

"We know." Miller hands Dempsey a plate of pancakes. "How is she this morning?"

Sitting at the table, he stares at his plate momentarily. "She was up half the night crying. She's still sleeping now. Owen woke up around four a.m., and I brought him into the bed with us. The kid's a kicker." He smiles lovingly at Owen.

Other than the four of us, Dempsey is the most constant male figure in his life. I'm not surprised to see the love he has for Owen shine on his face.

"What are we going to do about *him*?" The word "him" drips with malice from Dempsey's mouth. We're all feeling the same way.

"Bun-Bun." Owen's whine of distress has us all jumping to his attention. "Bun-Bun dirty." He holds up his prized lovie with a big smear of syrup down its ear.

"Oh no. Let me see if I can clean him." Owen watches me with big alligator tears streaming down his face as I attempt to carefully wash the stuffed animal's ear. "Oh, man. I think he might need a real bath, buddy. Can I give Bun-Bun a bath?"

Owen's bottom lip quivers, and he becomes inconsolable. Miller jumps up and runs out of the room. What's wrong with him?

Dempsey picks Owen up from his highchair, not caring that he's about to be as sticky as the stuffed bunny, and tries to calm him.

"There are extras at the pool house. I can go and grab—"

"I've got one." Miller bounds back into the room with a triumphant smile on his face. Owen lights up but looks a little confused. He looks at me, and I quickly hide the wet bunny behind my back, realizing why he looks that way. Seeing two of his favorite lovie might be disorienting.

"Bun-Bun!" Owen stretches his arms out to take the bunny back. I stop Miller before he makes a vital mistake.

"Let's get you cleaned up first, little man. We don't want to get Bun-bun dirty again."

"I'll run him to our bathroom and be right back. I should change his diaper too and check on Katy." I nod as Dempsey walks away with a slightly calmer Owen.

"You're a lifesaver, Fireball. Where did you get a spare lovie from?" I wrap my arms around his waist and pull our hips together.

"It was on their coffee table last night. I thought we might need it. And don't be a tease. We have company."

I trail a line of kisses down his neck. "And we have the entire second floor to ourselves. Who said I was being a tease?"

"The burning pancakes on the griddle."

"Shit." I pull away from his neck, and sure enough, the next six pancakes are on the crispy side.

There's a knock at the back door before Patrick walks in. Last night, he asked if he could sleep in the pool house to make sure it stayed secure with the broken window. We agreed, but I'm sure this man never sleeps. I think he's a robot.

"Morning, Patrick. There's pancakes and coffee."

He nods and helps himself to breakfast, sitting next to Miller at the table.

A crack rings through the air and a sting forms on my left ass cheek. I drop my head to my chest and breathe through the pain.

"It looked too juicy in these sweatpants. I couldn't help myself." Axel rubs his hand over the cheek, which I know is blooming with a handprint. He kisses my cheek and smiles, humming to himself while he piles his plate with breakfast. I open the refrigerator door and grab the whipped cream, placing it on the table in front of him. With wide eyes, he looks up at me, "Sprinkles?"

"You're adorable." I shake my head and open the spice cabinet. "Rainbow or chocolate?"

"Don't ask ridiculous questions, Lincoln."

I roll my eyes and pass him the rainbow sprinkles.

He shimmies in his seat. "This is why you're my favorite."

"Who's your favorite, Darlin'?" A hand wraps around Axel's neck, and Tucker's growl vibrates through the room. I bite my cheeks to contain my smile. Axel melts under Tucker's stare and licks his lips. His pupils dilate, and a devious smile spreads across his face.

"Lincoln. He gave me rainbow sprinkles *and* whipped cream."

He's purposely stepping into shit with Tucker. He's looking to get punished. I don't blame him. Tucker punishments are fun.

"Is that all it takes to be your favorite? You're that easy?" Miller is grinning ear to ear. He's also a fan of Tucker punishments.

"Morning everyone." Katy's sweet voice breaks up the lust and testosterone in the air.

"You have five minutes to eat, Darlin'. Enjoy the sweet stuff while you can." Axel's pupils dilate at the thought of what's to come.

"Did I just walk in on something?" Katy looks curiously around the room as she pours a cup of coffee.

"I'm about to get punished because I said Lincoln is my favorite."

"Yeah. Okay. You asked for that." Katy grabs a pancake and takes a bite. Tucker kisses her cheek and steals a bite.

"Hey! Get your own." She scowls at him for about three seconds before they're laughing. I've missed having Katy around here. She brings more lightheartedness to the house.

"Owen, don't run, buddy." Dempsey's voice booms down

the hall as a little body barrels into the room and stops. His eyes dart around, taking in all the bodies. He's trying to decide who to go to first. Much to our surprise, he toddles over to Patrick, who doesn't even realize he's there until Owen taps his leg.

"Uppies." Owen wiggles his fingers, and Patrick looks panicked as he looks at each of us, wondering what he should do. "Uppies," Owen persists more forcefully. With a look of almost horror, he reaches down and picks up the pleading child.

"I Owen. Who you?"

Has no one officially introduced Owen to Patrick? I suppose none of us thought to do it. He's barely two, but Patrick has been spending a lot of time with him, and you'd think there would have been an introduction at some point.

"My name is Patrick, remember."

"Oh. Pat-ick. I Owen." The corner of Patrick's lip tugs, but it quickly disappears. Maybe he has a heart after all.

"Time's up, Darlin'. I hope you got enough to eat."

With little protest, Axel stands, smiling, and is happily dragged out of the room by Tucker.

"As gross as this sounds, I missed you guys." Katy's comment makes everyone laugh, reaffirming how much we've all missed her.

Spencer walks into the room and looks back over her shoulder at the two men she passed on the stairs.

"What did Axel do now?"

25

Dempsey

L iving here is sweet torture. I get to share a bed with Katy every night, but there hasn't been anything sexual between us. Partly because Owen is in the room and partly because I have too much respect for the roof we're under.

I never expected anything from Katy when we were living in the pool house, and I don't expect anything here, but at least there, the possibility was always just a dirty thought away.

The biggest perk of being here is that Katy hasn't had any nightmares. I usually hear her at least twice a week. I don't think she remembers most of them come morning, but if she did, she's never said. I'd like to think being able to hold her in my arms while she sleeps gives her mind a sense of comfort and security that keeps them away.

I don't have to sleep in her bed. I could just as easily go back to the couch where I would sleep before we moved to the pool house, but after the first night when she fell asleep crying in my arms there hasn't been a question of where I'm sleeping. Katy expects me to be by her side, and that's precisely where I'll be.

Kissing. Our lips meeting each other in the darkness of night is all we've done for the past week. Kissing and hands exploring in comforting caresses. Katy told me it's like the beginning of one of her slow-burn novels with all the anticipation and build-up. I understand what she means by build up with the several times I've had to masturbate in the shower after her body rubbing up against me all night.

I won't push her for anything. This has always been about her and on her terms. It's what makes our moments together so powerful. Every time she's given herself over to me sexually, no matter how big or small, is her choice. A choice that was once taken away from her, and she gives me freely and willingly.

"Morning." Her sweet voice vibrates into my chest as she wakes.

This is my favorite moment of the day. When it's just Katy and me cuddled in each other's arms, and the world around us is forgotten.

I inhale a deep breath of her hair and pull her closer to me. Her palm splays flat on my chest over the organ that belongs to her. That beats only for her.

"I need to get out of this house. To and from work isn't enough. I'm going stir crazy."

"Are you ready to have a calvary with us if we go?"

Katy sighs. I understand how she feels. Having Patrick follow us around gives me the sense I also have a bodyguard. But I'm feeling the same restlessness as Katy.

"Is there anywhere we could go that we wouldn't have to

have a posse?"

Is there? I'm so frustrated with going through life acting like we're walking on eggshells. Katy is nineteen and deserves to be a teenager sometimes.

"I have an idea." I reach behind me and grab my phone.

Dempsey: Katy needs a night out without an entourage. Any chance I could bring her to Midnight Moonshine to blow off some steam?

Tucker: Of course. Tonight?

Dempsey: I think she'd love that.

Tucker: I'll set it up and make it a great night for her.

"What are you smiling about? Who are you texting?" Katy tries to snatch the phone from me, but I move too quickly, and my arms are longer than hers. I raise the phone in the air and use my shoulder to hold her back.

We wrestle for the phone while trying not to laugh too loud because Owen is only across the room in a pack-and-play.

I'm struggling with the feeling of Katy's full breasts brushing against my side over and over. Her soft skin sliding against mine, when she cheats. Katy swings her leg over my hip and straddles my waist. She leans forward, bracing a hand on my chest to reach for the phone and the string that my resolve has been hanging onto snaps.

I willingly give her the phone because my hands have a better idea. Katy gasps as I cup her breasts in my palms and my thumbs sweep across her nipples. I lick my lips and swallow hard, trying not to ravish her right here and now.

"More." Katy's hands cover mine, and she adds pressure, encouraging me to squeeze harder.

Fuck, that word should be illegal. I want to give her so much more right now. Tomorrow, Next month. The next fucking decade. This woman has captivated me, mind, body, and soul.

"May I?" She nods, not needing any more context to my question. I pull down the front of her tank top and almost drool as she spills over her black straps. Her nipples glisten from the milk that's leaked out, and I'm starving for it.

Sitting up, I almost knock her back, and she giggles, quickly covering her mouth to muffle the sound. I growl as the meal I've been dying for finally crosses my lips. She's as sweet and decadent as I remember.

Katy's hands push through my hair, tugging out my hair tie to free it. I love the feel of her fingers on my scalp. The light scratches her nails make drives me wild.

Katy's hips move in time with my tongue, and she's riding my cock over my pants. I'm already hard. I'm hard every morning waking up with her soft body curled into mine.

Switching breasts, I growl her name. Her body is taunting me with things I want but can't have right now. My little temptress seems to be enjoying herself as much as I am. Her hands leave my hair and brace on my shoulder. She adjusts herself so she's directly rubbing her pussy over me.

"Katy." Her name is a whine on my lips. She's killing me.

Her lips come to my ear, and her words make my stomach drop. "Shhh, Viking. If you wake him, we can't get our pleasure. Think I can make you come like a teenager just by sitting on your lap like this. I know I can."

My lips leave her nipples to capture her mouth. Her tongue darts out the moment our mouths fuse. Fucking heaven.

"You want me to come in my pants? I think I have more

198

restraint than that."

The smile that grows on her face is devious. It could move mountains. Solve world hunger.

"Is that a challenge?" Her hips dip, and she shifts over my entire length.

"Fuuuuck."

"I think I'll win. What do I get if I win?"

My heart, but you already have that.

"What do you want, Pepper? You're already breaking the rules because the sun is up. It's *my* time." I punctuate my words with a thrust of my hips, and her eyes close on a quiet moan.

"I want a date."

Her eyes open, chocolate decadence assessing me. She wants a date? Between us.

"You want me to take you out?" It's a line we haven't crossed. I want her to be mine. We do everything together, and from the outside, I'm sure we already look like a couple. A date would change the dynamics between us.

My silence gives her the wrong impression, and I watch the mischief in her eyes turn to unease.

"Or something else is fine. I didn't mean to—"

"Stop." Her body stiffens at my commanding tone. "Look at me."

"I'm sorry."

"I said stop. I would love to take you out, but it could and probably would change things between us. I need you to be sure, Katy. You're more than a job for me, and I think you know that at this point. You're still young, and you said it yourself: you want to date and go out. You want to be a teenager. I'm going to go out on a limb here and tell you I have happily fucking ever after feeling for you, and I'm willing to wait."

I've said too much. She's staring at me like she's never seen me before. Any moment and she's going to crawl off me and tell me to leave. I didn't even mean for the words to come out; they just did. I can't take them back now that I've said them, but I'd like to know what she thinks.

"Okay."

"Okay?" That's what she's giving me after my confession. I can't help but feel defeated.

"So if I win, I get my date. If you can hold out, you get the girl."

"I don't understand."

Katy's hips gyrate in my lap, and I'm even more confused about what's happening.

"Spoiler alert, Viking. The hero always gets the girl. And I'm going to get your orgasm."

Katy's fingers dip to the hem of my shirt, pulling it over my head. Warm hands roam my chest, and I'm lost in the feeling of her moving hips and soft touches. I have no idea what's happening, but she took my words. She heard them and made a decision. I'm going to get the girl because, in her story, I'm the hero.

I let her have my orgasm. Like she wanted, she dry-humped me into spilling in my pants. But not until after she rubbed herself into one by riding my cock. I wanted to hold out, but when she came with her head buried in the crook of my neck and I could feel her pussy pulsing on me, I caved. I'll always give her what she wants, even if that is a sticky mess in my pants because the pride on her face is worth it.

I guess my evening of country line dancing will be our first date.

26

Katy

"Why won't anyone tell me where we are going? You all suck." I've primped and preened. I took a deep dive into Spencer's closet, which has a disturbing amount of dresses for someone who mostly walks around in sports bras and leggings.

I chose a pretty, flowy pale blue dress with small ruffled sleeves. Spencer told me to wear comfortable shoes, so I pick silver sandals.

"You'll find out soon enough. Stop being impatient."

Huffing, I walk over to the mirror and check my makeup one last time.

"Mama, you pitty." Owen toddles over to me, and I pick him up, tickling his belly.

"Thank you, little man." Owen's brown eyes stare at me through the mirror. I'm so thankful that he looks like me. I don't know what it would have been like to stare at the face of my assaulter every day. Though I'd never love him any less; this boy has my entire heart. And somehow, it seems like that heart is expanding to let a tall, tattooed Viking have space.

"I'll take him. Dempsey is waiting downstairs." Spencer reaches out and takes Owen.

"I'm not crazy, right? Am I crazy for doing this? We're crossing a line. You pay him to spend time with me. What if that's all this really is?"

Spencer stares at me with a blank expression that says more than any words could.

You're being an idiot.

The man is infatuated with you.

He's not being paid to take you out.

Shut up and enjoy yourself.

"Okay, fine. I get it. Since you know where I'm going, will this outfit work?"

"You look beautiful, Katy." A masculine voice turns my head, and Tucker stands in the doorway to the bedroom. He enters the room and kisses Spencer, Owen, and then me. "You look beautiful as always, so stop being nervous. Patrick is going to follow you but stay in the parking lot. I think he's happy he isn't on Owen duty tonight." Tucker tickles Owen's neck, and he giggles. "No offense to you, buddy."

Wait. Why is Tucker giving me the details of tonight? Unless…

"Tucker, do you know where we're going?"

He smiles a devious smile, and that's all the answer I need. I can't help the excitement that radiates through me. We're going to Midnight Moonshine. It makes total sense. It's safe. Tucker has incredible security. I'm sure he's instructed his staff to keep an eye on me without needing a Patrick or Viktor there to do it. I'm so excited to dance and let loose.

"Oh my god, please let me do a Kickin' Cowboy. Please, please, please." I fold my hands, begging Tucker.

A smile tugs at his lips. "I think I can arrange that. Let me get going so I can make sure everything is set up. If you want to ride the bull, make sure you bring shorts to put on under this dress. You can leave anything you bring in my office." Tucker kisses my forehead, tickles Owen, and caresses Spencer's cheek before leaving us.

"Well, now that you've spoiled the surprise, your date is ready and waiting."

"You're sure it's okay if I leave Ow—"

"Don't finish that sentence, Katy. You don't ever need to finish that sentence. Have fun."

Have fun. It seems like such a foreign concept. It's not a luxury I've been afforded for most of my life, but tonight, I will take it. Owen will be here, safe with family, and I'm going to the safest place I could possibly go.

I say my goodbyes to them and force myself to take the steps slower than my excited body wants to. I'd hate to start the evening by tumbling down the stairs.

As I approach the bottom and look into the living room, I see several male bodies lounging around, but not the one I'm looking for. At least not until I fully come into the room and realize the cowboy hat sitting on the couch with a bouncing knee is my Viking. He looks delicious in dark denim jeans, a black button-down dress shirt with the sleeves rolled up, and a black cowboy hat. I didn't recognize him because of the hat, but all the dark makes his eyes sparkle, taking my breath away.

He stands when he sees me, and I'm speechless. The total package is more than I could have expected. He's my sexy bodyguard every day, but tonight, he's my breathtaking date.

"You look…"

"Nowhere near as stunning as you, Pepper. Let me see you." He motions with his finger to turn, and I give him a slow spin. There's general grumbles around the room about locking me up, never letting me leave the house, and how Viktor better be a gentleman. All of which makes me smile, but nothing warms my belly more than Viktor's look of awe shining back at me.

"You're missing something?"

I look down at my outfit, checking my ears and chest for jewelry and my hip for my purse. I have everything I need for the night. What is he referring to?

When I look back at Viktor, he's holding a white cowboy hat with a massive grin on his face. Where did that just come from? I dip my head for him, and he places it down and brushes the hair out of my face.

"Perfect."

"Thank you." I trail my fingers along the brim and feel the soft velvet. "I love it."

"Ugh." A groan of protest snaps my attention across the room. Lincoln strides toward us and gives Viktor a stern look before turning a soft gaze to me. "You're beautiful, Katy." He eyes Viktor again, and I wonder what's going on. *"Just for tonight,* the window is fixed on the pool house. If you'd like to stay there, *just for tonight"*—he shoots a glare at Viktor, and I understand now—"you can. Just let us know so we don't worry where you are."

"Was that hard to say?" I purse my lips to hold in my laugh at his sour face. "Was it hard to offer me an empty house to do naughty things with my bdgrd." Lincoln clamps his hand over my mouth, muffling my last words.

"Don't push your luck, woman. I'll change the lock code, and you won't have access to the pool house at all." I pout, and he shakes his head at me. "You're trouble. Have fun. Keep her safe Dempsey." Lincoln kisses my cheek and waves a hand of offering to Viktor.

"Always, Lincoln. Always."

It's been two years since I've been here, and it looks so different from what I remember. Maybe it's the excitement of knowing I can go on the dancing side of the club. I've only ever been in the restaurant side because I wasn't old enough.

Viktor and I hand our I.D.s to the young man behind the front counter, and he scans them into the computer. His eyes widen, and he picks up his walkie, talking in a hushed voice. I glance at Viktor, and he shrugs, not understanding his reaction either.

"He'll be right out?" Why does this poor boy look nervous?

"He? Who's he?"

"If you could just step right over there, please." He gestures to a door off to the side and Viktor guides me with a hand on the small of my back.

"What's going on, Viktor? Why can't we get in?"

"Just hold on a minute."

The door next to us opens, and Tucker steps out. Now I understand. He embraces me and nods to the boy behind the counter, who gives him a nervous smile.

"What did you do to that poor kid to make him look petrified when he scanned my I.D.?"

Tucker's brows furrow, and he looks behind me at the counter. "Will? Nothing." He pauses, and realization dawns on his face. "Oh. I have alerts on all of your I.D.s to contact

206

me immediately if they are scanned. It's the same alert for people that have been banned. He probably thought you were about to get kicked out. He doesn't like confrontation. Come here."

Tucker takes my hand and walks me back to the door.

"Will, this is my daughter, Katy, and my associate, Dempsey. I didn't mean to alarm you. My apologies for not warning you. I was expecting them." Will's body visibly relaxes.

"Hi. Nice to meet you both. It's alright, Mr. Bennett. I'm just not a fan of confrontation. I didn't know the alerts were the same. I won't jump to conclusions next time."

Tucker cups Will's shoulder. "No. Always assume the worst and hope for the best. I'll be more vigilant of my visitors and talk to IT about making the alerts different. I'd hate for this mistake to happen again. You're doing a fantastic job. I'll take them in now." Tucker nods his head toward the door he exited from and scans a card, opening it.

The air inside is instantly different. It's thicker; humid. The music is loud, and the bass is low, making my feet feel like they have a heartbeat. I can't contain the smile on my face as I watch, mesmerized, at the bodies dancing in perfected unison on the dance floor.

"Wow. How do they do that?"

Tucker chuckles and leans closer so I can hear him over the music. He points to a corner of the room where a group of people linger that don't seem as coordinated as the rest.

"People usually stand off in the corner to watch and practice. When they think they have the hang of it, they join the big group. No one is going to judge how well you do. Just try and stay to the edges. The regulars all hang out in the front near the main bar and can sometimes get grumpy when new people get in their way."

We follow Tucker down a small hall and into a door marked "OFFICE." The noise almost disappears when it shuts behind us.

"That's crazy. Where did the noise go?"

"Really good soundproofing." He claps his hands and gestures around the room. "Welcome to my home away from home. You can leave your purse here. I have a private bathroom that you're welcome to use instead of the public ones. You have open tabs at both bars in the club and the restaurant if you decide to eat." He hands Viktor a magnetic card. "This will give you access to my office and what the employees will scan when you order anything."

"Tucker," Viktor protests. "You didn't have to go through all this. I'm happy to pay for everything we need."

"Dempsey, I won't insult you if you don't insult me. Katy is my daughter and won't spend a dime here. You're an extension of her. I want you to both have fun and not worry about anything."

"I respect that. Thank you."

I'm vibrating with excitement and energy to get out on the dance floor.

"Hey Tuck, do I get my request?"

He chuckles and his eyes flash to Viktor before he responds. "Of course. Now?"

"Today is my favorite day. Let's go!" I take Viktor's hand and pull him behind me toward the door.

Tucker laughs this time. "Patrick can drive you home, Dempsey. I've already told him to be prepared.

"Prepared for what?"

Katy giggles, and as much as I love the sound, I know it's

laced with mischief.

27

Dempsey

F uck.
　　Me.
　　I wasn't prepared.
I know I'm a big man that gives off an air of superiority.
People don't generally look twice in my direction. When I'm
in full work mode, the only expression you'll get from me is
a scowl.

Why?

Tell. Me. Why? This gorgeous bundle of sex just slapped me,
and all I want to do is strip her in the middle of this fucking
club and make her come so hard she forgets her name.

"Again." I don't even recognize my own voice. Was that a
growl? It was low and husky, but she understood me. Katy
tips her head to the bartender and motions for another round.
Moments later, the blonde puts two more cups on the bar
top next to Katy's ass.

I drink in the woman before me. Her lean body sits on
the bar, legs spread, surrounding my hips. Her hair is in soft

waves flowing down her chest, and I take a lock between my fingers and twirl.

"Fuck, you're stunning, Pepper." My chest hurts looking at her.

Katy's smile takes my fucking breath away. She's so happy and carefree right now.

"Are you sure?" She holds up a shot glass-sized plastic cup, and I take it from her hands.

"Are you?" I take a step back and shoot back the amber liquid. I could care less what's in this cup because the next part is what I'm aching for. I brace myself as Katy splashes the cup of cold water in my face and wait with anticipation for the bite of her hand as she slaps me across the cheek. It's more euphoric the second time, knowing what's coming.

She didn't tell me what was happening the first time. All I was told was to drink and put my hands on her knees. I had zero issues with that.

Chug. Knees. Water. *Slap.*

My dick was instantly hard, and this second time turns me into fucking steel. I can feel it pressing against the zipper of my jeans.

I step back between her legs and revel in the joy that radiates from her entire body.

Katy gently caresses my cheek, and the warmth of her hand, mixed with the heat of the sting, leaves me on fire. She's my fucking flame.

"Are you okay?"

Is that a serious question?

I grab her hips and pull her to the edge of the bar.

"Do you feel how *okay* I am, Pepper?" I shift my hips, rubbing my erection on her heated core. Her eyes dart down to where we're connected, and a beautiful blush creeps up her cheeks.

"Just from a slap?"

"Just from you. You turn me on constantly, but that slap... Fuck it did something to me. Why do I fold so easily for you, Pepper?"

Katy's delicate fingers dance along the jaw of the cheek she hasn't slapped yet.

"Do you need a matching set?"

My entire body goes up in flames. I want to tell her yes a thousand times, but I'm not sure I could contain myself if she slapped me again. I'm already barely hanging on.

My pulse races, and my breathing is erratic. Being in public with her and having the feelings that I never allow myself to have outside the bedroom heightens every sensation in my body.

"I want you to do everything to me, but not here. I can't take much more. We need to get out on that dance floor and burn off some energy."

Katy pouts as I lift her from the bar top and place her back on the floor.

"Party pooper." She slaps my chest with an audible thwap. "Hmm. Did you bring a change of shirt? This might get uncomfortable." Katy pushes on various spots of my shirt, and water pools around her finger.

"Katy?" We turn our heads at the bartender's voice. "Boss-man said there's a shirt in his office if your man wants to change."

Your man? There's no way Tucker referred to me as Katy's man.

Katy laughs and looks up at me. "Why doesn't it surprise me

that he would think of bringing you a shirt? Wanna change before we dance?"

Grabbing Katy by the waist, I attempt, with little effort, to pull her into my chest. She squeals, not wanting to be wet. I lean close to her ear, and she shivers from the heat of my breath. "I thought you liked it when I got you wet?"

Her mouth drops open in mock horror.

"Sir, I am a lady, and you should not speak to me like that." She fakes a Southern accent, and it's adorable.

"Well, my southern belle, shall I go change so you stop looking at me like I'm your next meal?"

"I-um. I wasn't..."

"Uh huh. Let's go, Pepper."

After changing my shirt in Tucker's office—which I had to lock myself in the bathroom to do because if she kept looking at me with those hungry eyes, we were going to have to leave—we got on the dance floor.

Katy is much more coordinated than me and picks up the dances while I watch. I'm able to fake my way through the two-step, and a few slow, couple dances were played where I got to hold her close to me.

"Are you enjoying yourself?" Katy's head rests on my shoulder as we dance to a slow song. We've been here for hours, enjoyed dessert in the restaurant, and, at my request, one final Kickin' Cowboy sans water. I'm feeling light with the alcohol and the pheromones floating between us.

"Yes, but I'm ready to go home...to the pool house."

Fuck.

"Are you sure?" Please fucking say yes. I'm aching for her. Tonight has been beyond my wildest expectations.

"Positive."

Taking Katy's hand in mine, I pull out my cell phone and text Patrick. Three shots and a beer during dessert is more alcohol consumption than I'm willing to drive, Katy.

I pause to look for Will when we walk out the front door into the foyer. He quickly stands from the chair he was relaxing in, looking nervous.

"Will, could you contact Mr. Bennett? We're leaving and would like to say goodbye."

"Of course." He calls Tucker on the walkie, and a few minutes later, Tucker exits through the restaurant door toward us with a big smile.

"Heading home or…" He has a gleam in his eye as he leaves his sentence open-ended. I stay quiet, hoping Katy will answer his silent question, and I internally leap for joy when she does.

"We're heading to the pool house if it's still alright?"

Tucker takes her hand in his. "Is it your choice?"

A mild annoyance bubbles in my chest at the insinuation I could be persuading her, but the bodyguard in me knows it's the right question to ask, and I respect him for it.

Katy smiles at me sweetly and pulls me closer to her. "It is."

"Then have fun. Owen is well taken care of, and breakfast will be waiting in the morning. Lincoln made an overnight French toast casserole."

Katy hums her appreciation, and we say our goodbyes. Patrick is waiting for us at the curb when we step outside, and I wave him back in the car when he tries to step out to open the car door.

Patrick eyes me only once when I slide in next to Katy and take her hand. I'm sure this situation is strange for him. I'm paid to keep her and Owen safe, but tonight we are breaking all of the rules, and I don't even fucking care.

I got my approval from Katy's pseudo-parents before I made the official plans for this evening. I know Katy has shared some of our developing relationship with them, and I've spoken to a few as well, but this is an official date. I wanted their blessing because, at the end of the day, her safety is my priority. I won't ever jeopardize that for my feelings, and I needed to make sure they knew that.

I'm sure they saw the feelings developing between us over the past few years, but I never pursued them. I had no intention of crossing that line, but I'm not sure there even is one anymore. It's so blurry that it's blended.

Even the boundary of day and night seems to have lost its luster; Katy breaks the rules more than I do. Ultimately, her happiness is a close second to her safety, and I can provide her with both of those.

"Take us to the pool house, Jeeves!" Katy giggles at her own joke, and Patrick grunts his usual grunt. She's never sat in the back seat while I drive unless she was attending to Owen when he was an infant. So now, riding in the back and having me here with her is a whole new experience.

Katy laces her fingers through mine and sits as close to me as the seat belt allows. I feel like I'll get in trouble for being this close to her, but tonight isn't about the job. It's about Katy and a potential Katy and me.

As we pull up to the house, Katy suddenly looks nervous.

"What's wrong, Pepper?"

"Patrick, are you okay with this? I know you've been sleeping here?"

Oh, I had forgotten that fact.

"I don't sleep much. I'm fine."

"Are you sure, Patrick? I don't want to put you out." Katy's concern for his feelings is admirable.

"I'm sure. Have a good evening." Patrick holds my eyes in the rearview before stepping out to open Katy's door.

"Can we sit outside for a little bit? It's so nice out tonight."

I look at Patrick and nod. "I've got her. You don't need to stay." Patrick nods his acknowledgment and disappears up the driveway. Katy and I sit on the bench near the front door, and she curls into my side.

"We don't have to do anything tonight, Pepper. I don't want you to think I have any expectations."

She sits up, a devious smile lighting up her face.

"I do, Viking. I want to explore some of the things we bought at the toy store. If you're up for it, of course."

Oh fuck. If she's asking for my permission, she isn't thinking about things like the blindfold or the ropes we bought. She's looking to go big or go home.

"I'd be lying to you if I said I wasn't a little apprehensive about some of the more risque things we bought, but I made you a deal, and I won't renege on it."

Katy curls back into my side, and we silently enjoy the night sounds around us.

"Can I ask you a question, Pepper?"

"Anything."

"There's no wrong answer, but I'm curious if there's a reason why you want to…for lack of a better term, dominate me. This isn't me saying no, I'm just wondering if there's something behind your need to do it."

Katy sits up again, curling her legs under her on the bench. She takes my hand and toys with my fingers, deep in thought.

"I'm not a freaky bedroom person. Well, I guess I can't really say that because I don't have any frame of reference." She giggles and peers at me through her dark lashes. I can't help but smirk at her innocence and her boldness. "I feel safe with you. I've never questioned that. I want to explore…things that make me feel powerful…in the bedroom. My choice was taken away from me, and I think maybe—"

I grab her chin and stop her. "Be confident in your next words. No maybes."

She blinks at me several times. The moonlight makes her eyes shine gold.

"I want to be able to control a situation. You're bigger than me, and even though I know you'll be a willing participant, I want to take that part of my life back. If that's okay with you? You don't have to say yes. I'm asking for a big thing that probably isn't something that you've ever thought about or maybe even want to do. You can say no."

"Katy."

Her rambling words stop, and her eyes snap to mine. I take her cheeks in my palms and smile before I kiss her—tender and gentle.

"I will always be whoever you need me to be and do whatever you need me to do." I look up to the sky and back to her. "It's the nighttime, my princess. You own my nights."

Katy flings her leg over my hips and straddles me. I know this isn't the best position to be in because even though it's dark, we're under the pool light, and anyone in the big house could look in our direction from the porch and see us. But at the moment, with Katy's lips on mine, I'll take whatever disciplinary action comes my way.

28

Katy

"I will always be whoever you need me to be and do whatever you need me to do. It's the nighttime, my princess. You own my nights."

Who says something so freaking romantic? Viktor, my Viking.

I climb onto his lap, straddling his muscular thighs that bunch up below me, and kiss him. My emotions are too big right now to use words, so I'll convey with my body how much he means to me. We kiss for several long minutes—tongues tasting, lips smacking.

"We should go inside," Viktor says breathily.

"We should."

Neither of us makes any movement toward getting up. I can't help my hips from rocking over the bulge growing in Viktor's pants. This man devours my every thought, and all I want right now is to strip naked and take him for a ride.

We continue to make out like teenagers on a first date when we hear a throat clear.

"Oh shit." I jump off Viktor's lap, my legs getting tangled in his, and fall on my ass.

Panting from exertion, I look behind me and see Patrick standing several feet away as Viktor scoops me up off the ground.

"You should take that inside."

"Oh my god, Pepper. Are you okay?" Viktor's eyes frantically sweep across my body, looking for injuries, not bothered at all that we were interrupted.

"Sorry, Patrick."

"You should take that inside," he repeats and walks away.

"Pepper, talk to me."

I begin to giggle at the absurdity of our situation. Patrick just caught us making out and basically told us to get a room. My Viking is freaking out over a little tumble, and through it all, I'm still horny as hell.

Gently, I cover Viktor's mouth with my hand and see his panicked eyes.

"Relax. I'm completely fine." I slide my hand down his chest and softly kiss his lips. "We should probably listen to Patrick and go inside. He is in charge tonight, after all."

Viktor's eyes narrow as he stands with me in his arms and grunts at my comment.

"*He's* in charge? Do you really think that?"

I stare into his stupidly handsome face as he types his code into the keypad, unlocking the door.

"No. Not at all."

Viktor walks us into the bedroom and places me on the bed. I quickly jump to my feet, towering over him, and cup his bearded cheeks between my palms. I lean down, almost grazing his lips, and whisper my promise. "I know he's not in charge because tonight *I* am. Tonight you're mine, and if I get my way, so is your ass."

I scan Viktor's face for a reaction but don't find one. A smile slowly creeks across his cheeks, and I wonder what he's thinking. He doesn't make me wait long.

"And yours? Do I get to take yours once you've had your fun with mine?"

I feel my face flush and sweat prickle under my arms. It never dawned on me that he'd also want to do it. I've obviously never done that, but I'm not opposed to it.

"Could we work up to it? Maybe not tonight? I mean, I'm barely not a virgin in the front door, and"—I glance down at the prominent bulge in his pants—"you're a little, ahem, big to just shove it in the back door." I hate that I went from a confident queen to a meek little mouse just from a simple question.

Viktor lifts his chin and kisses the tip of my nose. "Always, Pepper. We'll always go at your pace."

I drop to my knees so I can bury myself in his arms.

"Thank you. Thank you, Viktor, for everything." I take a moment to put my big girl panties back on and inhale his rich, spicy scent.

"Viktor?"

"Hmm."

"Strip." I feel his laugh vibrate against me. "I'm serious. Strip." I pull back so I'm sitting on the bed and cross my arms, waiting.

"Oh. You are serious. Yes, ma'am."

He takes a step back and painstakingly slowly, removes his clothing. His body is a work of art, and I'm continuously marveled by his leg tattoo every time I see it, which isn't often enough.

"How about you, Katy?"

"Miss."

"What?" His head tilts in confusion,

"Call me *Miss* Katy. I'm in charge and want to be respected as such." I hear the huff of air and the muttered fuck that escapes him.

"Yes, Miss Katy."

Sitting up on my knees, I caress his beard and give his cock a feather-like stroke. Viktor's eyes flutter shut, and he licks his lips.

"Good boy, Viktor. Now, let's go shower before I ravage your body."

I squeak as my body lifts from the bed and lips crash into mine. His kiss is hungry as he expertly maneuvers us to the bathroom. With ease, he releases one hand from his grip on me and turns on the shower.

"Are you really going to let me do all the things I want to do to you? Bunny works for you as a safeword, too. You can use it before we even get started if you're not okay with anything."

"Miss Katy, my body is yours to do with as you please. Period." He says the last word with conviction.

"Alright, Viktor. Let's get this body washed; I have work to do."

We step into the shower and do our best to do all of the shower things between kisses and touches.

My hands roam down Viktor's back onto his muscular ass cheeks, and I give them a firm squeeze.

"Have you ever done anything back here?"

"No."

I slip a finger down the edge of his crack, and his body tenses then relaxes.

"So anything I do to this ass is…virginal?"

"It's all new and all yours."

Viktor kisses me as my fingers explore. With my free hand, I spread his one cheek and venture my fingers lower until I feel his breathing change.

"Viktor?"

"It's new and feels different. I'm all good. Keep going, Miss Katy."

The feeling of the puckered skin under my fingers is a strange sensation. A grunting moan fills the space around us as I put pressure on his hole. I smirk and continue my exploration.

"Do you trust me?"

"Implicitly."

I take a step to the side and round his body, trailing kisses as I turn. I nip and lick at his back as I lower myself down his body.

"Katy?"

"Hands on the wall, Viktor."

"Katy, what—"

"*Miss* Katy and I said, hands on the wall, Viktor. Be a good boy and listen."

Without further hesitation, he leans his arms against the wall, and his hips pop out, giving me better access to his ass.

"Open your legs more. Mmm, just like that."

Viktor gasps in shock when I bite his left ass cheek, but it turns to a growl when I lick the sting away.

"Use the safeword if you need it, Viktor."

I'm fully aware of the power this man is letting me hold,

the trust he's putting into me. Did I ever think I would find myself at eye level with a man's butt about to eat his ass? Hell no. But something about having control over this man, knowing that he could overpower me in the blink of an eye, is euphoric. The trust he's giving me and allowing me to take from him is what my body is craving.

"So fucking ready."

He rests his head on his bicep and takes a deep breath when he feels me pull apart his cheeks, exposing him fully.

With a delicate touch, I sweep my tongue across him, and his muscles tense in my hands. Growing bolder, I flatten my tongue and move again through his cheeks. Viktor's head falls forward as he moans a sound I've never heard from him before. It's low and guttural, and my instincts want me to ask him if he's okay, but I trust that he'll tell me if he needs to stop.

I continue to lick and circle his hole, enjoying the sounds he's making. His muscles have relaxed, his body telling me he's enjoying what I'm doing. Knowing I wanted to try this with him, I did some research on the good ol' interweb. I'd be lying if I said I didn't practice some techniques on the side of my closed fist. It's a great comparison to what I'm feeling right now under my tongue.

"M-miss Kaaaaty." I smile at the whine that comes from him. "Fuck."

"I need to get you ready, Viktor. All the lube is in the other room, but I have Aloe under the sink. I can start to prep you right now since your ass seems to be eager for me if you want to."

This man practically trips through the shower door, soaking the floor as he rummages through the cabinet for the Aloe.

I'm hysterically laughing as he's so deep under the sink he almost hits his head when he tries to come out with his prize. A half-full bottle of green gel rests proudly in his hands.

"Are you sure this will work?"

"Mhmm. I did my research. I thought about putting some lube in the bathroom, but when I read Aloe is safe to use, I knew I had some in here."

I shiver as the cool air from the bathroom sweeps through the shower with the closing of the doors. Viktor hands me the Aloe and resumes his position against the wall.

"Last chance to back out." I sweep a finger through his cheeks, teasing him.

29

Dempsey

"Not a fucking chance." I widen his legs and arch my back, giving her full access again. I'm at her mercy. At least my ass is. Her tongue between my legs was shocking and fucking incredible. I was serious when I told her I was all hers. I'm willing to explore all of Katy's fantasies, and if playing with my ass is something she needs to take her power back, she can have it.

"Okay. I'll go slow. Don't be afraid to tell me if you're uncomfortable."

"Of course." I won't. I don't think there's anything she could do to make me feel uncomfortable, but even if she did, I'd never tell her.

I hear the telltale clicking of the cap and smell the Aloe. It reminds me of summer days and sunburnt shoulders. I'm sure that's why she has it in the first place—her pale skin burns easily in the sun.

My breath hitches as the cooling sensation runs through my ass crack, but it's quickly warmed by Katy's fingers. I've never done or had anything in my ass before. Katy will be my first and only, and I like the idea of sharing a first with her. I'm giving her my trust as much as she's giving me hers.

I steady my breathing and close my eyes, concentrating on relaxing. I've done my research as well and am prepared for the initial burn pushing past the first ring of muscle. When Katy's finger slips in, I bite my lip to keep myself from tensing up, reminding myself that the pleasure comes after the pain.

As Katy's whispered words brush across my shoulder, a soothing hand runs up my spine. "You're doing so well. How does that feel?"

I concentrate on her finger shallowly pumping in and out....of my ass. I should probably feel weird about this, but the pre-cum dripping from my aching cock tells the true story of how I'm feeling.

"More. I can take it."

"You want another finger?"

A grunt and nod are all I can manage as she's already pushing into me. I feel my body relaxing the more turned on I get. It's accepting her invasion easier as she begins to scissor her fingers inside me. We may have done the same research.

"Viktor, I…god this looks so wrong and so fucking sexy at the same time. My fingers are in your ass. My big Viking man's ass."

Her fingers are in my ass, and soon there will be a silicone cock in there. I'd be lying to myself if I said I wasn't nervous about that one. We picked a moderate-sized dildo with a vibrating option for Katy.

"*Am I* yours, Miss Katy?" I want to be hers so fucking bad, and I know we have the blessing from the adults in her life.

We've clearly been taking full advantage of each other, but we haven't spoken about an *us*.

"Viktor, do you really want to have this conversation now, like this?" She wiggles her fingers farther into my ass to punctuate her point. I feel pressure as she works another finger inside me, and it momentarily takes my breath away.

"Y-yes. I can't possibly get more vulnerable than this. Make me yours, Pepper. I want to be only yours. Please."

Well, I didn't expect begging to come with ass play, but it appears that's where I'm at. This woman has my heart. I've loved her for longer than I'd like to admit. I won't tell her now or anytime soon, but my heart shattered the day Justin told me her story and hired me. She's been putting me back together little by little through her strength, bravery, and light.

"Viktor," she breathes out. Her fingers slip from inside me, and I instantly feel the loss. She rounds my body and places a hand on my cheek. "It's nighttime, isn't it? You're mine when the sun is down."

I take her hand in mine and kiss her wrist. "I want to be yours always. When the sun is up or down. When there are clouds in the sky or snow falling to the ground."

Confusion washes over her features. "You do?"

How could she not see it? I worship this woman's every move. I would have happily given my life for her in the car that night if it stopped Shane from taking her. But I didn't have to. She did it herself, and I'm still proud of her for thinking smart and bashing his nose with the back of her head. The seconds he was stunned allowed her to grab the gun and shoot.

I barely remember the moments in the car between getting

shot and waking up in the hospital, but I remember her. I remember the warmth of her body smashing into mine after she got her shot off, and Shane ran away like a pussy afraid to finish what he started. I knew she was brave, but seeing the recording from the dash cam after the fact set her on a higher pedestal in my mind than I thought possible.

"I fucking do."

"Um, okay. This feels like a conversation that maybe *I'm* not ready for with my fingers having just been in your ass." She frantically waves her hands in my face. "Before you have any negative thoughts, I feel the same way, but my head isn't in the right place at this very moment to think of anything other than the neon green dildo I want you to help strap around my waist so I can rail your ass."

I choke on nothing at her bold statement. "Holy shit, Pepper. Okay. I got it. Let's get out of this shower and pin that topic for another time. My girl has needs, and I'm going to fulfill them."

She said she feels the same way, and that's enough for me right now. I grab towels and wrap one around her before covering myself.

"We better hurry, or we'll lose all my progress." She gives me a sly smile and wiggles her butt as she walks out of the room. I happily follow her as she approaches the nightstand and opens the top drawer where we put our purchases from S'morgasm. Katy pulls out the black strap-on underwear and holds it up to me with a smile.

"Let me help you with those." She hands them to me and pulls the dildo out of the drawer next. We work together to attach the neon green monster, and I hold the underwear while Katy steps into it.

"This is fascinating." I run a finger under the waist of her contraption. At first glance, they look like a regular pair of underwear with a pouch and a reinforced O-ring low on the front. The back is a thick piece of elastic that sits under each of her ass cheeks, beautifully accentuating her firm globes. Another thin strap sits about an inch above the waistband that we quickly realize is more for show than function.

Katy wiggles her hips, and her eyes widen in shock. "This is...weird. How do you walk around with a boner?"

"You look fucking hot, and believe me, it isn't easy. You learn to tuck up if you're in public, but it isn't comfortable." She's adorable as she giggles and swivels her hips side to side, up and down.

"Katy." I stop her with a firm hand on her shoulder. "Progress, remember?"

She looks at the bed, then at me. Then back to the bed, and to my waist where my towel still sits.

"I hate to make this impersonal but our height difference is a bit concerning for this. Maybe you should lean over the edge of the bed."

It's my turn to look at the bed and then at her hips, and she's probably right. It will also put both feet on the floor, giving her the most purchase.

"I think you have the right idea. And nothing about this is impersonal, even if my face is in the mattress."

She giggles again and pulls my towel away, leaving me naked and with a sight matching hers.

"We both have boners!" Her hands fly to her mouth, and I watch her face turn red as she tries to hold in her laughter but fails. "Sorry. That was thirteen year old boy humor. I couldn't help myself."

I pull her into my arms and feel our "boners" smash between us. "Well, thank fuck you aren't a thirteen year old boy because that would make what's about to happen very awkward."

Katy pushes against my chest, and I allow her to move my body. I fall onto the bed, and she crawls onto my lap, her green dildo slapping against my hardened cock.

"This is a little intimidating." I chuckle as I flick the tip of the appendage that's about to be in my body.

Katy leans in and nips at my ear before whispering, "Don't worry baby, it will fit. I promise."

I can't believe she said that. I want to laugh hysterically but hold it in, not wanting to spoil the mood.

"I'm ready whenever you are, Miss Katy." The fire flashes in her eyes at the word Miss, that at one point, she hated. Tonight, it seems to bring on a different emotion, and I'm here for every bit of it.

She slides her body off mine, and I kiss her one more time before turning onto my stomach and hang my legs off the bed. An instant sense of vulnerability washes over me, and I close my eyes to tamp down the panic. I don't like feeling vulnerable. I joined the military to always feel in control of myself and my surroundings.

I don't know what Katy sees, but a soothing hand runs up my spine.

"Shh, Viktor, I've got you. Relax. You're safe."

Safe?

Was I feeling unsafe and not vulnerable? Or was it both? Whatever emotion was taking over is instantly smoothed over by her touch and words. This is why I want this woman to be mine. She understands me.

Katy walks to the nightstand and takes out the lube. My body shivers as I think of what's about to happen. I'm ready. I know what this means to her.

"Last chance to back out Viking?"

"I'm all yours, Miss Katy. Take your power back."

The cool gel runs down my ass crack, and her warm hands spread it around. She adds some to the dildo, and I'm fascinated with the concentration she uses to apply it to every inch.

Katy grabs the base and lines it. I turn my head to the mattress, wanting to feel and not see. This is for her, not me.

The pressure on my hole feels foreign but also familiar as I think of her fingers inside me in the shower. I inhale a deep breath and slowly release it, relaxing my muscles as I do. Katy sees it for what it's meant to me—access and permission.

Pressure increases as she pushes her hips forward, and the burning starts.

"Don't stop. Keep going." I know the feeling will change with just a little more pressure. Through the first ring of muscle. Push through Pepper. You've got this.

Relief.

The air leaves my lungs as she pushes herself to the hilt, and I feel her hips against my ass.

"Holy shit." Her words come out in a whoosh of air. "I'm-I'm in. Viktor, I'm in. Are you all right?"

"Fucking phenomenal, Miss Katy. Move whenever you're ready. I'm eager to feel you move inside me."

It feels...I can't describe it. I'm full; that's the biggest sensation right now. I'm more than ready for her to move, but she needs this to be about her and her pace.

Slowly, she pulls out and pushes back in. She's testing her

harness and my reactions. I can tell because when I moan, so does she. This feels like nothing I've ever experienced before. Katy's petite hands grasp my hips, and she thrusts forward a little harder.

"You don't have to go easy. Do what feels right, Miss Katy."

Everything she's doing feels amazing because it's her.

30

Katy

This....is...
Strange.
Exhilarating.
Awkward.
Fucking. Powerful!

I'm inside Viktor. I'm inside his body. He's letting me fuck him. I have all the power over this man who could so easily overpower me with the blink of an eye—but he won't. This man has given me all of his trust and vulnerability.

I want this. I want him and everything that comes with him. Each thrust of my hips forward feels like I'm digging deeper into his soul, his heart.

I'm not oblivious. I see the way he looks at me, but I still see myself as the naive sixteen year old that got into a bad situation and needs a big burly man to watch over her.

But now, in this moment, we are equals. He's giving of himself as much as I'm taking and vice versa. He's giving me strength as I'm taking it. Taking my power. Power that was stripped of me while I was forced on my hands and knees in that alley. Power that Shane used over me to take my virginity, my dignity, and the last piece of my youth.

Viktor, my bodyguard, my savior, my lover.

Viktor is giving it all back to me. Each thrust of my hips put a little piece of me back into place with a little piece of him molded into it. Weaved and intertwined. Blended colors mixed together to make a beautiful new image.

Fuck. I need to stop waxing poetic and get back to the moment.

Reaching into the pouch of the harness, I push the button to turn on the vibrating feature on the dildo.

"Holy fuck, Pepper. Fuck. God dammit."

I chuckle as I push harder into him. The vibrations affecting me as much as him, but his reactions are incredible, and I bite my cheek to contain my laughter.

"Feel good?" I coo close to his ear. The angle of my leaning over must rub something inside him because he moans out a guttural "fuuuuuuck," and I stay in the position and continue to thrust inside him.

I don't know how men do this because my abs and upper thighs are on fire, but I'm not stopping. The vibrator has me close to orgasm, and if the sounds coming from Viktor are any indication, so is he.

"How do you want to come? I can keep going." I pump my hips a few times and listen to his moan. "I can pull out and finish you with my mouth, or I'll let you come on my pretty tits, your favorite body part."

"Fuck. Tits. I want your tits."

His answer is frantic, and he moves his hips, wanting to get to them.

"Shh, me first." I stand, adjusting myself so the vibrator is angled right over my clit, and I brace a hand on Viktor's back as the warm sensation begins to wash over me. I'm struggling to control my hips when the orgasm finally takes hold. My movements become frantic, and I must be hitting something inside Viktor. His mutters, moans, and curses increase, and when I finally pull out, the rush of air that leaves him is full of relief.

"Get on your fucking knees, Pepper."

Without hesitation, I drop to the floor and arch my neck back, giving him access to my body. Viktor's hand moves frantically over his cock, stroking himself toward relief. With a grunt, his hot come coats my chest and neck. When the last spurt drains from him, he joins me on his knees and grabs handfuls of my breast.

Viktor's mouth sucks in one nipple while pinching the other. My milk joining with his come on my chest. When he switches sides, he licks up the underside of my breast, tasting the mixture of us.

His moans of appreciation make me feel loved and cherished.

"You taste like fucking heaven."

My giggle makes him look up, nipple still in his mouth, and I burst into laughter.

"You're ridiculous."

He releases me and attacks my lips. We tumble to the floor with his hasty assault, laughing through kisses.

Viktor looks between us and smirks. "I think we need another shower."

I run a hand across his cheek and look deep into his blue eyes. "How are you?"

"I'm good, Pepper. I'm really fucking good. Let's get cleaned up, and we can go to bed."

Viktor stands and extends his hand to help me. When he pulls me up, he wraps his arms around me, smearing his come between us. We kiss our way to the bathroom, and when he gives me his back to start the shower, I see something on the counter and get an idea.

As Viktor turns toward me with a smile, I slap a rainbow star sticker on his forehead. "You were a good boy and earned your reward."

His brows scrunch as he tries to look up at his forehead before he gives up and looks at his reflection in the mirror. He huffs and shakes his head when he sees I've placed one of Owen's potty reward stickers on him.

"You're gonna get it for that, Miss Katy."

Don't tempt me with a good time.

Babs: I'm so sorry, sweetie. I didn't mean to assume my role in yours or Owen's life. Please give me another chance.

I read the text message for what feels like the dozenth time while sipping my coffee. I woke up to my alarm wrapped warmly in the arms of this nakedly gorgeous man who wants to be mine, and for a few minutes, I wished I had no other responsibilities and could stay in his embrace forever.

Viktor rolled over at the sound and kissed my forehead, telling me he'd get Owen. I still had thirty minutes until we needed to get him, so I hit snooze and cuddled closer.

"Can you make love to me in the next nine minutes?"

"What?" Viktor chuckles as he looks at me.

"Nine minutes. That's how long my snooze is. Think you can get us both off in nine minutes?"

"I could, but I don't want to. Can you give me eighteen? One extra snooze."

"You're on!" I roll to my back and rest my hands above my head. "My body is all yours, Viking."

Viktor dives into my neck and growls. "I fucking love it when you call me that."

Blindly, he reaches out toward the nightstand drawer in search of a condom. I'm on birth control and want nothing more than to tell him we don't need it like our first time, but there's still a part of me traumatized about how Owen came about. I want him to have siblings. Growing up as an only child was lonely, but there's plenty of time.

Why do I feel like now is a good time for conversation? I have no idea, but my mind is running a mile a minute, and I need answers. As I watch Viktor roll on the condom and slowly lower himself to me, the words are out before my brain catches up.

"Do you want kids?"

Viktor pauses mid-moan, cock half inside me, and looks between us. "Really? You ask that now, Pepper." He pushes the rest of the way in and sits up on his knees, running his hands along my inner thighs.

"Sorry."

Gently, he thrusts in and out of me with a serious look on his face.

"Don't ever be sorry for asking an honest question. If you remember, you've asked me this one before."

"I did?" Why don't I remember his answer? Although, with the

237

torture of him languidly sliding inside me, I can barely remember my own name.

"Well, not you, exactly. Blake asked me for you. You were extremely embarrassed she asked. Your cheeks were this beautiful shade of scarlet. It was the day of your birthday party."

Oh god. Now I remember that embarrassing moment.

"Wait. Oh fuck that feels....oooh. She asked if you liked kids. I asked a different question." I close my eyes, and my head lulls to the side as he continues to pump into me. "You...you said something about dreams are—Fuck, Viktor. Right there."

Beep-Beep. Beep-Beep.

I slap the snooze button on my phone, not caring if he takes another nine minutes or nine hours. I'm in heaven right now.

"Futile."

"What?" Did I say something?

"Futile. I said sometimes dreams are futile. Yes, I like kids, and I'd love to have some of my own someday. But I never saw a life for my future that allowed me to have them...before you."

I want to question his answer. I need a lot more information, but he tilts his hips and pinches my nipples, and my teetering orgasm crashes into me.

"Viktor. I-I...fuuuuck."

"I know, Pepper. Believe me, I know."

His body leans over mine, and a few deep thrusts later, he's moaning his orgasm into my neck.

"Katy?"

"Hmm?" I look up from my coffee, Viktor's voice pulling me back from this morning's session.

"Are you going to respond to your mother?"

"Mama! All done." Owen waves his hands in the air, signing

he's done eating his breakfast. Viktor picked him up while I made us omelets to eat.

Grabbing the wipes to clean Owen of his egg mess, I contemplate his question like I've been doing for the last hour since the text came in. I want to say no. Every fiber of me wants to forget she exists, but despite my knowledge of her toxicity, I can't walk away.

"Should I? I can't come up with a good enough reason not to."

Viktor steps next to me, and I see the hesitation as his eyes dart to Owen. Things changed between us last night, but we still haven't talked about it. I pull Owen out of his highchair, and he takes off to his room in a flurry of giggles with Bun-Bun in hand.

"Come here." I open my arms, and Viktor closes the distance between us. "You're already an important figure in his life. I don't think some hugging will make a difference in his eyes."

His arms tighten around me, and I feel his warmth as he kisses the top of my head.

"I'll be right here no matter what decision you make for your mom. It can't hurt to hear her out one more time. She was excited at the coffee place. Not that it was an excuse, just an outside viewpoint."

"Gah. Why do you have to be so logical?"

"Because I'm older and wiser." He peers down the hall before leaning down and brushing his lips against mine.

"Only five years. And I'm happy to call you Daddy anytime you want me to."

Viktor suddenly steps back in a coughing fit, and I realize it's over my comment. I guess I shocked him.

Owen comes running into the room, concern lacing his face, and he pats Viktor's leg.

"You k, Vik? You k?"

My heart melts as Viktor picks up Owen and clears his throat after catching his breath.

"I'm good, buddy. I'm okay. Thank you for checking up on me."

"Arms up?" Owen raises his hands over his head like we tell him to do when he coughs. Viktor raises one arm and fakes another cough before wiping his hand across his forehead and presenting Owen with a relieved smile.

"You're the best. Thank you, little man. High five?" Owen smacks his tiny hand against Viktor's, which looks abnormally large in comparison.

I'm a puddle on the floor. How could I even question if he wants kids? He practically raised Owen with me. Short of a signature on a piece of paper and actually calling him Dad, Viktor is his father figure.

"But I never saw a life for my future that allowed me to have them...before you."

I need to explore that more with him, but right now, I'm sure there are hearts in my eyes watching the interaction between them. He's so fucking good with Owen.

"Are you okay, Pepper?"

"Yeah. I'm perfect."

31

Miller

"Cupcake! You look strange."

Katy looks down at her outfit—navy shorts, a yellow shirt with white polka dots, and tan sandals. "What's wrong with my outfit?"

"Mama pitty." Katy reaches down and strokes Owen's hair in his stroller.

Katy asked me to go out to lunch, and I was all too eager to have some one-on-one time with her. She walked up to meet me at the house, and since I'm driving and Axel is babysitting, she wheeled Owen with her.

"Yes she is bud, but she's missing her hemorrhoid."

"My what? Oh. Miller, don't be an ass."

Katy swipes at my arm when she realizes I'm referring to Vik. She asked if it could just be me and her, and of course, I can watch over her without a bodyguard following us, but with everything going on, we asked Patrick to join us since I have a feeling I know where this conversation will lead.

"Sorry. I had to. Did you bring an extra pair of shoes?"

241

Her sandals won't be appropriate for where we're going. She grabs the strap on her shoulder and shrugs, indicating they are in her bag. "Perfect. Axel is waiting inside with sugar and cartoons."

"Wonderful. It's like the hyper watching the hyper." She rolls her eyes, but I know she's just picking on him.

"Lincoln is here too. Spencer is visiting her dad with Tucker and you know Dempsey went with them. Let's get Owen inside and head out, or we'll be late. We have an appointment."

"Appointment? For what?"

I give her my most devilish grin. "You'll see."

We get Owen settled, and I grab the duffle bag from the front closet, hoping she doesn't recognize it. It contains everything we need for our outing. I send Tucker a text letting him know Katy and I are leaving the house so he can contact his friend Chip to let us in the gate when we get to our destination.

After the initial incident with Shane and a lengthy discussion with Spencer, we decided Katy needed proper gun training. Firearms play a healthy role in all of our lives. Tucker's property near Midnight Moonshine allots us a safe and private place to practice our skills, but more specifically, for Katy to learn since she's too young in the eyes of the law.

When she asked me to hang out, I could tell that something was on her mind. This sounded like the perfect way to blow off some steam, and it's been a while since anyone has taken her up here.

"Are we…?" Katy looks into the back seat where I put the bag and back at me. I see the smile grow on her face through my peripheral, and I can't help but match it. "It's been forever. This is perfect. Thank you!"

When we arrive, Chip's SUV is already at the gate waiting. Chip is Tucker's security guru. He is in charge of the systems at Midnight Moonshine, as well as the pool and main house. We see him fairly often, as Tucker has him maintain the systems monthly at the houses.

"Chip. Good to see you." We shake hands when we exit our vehicles. He dips his head and acknowledges Katy but doesn't say anything. Chip looks over our shoulders nervously at the vehicle that pulled up with us as Patrick steps out. He knew Patrick would be here as well. Does having a security detail put him on edge?

Chip is your average twenty-something kid with more brains than he knows what to do with. He looks like he should be selling insurance behind a desk with his dirty blond hair and brown eyes.

"Hi, Chip." Katy's bubbly greeting makes him blush, and he nods again and turns to the gate to unlock it. He peers at us over his shoulder a few times, his cheeks still pink. I have to ask Tucker about that. Does he have a crush? It's cute, but she's taken. I think.

"Okay, so the gate will lock automatically when you leave. You don't have to do anything special but close it. I'll get a notification when it's locked." He motions to a camera at the top of a light pole. "We've added extra security out here recently, so you'll see new poles like these."

"Awesome. Thanks, Chip. You ready, Cupcake?"

"Hell, yes! Bye Chip."

"Impressive. Have you been practicing without me?" Katy has always been a good shot. Some people are just naturals and once we found a few guns that she was comfortable handling, her skills improved even more.

"Other than Axel forcing me to play first-person shooter games with him, nope."

"Ugh, those games are made for people with high definition brains. I can't keep up with everything going on around the screen."

Katy chuckles as I hear the ping of her hitting another steel plate on the target tree.

"Okay, Cupcake. You didn't ask me to hang out for a random date. What's going on?"

Her shoulders slump, and she lowers the Glock to the table. "Can't I just want to hang out with you?"

I pull her into a hug. "Always. But that's not what this is about. Let's take a snack break and talk."

Katy heads toward the small structure that Tucker built out here for shade and relaxation while we practice. It's a three-sided building with chairs, ceiling fans, and a stone fireplace for when it's cold.

I grab the cooler from the bed of my truck and join Katy. She gives me a puzzled look as I pull out a foot-long sub, fruit, condiments, and chips.

"I thought you said a snack? This is a full blown meal."

"Tucker. Need I say more?" Katy laughs and shakes her head. When I asked Tucker about using the property with Katy, he had the cooler ready and waiting for me this morning. I'm honestly surprised he hasn't equipped this building with a full kitchen yet.

"Okay, missy, spill the beans."

"The what?"

"Oh, man. Am I that old? What's the latest lingo? Spill the beans, the tea, the skinny. I have no idea. Or, like Axel, I just want all the gossip. Tell me why we're here."

"Yeah, Miller. You're old."

I pick up a grape and toss it at her shoulder. "Brat."

Katy sticks her tongue out at me, picks up the grape from her lap, and pops it in her mouth. She looks off into the trees for a moment, then at Patrick's car next to my truck, where he's sitting guard.

"Am I a cliché?"

I take a bite of my Italian sub as I try to figure out what she means. "Explain what you're asking. I need more context."

"The damsel in distress falls for her bodyguard. The 'will they, won't they.' Forbidden love. I feel like I've read this trope a hundred times."

"Ah. So we're talking about you and Vik. Are things progressing there? You know he recently spoke to all of us, right?" I can tell she didn't know by the shock on her face.

"Um, about what?"

I have to look away as her cheeks pinken. What does she think he spoke to us about that's making her blush?

"He had a similar concern. He told us he was developing feelings for you and wanted to know if he should excuse himself as our employee in order to pursue things." Katy sits up in her seat, wanting to speak, but her mouth is full. "Don't get yourself in a tizzy. We wouldn't let him quit." She slumps back as she finishes chewing the food in her mouth.

"Okay, good. Thank you."

"I take it that means you feel the same way? Is that why we're here?"

Katy stares off into the woods, absentmindedly eating her food. She's deep in thought about her answer, and I appreciate it. She's never been a regular teenager, but at her age, it's so easy to let your emotions get the best of you when

245

it comes to a romantic relationship.

"I...I think I love him."

I choke on the strawberry that I'm chewing. I did not expect her to say that. I can't say I'm surprised to hear it, but now is not the time. I beat my chest with my fist as Katy reaches over and pats my back.

"Don't die on me, old man."

I shoot her an evil glance as I compose myself. Grabbing my water bottle, I take a big swig and think carefully about my next words.

"Tell me why. Why do you only *think*?"

"It's a feeling I don't quite understand. I think it's real, but how can I tell? Are the warm fuzzies I'm feeling because I basically live with Viktor and have spent practically every day together for over two years? Because he treats me amazing, but it's probably because I'm his job, and he's paid to? Do I have some kind of survivor's guilt PTSD because he was shot while protecting me? Or..."

I want to shut down all of her questions because none of them are true. We've all watched their relations blossom and grow in a purely natural way. Their feelings are real. But what is her or?

"Or what, Katy?"

"Or, do I really love Viktor?"

I let her question hang in the air. I can tell her all that I've observed, but I can't tell her how she truly feels. She has to realize that on her own.

"What's your reservation, Cupcake?" I reach into the cooler and grab my secret weapon. Tucker knows Katy so well and must have been as suspicious of her wanting to meet up as I was. "Capri sun?" Her eyes light up as she snatches it from my hand.

"It's still slushy. Yes!" Her shoulders do a little shimmy happy dance as she expertly stabs the straw into the drink.

"Always a kid at heart."

With the straw in her mouth, she pauses and looks at me. Slowly, she lowers the pouch to her lap.

"That's the problem, though, isn't it? I was sixteen and pregnant when I met Viktor. He carted me to the bookstore and library so I could finish high school. Hell, he *still* won't even let me drive myself anywhere. Could he really think of me as anything but a job?"

"Katy, from what I've heard, you've been engaging in adult activities with Vik already. I hope to fucking god he thinks of you as more than just a job or a kid. Otherwise, I'm going to have to have a completely different conversation with him."

It's my turn to dodge a grape that bounces off my shoulder and rolls to the grass.

"You know too much, Miller."

"I know enough to know you're happy. So I ask again, what are your reservations?"

Her shoulders fall, and she sighs.

"Am I worthy of someone else's love? I know you five crazies love me, but that's familial. You're my family. I think even my mother loves me in some small, warped way. But Viktor has no obligation. Am I enough for someone to love me for...me?"

She's been so happy since we rescued her from her neglectful mother. Sometimes, I forget that she had a completely different life three years ago. Katy is such a strong woman and mother.

I reach over and take her hand. "Look at me, Katy." When

she looks up, her eyes glisten with unshed tears. "Hey, none of that."

She wipes at her eyes and inhales a stuttered breath. "Sorry."

"None of that either. There's no need for tears or apologies. Vik is still with you because he wants to be, both for his job and for you. Shane is still somewhere out there and of course we will always have yours and Owen's safety as our number one priority. But Katy, your feelings are valid but aren't warranted. If I've learned anything from watching each of us fall head over heels for Spencer, I can tell you this. Vik is a love-sick puppy, and you deserve every ounce of love and affection he gives you. *You* are enough in every way for that man. You're incredible and strong. A phenomenal mother and daughter." Her lip tilts at the word daughter. She loves when we call her ours. "If I, or any of us, had any doubt that Vik wasn't a good man for you, we would have had him replaced when we saw his feelings start to change."

Katy shakes her head and scrunches her brows, not understanding what I mean.

"What-I don't understand. What do you mean you *saw* his feelings change?"

"Vik isn't as hardened as he might seem. At least not when it comes to you. Tucker noticed at the hospital when he came out of surgery after Shane's attack. The first thing he said was, 'Is she okay?' He didn't care about himself, only you."

"But I was still a kid?"

32

Katy

This conversation is going in a completely different direction than I initially planned. I thought I would talk to Miller about my personal feelings, but hearing about their observations of Viktor falling for me sheds an entirely new light on things.

I probably wouldn't have thought anything out of the ordinary, knowing Viktor asked about me after surgery. My protection was part of his job, and he felt like he failed because Shane got to me. But Miller said Tucker felt it was more. Was it?

"Which is why we've been keeping a close eye on things. Owen was his turning point."

"Owen? What do you mean?"

"Vik was there for you when we couldn't be."

On the day of Owen's birth, there was a structure fire in town at an apartment building just after midnight. Everyone was on nights, including Lincoln, who was filling in for a dispatching shift. I had no idea I was having contractions until my water broke, and everything happened so quickly. No one was answering their phones while Viktor was rushing me to the hospital. I still had three weeks to go and was completely fine when everyone left for work that evening.

When we finally made it to the hospital and were able to contact Axel, he couldn't leave the ED. They were swamped with injuries from the fire, which explained why everyone else wasn't answering. We didn't know about the fire until he told us.

Tucker wasn't answering his phone because he had broken up a fight earlier in the night at Midnight Moonshine, and his phone had gotten shattered in the process. It was a crazy series of events that led to Owen's birth just being Viktor and me.

But I never felt alone. I knew Viktor was there, and I knew as soon as everyone else could, they'd be there for me.

He held my hand. He whispered words of encouragement when I thought I couldn't push any longer. And despite the staff knowing that Viktor was only there for moral support, when the doctor asked if he wanted to cut the cord, I said yes before he had a chance to protest. Viktor had been there for me my entire pregnancy, and having him be a part of the birth felt right.

"He looked at you differently after that. There was more affection in his eyes. There was love in his eyes for Owen and adoration for you. Vik is an honorable man. His feelings for you are real. I have no doubt, and I hope you don't either. Do you think he loves you?"

I do, and that's the scary part.

"Yeah. I think he does."

"Well, Cupcake. Does that answer whatever questions you

needed answered today?"

"Shit, I think it does."

Miller reaches over and tugs at one of my French braids. "I love when you wear your hair like Spencer. She does, too."

I fucking hate cramps. No one tells you after you have kids that they can get worse. My periods were always normal before I got pregnant. I love my little vagina trophy, but damn, did he do a number on my body.

I hoped that drinking some tea and reading a book would help calm my uterus, but she seems to be protesting violently tonight.

"Hey Pepper, Tucker needs to see me at the big house. Will you be okay for a bit, or do you want me to send Patrick over?"

"I'll be okay. I'm heading to bed anyway."

"If you're sure? I'm just a phone call away." I nod, and Viktor kisses my forehead. The alarm chimes as he sets it before he leaves, and the lock clicks behind him.

Owen's asleep, the house is locked up, and I'll deal with my mug in the morning. I'll use my heating pad to hopefully calm my cramps before I try to get some sleep.

As I slip into bed, I open the bottom drawer of my night-stand to grab the heating pad. Sitting next to it in the drawer is my bright pink vibrator. I haven't had a need to use it in a while, but the memory of an article I once read saying orgasms help with cramps flashes through my mind. At this point, I'm willing to try anything.

I peek at the baby monitor and see Owen is still sound

asleep. I'm sure if Tucker wanted to personally see Viktor, then it's more than just a phone call conversation, and he'll probably be gone for a little while.

Why the hell not?

Pulling the vibrator out of the drawer, I settle myself on my back and relax my legs. I know it's fully charged because it was still plugged in through the hole in the back of the drawer. That was the best tip Blake ever shared with me, and Axel giggled the entire time he drilled it because he knew exactly what it was for but didn't question it.

There are a few different vibrators in the drawer, but this one is my favorite because it's simple and basic. When I want a quick orgasm, this is my go-to. It's a little bigger than a bullet, and instead of the tip being completely rounded, half is flat.

My breasts are sensitive because of my period, and I don't really feel like cleaning up a mess, so I go right to the source. The initial shock of the vibrations always makes me gasp, but it must be extra powerful because it's fully charged. My stomach muscles constrict as my body gets used to the sensation. I slowly rub the vibrator up and down over my clit and feel my body relax as it does its job. My triangle piercing makes everything feel more intense.

As my body begins to heat with my impending orgasm, I turn the speed up and gently graze my nipples for the extra stimulation. I try to stay quiet despite Owen being on the other side of the house. When my orgasm finally crashes into me, it's hard, and every part of my body tingles.

"Fuck, fuck, fuuuuck," I hiss through gritted teeth.

I'm panting by the time I pull the vibrator out of my shorts and flop my arm on the bed. My eyes are closed, but the room around me spins.

So strange. It almost feels like I've been drinking. I roll over to put my toy back in the drawer; I'll take care of cleaning that tomorrow. My cramps have settled, but my tongue sticks to the roof of my mouth from all the panting. I need water.

As I sit up and place my feet on the floor, the room spins faster. I brace my hands on my knees so I don't fall over and take several breaths.

What the hell? Am I suddenly coming down with something?

I manage to stand, but as I'm walking to the bathroom, my body keeps tipping left. The counter holds me up when I finally make it to the sink and drink down some water. My mouth is no longer dry, but now it's filled with extra saliva, and my stomach turns.

First, I'm dizzy, and now I feel like I'm going to throw up. What the hell is going on?

I stand in the bathroom, hoping the nausea and dizziness goes away soon. I left my phone in the bedroom, so I can't call Viktor. What could this be?

The tea? No, I drink it all the time.

My period? I've never had anything like this before.

What did I do differently?

The masturbating? Did I orgasm myself into this?

Fuck.

I slowly walk back to the bedroom and grab my phone. Opening the search bar, I type, *"Why am I dizzy after an orgasm?"*

Okay. It appears it's not uncommon. Causes could be: lack of oxygen from rapid breathing, increased blood pressure, elevated heart rate. All of those can cause vertigo. The nausea is also a symptom of the dizziness.

The internet recommends hydration, rest, and eating a banana. I already hydrated. I have bananas in the kitchen. I cautiously stand. It's been several minutes but the room still spins around me. Was it because my vibrator was fully charged? This is wild.

I'm making my way toward the kitchen, stumbling as I go, when I hear the door unlock. Viktor resets the alarm before he sees me frozen in the living room.

"Pepper. I thought you were going to bed?"

I can't stand still any longer. It feels like the floor is trying to topple me over, and that's what I almost do, but I manage to stop myself from falling by gripping the arm of the couch.

Viktor is at my side before I even see him move.

"Katy, what's wrong?" He's holding me up, but my body still sways in his arms.

"Need to sit."

"What's wrong? Talk to me. What happened?" He sweeps me up in his arms bridal-style, which only heightens the dizziness.

"Sit. Please sit." The nausea is coming back from all the sudden movement.

Viktor listens and sits on the couch, holding me tightly in his arms. His eyes are darting all over the room, looking for danger or the cause of my outward symptoms.

"Dizzy."

"You're dizzy?"

I nod into his chest, and his body relaxes a fraction. I don't know if it's better or worse with my eyes closed, but I feel exhausted, and it's hard to keep them open.

"Katy. I need you to talk to me, Pepper. You're worrying

me."

I'm trying to take deep, steady breaths, which is making it hard to talk. The breathing is helping my body regulate.

"Cramps."

"You have cramps? Are you on your period?"

"Yes. I...used my vibrator. Orgasm...was hard. Dizzy. Nauseous." I begin to giggle because saying the words out loud sounds absolutely ridiculous.

"Katy, I'm confused."

"I masturbated myself into a vertigo spell." My little giggle turns into a full-blown laugh, and I can tell Viktor is still confused.

"Pepper?"

I take several calming breaths, my laughter subsiding, and my dizziness seems to be leaving with it.

"I'm sorry, Viktor. Okay, so...I was having cramps, and I read once that an orgasm can help make them go away. I figured, why the hell not? But somehow, I orgasmed so hard I gave myself vertigo. You found me stumbling my way to the kitchen because the internet said a banana could help."

Viktor glances at the island where a bowl of fruit sits. He stands with me in his arms and brings us to the bowl, motioning with his chin for me to take a banana. I grab it, and we turn back to the bedroom. Viktor stops at the side of the bed and toes off his shoes. He carefully climbs onto the bed and sits against the beadboard, positioning me between his legs so my back rests on his chest.

"Eat."

"Viktor?"

"I need a moment. Eat, Pepper."

There's an edge to his voice, and it worries me. I open

the banana and eat it. I already feel better. The spell only lasted about ten minutes, but I've never had anything like that happen to me before. Viktor gently massages my shoulder while I eat, and I allow him time to process.

"So you're okay? How are you feeling now?"

I place the banana peel on the nightstand and turn to face him.

"I'm completely fine. It was a weird fluke. I didn't mean to worry you."

"I'm man enough to admit you fucking scared me, Pepper. I left you here alone, and when I saw you stumble, I just…"

I see the fear flash in his eyes, and I feel guilty that I put that feeling there.

"I promise I'm alright." I crawl into his lap and straddle his thighs. Bringing his hands to my hips, I squeeze them around me. "I'm all good."

Viktor's hands move to the front of my body and cup my abdomen. "Do you still have cramps? Do you need more help?"

I watch as the fear in his eyes turns to lust. His thumbs brush across my pubic bones, and my body lights up.

"I-I'm good right now." Viktor's lips trail along the bottom of my jaw, and I tilt my neck to give him better access. "I think I have PTSD for the moment."

"Okay."

He removes his lips, and I want to tell him to continue, but I won't. My body may be telling me I want this, but my mind knows I can't handle it right now.

Viktor reaches up and grabs my chin. "Next time you need an orgasm, you come to me. Got it?"

"But I'm on my period?"

"Pepper, I was man enough to admit I was scared, and I'm man enough to tell you I don't give a fuck about your period."

"But—"

"I. Don't. Give. A. Fuck. And if I thought you could handle it, I'd show you right now, but you need to rest."

He kisses my forehead and lifts me from his lap. I watch as he stands and strips down to his boxers. My eyes linger on his bulge, only a few feet in front of me.

"Put your tongue back in your mouth and move over. It's time to sleep."

I huff and reluctantly roll as he crawls in behind me and cocoons me.

33

Dempsey

She's fine. She'll be fine. I'm less than a football field away.

I hate leaving Katy alone in the pool house, and when I pass by Patrick, I ask him to keep an eye on the house. I get my usual grunted response.

Katy is locked and alarmed in. We are close enough to the house that even if something happens, we are right here.

I knock on the back door and walk in. Tucker and Lincoln are waiting for me at the kitchen table.

"Tucker. Lincoln."

Tucker nods and gestures to a seat. As I sit, I notice pictures on the table. I don't even have to look to know what they are.

"When are we going to be done with this fucker?" I roll my shoulders, trying to loosen the instant tension.

"These are different. Look." Tucker spreads them out further. Unlike older pictures, which were random locations and different people from our households, every picture is of Katy and Owen. Every. Picture. He followed her to work, to the park, and to the mall when we bought him new shoes. Patrick and I are both in multiple of the shots because Katy is never alone.

I spread them out further and can map every place Katy and Owen have been for at least the last two weeks.

"How the fuck is he following us so closely. If he's watching her, how have we not seen his vehicle." My frustration is boiling.

"That's what we're trying to figure out. Have you noticed anything out of the ordinary?"

I currently notice that Lincoln is being suspiciously quiet during all of this.

"Lincoln. What's wrong?" He looks up at me as if I broke him from a trance.

"Sorry, Dempsey. I'm trying to see what links all of these photos together. We've checked your car multiple times for trackers. Does Katy have a new purse? Maybe we should check the diaper bag. Did it get left in the open anywhere?"

"Now that Owen is mostly potty trained, she doesn't carry a diaper bag. She has a small backpack that she wears when we're out. If she needs to take it off, I carry it."

Tucker huffs, as lost in this situation as the rest of us.

"Anything from Montgomery?" Tucker's private investigator has been working on this case for a while and, like us, is hitting dead ends.

"He thinks Shane isn't working alone. We discovered he was a computer nerd in high school, so getting into the basic cameras that Eddie installed would have been easy enough. To our knowledge, he hasn't been able to get into Chips set up."

"Dempsey," Lincoln starts. "I know I don't need to tell you

this, but Katy and Owen are our world, and I have a feeling you feel the same."

"Without a doubt."

"I have two questions. As her bodyguard, how do we keep them protected?"

"Ideally, locked in a bubble until this asshole is found, and he can't hurt or scare either of them anymore." Wouldn't that be wonderful? "Practically, I don't know how we can do more than we're already doing without alerting the neighbors. Patrick already gets suspicious glances. Katy's preschool has been accommodating of us both being there, but any more muscle around, and there would be no point in leaving the house."

"My thoughts exactly. Now, my second question. As her lover, how can we keep them safe?"

My head shoots up from the pictures. I've spoken to them about my relationship with Katy, and I know she's spoken to them as well, but hearing Lincoln acknowledge there's something going on between us catches me off guard.

"Do you love her, Dempsey?" I'm getting whiplash as my head snaps toward Tucker's question.

"Do I get to keep my balls if I tell you yes?"

"As long as you continue to treat her the same way you have been for the last two years."

"Two—"

"Don't play me for a fool. I know your eyes have been only for Katy, and I respect that you waited until she was ready—most days. I'd be a shit father if I didn't worry about my daughter with *any* man. I know you'll do right by her. But what can we do now?"

"I should probably start by getting back to the pool house.

Patrick is keeping an eye out, but she's alone, and I hate it."

Tucker stands, and Lincoln follows. I take it as my permission to leave and stand to shake hands.

"We're going to get this fucker so Katy and Owen can have peace. I promise you both. I've taken a bullet for her once, and I'd do it a hundred times over if that's what it takes."

"I know you will." Tucker tightens his hand and leans in to slap my back. "Just don't ever try to call me Dad."

A laugh bursts from my chest without permission. The hilarity of the situation is Tucker is almost old enough to be my dad.

"Never, Sir."

As I step out the back door, I see all the lights are off in the pool house. I nod at Patrick, who acknowledges me and turns his attention back to the main house.

Tucker approves of me being with Katy. I told them I loved her. It wasn't a lie, but shouldn't I have told her first? Our relationship has shifted, and I think she feels it, too.

Quietly, I unlock the door and reset the system. I hope Katy's sleeping. She looked tired. When I step into the living room, Katy stands frozen, staring at me.

"Pepper. I thought you were going to bed?"

Katy's face falls, and she sways, almost falling into the couch. I'm across the room in four steps and take her in my arms.

"Katy, what's wrong?" Her body feels like jello in my arms.

"Need to sit."

"What's wrong? Talk to me? What happened?" I sweep her up as I scan every inch of her body that I can see. Why did I leave her alone? Something happened while I wasn't here.

"Sit. Please sit."

Sit? I can't sit. Where's the danger? What the fuck

happened?

I can feel her body swaying despite being in my arms, so I do as she asks and sit us on the couch. I don't like being vulnerable, but I don't see any sign of danger.

"Dizzy."

Okay, she's dizzy. What caused her to be dizzy? I know I'm carrying on a conversation with her, but my body is on autopilot. My eyes assess the situation, my mouth moves to ask and answer questions, but my mind feels like a hamster running on a wheel.

"I masturbated myself into a vertigo spell."

"Pepper?" She's giggling. No, she's laughing. How is any of this funny? Fuck my heart is full steam ahead like a runaway train.

Vertigo.

A dizzy spell.

No danger.

No. Fucking. Danger.

"...read once that an orgasm can help make them go away... the internet said a banana could help."

I glance into the kitchen and see the fruit bowl. Bananas. Standing, I bring us to the counter and motion for her to take one. When she securely has a banana in her hand, I bring us into the bedroom. I take off my shoes and sit against the headboard, adjusting Katy in my lap.

She's here and she's okay.

"Eat."

"Viktor?"

"I need a moment. Eat, Pepper." I need more than a fucking moment. Flashes of her panicked face as I bled out in front of her swept through my mind when I saw her stumble. I thought Shane had gotten to her. I haven't even told her how I feel yet, and I thought I had already missed the opportunity. This isn't the moment to confess my feelings, but soon. Really fucking soon.

"So you're okay? How are you feeling now?" Katy puts the banana peel down and turns to look into my eyes.

"I'm completely fine. It was a weird fluke. I didn't mean to worry you."

"I'm man enough to admit you fucking scared me, Pepper. I left you here alone, and when I saw you stumble, I just..." I just thought I failed you again, and I can't do that. I'll never fail you again. Please know that, without me having to say the words out loud. That day in the car is my biggest regret, and I'll spend my entire life and yours making up for every ounce of pain you felt, every second you were scared, and every drop of blood that I spilled. I'll never forget that day. That was the day I fell in love with you.

"I promise I'm alright. I'm all good." She straddles my lap and places my hands on her hips. She's here. Flesh and bone under my hands.

She had cramps from her period.

I move my hands to the front of her body. "Do you still have cramps? Do you need more help?" I need to feel more of her. Leaning forward, I brush my lips against her jaw. She tilts her head to allow me better access.

"I-I'm good right now. I think I have PTSD for the moment."

"Okay. Next time you need an orgasm, you come to me. Got it?"

Her eyes widen in shock. "But I'm on my period?"

"Pepper, I was man enough to admit I was scared, and I'm man enough to tell you I don't give a fuck about your period."

"But—"

"I. Don't. Give. A. Fuck. And if I thought you could handle it, I'd show you right now, but you need to rest."

I kiss her forehead and stand to strip down to my boxers. I can't help but notice her lingering eyes on my bulge, but not tonight.

"Put your tongue back in your mouth and move over. It's time to sleep."

I crawl in behind her and wrap her into me. I place my hand above her pubic bone and hear her hum from the warmth. I'll protect this woman from anything, even if it's her own body.

"Viktor...Viktor, wake up...Oh my god, please wake up...Open your eyes."

I open my eyes just in time to get an elbow to my gut. Katy is flailing around, and every nerve in my body lights up with adrenaline. A quick search around the room shows we're still alone, and the yelling and flailing is a dream. She's dreaming about me and not in a good way.

I trail a gentle hand along her arm and quietly say her name. She never comes out of her nightmares the same way. Sometimes, it's as simple as a gentle touch. Other times, I've had to yell and shake her.

"Pepper, wake up."

I quickly lean back as she jolts up in bed. "V-Viktor." Her head whips around the room as she becomes aware of her surroundings. "Oh, thank fuck. Viktor, you're okay."

Katy climbs into my lap and begins assaulting me with aggressive kisses. It takes me a moment to respond to her quick movement. When I do, I hungrily take her all in. Her body is sweaty, and I can feel her heart racing.

She leans back, and I kiss her neck and shoulders as she pants, still catching her breath from her dream.

"Need…you."

Her arms cross and she reaches for the hem of her tank top, pulling it off.

"Katy, I think—"

"Night time. My time. I need you."

"Okay. Okay, I got you, Pepper. I grab her breasts as she rocks on my rapidly hardening cock. I bring her to my mouth and suck on her perfect nipples. The sweetness of her milk mixed with the salt from her sweat almost turns me feral.

"Let's go. Shower." I wrap my arms around her thighs and stand with her. We stroll into the bathroom, stumbling through kisses and touches. I turn the shower on, and with a whine from Katy that makes me chuckle, I place her feet on the floor.

She stares as I crouch in front of her, and she pulls my hair tie out to run her fingers through my now messy hair. My thumbs dip into her sleep shorts, and I pull them down her legs along with her plain black underwear. I should have known she had her period. It's the only time she wears these.

"Oh shit. Viktor, no. My period." It seems she's just come up from her sleep and lust fog to realize what we're doing.

"I don't think so, Pepper. You told me you needed me, and that's what you're getting. All of me, no matter what."

I slide my hand from her ankle, up her calf to her knee. I lift her leg and set it on the edge of the toilet seat. She wobbles to catch her balance and grabs my shoulders.

"W-what are you doing?"

265

Sliding my hand up her inner thigh, I capture her eyes. I want her to see I have no hesitation with my actions. "Removing your tampon."

Her face immediately turns red. She's embarrassed, and I won't allow her to be.

"Pepper, you always have a safeword, but I promise I'd never do anything I'm not comfortable with.

34

Katy

He's going to take my tampon out. Someone other than me is going to take the tampon out of my body. It's okay.

You're fine.

You trust this man.

"I trust you."

Viktor continues to caress my inner thigh, slowly trailing his fingers higher and higher. His thumb brushes across my piercings, teasing my clit, and it already feels like fireworks exploding through my body.

"Fuck."

"You're overly sensitive because of your period. Everything is going to be heightened."

Viktor's other hand moves between my legs, and I feel the slight pressure as he grabs the string between his fingers.

"Deep breath, Pepper, then exhale."

As I breathe out, I feel the familiar yet foreign sensation of the tampon being removed. I tip my head back and stare at the ceiling, willing my embarrassment to go away. I hear Viktor moving around under me. It sounds like he's wrapping the tampon in toilet paper, and I hear the rustling when he drops it in the trash.

"It's done. You can look now." His finger brushes over my clit again, and I squeeze his shoulders as I inhale a stuttered breath.

"I'm good."

I hear him chuckle as he stands. Viktor grabs my chin to lower my face, and I close my eyes.

"You're going to have to look at me at some point. Don't be embarrassed."

"Ugh. But I am. Don't laugh at me, you big Viking." I flail my hand and smack his chest. He grabs my wrist and holds it over his heart.

"Katy. Look at me."

With reluctance, I open my eyes, and sincere silver-blue eyes stare back at me. He opens his mouth to speak, and I cover it with my hand.

"I-I'm not ready. I know, but I'm not ready. I know and...I do, too, but not yet."

He nods in understanding, and a half smile creeps up his face. "Okay, Pepper. I'm ready whenever you are. I've been ready, and nothing is going to change it. Let's get in the shower so I can show you how ready I am."

He boops my nose and turns to check the temperature of the shower before removing his boxers and stepping in. A hand extends for me to join him, and I take it, stepping into the steamy water.

Viktor's body surrounds me as my back is pushed against the cool tile, and his lips suck on my neck. I don't have time to respond before he hoists me into his arms, and I feel his cock rubbing against my swollen pussy.

"Fuck, Viktor."

"That's the plan. Will you let me fuck you, Pepper? I want to take you right here. I want to take away whatever bad images were just in your dreams. I'm here, and I want to prove it to you." He takes my hand and places it over his scar. "I'm here because you saved me. Let me save you this time."

His words are poetry to my soul. "I'm yours." *In more ways than one.*

With a quick dip of his hips, he lines himself up perfectly and glides inside me. I try not to think about the fact that my blood is probably providing the lubrication to allow him easy access, but if he doesn't care, then neither will I.

Every nerve in my body is on fire. I never knew period sex could feel like this. It's so carnal yet sensual. Viktor's groans of pleasure even sound different.

"Tell me about your dream, Pepper."

"W-why?"

"I said I want to erase it. I need to know what I'm taking away."

I don't want to relive the horrible memories. Once was enough, but the memories still haunt me at night.

"It was about you. Fuck, right there, Viktor." My head falls forward onto his shoulder, and his mouth trails kisses over my shoulder and neck.

"Tell me."

"You-you were lifeless in front of me...They were doing CPR, and I felt so...so helpless."

"I'm." *Thrust.* "Right." *Thrust.* "Here." *Thrust.*

"You are. God, you are."

He leans down and squeezes a breast, bringing it to his mouth. He hums his approval as I feel my milk let down. Fisting his hair, I hold him to me. The hot water sloshes around us as he pushes the bad memories from my mind.

"You're not helpless," he mumbles around my nipple.

"I was. I couldn't do anything but watch and cry and hope."

"You saved me. Fuck. You fucking saved me." He's relentlessly pounding into me. I can feel his emotions in every thrust of his hips. "You were all I thought about. Seeing the fear in your eyes before I blacked out kept me alive. Every conscious and unconscious thought I had was of you. I couldn't die. I wouldn't. I never wanted to see that look on your face again."

"Fuck, Viktor!" My cry is one of pleasure and pain. His words are tearing me in two, and his cock is hitting my sweet spot over and over.

"Are you going to come for me, Miss Katy?"

"Fuck yes. Oh fuck, fuck yes." I lock my ankles behind his back to pull him as close as possible.

"Come for me like a good girl. I want our come to mix with your blood. Mark me as yours. Make me your fucking dirty boy."

I can't hold it. Viktor's filthy words fizzle my brain, and I explode hard around his cock. The orgasm is so intense it takes my breath away. I'm flying. Floating. Fucking soaring.

"Fuck, Pepper. Fuck. I...I. Fuck! I won't fucking say it but goddammit, so much. So fucking much." He slams into me one last time before I feel his orgasm jerk inside me. I capture his lips and convey his sentiment.

"So fucking much, my Viking."

When our breathing has settled, Viktor gently pulls out

and sets my feet on the floor.

"Fucking exquisite." He stares down at his softening cock streaked with blood and come. With reverence, he strokes his hand up and down his shaft, smearing it in before it washes away in the water.

As if snapping out of a spell, his hand shifts to my lower abdomen. "How are you feeling? Any cramps?"

I stare into his eyes, shake my head, and he smirks.

"Good. Let's get washed up and back to bed."

I rest my head on his chest and close my eyes. "Thank you for scaring the demons away and sharing yourself with me."

He tips my chin up and gently brushes my lips. "I'll always scare your demons away, real or imaginary." Viktor kisses my temple, and I know he means every word. Even the half-spoken I love you.

I can't explain why I'm not ready to hear it. I feel it. I know he feels it. We just said it without the "L" word itself.

Maybe I'm scared. Maybe I'm waiting for the other shoe to drop because this can't be real. It's too good, and even after close to three years, I still have trouble believing this reality.

But I need to. I'm not scared, neglected Katy North anymore. I'm Katy Coble, Spencer Coble's daughter. The daughter of a strong, confident, kick-ass woman who deserves every good thing and man in her life. That's exactly what I deserve...and what I have.

I need to stop running from my past and lean into the future that's right in front of me. A future that includes this beautiful man and the adorable almost two-year-old in the other room.

✧ ✦ ✧ ✦ ✧

"I'm going to do it." Maybe if I say it out loud, I'll have more confidence.

"Do what, Pepper?" Viktor looks up from his phone at the kitchen counter as I cut bananas for Owen's breakfast.

"More nanas, Mama." Owen signs more with his hands, and I mimic the movement back to him.

"Good job. More bananas for Owen."

I'm going to do it. I think.

"See my mother again. I think I'm going to give her one more chance. I want her to meet Owen in a controlled setting. I don't ever want to have regrets or feel like I was selfish and never gave her a chance."

"You don't owe her anything, but I understand your reasoning, and I'll respect and be there for you, whatever you decide."

"Owen has a tumble play class at the gym tomorrow. I thought I might invite her if you wouldn't mind doing it with him. Then I could sit and chat with her, and she could watch him play. It's only an hour, so there's a time limit to my interactions with her, and I can decide at the end if I want them to meet. What do you think?"

"Mama, boo-boo."

"What? *Shit.*" Without realizing it, I accidentally cut my finger with the knife. Turning toward the sink, Viktor is at my side before I take a step.

"Let me see."

"It's okay, Viktor. It's just a little nick."

He takes my hand, turns on the cold water, and runs my finger under it. The water runs pink, and I feel the heat radiate off his body as it's pressed against mine.

"Naughty, naughty Pepper. Get your mind out of the

gutter." A shiver takes over my body as his whispered breath grazes my ear.

I peer at him over my shoulder and smirk. "You wouldn't know what I was thinking if you weren't thinking the same thing."

"Touché. I think you're right. You just nicked yourself. I'll get you a bandaid." He hands me a paper towel and heads to the bathroom.

"Mama boo-boo K?"

"Yeah, little man. Mama's okay. Viktor is gonna give me a bandaid and make it all better." Owen gives me a toothy smile, and I'm so grateful he looks exactly like me. One of my fears that I silently struggled with during my pregnancy was how I would feel if he didn't look like me. If he looked like my rapist. The moment he was put on my chest, that fear went away. Even if he hadn't looked like me, Owen is mine and only mine. I would love him no matter how he came about.

I get an idea and quickly step over to my purse hanging in the foyer. Digging through, I grab what I need and return to the kitchen.

"Your choices are trucks or neon green. Which would you prefer?" Viktor's voice comes from down the hall, waiting for my answer.

"Surprise me."

A moment later, he appears with a neon green bandaid in his hand and a smile on his handsome face. I extend my hand, and Viktor gently covers my wound. I pull my other hand out from behind my back and place a star sticker on each of Viktor's cheeks. He huffs and looks down at me with dominance in his eyes.

"I told you the last time you were going to get it for putting a sticker on my forehead. What are these for?"

"One is for last night, and one is for right now."

He opens his mouth to protest, and Owen claps and squeals. "Yay Vik Vik. Poo-poo potty. Yay!"

My hands fly to my mouth to cover my laugh. Fire burns in Viktor's eyes before he turns his attention to Owen.

"That's right, big guy. I got two stickers because I did a good job in the bathroom." He glances at me, and my face flames. He *did* do an excellent job last night in the bathroom. "Finish your bananas so we aren't late for school."

Viktor turns his back to Owen and steps into me. "Your time is coming, Pepper. Just you wait."

35

Katy

I'm distracted at work, which is never good when you're dealing with a bunch of toddlers and glitter. My mind keeps wandering to the shower sex Viktor and I had this morning. I can't seem to connect how his body could be so rough, but his words simultaneously tender.

We're just getting the kids settled for a snack when I hear a commotion in the hallway. I try to ignore it so the kids don't notice and turn on some music, but when I hear Viktor's voice rise, I get nervous. Callie, my lead teacher, and I exchange a look, and I raise the volume on the radio.

I tentatively walk to the door and try to peer out the small rectangular window, but it's blocked by a body.

A firm "No" comes from Viktor, and I hear the muffled sounds of my director speaking back to him, but I can't understand what she's saying.

I turn the knob and crack the door open a few inches before Viktor spins, and I see a look I haven't seen on his face since…

"Close the door and stay inside." I'm startled, frozen by the authority in his voice and the memory of a similar situation the night I rolled down the window in the rain.

"Oh, Katy. There's someone here—" Viktor quickly cuts my director off in her attempt to speak with me directly.

"I said no, Miss Holly. Call the police."

Police?

"Viktor, what's—"

"There's a man here claiming to be Owen's father and…" I know Holly is still saying words, but I hear nothing. My eyes flash to Owen's classroom, where Patrick stands firmly in front of his door. I see his fingers twitching, and I know it's because Miss Holly doesn't allow them to bring their guns into the building. Bodyguards she tolerates, firearms around children she won't. Ordinarily, I'd agree with her, but right now, I wish I had one of my own.

"Is he…He can't be right?" I'm keeping my panic in as best I can so I don't scare any of the children behind me.

"I don't know, and I don't care to find out. I'm not moving, and neither is Patrick. Whoever it is isn't on his pick-up sheet. Miss Holly already confirmed that, so she won't be letting him in the building."

"Miss Katy, he says he's Owen's father. Do you want to come speak with him?"

My body trembles with fear and adrenaline. My eyes dart between Holly and Viktor. Holly knows my story, and I can't understand why she would even entertain the idea that I would want to speak to a random man who claims to be Owen's father.

"I said call the fucking police. He's trespassing on private property."

"Mr. Dempsey, I will warn you only once to watch your mouth. This is a preschool full of children." She may be chastising him, but there's no conviction behind her voice. She's afraid of Viktor.

"Exactly. There are children here and you're acting like you're going to allow a strange man into this facility when I've told you to call. The. Police."

Holly looks frazzled. She's attempting to keep her composure but failing. She keeps running her hands down the front of her pink blouse, and her hair is askew because she's continuously pushing her glasses further on top of her graying hair.

Conversations stop when the bell, indicating the front door has been opened, pierces the tension-filled air.

Did he leave? Was it actually Shane?

"I hope so. If he knows what's good for him, he left. I don't know who else it would have been."

I guess I spoke out loud because Viktor answers both of my apparent non internal thoughts.

"Patrick, grab Owen. We're leaving."

"Viktor, I can't leave. There's still another hour of school left."

Now that the threat is gone, he pushes the door open. His large hands grip my cheeks, and I can see the desperation in his eyes.

"Katy, yours and Owen's safety have been compromised. We need to get you both home. Please don't argue. Miss Holly can take over for the last hour. It's the least she can do after almost putting you both in danger."

Dempsey glares at her and Holly scoffs. "I did no such thing."

"Katy, grab your bag, please."

I nod, and he releases my cheeks. He turns his body to face

Holly, and as he's about to speak, Owen excitedly yells his name from down the hall. Viktor's face immediately changes when he sees my son. All the anger leaves his body in a rush, and when Owen crashes into his legs, he scoops him up and gives him a big hug.

My heart threatens to swell out of my chest. Patrick and Viktor share a quiet exchange, and Patrick leaves with my car keys in his hand. I say goodbye to the kids in my class and join Viktor and Owen at my classroom door.

"Goodbye, Holly. I'm not sure if Katy will be back the rest of the week, or ever. We'll let you know." Despite Viktor's softer features while holding Owen, his comments to Miss Holly hold his distaste.

I want to argue about returning to work, but there's no point, at least right now. He's in bodyguard mode, and saying yes is the only word he will hear.

I leave the classroom, and Holly walks in as we head toward the lobby. Two locked doors separate us from the outside world. Suddenly, I feel frozen.

"Are we sure he's gone?"

"Patrick went to check, and he's bringing your car to the front for us. We're taking every precaution."

"Bun-bun!" Owen shrieks.

I look into his sweet face and see him staring down the hall. Patrick must have forgotten to grab his bunny.

"I'll get him for you." Viktor nods, and I feel his eyes watching me as I retrieve his comfort toy. I apologize to Owen's teacher for the interruption and quickly return to Owen and Viktor at the door.

My car sits in front of the door, but we aren't moving.

"What's wrong?"

"Nothing. Patrick brought your car to the front. Now we wait for him to get his, and we'll leave."

This feels like so much dancing around just to exit the building, but I know Viktor and Patrick are the best of the best and know what they are doing.

Shane was here. How? I know he's been following us, but how could he be so bold as to show up at my job, Owen's school? If he's really watching us this closely, wouldn't he know that we have bodyguards? He knows about Viktor.

My phone jingles in my back pocket, but as I reach for it, Patrick pulls up, and it's time to go. Viktor takes my hand as he pushes through the first set of doors. Patrick waits with a gun in hand on the outside of the second. This all feels so surreal.

"Bang bang!"

I freeze, my body instantly trembling. I hear Viktor mumble something and a grunt from Patrick before my body is wrapped in warmth.

"Katy, look at me."

I can't physically make my body move. I'm trying. It feels like the world is crashing around me.

"Breathe, Katy. Deep breaths, or you're going to hyperventilate. You're safe. It was Owen."

"Owen?" My baby's name snaps me out of my spiral. "Is Owen safe?"

"He's perfectly safe with Patrick. Owen made the sound. He saw Patrick's gun and said bang bang. I'm assuming that's what scared you?"

Owen made the sound.

I'm such a fucking train wreck. I'm stronger than this. Taking a deep breath, I straighten my back. Viktor wipes his thumb across my cheek, and I realize I'm crying. No more.

"I'm sorry. I'm good."

"You sure? We can take another minute. Patrick and Owen are safe in your car. They're waiting for us. Take however long you need."

"Positive." Without thinking, I lean in and take Viktor's lips. He doesn't hesitate to return the kiss, and I'm thankful. We don't do public displays of affection, especially not during the day, but I need this. I need his connection to feel grounded.

"Come on, Pepper. Let's get our boy home."

Fuck. That sounds so right coming from him.

Viktor opens my door, and I slide in. He secures my seat belt for me, and I'm not even upset about it. He exchanges a nod with Patrick, who retreats to his car, and we leave my job for possibly the last time.

I feel like I should be sad about that fact. My job was the little bit of freedom that I got, the extra money in my pocket, so I didn't feel like a complete burden. Right now, all I can think about is Viktor calling Owen "ours."

Viktor has been with Owen since the moment he was born. He's never backed down from his assumed role as a parent. It was never his job to help with Owen, but he did. His job has always been to protect me and then my son once he was born. The diaper changes, making breakfast, letting me sleep in, none of that was in his job description, but he did it. He does it. He does it all and so much more.

Why?

"Why what, Pepper?"

Shit. Where has my internal monologue gone?

"You okay over there? You've been staring at me for a while."

I have. Damn, I must be losing it.

"What's going on in that head of yours?"

Can I tell him? There's so much already going on between us. It feels like our relationship has developed overnight, but in reality, years. Maybe I never noticed how he treated Owen because I never had a father growing up. Justin was the closest thing I had to a father figure, but as quickly as he came, he was gone, and I was alone again. It wasn't until Spencer came into my life that Tucker, Axel, Miller, and Lincoln took on the roles of my fathers. I don't know if I could ever refer to any of them as Dad, but that's what they are.

"Pepper?"

"Why are you so good with him?"

"Him?" I glance into the backseat, not wanting to say Owen's name and alert him of our conversation. "Oh. Why wouldn't I be?"

"Because you're paid to be our bodyguard, but you do far beyond that for him."

Viktor stares out the windshield, deep in thought. Maybe this is as hard of a question for him as it is for me.

"Because he's a part of you."

"And you're paid to be *my* bodyguard, yet you go above and beyond for me, too. Why?"

His sigh sounds like it comes from the depths of his emotions.

"You've never really been just a job. At first, you were. When Justin told me your story, it was easy to be your protector. You were so young and innocent, or so I thought. I don't know how or when it changed. I help because I love him. How could I not? He's an extension of you."

He loves Owen because he's an extension of me; therefore,

he loves me. He's saying the words again without actually saying them.

"Okay." I don't know what else to say because what I really want to do is jump in his lap and tell him how much I love him. How I loved him the moment he cut Owen's cord and I saw the love he already had for my brand new baby boy.

"Okay." He accepts my answer as we pull into the driveway.

"Can we hang out here?"

"Of course." Viktor pulls the car toward the big house, and Patrick follows.

I have a lot of big feelings right now, and while I should probably sit alone and stew with them for a while, I'd rather be surrounded by family.

"Who's car is that?" There's a little blue sedan that I don't recognize parked amongst all of the big pickups.

"That's Chip's car." My head whips around to the voice I rarely hear. Patrick answered my question.

"Oh. Okay." *Patrick* answered my question. Patrick. He never speaks. And how does he know that's Chip's car? I thought he had an SUV. Before I can question my mostly mute bodyguard, he disappears around the house to patrol. I'll have to look into that later.

As we walk into the house, Owen runs between our legs, not caring that he pushes me out of the way.

"Hello I here!"

"Do I hear my favorite little guy?" Axel rounds the corner with a huge grin on his face. He grabs Owen by the waist and lifts him into the air. "Hey there."

Owen giggles, and I see Axel look at the clock and then at me. "Shouldn't you be at work?"

The smile on my face falls, and I look at Viktor.

"We had a situation at the preschool," Viktor responds in his authoritative voice. "Who's home? I'd like to brief you all."

"Everyone and Chip is here in the kitchen with Tucker and Lincoln. Hang on." He puts Owen down and cups his hands around his mouth. "Family meeting in the kitchen."

He turns back to me with a smile and pulls me in for a hug. "You okay, Katy girl?"

I shrug, not really knowing how I'm feeling, and he kisses the top of my head in understanding. I peer around Axel's shoulder when I hear footsteps bounding down the stairs. Miller sees me and smiles. He tugs my arm when he reaches us, and Axel reluctantly lets go.

"My turn."

Miller crushes me against his chest. His body is warm, and his shaggy brown hair is wet. He must have just gotten out of the shower.

"You're dripping on me."

"Oh, am I?" He shakes his head like a dog, and water droplets rain on me.

"Ugh! Yuck." I try to pull away, but his grip won't allow me. "Viktor, do your job and save me from the Golden Retriever."

"Not a chance, Miss Katy."

Oh, screw you with your *Miss*. I hear him laughing at me. I'm gonna get him later.

"My turn. My turn."

Owen jumps at our legs, and Miller releases me to pick him up, rubbing his wet hair all over Owen's face. My heart lights up at the giggles that fill the room.

"Who needs a family meeting?"

I look up to see Spencer coming down the stairs. Her hair

is also wet and down. Based on Miller's heated look, they must have been in the shower together. I love everyone's relationship in this house. It was always entertaining to make fun of and embarrass them when I lived here.

"We all do," Viktor replies to Spencer. "We had a situation today at Owen's preschool."

"Okay. Kitchen, everyone."

Spencer kisses Owen on the cheek, saying her hellos, and disappears into the kitchen to join everyone else. Miller puts Owen down, and I move to follow him into the kitchen.

"Pepper, wait."

I stop and turn toward Viktor. "What's wrong?"

"Stay here with Owen, and let us talk in the kitchen."

"Why can't I be involved?" Viktor brushes a lock of hair behind my ear and kisses my forehead.

"Because I have trouble concentrating when you're in the room. Because if you're there, I can't make the best plan of action for you and Owen. You distract me in the best way."

Dammit. Why does he have to say dreamy things like that?

"Fiiiiine. But only because you drive a hard bargain." I kiss Viktor's cheek and plop on the couch. Owen crawls up and cuddles into my side. It's close to nap time. I should lay him down in his crib.

"Mama, bun-bun seepy."

That's my cue. "Come on, little man. Let's lay bun-bun down for a nap."

Once Owen is settled, I rest back on the living room couch. Now, what do I do? I see Tucker's laptop on the end table and grab it to watch some mindless videos. I don't want to turn the TV on and disturb everyone, and a laptop screen is much bigger than my phone's.

I open the screen and easily type in his password. When I started homeschooling, I used Tucker's laptop for the first few days until he bought me my own, and his password hasn't changed. As my finger scrolls over the pad to click on the internet icon, I see a folder labeled 'Katy.' Why would Tucker have a file with my name on it?

Despite knowing that I should mind my own business, I can't help but click the icon. A document opens with more folders, each labeled with dates. I click on one and see pictures; some look familiar, others don't. It's obvious the Katy folder is filled with things related to Shane. I want to close it and the laptop, but I know there are things they aren't telling me, and I want to know. Several more folders hold pictures. I find one with information of Shane's police career.

I continue to look at different things until I come across a date I'll never forget. The day Shane tried to take me and shot Viktor. The mouse hovers over the folder icon. What could be in here? Viktor's medical records? The damage done to the car?

I'd rather forget this day ever existed, but if information about the second worst day of my life exists, I want to know. Clicking on the mouse pad, a video pops up. I gasp as I realize it's the dashcam footage of Viktor being shot and Shane almost taking me.

36

Dempsey

The tension in the room is thick with anger as I tell everyone the details of Shane's appearance at Katy and Owen's preschool.

"He claimed to be Owen's father and wanted to talk to Katy. The dumb director at the preschool almost let it happen."

"She's not going back there." Tucker runs a furious hand over his beard, and I can hear the heel of his boot tapping on the floor.

"I told the director she would be out the rest of the week and probably wouldn't be back."

"She won't be," Lincoln confirms. "Katy can have my entire salary if she needs money."

"That's a generous offer, but you know she won't go for that," Spencer states blankly. "Her job has been her only independence."

"Fuck!" Miller exclaims. "We can't take her independence. She'll hate us."

Silence fills the room as Miller's statement sinks in. He's

right. Work is the only time she gets to do something that me or any of the others aren't actively in the room with her. She loves working there, and she loves Owen getting the chance to play with kids his own age.

The song *Brown Eyed Girl* breaks through the room, and everyone looks at Axel while my head whips toward the living room. That's Katy's text alert tone on his phone. Why is she texting him from the next room?

"Katy went back to the pool house but left Owen here asleep in his crib."

Another alert comes through.

"Fuck. Look." He turns his phone to show us the text sent from Katy.

Unknown: I was so close today. I couldn't decide who I wanted to see more, you or my son.

Once again, his phone buzzes, and everyone in the room is on high alert. Axel jumps from his chair, and it crashes to the floor.

"Tucker, where's your laptop?" Axel charges toward the living room, and everything in me wants to go to the pool house and make sure Katy is okay, but there's so much going on right now I don't know which way is up.

"Fuck!" Axel roars. He slams Tucker's laptop closed and spins to face us. "She watched the video."

Everyone but Tucker looks confused. What video did she watch? Why is she contacting Axel and not me? I pick up my phone and hit #1 on my speed dial.

"I've got her." Some of the tension leaves my body.

"She made it safely back to the pool house?" Patrick grunts. "Is she okay?"

"No."

"No? Why the fuck not?" Everyone's attention turns to my phone conversation.

"She told me not to let anyone in?" I storm into the kitchen and out to the three-season porch. Patrick's hulking figure stands outside the door to the pool house.

"I'll be right there."

"No."

"Why the fuck not?" My rage seeps through my voice. Who does he think he is telling me no?

"She specifically said not to let *you* in?"

I hang up the phone and spin to walk back inside, but everyone is already behind me. "What was on that fucking laptop?"

Guilt.

Shame.

Trepidation.

Finally, Tucker sighs and gives me the answers I need. "It was open to the video footage from the dashcam of the shooting.

"Fuck. And Katy watched it." There's no reason for anyone to answer. It wasn't a question. It's the only reason she would have left here, on her own, without Owen, and now doesn't want to see me.

I've seen it. Once. That was enough for someone like me who's seen combat and death. I can't imagine how she's feeling right now. "And the text?"

"I'm looking into it, but since it's from Shane, I'm sure it's a dead end as usual."

"Thanks, Chip."

I look back across the yard. I want to go to her. I need

to go to her. She can't just shut me out like this. We can work through this together. We have to work through this together.

I turn to walk out the back door and hands grip my shoulders.

"Get your fucking hands off me." I don't care who's grabbed me. Right now, I'm not in the mood for anyone's shit.

"Dempsey."

My head falls forward. Of course it's Tucker. The fucking voice of reason.

"Respect her wishes. You can hate it now but she'll appreciate it, and you, later."

"How did you find out?" I barely just heard she doesn't want to see me.

"Patrick texted me."

All the fight leaves me. "Can I go and stand with Patrick? I won't bother her. I just…I just need to be near her."

"Dempsey, I'm not sure—"

"Please." I'm clearly not above begging. I know she's hurting right now. The video is fucking horrible. She still has nightmares about me, and now she doesn't even want to see me. "Tucker, please."

He finally releases his grip, and I feel my entire body deflate.

"Don't push her. You can stay in Katy's room if you decide you're going to sleep at all tonight."

"Thank you. Can you let Patrick know I'm coming so he doesn't try and shoot me?"

"Sure."

I walk straight out the back door toward the pool house. Patrick lifts his hand then glances at me, and I silently thank Tucker for announcing my arrival.

Patrick eyes me suspiciously as I approach, and I lift my arms in surrender.

"I'm not going to cause any problems. I just need to be as close to her as I can. She's hurting, and on the off chance she decides she needs me, I'm going to be here."

He nods and ignores me. That's fine by me. I have enough thoughts swirling around in my head. I wouldn't be good conversation anyway.

One hour passes, then two. I watch the shadows as they change across the yard. At hour three, Patrick answers a series of texts, and hope blooms in my chest when he punches his code to unlock the door. It quickly plummets when he reaches in, picks up Owen's diaper bag, and quickly closes the door.

Miller walks toward us and retrieves the bag from Patrick, giving me an apologetic look.

"Is Owen spending the night with you?"

"He is. Do you want to come have a beer?"

"No. I'm good here."

"Okay. It's a standing offer." I nod, and he leaves to return to his house.

"Wait. Are his stickers in the bag?"

Miller turns, giving me a confused look. "Stickers?"

"His potty stars. He gets one for peeing in the potty and two if he poops."

Miller rummages through the bag and pulls out a sheet of holographic stickers. *Shit.* I was hoping it would give me another chance to see her.

"Okay, well, he really likes getting them as a reward." He smiles his thanks, and as he turns, the doorbell microphone crackles behind us. I turn with hope that I'm going to at least hear Katy's voice.

"Go with him, Viktor." My heart sinks that she's sending me away. I just want to be near her. "Go be with Owen." She says the one thing that will change my mind.

"Okay. Okay, Pepper. I'll go be with Owen. I'll go be with our boy."

As I leave, the mic crackles one more time. A quiet "So much" whispers through the air, and I smile. I repeat the words back into the silence with a smile. It's her way of reassuring me that we will be okay. I'll give her the space she needs, at least for tonight. Tonight, I have a little boy to take care of.

"Patrick. Guard her with your life. Your. LIFE. I don't need to tell you how important she is to me."

"My life." He nods, and I already know he takes his job as seriously as I do, but I needed to hear it out loud.

I catch up with Miller and take the diaper bag from him. He throws his arm over my shoulder and smiles.

"Guess you're coming for that beer after all."

37

Katy

That was too much to watch. I don't want to think about it anymore. I quietly leave the big house because seeing that video brought back more memories than I remember from that night. I had pushed as much as I could out of my mind. All I saw were the flashes in my dreams, but what I just saw doesn't compare to my memories of the event.

Patrick catches up with me halfway across the yard. He doesn't say anything—just follows me after realizing I'm alone. When I reach the door, I punch in my code and turn the nob, pausing once it's open.

"Patrick, I want to be alone. Please don't let anyone in." I look at him over my shoulder and understand his silent question. Tears burn the back of my eyes, and my stomach churns as I say the next words. "Don't let Viktor in. No one."

I pick up my phone to text anyone needing a distraction and see a missed notification from earlier that I had ignored.

Unknown: I was so close today. I couldn't decide who I wanted to see more, you or my son.

"Fuck."

I want to throw my phone across the room, but I need to let everyone know about this text. Shane has gotten into my phone now. He's cornered every aspect of my life. He wants Owen, but he'll never have him. In light of what happened today, I think Owen should stay in the big house surrounded by everyone. He'll be the safest there.

Who should I text?

Logically, it should be Viktor, but I can't even think about him right now. Who would be the best person to pass along the message?

Katy: Hey Axel, I walked to the pool house. Owen is napping in his crib. Could you please keep an ear out?

<Forward Message> Unknown: I was so close today. I couldn't decide who I wanted to see more, you or my son.

Katy: I saw the dashcam video on Tucker's laptop. I need some time to process what I watched. I'll be okay.

I know that last one won't go over well, but I needed to tell someone so they understand how I'm feeling right now. But I don't want to feel it. I want to forget and be a teenager.

Group Chat: Blake, Nicole, Meghan

Katy: I know it's last minute, but I desperately need a girl's night tonight. Anyone want to come over and be irresponsible with me? ...and bring the booze for the underagers?

I pause for a moment before hitting send. Annie and Spencer aren't included in this message, and I don't want them to feel left out, but I want to let loose, and they aren't exactly the biggest party people.

I hit send. I'm sure they will both understand, given the circumstances. I don't have to wait long before bubbles appear.

Nicole: I'm in, but since I can't do any of the drinking, I'll bring the booze. I can watch you all get drunk and stupid.

Blake: Hey. I resemble that remark. ;) I'll be there. I assume there's gossip if we're midweek drinking. I'll bring snacks!

Meghan: Katy, this is Meghan. Did you mean to include me in this message?

I can understand why Meghan is confused. She doesn't know the other two numbers, and we rarely hang out, but someone my age sounds like the best kind of girls' night. Blake will be a blast, and despite Nicole being pregnant, she will bring the fun.

Katy: Absolutely! Come to girl's night. Got any fun card games? You can crash here so you can drink and have fun!

Meghan: I'll be there. What time?

Katy: Does 7 work for everyone?

My phone dings with confirmation texts, and my excitement grows.

I get a notification that there's motion at the front door, and the quick snapshot from the camera shows me Viktor has arrived. I knew he would, but I hoped he'd give me more time. I wait to hear the lock engage or the ring of the bell, but nothing comes. Opening up the camera, I see he's just standing there mirroring Patrick. Did he come to stand watch with him?

A few hours later, Miller texts to ask me for Owen's diaper bag and whatever he needs to spend the night. I let him know I'll pack it and have Patrick waiting with it outside.

When Miller arrives, I watch the interactions through the camera and hope that Viktor will go back with him. He doesn't. He can't just stand here all night.

I click the voice button to talk. "Go with him, Viktor. Go be with Owen." I know he wants to stay for me, but I also know he'll go for Owen.

Without a fight, I watch him agree to go. I need him to know we're okay. He looks so defeated, and I want to comfort him, but I need to process. This needs to be about me.

Clicking the talk button one more time I reassure him the best way I know how. "So much." It's a whisper from my lips, but he hears it. I know he does. He walks up to Miller, who slings his arm over Viktor's shoulder, and they head to the big house.

Katy: Girl's night tonight at 7. Blake, Nicole, and my friend Meghan are coming over.
Patrick: Copy.

Even via text, he's a man of little words.

At six-thirty, Patrick knocks and enters the house. I ordered a grocery delivery with some extra supplies for tonight and some hangover supplies for the morning. Meghan and I have been texting, and she plans to stay the night. I thought we might need some greasy foods for the morning to soak up all the alcohol we plan to drink tonight.

Viktor: This will be my only text unless you reply back. I respect your need for the night off and I'm glad to hear you won't be alone. Please know if you need me I'm right across the lawn and will be there for you in a heartbeat. So much.

My eyes blur with tears. I'm not surprised he knows about my girl's night. Patrick would have told someone at the big house to expect the cars. My anxiety creeps up at that thought.

Katy: I'm second-guessing myself. Should I invite Annie and Spencer? I don't want to hurt anyone's feelings.

Blake: Annie completely understands and knows I'm the fun one. Besides, getting shitfaced on a Tuesday isn't really her thing. LOL. See you soon!

Nicole: I already spoke to Spencer. She called Justin, and he mentioned I was coming over. She's just happy you're having us over and won't be alone. I wouldn't worry. :)

Their responses make me feel better. While I love them all equally, I also love them differently. I'm not surprised to hear that Annie and Spencer understand what I need tonight. That's the nature of their personalities.

Blake said she was bringing snacks but I wanted a few specific things. As I'm setting everything up on the kitchen island, my phone notifies me of motion at the front door. I catch myself bouncing on the balls of my feet and chuckle when I think of Axel doing the exact same thing.

Hmm. He might be a fun addition later to our girl's night. I'll have to see what everyone else thinks about that.

"The party is here, Bitch!" Blake rounds the corner with Nicole on her heels, and her expression is mixed with shock and horror as she sees me. "Oh, this won't do."

I contain my need to laugh hysterically as I look over their outfits. "What are you wearing?"

"What are *you* wearing? This is a party and you are severely underdressed. Let's go." Blake walks to my bedroom and I'm left standing dumbfounded with what just happened.

"Don't fight it, Katy. She did it to me, too."

Nicole makes a slow turn, and I take a good look at her shiny, silver, one-shouldered dress. It's ruffled at the bottom and across her shoulder, and the entire thing is ruched, perfectly accenting her baby bump.

"She did this to you?"

Nicole begins to nod when Blake pops her head out from my bedroom door. "What are we waiting for? Let's get you dressed for the occasion."

I drag my feet toward the crazy woman wearing a bright yellow sequin mini-dress. Why does she even own that? My phone buzzes again, and I perk up.

"Meghan's here."

"Who? Oh, the other number in the group chat. Who is she?" Blake's curiosity is piqued.

"She's a friend from high school, and I'm sure she didn't adhere to tonight's absurd dress code either, so it seems like you have two Barbies to dress."

"Yesssssss." Blake pumps her fist like it's the best thing in the world.

"Katy?" Meghan's voice hesitantly flows through the room.

"Oh-M-Geeeeee! You are so pretty! Nicole look at her hair."

I laugh as Blake accosts my poor, unsuspecting friend.

"Um. Hi, I'm Meghan." Meghan turns her head in every direction, trying to keep track of Blake as he bounces around her before finally looking at me in complete shock.

"Meghan, this is Blake, and the sane, pregnant one over there is Nicole. Crazy ladies, this is my friend Meghan." Meghan lifts her hand in a shy wave.

"You were right. She's underdressed. Makeover time!" Blake takes Meghan's hand and drags her over to me before taking us both to my room.

For the next hour we all laugh and drink while Nicole does our hair and Blake dresses us like we're her new favorite dolls. Meghan ends up in my little black dress. She's shorter than I am so instead of the dress coming mid thigh it stops just above her knees. It's hip-hugging with spaghetti straps and a deep plunging V in the front. She looks stunning.

When Blake went through my closet looking for something I could wear, I heard lots of sighing and tsking. Finally, she walked over to her large bag and pulled out a scrap of fabric that looked more like a scarf than a dress.

"I knew I'd need this backup."

I stare at my reflection in disbelief. The dress is a satin material in a deep green color. I'm completely covered in the front with a halter-like top, but the back of the dress is open dangerously low to my ass crack. The front has dueling slits up both legs. I have to go commando with how much skin this dress shows.

"Blake, this dress is..."

"Fucking stunning? Nah. *You* make the dress, Katy. Smile!"

Blake takes a few pictures with her phone and sends a text. I eye her suspiciously until her phone buzzes in her hand, and a smile takes over her entire face.

"Meghan, come over here and get in the picture."

The next several minutes are spent taking pictures of the four of us dressed in our best. We make it back in the kitchen, and Blake and Nicole prepare for our next round of drinks as I watch Meghan's gaze dart to the front door several times.

"You okay? Did you need to head home? You don't have to stay if you don't want to."

"Oh no. I'm good. I'm staying."

"Shots!" Blake puts a glass of something blue in front of each of us, and I arch a brow. "Just trust me."

Meghan shrugs and chugs it down. I laugh at her exuberance when she asks Blake for another.

"Um, can you tell me anything about the uh, guy at the front door?" Meghan tries to ask her question quietly but between the buzz we already have going and Blake's superhuman hearing, her question isn't only heard by my ears.

"Hunky Patrick. He's more cryptic than the Mona Lisa. A man of little words and lots of grunts." Blake hands Meghan another shot, and we each click glasses. Nicole joins in with something not blue in her glass, and we down our shots.

"He spoke to me when I came in."

Nicole laughs and beats her chest a few times, her blonde curls bouncing around her face. "Me Patrick, you Meghan." Blake and I giggle, and Meghan looks confused.

"Well, no. He said hi and introduced himself as Patrick. He told me that he would be watching over us tonight, and if I needed anything, I could just step outside and let him know."

You could hear a pin drop with the amount of silence from Nicole, Blake, and me.

"Did I say something wrong?" Meghan shoots a worried look between us.

"Just to be clear," Blake starts. "You're referring to that hunk of man meat that looks like he wants to rip your head off if you even breathe in his general direction. Tall as a tree, dark hair, dark eyes, permanent scowl and usually communicates in grunts? He spoke in more than one-word sentences and even offered to get you anything you needed?"

"Um…" Meghan looks embarrassed, and I don't blame her. Blake has her in the hot seat.

"Let's settle this." Nicole stalks toward the door, and Meghan turns instantly red.

"Hey Patrick, could you come in here for a minute."

Nicole walks back in the room, followed by Patrick. When he does his usually visual scan of the room, his eyes stop dead when they see Meghan in my little black dress. He roams her body and I can't blame him. She looks hot.

Meghan's breath hitches at his heated stare, and the sound seems to snap Patrick out of his trance.

"Miss Nicole?" His voice is hoarse, having not used it for a while, and Meghan shivers next to me.

"See, two words." Blake plants her hands on her hips and looks between Patrick and Meghan, obviously seeing what the rest of us are. There's an attraction.

"Would you take a picture of the four of us together?" Nicole hands him her phone and I'm thankful for her quick thinking before the room got anymore awkward.

"Uno. Bam." Nicole slams her last card down, and the rest of us groan.

"Isss no frair." *Hiccup.* "You're soooooober," Blake whines to Nicole as she tips her head onto her shoulder.

We've danced, we've drank, we've sang karaoke poorly, drank some more, and ended up sprawled out on the floor in our PJs playing *Uno.*

"On that note, I'm going to quit while I'm ahead and leave the three of you to continue your evening." Nicole rubs her baby bump. "Me and this little one need to get home and into a comfy bed with my full-length pregnancy pillow. Maybe we can even convince Daddy to give us a foot rub."

"I should go home, too." Blake pulls out her phone and types a text. She gets an instant response, and the look on her face is pure love as a dreamy smile lifts her lips.

"Puke. Gag." Nicole playfully pushes my shoulder at my exaggerated noises, and I topple over onto the floor. "Go home and be party poopers."

"Hey, G.I. Joe! We need you." Blake cups her hands over her mouth and yells at the front door. A moment later, the door opens, and Patrick steps inside. "Nicole is ready to go home. Can you walk us out to her car, please?"

Patrick nods at Blake's question, but his eyes are on Meghan. I nudge her shoulder, but she's staring right back, and I let them have their moment.

Nicole and Blake say their goodbyes and Meghan and I clean up the mess in the living room before having one last *Uno* battle, then heading to bed.

"Thank you so much for coming. The kitchen is free reign whenever you get up. There's lots of breakfast options." We embrace in a hug and she retreats to the guest room.

"Let me go. No. NO! He's losing too much blood. He's not breathing. No."

"Katy."

I shoot up in bed as my bedroom door crashes open. The man staring back at me isn't the one I want to see. Patrick's eyes scan the room for danger, seeing none.

"Viktor," I pant out. "Want…Viktor."

Patrick picks up his phone, and I see his lips moving, but I can't hear anything. The blood rushes through my ears, and I struggle to catch my breath.

"He's coming."

"Katy?" Meghan's worried voice drifts into the room and Patrick's gaze bounces between the two of us.

"Go," I whisper, and I wave for him to take care of Meghan. I know he called Viktor.

Viktor is coming. Viktor is coming.

I pull my knees to my chest and rock, repeating to myself over and over that he's coming.

It feels like hours, but I know it's only minutes when I finally hear the front door open, and he appears in the doorway. He pauses for just a moment to assess the situation before he's at my side, and I'm scooped into his arms. He settles us onto the bed, and I bury myself into his chest. The tears begin to fall, and I feel the dam burst.

Viktor's arms tighten around me, and my hand desperately reaches for the hem of his shirt. I need to feel him. My hand finally slinks under, and I search for his scar. My fingers brush the jagged edges that are a little rougher than his normal skin. I can feel the tiny spots where the staples left their scars. Something that isn't visible to the naked eye but I know intimately.

38

Dempsey

I tried to be social all evening. I drank the beer I was offered. I ate the dinner that Miller made, but my focus was on Owen. I took care of him because Katy told me to, and if I can't be with her tonight, I'm going to be with him. I'll take care of our little boy. I will always take care of him and her.

I retreated to bed early, almost wishing I had chosen to sleep on the couch because the bed smells like her and makes me long to be with her even more.

She's hopefully having a fun evening with Blake, Meghan, and Nicole.

I lay in bed staring at the ceiling for hours, listening to Owen's quiet snores across the room. It's after midnight when my phone vibrates, and I'm instantly on my feet when I see Patrick's number.

I exit the room, quietly closing the door behind me. "What's wrong?"

"Nightmare. She wants you."

I hang up and grab my shoes at the front door. Axel sees me from his place on the living room couch, shooting me a concerned glance at my hurried pace.

"Patrick called. Going to Katy. You got Owen?"

"Of course."

I nod my thanks and rush out the door. Axel is usually up late on his nights off since his body is used to being awake for work. I'm thankful that I didn't have to add waking someone up to the tasks I had to do before getting to my girl.

I force myself not to run across the yard, but barely. Patrick isn't standing outside, but it makes sense since he called me from inside. When I walk in, Patrick and Meghan are standing near the hallway talking, and he nods toward Katy's bedroom. I walk up to the door and quickly look around the room before I lock eyes with her. She looks so small and I quickly grab her in my arms and settle us on the bed. She buries herself into me, and quietly sobs.

I pull her closer and feel her fingers roam under my shirt and skim my bullet scar.

"Pepper, I'm here." Her tears come harder.

"I saw—" Her words cut off with a sob.

"I know. I wish you hadn't. I'm sorry you did. I'm so fucking sorry."

She tries to bury herself farther into me. It feels like she wants to burrow into my skin.

"I was there. I saw it happen, but somehow that video was...was."

"Worse?"

"So fucking worse."

"Pepper, let's get you back to sleep. Can I get up to take my clothes off and get comfortable?"

"What if I don't want to sleep?" Katy tips her head up, and her lips graze my jaw. The connection sparks a fire in me, but I know she needs comfort. I can smell the alcohol on her, and as much as my body wants to do all of the dirty things that her heart desires, tonight isn't the night. Katy's friend is also here, and I think her nightmare might have scared Meghan.

"As much as I'd love to take you up on your offer, you'll feel better in the morning if you get some sleep."

Her bottom lip pops out, and I want to give in. I want to give her the world, but not tonight.

"Pepper, you know I never tell you no, and I feel bad enough. Please be a good girl and listen to me. You need to sleep."

"Or you could be my good boy and let me suck your dick for coming to my rescue."

"Katy," I sigh out her name. She's testing my patience and resolve. Her hand that was trailing over my scar now grazes the top of my jeans. I allow her to unbutton them. I need to take them off to sleep, so it's okay.

"You came running when I needed you. My Viking to the rescue." She nips at my jaw as my zipper lowers.

A huff of air escapes me as her hand brushes over my thickening cock.

"Will you let me thank you? Please?" Now she's begging. I have no defenses against her. "Pleeease." She squeezes me, and I'm gone.

"Yes. Yes, Miss Katy."

"Mmm, good boy." My arms relax as she slides down my body. I should protest, but I'm putty in her hands. I'm a weak man for her. I adjust my hips so she can pull down my pants, and she takes my underwear with them. I'm naked and at her mercy from the waist down, and she smiles up at me.

"You're breathtaking, Katy." I rub my thumb along her cheek as she takes me into her mouth. I do my best to contain my moans, knowing we aren't alone. She takes me further, licking and sucking my shaft. I run my hands through her hair and enjoy the feel of her head bobbing.

Katy hums in pleasure, and it sends a shock wave straight to my balls. I want to touch her, but she needs this for herself. I know this is more than her wanting to thank me for coming to her rescue. She knows I'll always be here. This is Katy taking her power back from her dream and reminding herself that I'm here and whole despite what she saw on that video.

"Katy, your mouth is incredible. God, fucking shit." She does my favorite swirl thing with her tongue, which I can't even describe, and I involuntarily fist my hand in her hair. She moans her approval.

"Do you want the pain, Pepper?" I tighten my fist, and she moans again. "Okay. I've got you, but don't get too loud, or you'll wake your guest again." I tighten my grip further and lift my hips to meet her bobbing head. She squeezes my thigh in appreciation.

"Fuck, Katy. So much. So. Fucking. Much." My hips thrust, but she's still very much in control of everything happening. Her hand tightens on the base of my cock as she pulls me closer to the edge.

"I'm close, Pepper."

Katy increases her efforts and reaches her other arm between us to roll my balls in her hand, and I'm a goner. I come hard. Katy eagerly takes it all in, and when I'm done, I have to pull her off me as she continues to suck on my deflating cock.

"You got it all. You're killing me."

She smiles as she crawls up my chest.

"Thank you, Viking. I needed that."

"I know, Pepper. Any time." I pull her in for a kiss, tasting myself on her lips. "Are you ready to sleep now, or would you like me to reciprocate?"

She nuzzles into my chest, inhaling deeply.

"Sleep."

I chuckle as she tries to fall asleep. "Can I put my underwear back on?"

Katy reaches between us and wraps a gentle hand around my cock. "No. I like it easily accessible."

I kiss her forehead as I shift us lower onto the bed. "Anything for you, Pepper."

The smell of coffee wakes me up, and for a split second, I'm on alert. I'm not used to anyone being in the house other than Katy and me. I wonder if it's Patrick or Meghan that's up?

Carefully, I untangle myself from Katy and pick up my clothes, getting dressed in the bathroom while I do my morning routine. She's still asleep when I'm done, and I leave the room, hoping she'll sleep for a while.

Patrick stands at the counter drinking a cup of coffee, but I hear the shower in the guest bathroom, so Meghan must be up as well.

"Morning."

He tips his cup at me in greeting and reaches behind him to take down a mug for me.

"Did you have a good night?" I never heard the door open

last night, so I assume he stayed in the house. The couch doesn't look like anyone slept on it, and I know there's only a small pull-out couch in Owen's room now that it's a nursery.

"Sure."

"Thank you for calling me last night. I know Katy asked for me, but I appreciate all you do, Patrick."

The shower turns off, and our eyes drift down the hall. A few minutes later, the bathroom door opens, and Owen's door closes. Patrick opens the refrigerator and pulls out eggs, sausage, and hashbrowns. I watch him with a curious eye as he makes a full breakfast in Katy's kitchen like it's the most natural everyday task. I wonder if this is how I looked when Katy first moved into the pool house, and I essentially moved in.

"I smell coffee. Need coffee." Katy's scratchy morning voice drifts through the room as I hear her dragging footsteps heading our way. Patrick takes down another mug and pours coffee into it. He slides me the mug and retrieves Katy's flavored creamer from the refrigerator. I'm impressed with his observation skills.

Katy walks into the room with her bathrobe haphazardly over her shoulders at the same time Meghan exits from down the hallway. Katy and Meghan's eyes meet, and Katy playfully scowls at her.

"Bitch, you've had time to shower? How are you functioning?"

As Katy comes closer, I extend the mug in her direction, and it becomes her sole focus. She sits beside me at the kitchen counter, and Meghan joins her.

"Don't worry, I feel like ass. I sat on the floor for half of the shower."

I watch in fascination as Patrick pours another cup of coffee, tops it off with creamer, and hands it to Meghan. She thanks him as her cheeks tint pink, and he gives her a small smile.

The man just fucking smiled. What the hell? He turns back around, and plates four delicious breakfasts, and the girls moan their appreciation.

"Viktor, can we still go to the play gym today for Owen's lesson and to see my mom?"

Patrick arches his brow. I hadn't mentioned it to him yet since yesterday's events at the preschool. There had been so much going on it slipped my mind.

"Did you already ask your mother to meet us there?"

"I did, and she's more than excited."

I'm not too thrilled about going out in public so soon, but like Miller said, she'll hate us if we try to keep her in a cage.

"It shouldn't be a problem."

"I need like fifty more hours of sleep. I have no idea why I'm even up this early." Katy laughs at Meghan as her head slumps into her hands. I watch Patrick keenly as his expression turns to one of concern. He reaches above the stove and grabs a bottle of pain medicine. Grabbing two glasses, he puts water in both, sets a glass down in front of each girl, and pours out two pills for each of them.

Meghan's cheeks darken. She picks up the glass and pills and offers him a quiet thank you in appreciation.

Very interesting. I'm not one for gossip, but I'd say my curiosity is piqued.

Tucker: Montgomery has some information for us.

Demspey: Be over in a few.

Tucker: Take your time. Owen is eating breakfast.

Leaning over, I kiss Katy's temple. "Owen is awake, and Tucker has some information for me. Why don't you shower? I'll go take care of that. Spend a little more time with Meghan while Patrick and I see what's going on."

"Okay. A shower sounds heavenly."

"I can get out of your hair." Meghan moves to stand, and Katy throws her arms around her neck.

"Noooooo. Don't leave me yet. Let's gossip while the boys are gone, and there aren't any middle-aged women here. I love Blake and Nicole, but I'd rather not hear or share bedroom activities with them."

Meghan dips her head, but I see the tips of her ears darken. I glance at Patrick, whose back is turned, but his posture seems stiffer than usual.

"Okay, I'll stay."

"Don't leave without texting me to walk you out." I think that's more words than I've ever heard Patrick say. Katy must be in as much shock as I am because we both stare as Patrick slides his phone to Meghan and without hesitation, she types her number into his cell.

Now I'm very much interested to know what happened last night.

"Same goes for you, Pepper. Do not leave the house. Lock up behind us. I'll bring Owen back with me, but if you decide you want to come to the big house, text me."

"Can I not walk across the lawn alone?" I pin her down with a stare that she knows means I'm not taking no for an answer. "Ugh fiiiiiiine."

Katy hops off the stool and, with a bit more pep in her step than she walked in with, she retreats to her room.

"Make yourself at home, Meghan. I'll be out in twenty."

"Thanks." Meghan turns to Patrick and smiles. "Thank you for breakfast." His response is a nod. He collects all the empty plates and places them in the sink.

"Ready?" I drink the last of my coffee and add it to the dishes I promise myself I'll do when we return.

We say our goodbyes to Meghan and walk in silence to meet Tucker. I want to ask Patrick about Meghan and what happened after I left him alone with her, but I doubt I'll get any information from him. I'll talk to Katy later and see if Meghan gives her anything.

"Gentleman, this is Montgomery," Tucker greets us as we walk into the kitchen from the back porch. Next to him sits a man weathered by age and too much sun. His thinning dark hair and wire-framed glasses make him look even less attractive. I've never met him before, but his reputation precedes him, and I know Tucker trusts him implicitly.

On the opposite side of the table sits Chip, who squirms in his seat as Patrick walks in and passes by me. His eyes follow Patrick as he takes a position in the corner of the room. Is he blushing?

What the fuck is going on around here?

"Montgomery thinks Katy has a tracker on her somewhere."

39

Katy

My social battery is low, and I wish I had canceled on my mother. Hanging out with Meghan, Blake, and Nicole was exactly what I needed last night, but today, I could use a day of cuddling and movies.

Between the stress of having Shane show up at my work, getting the text, seeing the video, and then the nightmare, I have nothing left to give, but I'm not heartless, and I know my mother is looking forward to our meeting today.

I look over at Viktor and smirk. He sees me and gives me a knowing glance.

"What's so funny over there?"

"You. You look...different." Knowing that he's going to be crawling around on the floor with other kids, he's wearing a more casual outfit than usual. A light blue t-shirt hugs his sharp angles and curves of his biceps, and I see some definition of his abs where the seat belt has pulled his shirt tight.

"I've never seen you in shorts." My eyes drift over his

khaki cargo shorts and follow his tattoo down his calf as it disappears into his sneakers.

"I'm a person, not a piece of meat, Pepper. Stop drooling."

"You make it extremely hard, Viking."

Viktor clears his throat as he not so subtly adjusts himself. "No, *you* make it extremely hard, Miss Katy."

His eyes flash to Owen in the back seat and back at me. I don't know if it's sexier that just my perusal of his body made him have to adjust himself or that he thought to look back to see what Owen was doing at that moment.

"So, your mother is meeting us there, and you are both going to sit in the stands and watch, correct?"

"Mood killer," I huff. "Yes, that's the plan."

Viktor gives me a knowing smirk before reaching over and squeezing my thigh.

"I haven't forgotten that I need to return the favor from last night. Don't worry."

I place my hand over his and lace our fingers together. "You better not."

Viktor glances in the rearview mirror. "Patrick is going to wait outside in his car. Do you think you'll let Babs meet Owen?"

I don't know the answer to that yet. For so long, I was adamant that she never have anything to do with him. The longer I'm a mother, the more I can't understand how she treated me the way she did for all those years. But I also know people can change, and I don't ever want to look back and not be confident I didn't give her the chance she deserved to at least try.

"I'm leaning toward yes. If she's still there at the end of the hour, then assume it's okay for them to meet. If I'm uncomfortable, I'll ask her to leave before it's over."

I already asked her to arrive ten minutes after the class starts. She understood my reservations, and I'm glad she respects my boundaries.

"That sounds like a good plan." Viktor squeezes my hand, and I appreciate his support on this matter. He could have easily tried to talk me out of today, especially after yesterday. He knows how much my independence and being able to make my own decisions means to me.

As toddler tumble time begins, I sit nervously waiting for my mother to arrive. I chose a seat closer to the back of the viewing area but still close enough that I can watch Owen, and she can see him when she gets here without being directly in Owen's line of sight.

I absentmindedly rub the soft ears on Bun-Bun. Owen loves this class and doesn't mind putting down his favorite toy as long as I hold it for him and promise to keep him safe. Feeling the fabric under my fingers stops my leg from bouncing and my eyes darting everywhere looking for her. I shouldn't be this nervous to see my mother.

"Katy." I stand at my mother's voice and almost drop Bun-Bun.

"Shit. I mean, crap. I mean…hi mother, Babs." Get it together, Katy.

"Hi, sweetheart. I didn't mean to startle you. You were deep in thought."

My mother looks as nervous as I feel. Her eyes dart between the gym floor and me. I can understand her nervousness. I yelled at her the last time we met, and allowing her to even be in the same room as Owen is a big step for me.

"Sorry. Have a seat." I motion to the empty chair beside

me, and she smiles and joins me.

She looks out into the gym, and I wonder if she can pick Owen out. When her face lights up, I realize she's spotted him. I remember she's met Viktor before, and that's probably how she figured out who Owen is.

"He's beautiful, Katy. He looks just like you."

"He does." I don't know what else to say. Owen looks like me. It's a fact and one I'm thankful for.

"Katy, I'm sorry I overstepped the last time we met."

"Let's just forget about it." I grip Bun-Bun a little tighter, and my mother watches my every move.

"Okay. Sure."

"Babs, are you okay?" Her eyes snap to mine and she looks... guilty, defeated, worried?

"Of course I'm fine. I wish you wouldn't call me by my name. I'm your mother, Katy."

"Not anymore."

Her face turns red, and I want to feel guilty for my comment, but it's true. In the eyes of the law, she is no longer my mother; Spencer is. She gave me away.

"Katy, that's not true. I gave birth to you. I will always be your mother."

"No."

"No?"

"No. You're correct. You gave birth to me. That's it. It doesn't make you my mother. I've found more love and support from my newfound family in the last three years than I ever did in the sixteen years you were my mother." I use air quotes around the word mother because I no longer consider her in that role.

She opens her mouth to speak, but a jingle comes from her

purse, and she reaches in and takes out her phone. For just a moment, her face falls before she composes herself again.

"I'm sorry you feel that way, Katy." Her entire posture changes, and she stares out into the gym. I don't think she is watching Owen. She seems to be looking at nothing. I want to tell her to leave. I don't think her meeting Owen is a good idea. Not today, anyway. I don't want to make a rash decision, though. I need to calm down before I decide anything.

"I'm going to go to the bathroom. Please stay here and don't get any closer. Viktor won't allow it anyway."

She looks back at me, panicked for a quick moment. I stuff Bun-Bun into my purse, not wanting to leave him alone with her.

"Is that the one I gave him?"

It takes me a moment to understand what she's talking about, then I remember she gave Owen a bunny identical to his comfort animal.

"Oh. I'm not sure. He has several that are the same. I'll be back." I look into the gym to see if I can catch Viktor's attention and let him know where I'm going, but he's engrossed in the foam pit on the far side and isn't looking my way.

"I'll wait right here." She pulls her phone out of her purse as I walk away, and I hope she doesn't get any ideas of taking pictures of Owen.

The bathroom is at the back of a long hallway. This building is a large warehouse sectioned off for gymnastics and parties. I walk into the bathroom and go right to the sink. I don't have to actually use the bathroom; I just need a moment to breathe and compose my thoughts. In the last few years, I've done a lot of work to get out from under her thumb and her belittling thoughts of me. Being in her presence for only a few minutes has already frazzled the edges of my finely curved corners.

I wash my hands and smooth my hair out in the mirror.

"Don't let her get to you, Katy. You're stronger than her. You can get through this and then send her home."

The bathroom door opens, and I step back from the sink, not wanting anyone to hear my pathetic little pep talk. I look up and freeze at the reflection staring back at me in the mirror. A tall man with eyes almost as black as night gives me a devilish grin.

My body remembers him. Both of my encounters with this man have been in this exact position. He's always behind me. When he raped me in the alley, he had me on my knees. When he grabbed me in my car, it was from behind, but it gave me the opportunity to bash his nose with my head. I notice the slight crooked slant to it, and a moment of pride washes over me before he takes a step forward, and fear crawls into every crevice of my body.

"I've waited a long time to get you alone again, my sweet, sweet Katy."

My body physically convulses at his voice. It's as thick as honey and smooth as silk, but I remember the allure it had on me the first time and know it means danger. I'm at the back of the warehouse, and no one will hear me even if I scream.

What are my options?

Viktor doesn't know I'm back here because I didn't tell him before I left. Why didn't I tell him? My mother knows, but she couldn't care less where I am.

"It's just us back here. I covered my tracks. Are you going to come with me quietly? I have a car waiting just outside the back door that's conveniently located right outside this bathroom."

I can't just walk out of here. I have to fight. I didn't fight the first time he had me alone, and I'll be damned if I'm going to let him take me now. I'm not the same scared little girl I was in that alley.

"I can see in your eyes you want to do this the hard way. Maybe this will change your mind." Shane pulls his hand out of the front pocket of his black hoodie and points a gun in my direction. I'm not as afraid as I once was of guns, but that doesn't make having one pointed at me any less scary.

"Wait. What do you want?"

"Not you, but you'll get me what I really want. I want my son, Katy. You're just a means to an end."

He takes a slow step forward, and I step back, bumping into the sink.

Shit.

A smile slowly creeps up his lips, and the chip in his front tooth becomes visible. I'm trapped, and he knows it. The already small room feels like it's closing in on me.

Control your breathing, Katy. You don't want to pass out and make it easy on him.

He takes another calculated step forward but slightly to his left, blocking the exit more. It's a testament to his police training. Close off any exits. I may be his perpetrator, but I'm also his victim right now.

Maybe if I can stall long enough, someone will need to use the bathroom.

Another step forward, but I have nowhere to go. I need to fight, but Shane is playing offense right now and has the advantage. He wants Owen, and I'm the key. I have time to make a smart decision, and right now, that might be letting him take me wherever he needs to.

Slowly, I raise my hands in surrender.

"That's a good girl. I want you to take your phone out of your pocket and toss it on the ground. Can't have any of your daddies following us before I get my boy."

Bile threatens to rise from my throat as he refers to Owen as "his boy." I pull my phone from my front pocket and drop it on the floor. He steps forward and smashes it with the heel of his foot.

I see a moment of distraction and kick his knee to the side, making him stumble. The gun tumbles from his hand and slides across the tile floor in the opposite direction of the door. I think for a split second too long about running toward the door or the gun. When I decide the door is my best option, I only make it a few steps.

Firm hands push me forward and grab my ankle as my knees slam against the floor. Pain radiates up my legs, and I cry out but quickly bite my tongue to contain the sound. I don't want to give him the satisfaction of my pain. I kick out my feet, trying to shake him off as I attempt to crawl my way toward the door.

A metallic sound rings in the air, and Shane's furious voice seeps into my bones. "Stop, Bitch. I have a knife to your Achilles tendon. If I slice it, you will be completely immobilized and in a world of pain. Do you want to continue to fight?"

"Fuck." I drop my arms to the floor and sprawl out in surrender.

I tried. At least I can say I tried.

Shane doesn't release me as he stands. Pain sears through

my head as he grabs a handful of hair and pulls me to my feet. He yanks me further into the bathroom until he reaches where the gun slid. Shane squats, taking me with him, and my head bends at an odd angle, wrenching my neck.

I hiss at the pain and stumble as he pulls me to the exit. Panic rises again as I realize he's about to take me from the building. The few scraps of safety I felt quickly fade as we leave the bathroom, and Shane pushes the emergency door open without an alarm sounding. He puts his hand in his pocket, and the trunk pops on the black sedan.

"No. No. No!" I try to scream and flail as a last-ditch effort before he takes me, but it's futile in the empty alleyway, and we both know it.

"Shut up." I hear the smack and the instant pain on my cheek just before I'm shoved into the trunk. I'm still dazed as zip ties bind my wrists and tape is placed over my mouth just before darkness falls over me when the trunk is closed.

I contain my internal urge to pull on the restraints. I need to conserve all of my energy. I have no idea how long I'll be in this situation, and I want to be able to fight for as long as I can.

40

Dempsey

I want this life with Katy. I want to bring Owen and our children to tumble class and get dizzy doing forward rolls with them into the foam pits. I don't think I've ever been so happy in life.

Katy and her mother don't look like they are having a great time. I supported her decision to see her mother once more, but I had my doubts it would go any better than their first meeting. I respect her desire to allow Babs and Owen to have their chance at a relationship, but if the glances I'm seeing are any indication of their future, it doesn't look promising.

Owen runs toward the foam pit, and I have to focus my attention entirely on him so he doesn't sink and disappear into the foam abyss.

This is the life I've always wanted. It's time to tell her how I feel. I know she's not ready, but I think she's scared, and I need her to know there's nothing to be afraid of with me. There will never be anything to be afraid of.

By the time I pull Owen away from the foam pit, I'm sweaty

and more exhausted than I think I should be for playing with a not even two year old. Joy beams on my face, and I look at Katy and her mother and find one seat empty. I feel my face fall as I look around the room, trying to find her.

She's not at the front counter or near the vending machines. Her mother still sits where I last saw them together but looks around nervously. When she sees me staring at her, she stands and spins in both directions, looking for a way out.

I snatch Owen up and speed walk to Babs. She takes several steps backward, tripping into the seats. She braces herself on the back of a chair before she falls over and clutches her cell phone to her chest.

"Where is she?" My voice is a growl as the feeble woman cowers below me.

"I-I-I…"

"Where. Is. She."

Babs stares at Owen in my arms with awe and momentarily forgets I've asked her a question.

"Babs." My sharp tone grabs her attention back to me.

"B-bathroom. She's in the bathroom." Babs spits out as she cowers under my stare. My eyes whip to the back of the building and back to her.

"Let's go."

"What?"

"If she's in the bathroom, I'll need you to check on her. Let's go." Her mouth flaps like a fish, but she sees the seriousness in my eyes and slowly walks toward the bathrooms.

"Maybe she didn't go to the bathroom. I might have heard her wrong."

"I guess we're about to see?"

Babs drags her feet as we walk down the long hall. I have a

terrible feeling. I knew seeing her mother wasn't a good idea. Katy should have been the one on the gym floor with Owen, and I would have been watching them play together.

I slam my hand into the bathroom door and yell, as it opens, "Man coming in the women's room." I coax Babs into the room ahead of me and see all the stall doors open. The room is empty, and my heart sinks.

Where is she?

Owen starts to squirm in my arms. I know he wants down, but I can't release him. I have to hold on to him for Katy. For myself. As I readjust him, something on the floor catches my eye.

No.

I bend down, carefully picking up the shattered phone. As much as I hope when I flip it over, Katy's sunflower phone case doesn't stare back at me, I know it will.

Turning it in my hand, Babs gasps when she sees it. It sounds fake, but I can't understand why.

"What do you know?"

"Nothing," she says too quickly.

"Fuck!" The word escapes me in a roar, and Owen bursts into tears. My heart breaks, and I apologize to him as I pull my phone out.

Who the fuck do I call first?

"I should go."

I hit the speed dial on my phone, not wanting to make this call, but it has to be done.

"Don't fucking move." Babs freezes in fear.

"Dempsey?"

"Tucker, she's fucking gone."

"Where are you?"

"He has her. I know it. I found her phone smashed in the bathroom at Rock Star Gym. We're here for Owen's tumble class."

"I'm on my way."

I stop him before he can hang up. "Tucker, Katy's mother is here with me. I have no proof, but I have a nagging feeling she's involved.

"I'm already in my truck."

The call disconnects, and I hit #1 on my speed dial, and Patrick picks up.

"Inside. Now. I'm walking Katy's mother out with me from the bathrooms. Meet me along the way." I hang up and glare at the mouse of a woman before me.

"*We*, meaning you and I, are going to walk out of this building. You are going to come with me quietly and without making a scene, or I won't be held responsible for whatever happens if you try to protest. Do you understand me?"

With fear in her eyes, she nods her head, and I'm glad. The less bloodshed now means the more I can spill when I get my hands on that motherfucker. And Shane's blood will be shed.

If I truly admitted to myself everything I know about the evil men in the world, I'd have to confess that Shane taking Katy isn't really a surprise. But fuck me if I didn't think I could protect her from this situation.

I failed her.

Again.

Fucking. Again.

I'd take the pain of bleeding out in a car again over this

feeling. Every fiber of my soul is being shredded over and over, leaving nothing but a bloody pulp, but I have to focus.

Katy's mother sits in a corner of Spencer's house, looking frailer than a piece of paper in a hurricane. Her skin becomes paler the longer she sits. We've offered her food and water, but she's refused.

Outwardly you'd think she was exhibiting signs of a mother traumatized by her daughter's abduction, but I'm calling bullshit. I'm not the only one who's noticed the slight signs of withdrawal paired with fear in her eyes.

When Justin barged into the house, the look of disgust he flung her way was palpable. All the women and kids are locked up at Annie's house, like Fort Knox. No one is getting in or out of there without a nuclear launch code. Cole stayed with them as our point of contact, so none of the ladies have to get direct bad news if any comes, and we can all check up on the kids without worrying them.

It's tearing me up even more not to have eyes on Owen every second, but I know he's safe at Annie's. I need to believe that so I can focus all my energy on Katy.

"She's not his ultimate goal," Spencer offers.

It's been my thought as well, but I'm trying to make rational decisions before I go off the rails. I feel like a caged animal ready to strike.

"What do you mean, Smithy? His pictures have been focused on Katy. I don't think he's after you anymore."

"He's not. It hasn't been me for a while. It hasn't been Katy either." She walks over to the kitchen table, where hundreds of pictures are spread out. "Look."

"You don't have to. It's not Katy or Spencer. He's after Owen."

326

Curses and grumbles fill the room as everyone realizes what I've been thinking for a while. Owen was with me, and he was safe, but I left Katy vulnerable.

"Fuck!" I slam my hands on the table, pictures fly in every direction, and no one flinches except Babs. A shriek echoes from the living room, and I charge into the room straight for her. I know I'm a mess right now, but she's reacting to me like she thinks I'll hurt her. I'm not entirely sure I won't, so maybe her reaction is accurate.

Bracing my arms on either side of her chair, she leans back as far as she physically can as I tower over her trembling frame.

"Listen, you little bitch. I don't fucking like you, and I think you know a lot fucking more than you're saying. I don't like to hurt women, but I might make an exception if I decide you have information you're holding back."

A firm hand clasps my shoulder, and I shrug it off.

"Dempsey."

Tucker can fuck off. I don't care who signs my checks; they can fucking keep their money for all I care. Babs knows something.

Babs starts to hyperventilate under my intense glare. Her eyes roll back into her head, and her body slumps over as she passes out.

I stand, crossing my arms over my chest. "Fucking great."

"Dempsey."

"I fucking know, Tucker. I need to calm the fuck down." I run my hands through my hair, pulling the hair tie out and chucking it across the room with a roar.

Dropping onto the couch, I fist my hair at my temples and pull. The bite of pain grounds me but does nothing to calm my rage.

I FUCKING FAILED HER AGAIN.

We have nothing. No leads. He hasn't contacted us. She could be anywhere.

"What does he want? Why hasn't he contacted us? He's never been shy about it before. Why now?"

It's obvious by the looks on everyone's faces they're feeling the same way.

"What are we missing?" I can see Lincoln sorting through the pictures on the table.

A soft moan draws my attention across the room as Babs wakes from her fainting spell. Before I can even move, Tucker stands in front of me.

"Let me try."

I nod, knowing I'm beyond rational thinking at this moment.

I never told her. I was too chicken shit, and then when I wasn't, I let her irrational fear keep me from telling her how I feel.

I fucking love her, and I will tear Shane apart inch by fucking inch when I find him.

As Tucker approaches Babs, she cowers as far into the corner of the chair as humanly possible. My lip twitches, seeing her fear, knowing I caused it. Even if she had nothing to do with Katy's abduction, she deserves every bit of fear she has right now. She neglected Katy growing up and used her for whatever she needed, then basically sold her.

"Babs, I'm inclined to agree with my friend over there that you seem to know more than you're letting on. Would you care to share with us what you know? It seems convenient that the one time our guard was down, Shane took the opportunity to take Katy. How did he know she went to the bathroom?"

Babs closes her eyes as if she can block out Tucker's words just by not seeing him. That's not going to fucking happen.

Justin enters the room and steps up to Tucker. "Let me try." Tucker steps aside, looking slightly defeated. It's how we are all feeling.

No one has even mentioned calling the police. At this point, we are beyond the law.

Justin squats in front of Babs, and she peeks her eyes open. Her body physically relaxes when she sees him, and it makes my rage boil inside again. She shouldn't feel an ounce of relief.

"Babs, you're a piece of shit mother. The only good thing you've ever done in your life is sign the paperwork allowing Katy to be free of you. If there's a fucking iota of a human being left inside you, and you know anything about Katy's abduction, I suggest you tell us right now. If we find out that you were holding back information, every person in this room will turn a blind eye to whatever wrath that Viking back there sees fit to dole out to you."

Holy fucking shit. I don't know where that came from, but every word Justin just said is accurate. I'll name my firstborn after him for that.

Babs begins to stutter, and her eyes start to roll again.

"Nope. Not happening." Justin slaps her cheek a few times, stopping her fainting spell, and whatever relaxation she felt in his presence is gone.

"Let me have my fucking chance with her." Justin puts his hand up to stop Lincoln, and I see the pain in his eyes that matches mine.

Lincoln is feeling the agony of failing Katy as much as I am. He thought he saved her from Shane once, and here we are, having to do it again.

Katy has a piece of every person's heart in this room. She's Justin's savior, Axel's safe space, Miller's joy, Lincoln's kindred soul, Spencer and Tucker's daughter, and my future wife.

"Okay."

What? Did Babs just say okay? Is she admitting to knowing something?

Her eyes dart around the room at everyone gathered around her. Tucker and I exchange a knowing look. We're about to get somewhere in Katy's disappearance.

"Sh-Shane took her."

No shit. That's not news.

With a trembling hand, she reaches into her purse and pulls out her phone, handing it to Justin. He takes it with a confused look.

"T-texts."

Justin glances at the phone and immediately sprints to the kitchen, handing it to Chip, who's been trying to access any cameras around the gym to see if he can find any suspicious cars. The house grows silent as Chip types away after plugging her phone into his laptop. I think everyone is holding their breath, waiting for even a scrap of hope of Katy's whereabouts.

"You fucking bitch." Chip shoots a scathing glance in the direction of Babs.

"What did you find?" Axel asks. His usual bubbly tone is laced with unease. Tucker walks up behind him and wraps his arms around Axel's chest, pulling him close. His vibrating stops as Tucker takes away some of his anxiety.

"Katy was being tracked."

"We already knew this." My words come out with more venom than I intend, but Chip lets it roll off his shoulders and goes back to his search.

"Bun-Bun."

"The fuck?"

"There are texts exchanged about Owen's bunny. She gave him one with a tracker in it."

"The fucking coffee shop," I growl. All eyes turn to me, waiting for an explanation. I charge back into the living room and put my finger in Babs' face.

"You goddamn fucking cunt. You conspired with your fucking daughter's rapist. Are you that fucking heartless? Are you so fucking hard up for a fix? What did he pay you because people like you don't do a damn thing unless they're getting something out of it? I'll double it. I'll fucking triple it. Every penny I have for every piece of information you know right goddamn now."

My chest heaves with the effort it's taking me to contain myself. I want to tear this woman apart. Words start spilling from her mouth, but I can't hear anything. The blood rushes through my ears so loudly it's all I can hear.

My phone buzzes, and I pull it out of my pocket. Everyone who would be contacting me is here in this room. It has to be...

"FUCK!"

I toss my phone at Chip, and everyone scrambles to see the reason for my outburst.

"Dempsey?"

Tucker calls out to me as I storm out of the room, but I'm

beyond reasoning right now. I walk through the kitchen and out the back door, straight to the first tree I come to. I take my aggression out, punch by punch. I see Shane, who took the woman I love. I see my CO that got away with raping a fellow Marine. I see…myself. Their brutality doesn't come close to the feeling of failure coursing through my body. I'm not good enough for her. I wasn't good enough to keep her out of Shane's hands. I'm no better than them.

He has her, and the picture he sent me is proof.

Unknown: Are you willing to share?

"God damn mother fucking asshole fucking cunt—"

A hand grabs my biceps, and on instinct, I spin, swinging my fist. Patrick ducks but sucker punches me in the gut as he straightens. I fall to the ground, my body exhausted. Tears flowing freely down my cheeks, and there's nothing I can do to stop them.

I scream.

Long. Loud. Agonizingly.

I scream until my voice becomes hoarse, and the tears stop. When I look up at Patrick, he offers me his hand. There's no judgment on his face. I feel the empathy, the camaraderie.

"Chip has a lead."

41

Shane

Twenty-four hours wasn't much notice to get my plan in place, but when that druggy bitch told me my sweet Katy agreed to meet her again, I knew it was finally my chance.

How easily Babs was to manipulate. All she wanted was a high, and I still have plenty of connection from being a street cop that I've been able to supply her with the good stuff and not the cheap bottom-of-the-barrel crap she's used to. A quick trip to a salon and a clothing store and she suddenly looked like mom of the year.

Fucking pathetic.

I glance in my rearview mirror at the back seats, knowing the treasure that lies just behind them. My Katy is quiet. Her determination in the bathroom was a turn-on. She didn't fight like that when I took her in the alley two years ago. She had been a helpless little doe. Much like Spencer. So easily pliable.

I know high school girls come through this parking lot for lunch. Such innocence just strolling around without a care in the world, naive to their surroundings. The girls usually come in pairs, but I'm patient. I'll wait for the right gem to come alone.

It doesn't take long before my present arrives. A pretty brunette strolls through the parking lot, more preoccupied with her phone than noticing any danger. Time to turn on my boyish charm. I flip my hat backward and pull the zipper half down on my hoodie to give myself a lazier appearance.

The brunette walks inside, and I wait on the side of the building. She doesn't keep me waiting long. My fingers tingle from the adrenaline of the anticipation.

"Hey, excuse me?" I rub the back of my neck to look insecure and innocent and flash her a half smile. Brown eyes look up at me from her phone.

"Oh, hi."

"I was just wondering if you'd seen a debit card lying around out here. I must have missed my pocket when I was putting it away, and I swear I'm blind because I can't find it." I shrug my shoulders and look around me, making sure no one is in the area.

"Um, no, sorry. I wasn't really paying attention." She chuckles and waves her phone in a knowing gesture.

"Damn." I sigh heavily, letting my shoulders fall. "I feel like I've looked everywhere. Would you mind being another set of eyes and helping me out? I got gas, then walked next door to get lunch, but I lost it before I could order my food.

"Um?" She looks down at her phone, assumingly to look at the time.

"You probably have to get back to class. Thanks anyway. I don't want to be a burden and take up any more of your time."

Take the bait, pretty girl.

"Sure, I can help for a minute or two. It must be around here somewhere."

Perfect. I just need to get her in front of the alley and—

Beeeeeeeep.

"Shit." I look up to see the light I'm stopped at has turned green, and I was lost in my favorite memory of *my* Katy. Shame I didn't get to finish the daydream. The surprise that made it an impossibly perfect moment. Spencer's arrival.

I can't help but smile as I drive through the quiet suburban neighborhood I've called home for the last year. A few phone calls to the right people, and I was able to get use of an old safe house that the city still owns. I offered to take over the utility payments, and they were all too happy to unload those bills. Fucking bureaucracy.

The garage door opens as I pull into the driveway, and I push the button again to cocoon us in darkness. No one outside these walls will be the wiser that I have my feisty baby mama in the trunk.

Stepping out of the car, I stretch from side to side, knowing she probably won't go willingly into the house. I'm eager for the next battle. My hand runs along the side of the car, and I bang the trunk before hitting the button on the key fob to pop it open. I ready myself to grab my gun if she puts up too much of a fight, but much to my dismay, she lies there quietly.

"Hello pretty girl. We're home."

Katy squeezes her eyes closed. Black lines stain her cheeks, letting me know she's been crying. Pity I didn't get to see it. There's still time.

"Only little bitches cry."

"Shut up." I scrub a hand over my face, wiping away the voices.

"You're never going to be good at anything being such a pussy. Man the fuck up."

"Fuck off. I'll show you who's a man."

Reaching into the trunk, I grab a handful of Katy's hair. It was effective earlier to get her to do what I wanted. Her eyes widen, protesting the pain, but she makes no sound, and I'm disappointed.

"Out you go." I grab her legs to help her sit up, but I have to do most of the lifting to get her out of the trunk.

Katy's eyes bounce wildly around the garage. There's little light to see anything, but I know where everything is without sight and guide us to the door that leads into the kitchen. A keypad adorns the door, and the lock beeps, allowing us entry.

I direct Katy to sit on a kitchen stool, and she glares at me. I'm a little disappointed she isn't putting up more of a fight.

"Before you get any ideas of trying to escape, the doors only open with a keycode both in and out. This is a safe house, so none of the windows open, and there are no knives anywhere to be found. I know you're resourceful, but unless you plan to try to dig a hole with a spoon, there's nothing here to use as a weapon."

She stares back at me in silence. Is it calculating or defeat?

"You can't even scare a teenage girl. What good are you?"

A growl escapes me, and Katy's brows scrunch at my random noise. I turn my back on her and squeeze my eyes shut. I've come this far, and I'm so close to getting my son. Keep your shit together, Shane.

Turning around, I open a drawer and pull out a burner phone. Another perk of this safe house. These things are like cockroaches. They seem to multiply in every drawer.

"Smile pretty for the camera." She closes her eyes and looks down, doing the opposite of what I asked her. At least there's a spark of defiance in her. She isn't completely defeated. I snap a picture anyway. Surely, her bodyguard knew what she was wearing at that gym. He only has eyes for her. It's a shame I didn't take him away from her that night in the rain. I thought for sure he would have bled out.

A shiver runs down my spine as I remember hearing Spencer's voice over the car speakers. Her fear and the thrill of getting what I wanted while knowing she couldn't stop me.

My nose tingles at the next reminder that I didn't complete my task. I glance at Katy, remembering the blinding pain when she reared her head and broke my fucking nose. I was so proud of her, but I never expected her to grab a gun from the glove compartment. That wasn't something I could have predicted. Or her lack of hesitation when she pulled the trigger and a bullet seared through my arm.

I slam my hand on the counter at the memory, making Katy flinch. I had to let her go and leave. There was no way I was getting her out of that car and into mine when I didn't have use of my arm.

"Fuck." I rub my arm over the bullet wound and open the refrigerator for a beer. I chug it down in a few long pulls and toss it in the blue bin by the garage door. That was two years ago—two long years.

I dial a number into the phone that I know by heart and type a message before I hit send on the picture. I smile knowing it will torture him to know I have her.

Katy watches my every move as I stalk closer. Her breath hitches as I straddle her legs and run my knuckles along her cheek. She's wearing a brave face, but I see the fear behind her eyes.

"You know. We could just let Spencer keep Owen and make another one." Her body begins to flail under me as I trail my fingers down her neck and over the front of her shirt.

"Ah. There's my little fighter. Keep it up. You're making me hard." Her body stiffens as I knew it would. I step away, and her body sags in relief.

Pulling out my knife, her eyes widen. As I get closer, she tries to slink away, but there's nowhere to go. She has nothing to worry about. I won't hurt her unless she makes me. Katy's eyes follow the knife as I cut the strap of her purse, and she gasps.

"I need to make sure you don't have anything in here to hurt yourself." A smile lights my face at the very first thing I see. I pull the stuffed bunny out of Katy's purse, and she whimpers when I close my fist tightly around its midsection. Laughter escapes me when I feel the tracking device hidden inside.

"Sometimes I'm a real genius." I stab into the back of the bunny, and Katy whines as I tear apart Owen's precious toy. Her eyes widen as I pull out the device the size of a quarter and place it on the table in front of her.

I see the moment she realizes the true betrayal of the

woman who birthed her. I quickly noticed the navy stuffed rabbit that went everywhere with Owen. He was never without it. It grew with him from his infant seat to the strollers on walks and carrying it in his hand when he could walk alongside Katy.

The day Babs met with Katy at the coffee shop and handed my gift to her, I nearly came in my pants at the exhilaration. Watching the red dot on my phone wherever it went had become my biggest thrill. I may not have always been able to track where Katy was, but she wasn't my priority. Owen was.

"It's a shame that I won't need this soon."

Katy's head shakes in disbelief. Her eyes plead for answers, asking why, how?

"Oh, Katy dear. Your mother is a druggy slut. It's easy to slap lipstick on a pig and motivate it with food. Oh, don't look at me like that. Did you honestly think, after nineteen years, she'd suddenly cleaned up her act because you gave her a grandchild? Fuck no. That was all me. That woman hasn't been sober since the 80's, probably earlier. She does clean up nicely, though. I thought about giving her a spin, but she looks like she's a leach and would get too attached." I look Katy up and down, licking my lips at the memory of her. "Besides, I prefer the younger model."

"Stop playing with your food, you lazy piece of shit."

I spin to the refrigerator and grab another beer, chugging it faster than the first. I have a job to do if I want to get my boy, and I need to think straight.

"Let me show you to your room. It's all yours if you decide to stay with me and Owen and be a happy little family.

Otherwise, the accommodations should be to your liking for your short-term stay."

Grabbing her bicep, I pull her up, and she comes willingly. More tears spill down her cheeks at all the information I just gave her. It's a lot to process. I'm honestly a little disgusted when I think of how easily Babs tossed her daughter to the curb.

We come to a door in the hallway with another keypad. Punching in the code, I listen for the beep and turn the knob. The door opens to a plain room. White walls and curtains cover a window facing the back of the house. The bedspread is floral and smells musty from sitting in here unused. A door leads to an en suite bathroom, and another is a closet that's long been empty.

"If you promise to behave, I'll give you back your hands. Can you be my good girl?"

Her body winces, but she nods her head. I pull the tape off her mouth and enjoy the whimper she gives me. Using my knife, I slice between the plastic of the zip ties, and they snap apart. Katy rubs her wrists but stays silent.

"I'll let you know when I need your services again. Until then, enjoy yourself here." The door locks behind me and I pause at the sound.

"Please don't lock the door. I don't want to be left alone. Please, father."

I know it's no use. It never is. I'll take his silence over his words or hands any day, but the unknown of how long I'll be locked in here is what terrifies me.

I slump against the door, slide down until I'm seated, and wrap my hands around my legs. I didn't mean to kill the cat. It ran in front of my bike, and its back leg was broken. The bone was sticking out, and it was crying for help. I helped it.

"You don't belong around people. There's something wrong with you," my father told me when he found me in the garage with the body. I couldn't convince him I had killed it out of mercy. Hadn't I?

Father told me I was destined to be alone. No one in my life could ever love me because I'm sick in the head. I'll prove him wrong. I'll be a better father to my son than he ever was to me.

As I walk down the hall, I stop at the nursery I have set up for Owen. It's everything I wanted as a child. Glow-in-the-dark stars line the ceiling, and everything is navy in color, just like his Bun-Bun. Unlike the closet in Katy's room, the one in here is full of toys and clothes, and I even made sure to pick up several packs of the colorful star stickers that he likes as a reward. He's going to be so happy here.

Katy has been with me for over two hours now, and I haven't heard from her worthless mother. I hope they took and tortured her for information. She knows nothing more than I wanted her to know, and that was jackshit. I have the bunny with the tracker, and I have Katy. Soon, I'll have my boy, and life will be complete.

42

Katy

I'm in a room, in a house, in some cookie-cutter neighborhood. I can see backyards with swimming pools and trampolines. The window is nailed shut, and it looks like there's a wired alarm, even if I could get the nails out.

The closet and bathroom are empty except for a toothbrush and toothpaste. Travel-size shampoo and a bar of soap are the only things in the shower. Dresser drawers are empty. There are no knick-knacks or even pictures on the walls. Unless I planned to smother him with a pillow that smells like a grandma or somehow sharpen my toothbrush into a shiv, I have nothing to defend myself with.

Think. Think.

He has a gun and a knife. Maybe I showed my hand too soon by fighting back in the bathroom. He doesn't see me as meek and defenseless like he did that day in the alley.

THINK. THINK.

There must be something. A loose nail or screw? There

are no lamps in the room, no books. I walk around testing all the knobs on the furniture, looking under everything. The bathroom is bare unless I want to beat him with a toilet scrubber.

I plop on the toilet seat in defeat and hear the shift of ceramic. Spinning, I grip the edges of the tank, and the top lifts.

"Holy shit," I whisper shout.

The top of the tank comes off. It's big, bulky, and definitely heavy, but if I can catch him off guard, maybe I can stun him long enough to grab the knife. No. I need to grab the gun. This is my only chance. There's nothing else in these rooms, but it seems like such an absurd plan.

It's the only plan.

The door has a locking keypad that makes a sound. I need to be on high alert for whenever he gets back. Fully removing the lid, I clutch it to my chest like it's my lifeline. My eyes assess the room again, but instead of looking for a weapon, I'm looking for a vantage point.

Channeling my inner Viktor and Lincoln, I inspect every corner of the room. Do I make him come to me across the room? I could hide in the closet.

No. Neither of those would work because I'm stuck in here if the door closes. My best option is the element of surprise as soon as he walks in the door, hoping I can stop the door from closing. I glance behind me at the hand towel hanging up. I can use that to hopefully prevent the door from latching while I try to get his gun. At least it gives me a second option. Run.

Next to the door is a tall dresser. If I hide behind it, he'll have to step into the room when he doesn't initially see me.

Fuck. I already feel the weight of the ceramic. It's going to be exhausting holding onto this for an undetermined amount of time. I'm glad I chose to save my energy earlier. I have a little boy and a hulking Viking to get back to, and I'll be damned if I'm going down without a fight.

43

Dempsey

I have no idea what the fuck Chip is going on about. I heard something about triangulating the texts on Babs' phone between her and Shane. Going back to the texts the day she gave the stuffed bunny to Katy. Honestly, I couldn't care less if he had to give a hand job to every nun in the city as long as he finds Katy.

"Can I look at it?" Spencer approaches me with caution and a small medical bag. My hands are torn up and aching. I wrapped dish towels around my knuckles in an effort not to get blood on anything, but I know it's not a solution.

"Sure."

She gestures to the kitchen table, and I move to sit, resting my hands on the table. I wince when she pulls away the first towel, reopening some of the cuts as the dried blood clings to the material.

"Did it make you feel better?"

Did it? Fuck no.

I jerk my head in response, and she nods in understanding.

"How are you doing, Spencer?" This is hard for all of us, but I imagine there's a different level of guilt for her.

"May I share something with you, Vik?" She dabs a cleaning solution on my knuckles, and I relish the sting. I'll gladly accept any feeling other than the gut-shattering heartache right now.

"Anything."

"Do you know I was once pregnant...with Shane's baby?"

It's not often that Spencer isn't one hundred percent confident, but that slight pause speaks volumes.

"I do. Justin filled me in on your past when things started to escalate with Shane. I'm sorry if that's a breach of confidence."

"No," she insists. "I've told my story several times lately. It saves me the pain of telling it again."

I nod, feeling like there's more to it than we all know.

"Emory."

"Who?"

"I had named my daughter Emory. I don't think I've ever said that out loud before." Our eyes lock, and I see the pain. Her mask is down, and she's completely vulnerable. This isn't a side of her I usually see unless she's with one of her men. This emotion is for me.

"I always liked having a unisex name because there were no preconceived notions about my gender. In fact, it was almost easier to hide because people assumed it was a male's name and would look me over. I stood out enough as a child already. Emory means "home strength" and refers to someone who has great bravery in challenging times."

"It's a beautiful name." Spencer nods in response. She's speaking to me, but there's a far-off look in her eyes as she tends to the cuts on my knuckles.

"It is. Although I had no idea when I chose it, I was the one who would need the strength through the challenge of her loss."

Tucker walks past us in the distance, and I lock eyes with him. I give him an almost imperceptible nod, but he understands and slowly walks our way.

"I never thought of her. It was a time in my life I wanted to forget. I knew I would never have a child of my own ever again, and it was easier to forget the pain ever existed than to deal with it. I compartmentalized my experience into a box in my mind and tucked it away."

Tucker hears her words and stops a few feet behind her, not wanting to stop the emotions her soul is unburdening.

"Until Miller, Axel, Lincoln, and Tucker came into my life, and I had to give them the option of living a childless life with me. But Katy took that burden away. She became ours and filled the hole in my heart that I had ignored for over a decade. I never even told my father, but I donated Emory's body to the hospital. If there was any part of her that could help another, I wanted that."

Spencer finishes wrapping my hands and cleans up her supplies.

"I'm sorry my past has put you in this position."

"Spencer, you—"

"I know I'm not the cause of this. He chose Katy randomly, and by some ridiculous fuckery of fate, she was linked to us."

Tucker smiles at her curse word. It's a rare occasion that Spencer resorts to cursing, but she's passionate about what she's saying right now, and I can't blame her.

"I'm grateful because he brought her to us, and that brought her to you. Katy belongs to us, and every person in this house will do everything in our power to find her and bring her home safely. For you Vik. I'm not losing another daughter to him. You deserve her future."

Tucker realizes she's done and steps up to her, kissing the top of her head tenderly.

"Y'all done here, Little Miss?"

Spencer looks up at him, knowing he was listening. He won't bring it up until she's ready to discuss it again. If she ever is.

"Fucking A. I found it! I found the location of the tracker." Everyone in the house rushes to the living room at the sound of Chip's exclamation.

"I know that address." Everyone looks at Lincoln. "It's a police safe house. Fucking shit. Let's go."

"Patrick, stay with the useless mother. I think she's about to see the inside of a jail cell." He nods and hovers over her cowering body.

"I'll stay, too. I think I'm more afraid of what my pregnant wife might do if she found out I put myself in danger than I am of a man potentially wielding a gun. Bring home our girl, Vik."

I give Justin a curt nod, and everyone heads to the front door. I see Chip sit back on the couch, and I grab the back of his shirt, pulling him up to his feet. I hear a growl across the room and look up to see Patrick scowling at me. Fucking weird.

"You're coming with us, Chip. We need to know if that signal moves." Chip glances at Patrick before stumbling his way toward the door, laptop in hand.

Wordlessly, we all file into our vehicles. I get into Lincoln's passenger seat with Miller and Chip climbing into the back.

Tucker and Spencer get into his truck and follow us. I want to tell Lincoln to floor it. I want to reach my leg over and slam my foot on his to make us go faster, but we have to get there safely.

A hand reaches from behind and clamps my shoulder. "She'll be okay," Miller says, trying to calm my nerves.

"She better fucking be." I'll rip every fucking inch of that motherfucker apart if he even touches a hair on her body.

"Chip, any movement?" Lincoln turns into a residential neighborhood, and I can feel my heart trying to beat out of my chest.

"No. It hasn't moved."

"Stay in the truck and lock the doors when we get there. All right, Chip?" Lincoln uses his stern cop voice, and Chip nods in understanding.

Lincoln pulls over a few houses down from the red dot on Chip's screen, and a silent look passes through all of us. This is it. Katy may or may not be inside the house. Katy had Bun-Bun, and the tracker was inside the toy. Shane could have dumped the tracker here and gone somewhere else, but I fucking hope he wasn't that smart.

We all climb out of our vehicles, and I hear the doors lock behind us. I see Chip slink down in his seat. Poor kid isn't made for this kind of stuff.

"Do we have a plan?" Axel asks as he looks around at all the perfectly manicured lawns and minivans around us. Each one of us is carrying at least one gun. I can guarantee Lincoln and Spencer have at least two each.

As we stand here trying to come up with a plan, two quick gunshots pierce the air.

"Katy!" I'm running before I even realize I'm moving.

"Dempsey, wait," Lincoln yells hot on my heels.

"Fuck that."

Tucker grabs me as I'm about to reach the bottom step of the porch and wraps his arms around my chest. I try to wrestle him off, but the fucker has me in a bear hug, and Lincoln steps up to my front, forcing me to give him all my attention.

"Look," Lincoln tells me.

He knows my background and knows I'm better trained than my emotions are allowing me to act. I don't want anyone else to get hurt, but my body is vibrating to get inside and make sure she's okay. She's alive.

"Fuck."

There's a keypad lock on the front door, like Justin and Spencer's house. Tucker releases me, realizing I've gained my wits back, and I bob my head in thanks. He returns it as a silent gesture, saying, " No problem."

"How do we get in?"

"Let me make a call and see if I can get a code."

Lincoln pulls out his phone, and I grab his wrist. "Two shots were fired. We don't have time for calls. We need action now."

Lincoln's eyes bob between mine as he considers my words. I see the moment he comes to a decision. I release his wrist, and he pulls his gun out.

"Fuck it. Everyone get ready." He raises his hand toward the door, and we all cover our ears. The gunshot pierces the air as the door explodes next to the lock pad.

I push past everyone and shove the door with my shoulder. It gives under my weight, and we pour inside the house in different directions. I follow the smell of gunpowder down a hallway and peek into doors as I pass them. The first room is a...nursery. Fuck. Next is a bathroom. I carefully approach the final door as the smell of copper stings my nose.

No. Fuck no.

I take a deep breath and approach the door. As I spin the corner, gun cocked in front of me, something crunches under my feet, and I have a split second to duck before a bullet flies past my head.

"Fuck."

Someone yells, "In here," before I'm slammed into.

44

Katy

Come on. Where is he? I've been sitting on the bed, clutching the top of the toilet, barely breathing. I don't want to miss a single sound, so I know when Shane is coming back. I became quickly fatigued holding the heavy porcelain and realized standing until he comes back isn't an option. I need to conserve my energy so I can get the best swing possible.

I jump when I hear a chair scrape along the floor, and Shane curses.

"Time to go, Katy."

Go? I can't leave. This is my chance. It has to be. I hide behind the dresser like I planned, and lock my jaw closed to keep my teeth from clattering in fear. I rest the toilet lid on my shoulder, preparing to swing it like a bat. Shane walks up to the door, and I lift the top and spread my legs, getting ready to attack.

The door beeps, and as expected, when he doesn't see me, he takes a step inside and looks around. I made sure to close the bathroom door so he would assume I was in there and direct his attention in the opposite direction of where I'm standing.

"We have to go, Katy."

He takes another step in, and I swing up and out. The momentum throws me forward, and when the lid collides with his chin, his head snaps back, and the porcelain shatters all around us. Shane's body falls forward, taking me with him. The gun he had in his hand lands under me as his body crashes on top of mine.

"You hucking itch," he screams, words slurred from the odd angle his jaw sits at. I think I broke it. Good.

He looks around the room, trying to locate his gun while using his body weight to keep me pinned down. He has no idea it's under my hip, but I can't lift him to reach it either.

Shane realizes he can't find it and shifts to grab his pocket knife from his back pocket. The movement gives me just enough wiggle room to reach behind me and grab the gun. I can't think. I just need to act.

I need to pull the trigger.

I need to get back to Owen.

I need to get back to Viktor.

I rip the gun out from behind my back, and as soon as it's free, I pull the trigger.

Once.

Twice.

Shane roars in pain and grabs at his side. He sits up on his knees, looking at me with a shocked expression. I shakily point the gun at him as he pulls down the zipper of his jacket, and his white t-shirt underneath is covered in crimson.

"You hucking cunt!" His speech is even more slurred as

353

I watch the color drain from his face. He stands on shaky legs and stumbles out of the room, clutching his side. Large pieces of porcelain stop the door from closing and locking me back inside the room.

I scramble back to the corner next to the dresser. I should try to storm my way out of here, but my body is currently in freeze mode, having already gone through the fight. I just need a few minutes to compose myself before I can get to the flight part.

I shot Shane...again. But he came back the last time. He came back, and I need to be ready. I have a gun, and I can defend myself when he comes back. I'm ready. I can hear him opening drawers in the kitchen; every noise is like a cheese grater on my nerves.

I have to move. Get the fuck up, Katy.

Get up. Get up. *Get. Up.*

I can't. I know I need to, but I can't. I look down at the gun in my hands and have no idea how I'll use it when he comes back. My hands are trembling, and tears take over my vision.

"Fuuuuuuuck. Get up you stupid bitch. You can do it. I can do it. I have to."

Just as I begin to believe my pep talk, a loud bang sounds from across the house. He's found another gun.

Get ready.

He's coming back.

You've lost your chance.

I have to survive.

Just shoot. He's coming for you. *Just shoot.*

I aim at the space just inside the door. I hear the crunch from the broken porcelain on the floor and pull the trigger.

"Fuck."

Viktor?!

I drop the gun and launch my body into him, slamming us into the open door as I hear someone yell "In here" across the house. Viktor's strong hands rip me off his body, but the moment he realizes it's me, I'm lifted off the floor into his arms.

"Oh my god, I shot at you. Did I hit you? Are you alright?" I try to pull back to see if he's injured, but his grip is so fierce I can't move.

"I'm fine, Pepper. You missed. Even if you didn't, I'd gladly wear your scar. Are you hurt?"

"No. No, I'm okay." Viktor's hands begin to roam my body as if he doesn't believe that I'm unharmed. "Look at me, Viktor. Look at me."

His wild eyes stare back at me, and I cup his cheeks. "I love you."

"No."

"Viking, did you just tell me no?"

"Yes."

"Why?"

"Because I love *you.*"

"Oh, well, can we love each other? And maybe when I'm not covered in blood?" My panic instantly rises. "Shane. Where's Shane?"

"All clear?" Viktor yells over my shoulder.

"He's dead." Tucker comes around the corner with concern in his eyes. "Are you okay, Katy?" I wiggle, and Viktor reluctantly releases me but takes my hand.

Tucker pulls me into a hug. "He's dead. It's over. I'm proud of you."

Viktor releases my hand, and as I turn to see why, my eyes

catch on the new bodies gathered in the hallway outside the bedroom. I'm passed around, and rounds of hugs and praises are whispered in my ear.

It's not long before sirens are heard outside, and Lincoln leaves our group to talk with the arriving officers.

"Am I in trouble?"

"Why would you be in trouble?" Viktor takes my hand and laces our fingers together.

"I ki–shot someone." I'm not sure I've fully processed what I actually did yet.

"No. No, Pepper. It was self-defense."

"And he's…"

"He's dead. It's over. You saved us again."

"What? What do you mean?" I stare into his silver-blue eyes. He takes my hand and presses it to his stomach over his scar.

"He shot me, and I survived because of you. You shot him, and he didn't. Because you were never his. You've always been mine, Pepper. Both of you."

We're both his.

"Owen. Is Owen safe?"

"Yeah. Hold on," Miller says behind me. He pulls his phone out of his pocket, and a moment later, I hear Cole's voice.

"Do you have her?" his voice comes through the speaker.

"Yeah, and we've got a mama bear here who would love to see her little boy."

Miller hands me his phone, and a moment later, Owen's sweet face appears on the screen.

"Mama!"

"Hey beautiful boy. Mama loves you."

"Love you, mama." Lips fill the screen as he tries to give

me kisses through the phone, and I giggle at his adorableness. Viktor hugs me into him, and I feel the safety his body engulfs me in.

I hang up with Owen and realize there's still someone that I need to ask about.

"My mother. She was involved with Shane."

"We know." There's a growl to Viktor's answer. "Patrick has her at the house. She won't get away with being involved with this, Pepper. I promise."

I believe him.

45

Dempsey

She's here in my arms. I fucking found her, and I'm never letting her go.

"Get an ambulance in here," one of the cops yells from the kitchen. Katy stiffens in my arms.

"Ambulance? Is he alive? You said he was dead."

"Shh, relax, Pepper. They have to have the paramedics out here to pronounce the body. It's okay. You're safe."

"I want to see."

"You want to see…the body. Why?"

"I need to know. I need to know it's over."

"I'm not sure that's a good idea."

"She needs it, Viktor." Spencer gives me a look that leaves no room for argument. It's Katy's choice. I'll deal with whatever the fallout is for her. If she needs it, I'll take her.

I walk us into the kitchen with Katy tucked under my arm. There's already a sheet on the floor over Shane's body.

"Are you sure?"

"I am."

Lincoln stands next to the body, realizing what we're doing. I nod at him, and he puts on a pair of gloves then slowly lifts the sheet. Katy's hand tightens on my shirt as Shane's face is uncovered. Lincoln stops the reveal once Shane's shoulders are exposed, and I'm glad he does.

Katy gasps and buries her face into my chest.

"Okay. I'm done."

I walk her away from the kitchen, glad she didn't look around the room. Blood covers several surfaces, as Shane must have been trying to find something to help stop the bleeding.

We make it to the front door that someone leaned against the inside wall from where I knocked it down. Nothing matters to me right now other than the woman in my arms. I almost lost her for a second time, and I swear on my life it will never happen again.

There's chaos around us as police cars litter the road and front yard. Red and blue lights flash amongst the fading sunlight, and navy blue uniforms wander in every direction.

"Marry me, Pepper."

"Viktor?" She looks up at me through her dark lashes, brown eyes full of confusion. "Are you sure my bullet missed you?"

I've never been more sure of anything in my life. I release her and drop to one knee, taking her hands in mine.

"I wish it had because I'll bleed any day for the rest of my life for you. I almost lost you today. Fuck, I *did* lose you. You were taken from me, and I almost lost my mind." For the first time, she notices the bandages on my hand and squints at them as she rubs her thumbs over the tape. "I pretended a tree was Shane's face."

"Did it help?"

"You helped. You killed that motherfucker. *You*, Pepper." I drop my head to our joined hands. "Marry me. I never want to be without you again. I want to make Owen a big brother. I want to have all the babies with you. Let me take care of you. Both of you. Let me love you the way you deserve to be loved. I want to love you so hard you get sick of me and then love you even harder. Please, Katy Coble. Marry me."

She's quiet. I don't know what I'll do if she rejects me. She consumes me. Every last fucking inch of me belongs to her. She has to say yes.

"But, Viktor."

Fuck please don't say no.

"If I say yes"—say fucking yes—"who will be my bodyguard? You can't also be my husband. That would be a conflict of interest." A chuckle escapes her, and I lift my head and look into her chocolaty eyes.

Fuck, she's saying yes.

"Say yes. I'll be your forever bodyguard if you say yes, Pepper. Be mine. I want to adopt Owen and be his, too."

Katy's eyes well up with tears, and I stand, pulling her into my chest.

"Say yes." I kiss her temple. "Say yes." Her forehead. "Say." Nose. "Yes." Cheek. "I love you." My mouth hovers over hers, waiting to hear those three little letters leave her lips.

Her eyes flutter closed, and the quietest "yes" breathes across my lips as she crashes her mouth to mine.

I lift her into my arms and kiss her with every bit of passion, love, and loyalty I have.

"You said yes. You'll marry me?"

"Yes."

"You'll be mine? Forever?"

"Forever."

I need to know. "And Owen?"

"Forever, Viking. Ours forever."

"Fuck. I need to take you home right now and make love to you, but you need to talk to the police. You're mine as soon as we leave here."

"Forever yours *after* we pick up Owen."

"Forever mine *after* shower sex, then we pick up Owen." I look down at her clothes splattered with blood, and she follows my gaze.

"Deal." She seals her words with a kiss.

"Are you going to make me wait?"

"For shower sex? We can do that as soon as we get home."

I laugh into her neck and inhale her sweet scent. "Not for the sex. To make you Katy and Owen Dempsey. I'd drag you to the courthouse right now if you'll let me. I know I'm being demanding, but I've never been more sure of anything in my life." I move a hand to her belly. "I want more little Owens and little Katys. As many as you'll give me. I want to take care of all of them. Of you."

She playfully slaps my chest. "I knew you had a lactation kink, but are you adding breeding kink to that as well?"

"Fuck yes. Courthouse then baby making." I possessively growl into her neck at the visual of both of those things.

She giggles, and it's music to my fucking soul. "Can we start with the shower first and a promise that I won't make you wait too long for the rest? Because I think I like the idea of dark hair, blue-eyed baby Vikings running around, but I also need to remove this birth control first." She lifts her arm and pokes at the small rod.

I echo her answer from earlier. "Deal." I'll take it out myself if I have to.

There are two police cars in front of Spencer's house when we pull up. Katy gave her statement at the scene, and they told her she would have to go to the station tomorrow to make a formal statement.

Justin bursts out the front door and almost tackles Katy. He lifts her off the ground in a bear hug that has her huffing.

"You scared the shit out of us. Couldn't you have a normal teenage tantrum and smoke cigarettes or experiment with drugs? You had to be all dramatic and get kidnapped. You overachiever." He puts her back on her feet but doesn't let go. Justin mouths "thank you" to me, and I smile back.

"This teenager is going to be a married woman," Katy proudly exclaims.

I momentarily panic realizing I didn't ask anyone's blessing for Katy's hand in marriage. I've spoken to each of them about my intentions on several occasions, but never marriage. Are they going to approve? If any of them tell her no, she'll listen to them, and I wouldn't blame her.

"Married huh? To this Viking over here? You think he's worthy of you?"

I wait on the edge of my seat for whatever answer she's about to give him.

"Well, I shot at him before he asked me, and he still got down on one knee, so I think he might be worthy?"

Shock washes across his face. "You what? Oh hell, I need this story, but you look like you need a shower. Let's get you inside." Justin gives me a smile of approval, and all the stress leaves my body.

As we walk into the house with Justin's arm slung over Katy's shoulder, she stops in her tracks, and I nearly bump into her.

"Pepper?"

"You bitch. I hope you rot in a jail cell and regret every decision you've ever made." A slap rings through the air, and Justin pulls Katy into his chest. Past them, I see Babs in handcuffs, being escorted out by two police officers with a bright pink handprint on her cheek.

My girl got her closure. I couldn't be more proud.

Katy scowls at her mother as she leaves the house, and a small smile tugs at the corner of her lips.

"You alright?"

"Never better." She smiles up at Justin, who kisses her forehead and releases her.

"I'm going to take Katy to the pool house to get cleaned up, and then we'll go get Owen."

"How about you take your time? I'll have Owen brought here, so you won't have to worry."

"Thank you, Justin." Katy gives him a final hug.

"I love you, Katy. Never forget that."

"You'd never let me, Justin."

"That's the truth."

Katy and I walk through the house and out the back door. For once, I'm not looking around for danger. It's dead. She killed it. She killed *him*.

"I fucking love you, Pepper. I'm so goddamn proud of you."

"Say it again."

"Which part?"

"All of it."

We stop midway to the pool house, the grassy area lit only by the stars. Brushing her hair behind her ear, I pull her close to my chest.

"I'm so fucking proud of you and everything you've endured today, this week, these last few years. Everything you went through to become the incredible, loving, compassionate person that you are. I'll spend every fucking day of the rest of my life making sure you know how proud of you I am. But…"

"But?"

"But if I don't get inside you in the next two minutes, I'm going to give everyone with eyes near us a show." I give her a little shove, and she giggles. I smack her ass to encourage her to move, but instead, I see the lust take her over.

"Make me."

Growling, I dip down and throw her over my shoulder, smacking her ass again. Her giggling continues through the house and straight into the bathroom, where I put her on the floor and immediately take off her shirt.

"I don't want a quickie in the shower. I want to worship you in the bed. We're going to make this strictly about cleaning up." Katy bites her lip as I turn on the shower, and I get the feeling she's up to no good.

"Do you understand?"

Her head shakes back and forth as a mischievous smile paints her face. With both hands on my chest, she pushes me into the shower. It's already heated to the perfect temperature thanks to the water tank Spencer installed when she lived here.

Katy's smile continues as we shampoo and condition each

other's hair. I love feeling her fingers massaging my head, and I don't hold back my moans as she scrapes her nails over my scalp.

My eyes are still closed as her hands move down my neck and over my chest. I don't realize she's sinking to her knees until she grabs the base of my cock and sucks the head into her mouth. I look down at this sinful woman, and that damn smile is somehow still on her face despite her lips being stretched around me.

"You're a goddamn fucking dream come true."

She hums, and I push her hair back to see her entire face. She teases and taunts me with her tongue. There's no urgency or end game in her movements. She's doing this purely for pleasure, and I love every second of it.

"Please," I plead. I need to be inside her. I need to feel our bodies connect. "Please, Pepper."

She pops me from her mouth and grabs the loofah. I pick up the soap and squeeze a generous amount onto the sponge. Katy lathers me up, and I do the same, finishing our shower between kisses.

I turn the water off and grab us two towels from the rack. We laugh and stumble through, drying each other off. When we're done, she takes my hand and walks me into the bedroom.

"Sit up against the headboard."

"Yes, ma'am."

"Miss Katy."

My lip twitches. "Yes, Miss Katy." I sit on the bed as she tells me to. My cock stands at attention for her next command.

Katy crawls onto the bed and up my legs. She pauses and leans down, licking my cock from base to tip, swirling her tongue around my head a few times.

"Hey Viking?" I hmm, because words aren't a thing in my head right now. "I'm about to sit on your cock, without a condom, and you aren't allowed to freak out after, alright?"

I give her a knowing smirk, realizing we're about to relive our first time. She wants to take her power back again.

"Never again."

Just like that first night, she moves up my body and positions herself over me. Her hand wraps around to line us up, and she slowly sinks down. My body lights up as her heat engulfs my cock. I feel every inch as her body consumes me and my head falls to the headboard.

"I love you."

"You love my body," she says through a giggle.

"I love you *and* your body." Opening my eyes, I cup both of her breasts in my hands and lean forward to take a nipple in my mouth. Her milk supply has been reducing since her nursing sessions with Owen have slowed, but soon, her belly will swell with my sons and daughters, and there will be an endless supply.

Katy and I get lost in each other's bodies. It feels familiar yet utterly new as neither of us hold back our emotions. The I love you's flow freely, and everything feels deeper, stronger.

"Marry me, Katy."

"I've already said yes."

"I want to hear it again because I'm not sure I believe it."

She leans forward and cups my cheeks. "Yes, I will marry your big, stubborn, Viking ass. But…"

"But?"

She wiggles her left hand in front of me. "But ask me again when you have a ring to make it *officially* official."

"Deal."

46

Epilogue Katy

3 years later

"How's my favorite Mama-to-be feeling today?" Blake pushes Nicole's shoulder and pouts as we find a table to sit at.

"Blake, will you let Katy have her moment? You get doted on enough by two partners. Besides, you have months to go, and she's got weeks." Nicole leans over and rubs my very large baby bump. The three of us are having coffee at the cafe inside Annie's building during my lunch break.

Two months after Viktor proposed, we had a little backyard wedding. Annie offered me a job at the nursery in her building, and I accepted it without a thought. I still want to return to school and get my teaching degree, but while I'm young and our children are little, this job provides me with all the experience and opportunities I need. She also offered Viktor a permanent security job, which meant he could be in the same building as me and our children every day, and he said yes before she even finished her offer.

"Have you told her yet?" Nicole sips her pumpkin spice latte and eagerly awaits my answer. I rub my belly and shake my head.

"Do you think she'll be mad?"

"Not at all. She loves you, and she'll love it." Blake pulls me in for a hug, making me feel more confident about my decision. "Are you going to wait until he's born? Make it a big reveal."

"That was my plan. Should I tell her beforehand? Will it be too much of a shock? I'm totally overthinking this, aren't I?"

I sigh and pick up my lemonade. Naming babies is so hard, especially when their names are so meaningful.

"It's going to be a wonderful surprise, and you know it." Nicole squeezes my hand in reassurance. "You've already asked Justin, and he's the Spencer guru. Now, how's my favorite niece?"

"You know, Nicole. You're going to give me and my kids a complex if you keep referring to all things Katy as 'you're favorite.'"

Nicole uses one hand to cup her mouth, pretending to direct her comment to only me, and sings, "Drama Queen" while looking at Blake. I laugh as Blake sticks her tongue out at Nicole and enjoy their interaction.

"Anyway. Let me redirect my question to spare someone's ego. Is Owen excited to have a little brother?"

"No. He wanted another little sister. He's absolutely enamored with Justine and is worried a little brother will try to steal all of his legos."

I got pregnant right after our wedding, and Justine joined

our family with blond hair and blue eyes like her daddy. He's her favorite person, besides her namesake, her Uncle Justin. I'll never forget the look on Justin's face when I handed my newborn daughter to him at the hospital and told him her name.

It was better than any mac n cheese he ever made me.

Nicole looks at her watch. "Is Meghan joining us today?"

"Not Meghan anymore. It's Lainey, remember?" Blake reminds Nicole. "She goes by her middle name now. New hair, new name. And no, she said she had a lunch date."

Nicole and I look at each other with smiles and say, "Sawyer."

After a little whirlwind of an affair with Chip and Patrick, *who knew*, Meghan took a life sabbatical. She confessed to me one night about her home life, and it was about as crappy as mine was; only hers involved physical abuse as well as mental. She took money she had been saving and experienced life how she wanted with all the freedom she needed.

When Meghan returned, she had dyed her hair a pretty shade of brown and decided she wanted to leave behind her old life, including her first name. My strawberry blonde friend Meghan became my brunette bombshell, who dropped her first name and chose to go by her middle name, Alaina, but wanted to be called Lainey.

Sawyer is the hottie she's been dating for over a year, and there's definitely a ring in her near future.

"Sometimes I'm jealous of young love." Blake gets a dreamy look on her face, and Nicole pops her in the knee.

"There was almost an orgy in my driveway the last time I babysat for you guys because you couldn't even leave before your hands were all over each other. Your sex life is fine."

Nicole rubs Blake's baby bump. "More than fine if this is any indication."

I love my weekly meetups with the girls.

47

Dempsey

"Y ou did it again, Pepper. And look at that dark hair. He might actually look like you."

"Gee, thanks."

I kiss my beautiful wife on the forehead and marvel at the precious gift she's given me of my second son. There's no greater gift in life than being a father. Owen became mine as quickly as we could file the paperwork. Justin and Annie made it happen without a hitch. And now, this new baby boy makes the third Dempsey in our little clan.

"Are you still set on the name?" She looks at me with hope and apprehension, and I brush my knuckles across her cheek for reassurance.

"I am. Are you having doubts, Pepper? She'll be honored, but we have the alternative name picked out just in case. I love both choices."

Katy thought long and hard about the perfect names for our children. She'd told me early on that she wanted to name our daughter Justine and I knew Justin would be honored, but I wept like a baby when she told me she wanted Viktoria to be her middle name. She understood if I wanted to wait and see if we had a boy to use Viktor, but it didn't matter to me if we had a football team worth of girls; my name would be immortalized with my first daughter, and that was good enough for me.

"Not doubts. Just nerves. I don't ever want to offend Spencer."

"Well, if she hates it, we have an alternative, and nothing is signed for yet, so it's easily changed."

"Signed for? You make him sound like a car."

I kiss her gently on the lips. "Well, I sure enjoyed taking his mother on a joy ride."

"Eww. That's a dad joke. Go get the crew before they start to protest in the lobby. You know they are only staying away out of respect. Any one of them can just barge in at any minute."

"I'm going." I kiss Katy one more time and brush my lips against my son's cheek, careful not to scratch him with my beard. I can hear everyone's laughter as I walk down the hall, send an apology glance to the nurses behind the desk, and nod toward the doors to let them in.

The laughter stops as everyone rushes in with words of love and congratulations.

"Mama and baby are both doing great. Can you all behave so you can go in together?" A few glances are exchanged with the nurses behind the desk, and grumbles of approval are heard.

Everyone files into the room, and suddenly, their voices change octaves to sound more like hyenas than full-grown adults.

"Who's first?

"Spencer is first and the rest of you follow her lead and go wash your hands." No one objects to Katy's instructions.

Spencer stepped into the bathroom before fully entering the room and is now ready for our big reveal. I take my son from Katy's arms, giving her a reassuring smile, and hand him to Spencer. Her face beams as it always does with a new baby. Katy already has tears in her eyes, and I take her hand, knowing that this is the make-it-or-break-it moment.

Everyone returns to the room after washing their hands, and Spencer turns to hand the baby to the next person who wants to hold him.

"Wait." Spencer freezes and turns to Katy. "Don't you want to know his name?"

"Of course."

Katy waves Spencer over. "Would you come sit for a moment?" She gestures to the chair next to the bed, and Spencer gently sits so as not to disturb the baby in her arms.

Katy takes a deep breath and looks at me. I give her a nod of encouragement, and I see Blake and Nicole each squeeze one of Katy's legs.

"Before I tell you, please know that we have an alternative name picked out if…"

Spencer looks at her, confused.

"If?"

"If you don't like it."

"Katy, you're allowed to name your child whatever you like. I'll love him even if his name is Bologna." Someone in the room snickers, but everyone knows this is an important moment. Katy confided in everyone for their opinions—everyone but Spencer.

"With your permission, we want to name him...Emory Tucker Dempsey." Katy's eyes flash to Tucker. He didn't know about her middle name choice, but his chest puffs up with pride as we all wait for Spencer's response.

She stares down at the baby in her arms, expressionless. She rocks slightly, and finally, after what feels like an agonizingly long time, Spencer looks up to Katy and smiles.

"Don't you think we had enough penises in this family already? Poor Justine."

She made a joke, but that doesn't answer Katy's question.

"Spencer?" Katy questions.

She extends her hand and places it on Katy's arm. "I'm honored, and I love it. Emory Tucker is beautiful. But you might need to ask Tucker because I'm not sure if his head will fit out the door after this."

"Smithy, that's two jokes in a row. Is the air too thin in here?"

Axel claps Viktor on the back with a big grin. "Are you ready, Daddy?"

"Ready for what?"

"You're gonna have to make three more of those to use up the rest of our names."

"Um, excuse me," Katy interrupts. "You're asking the wrong person. This vagina factory is temporarily closed. Two kids, so close together, and she needs a break."

Tucker removes his hat and runs his hand through his silvering hair. "I really don't need to hear my daughter talking about her vagina."

"He's beautiful, Katy girl." Lincoln slides over and wraps an arm around Miller. They both look at Spencer in awe as she holds Emory.

Blake stands in the middle of Annie and Cole, each of them holding a hand on Blake's stomach, cradling baby number four.

Justin smiles a goofy smile at Katy over Nicole's head. He nuzzles into her curls from behind, and I hear him whisper the word baby. Nicole playfully swats at him, saying, "No. Three is plenty." I disagree. Three isn't nearly enough for me, but for them, Hannah, Miles, and Seth are plenty. For now, at least. I know she'll give in soon enough.

Tucker slings an arm around Axel and whispers something in his ear, making him blush.

These are Katy's people. My people. And my sons' and daughter's people.

Our found family through love, and trauma, and healing.

They. Are. Enough.

The End

48

Author Notes

Well, here we are. The final book of the You're Enough series. My first *completed* book series. I know I should be sad, and I am, but my evil mastermind created a situation where I don't have to leave these characters just yet.

If you haven't already, you should hop on over to my other series, Tipsy Penny, and start with Hazel's Harem. The fourth and final book in that series will cross over into this world, and we will get to see everyone for one last book before getting to officially say goodbye.

Also, keep an eye out for some novellas!

I can't thank you enough for delving into my mind with me and these wonderful characters I've created. Your support and engagement have made this journey more incredible than I could have ever imagined.

Thank you from the bottom of my heart

~Casiddie

About the Author

Casiddie is a single mom to five wonderfully crazy kids. When she's not carting them to activities, she's getting lost in her head with her friends as she brings them all to life.

You can connect with me on:
🅵 https://www.facebook.com/casiddiewilliams
🔗 https://www.tiktok.com/@casiddiewilliams_author

Also by Casiddie Williams

Hazel's Harem
A new job opportunity brings curvaceous, single mom Hazel Gibson, back to her hometown where she finds her hands full with a little more than just her 12 year old daughter.

When two gorgeous men offer her a six week proposition to be with both of them together, no strings attached, Hazel decides you only live once, and why choose if you don't have to?

But life has a habit of throwing Hazel curve balls, and she finds herself having to make some major life decisions to protect her family. Curve ball #1: When you're already juggling two men, what's one more?

Caffeinated Passion

Stella has been the focus of Penny's desire for almost a year. She watches her work while silently longing for her, wishing she could make Stella hers.

Though Stella is a down-on-her-luck waitress, she makes the best out of life with her son Cooper. She's desperately trying to get out of her terrible situation with her drunk boyfriend, one shift at a time.

When Stella finds herself in need of an extra hand, Penny takes the opportunity to swoop in and help her, offering a job to nanny her daughter, a safe place to live, and a relationship if she's interested.